batting for
CHARLIE

Belinda E Edwards

ISBN: 9798452654162

Sparkling Creatives.

Unit G7 Beverley Enterprise Centre, Beck View Road,

Beverley, UK. HU17 0JT

Dedication

I can only dedicate this book to one person. She started writing a novel the same day as I started writing this and we wrote together every day for 6 weeks, then took a break. Little did I know she would not get to finish hers. She was taken from us far too soon. This one is for you, Yvonne.

Chapter 1

India stared at her watch as she tried to open the door to Bentley & Bentley. She was late. Her phone tucked into her shoulder, she struggled to juggle her handbag and coffee, plus her phone and the heavy door. Why had she answered her mother's call, when she knew it would be yet another attempt to control her life?

"Mum, I have to go."

"India Barrington Jones! Don't you dare put the phone down on me!"

"I need to get to a meeting." She pleaded.

"India, it is only 8 am. You can't be at work yet."

"Mum, this is London, not Hurst's Bridge. Things start earlier. I have to go."

India ended the call, realising she would pay for it later. She needed to get her brain straight for this meeting. She was a lowly assistant, however her boss Philip Bentley seemed to like her, and she was hoping to land a longer-term role soon. Working in the capital for a firm with a reputation like Bentley & Bentley had been a dream for too long to let it go. Her parents were not happy with her living so far away and in London to boot. India felt if she wanted to do well in PR, she needed to be where she was.

Slipping her coat and bag onto her chair, she grabbed a notepad and her drink, then hurried to the conference room. She could hear excited voices from inside the room, and she rolled her eyes, imagining the scene ahead of her.

Fudge! Alice will be gripping her hands together and her voice will have raised an octave or two. Malcolm Jenkins will be lowering his voice and trying to act cool.

As she moved into the room, her eyes met those of Philip Bentley himself at the end of the table. She apologised for her lateness and took a seat, checking out all the shots of sports stars spread over the desk.

"Good morning, India," said Philip, checking his watch yet smiling "I'm going to let Malcolm tell you about this project."

Malcolm grinned, thinking this was the boss showing faith in him. India grinned back, knowing that was Philip's way of testing how well Malcolm understood the task at hand. Leaning back in her seat, she watched both men with interest. Malcolm stood up from his place and walked to the board at the front of the room.

"This is the product we are looking to support the launch of. Gym Away is lightweight equipment to fit in your suitcase. The ideal client is the business executive who spends a lot of time on the road, living in hotels away from their regular gym. The client would like us to secure an athlete who is on the road. They want to showcase that the product is suitable for an expert, so the professional man believes it is suitable for them."

"Great Malcolm, so Alice, can you tell us who we think would be a good match," asked Philip.

India leaned forward and started looking through the photographs. There were tennis players, soccer teams and rugby teams, some she recognised. Alice offered her a condescending smile as she listed well-known names from soccer and moved on to rugby. India was feeling uncomfortable with the way this list was growing with household names, who played their sport in the winter, as it was now March.

"I know I was late, but can I ask a couple of questions so I can help with ideas?"

"Of course, India, fire away," smiled Philip obviously delighted with this interruption.

"Who brought the photos?" she asked, wanting to be certain it wasn't Philip.

"I saw Malcolm as I was leaving yesterday and spoke to him about this morning in person before I emailed everyone with the time for today. He found the images."

That made the next questions a little easier for India to ask. Malcolm was always making her feel uncomfortable, and much as she liked to play nice with everyone, she felt the need to state a few obvious things.

"OK. So, when is the launch, how long is our campaign and what is the budget?"

Alice and Malcolm exchanged glances, and they both sat down. Philip Bentley beamed at India.

"Three particularly good questions. We start next month and run until October. The money is tight, too tight if truth be told. I'm working on getting it increased. This company has a lot of other products to come; so, this could open doors to some very lucrative work if we can show what is possible."

"So, do we need to look at sports that are played during that time, or are we looking for players to come on board during their off-season? They might be more available out of season, but they won't be pulling column inches from their jobs. I would like to suggest we consider cricket and tennis anyway, as I think there may well be players we can get for a better price."

Malcolm was looking decidedly unhappy, he pulled out the tennis player's photos and the one cricket team he had. Philip was pleased India was there to talk sense. She did not just drop the names of famous sportspeople. He was fairly sure neither Alice nor Malcolm had much idea about professional sport, anyway. Of course, India was much more aware of who was who. Philip made a decision.

"I think cricket might be our way forward. There would be a bigger selection to choose from, and they specifically asked for a British player. With this budget, we are going to need someone who will get the coverage in one of the better teams probably not currently a star, maybe a 'rising star'?" He looked at the faces of his staff.

That left Malcolm clutching one image, a simple black and white squad photograph of the Yorkshire Cricket team. Despite looking at a monochrome photo, India saw the brown eyes and dirty blonde hair decorating a smiling face from her past. Without realising what she was saying, she blurted out, "Charlie Robertson!"

The other three were all staring at her now. Realising she had said that out loud it was India's turn to look sick, and she sank back into her chair.

"I take it that Charlie Robertson is in that famous address book of yours" sniped Alice, who could not understand how anyone had a paper address book in the 21st century. India's mother, on the other hand, lived and died by hers and she'd encouraged her daughter to keep one of her own for many years. Charlie did not have a place in India's treasured book, so she shook her head, still staring at his face. Philip, unused to seeing India withdrawn like this, pushed on regardless, wanting to make a decision and to have something to take to the new clients, Joe and Matilda Cookson.

"Charlie Robertson, why him? How long has he been with Yorkshire?"

Taking a deep breath, India thought he was an excellent candidate and if she could avoid seeing him during that process, so much the better. Malcolm seemed keen to drive this one so hopefully... "Charlie Robertson is from Scotland. He played rugby too for a short while. He started to focus on cricket when he left school. He joined Yorkshire full time six years ago. He isn't one of their stars, but he is an opening batsman, with Ben Woods, the Yorkshire captain."

Philip looked impressed, whilst Malcolm and Alice hit Google on their phones to beat her in this game of trivia. India carried on. "For our project, he is charismatic and gets a lot of attention in the press, not always for his cricketing skills!"

At which point both Alice and Malcolm flashed their screens, showing images of Charlie Robertson looking stunning with different girls on his arm. India closed her eyes. She hated to see these photographs that filled her screen every time she tortured herself by checking what he was up to now.

"Looks worth exploring. India, you seem to know a lot about him. Did you say his number wasn't in your book?"

"No, I don't have it." India was speaking quietly, and her eyes were fixed on her notebook.

"I bet one of your contacts could get it for you." *Damn, he was right.* Her cousin Robbie went to school with him. and they were still in touch. Charlie went to Robbie's house every New Year and had done for the last six years to India's knowledge.

"Yes, I can have it for tomorrow." She was reluctant but this was work.

"That's settled then. See you in the morning to see how we move forward with this. Same place, same time as today."

"OK, should we be working on other possibilities?" smirked Alice. Philip paused and, shaking his head, said, "Yes." Something in the way he left the room told India that Philip Bentley had already decided he liked the sound of Charlie Robertson.

Chapter 2

As India stepped into her flat at the top of Putney High Street, her phone was ringing yet again. A glance at her screen told her it was her mother for the fifth time that day and for the fourth time, India cancelled the call. Why hadn't she done that with the first one, she wondered? She knew she would answer it and face whatever conversation it was this time, but she had to get herself centred first. She had been caught in a cold March storm on the way home. Her clothes were soaked, but it was more than that, her body was beyond tired.

All day in the office, she had been aware of Alice and Malcolm watching her and sniping at every opportunity. She was tired of their jealousies. What was she supposed to do? Not ask the important questions? Pretend she didn't know the right person for whatever Philip needed? And now they had added blooming Charlie Robertson to the mess that her life seemed to be.

Tonight, she'd phone her cousin Robbie for Charlie's contact details and she'd call her parents. Right now, she didn't feel strong enough to do either. It was time for a shower, a glass of wine, and a chat with Katie, her closest friend. India stood longer in the spray than normal, letting the heat soak into her tired bones. She indulged in a favourite body gel smelling of orange flower; something about today made her appreciate this gift from her aunt. In her favourite pyjamas and wrapped in a fluffy dressing gown against the cold of her flat, she padded over to the kitchen and reheated soup.

This was a night to pull out all the self-comfort she could find. She took her meal to the table, collected her phone and a glass of wine. It was time to talk to Katie on video chat. The two girls often had dinner together like this. Even though she was 200 miles away, they still spoke most days. London still felt lonely to India. Although she had friends here, none of those friendships felt as deep as the one she had with Katie. India had met Katie on her very first day at university. Their first-year rooms were two doors apart and now, even though they had left university, they were closer friends than ever.

"Hey there." beamed Katie, she looked like she had been enjoying a better day than India.

"Hey."

"Crikey, that was quiet. Hang on! Are those your silk pyjamas? It's only 6:45. Tell me what happened?"

"You know me too well," sighed India "is it so obvious?"

"Well, it is to me. So, was it your mum or those two idiots at work?"

India smiled. Katie might know her well, but even Katie didn't know the full story about Charlie Robertson.

"Well, my mum kicked off the day by phoning me as I got off the tube in Earl's Court. I knew it would make me late for a meeting my boss had called. Still, it was so early in the morning I thought something was wrong."

"So, what did your darling mother want this time?"

"She wanted me to go to a dinner with some friend's son. He doesn't have a date for some work event, and she couldn't help but tell me what his prospects were. I think she is working on a list of 'suitable' husbands for me. Now she has my brother married off, I'm next on her to-do list."

"Maybe he is OK. At least this way you know the guy checks out and you will have no problem introducing him to your folks."

"I'm going to ring her back after I've spoken to you and before I have rung Robbie."

"Robbie, your sexy cousin Robbie from Scotland?" Katie's voice rose in anticipation.

"Yes, my married cousin Robbie! That is from the next part of my day."

"I can't imagine anything being horrible that involves Robbie."

"This morning's meeting was to look at a new project. They want a professional athlete for all the adverts. Bentley & Bentley's dream team had come up with lots of photographs of potential men, none of which were right for the job. Before I knew it, we were looking at the Yorkshire cricket squad."

"I'm still working on the link to Cousin Robbie. Oh wait, doesn't he have a mate from rugby who plays for Yorkshire? What was his name, Romeo? You were always drooling over him whenever he was in the paper at uni."

"Charlie Robertson, Romeo is his nickname, Charlie Whisky Romeo. Cricketers are all into nicknames. And I wasn't drooling!"

"So, if he is still as dreamy looking as I remember him, I'm guessing you suggested him for this project?"

"Well, I didn't mean to, I saw his face in the photo, that wicked grin, and said his name. I didn't realise I said it aloud, and everyone jumped on it. To be honest, he probably is right for the project. We don't have a massive budget, so can't afford one of the big stars. He has great looks so will be fine in all the photographs it's just…"

"Just what? So far, I can't see what the huge disaster of today is India. So, your Mum wants you to go to some fancy event with someone she approves of, you can check him out. If he seems OK, you can give it a try. If he knows your mum knows his mum, he will be on his best behaviour. If when you check him out, you don't like what you find, you tell your mum you're busy with work. And if Romeo is right for this project, what is the issue? I know you like him; I remember your face when he popped up on the TV News that time. Tell me, what is the problem?"

"One, you know as well as I do the odds are exceptionally long on me liking anyone my mother thinks 'suitable'. Two, I don't think I ever told you the story about Charlie, well not all of it, anyway."

"I know you met him at a New Year party at Robbie's, but you were what, sixteen or seventeen there can't be much more to tell, is there?" Katie paused, then gasped, "NO! Tell me he didn't...."

"No, he didn't touch me, well not like that anyway."

"OK, do you want to tell me now?"

"It's silly. Yes, I was seventeen and my mum and I were clashing, teenage hormones and all that over Christmas. My brother dragged me up to Scotland to stay with family up there, and we went to a party at Robbie's. In those days, we went around from one party to another all night. Andrew was trying extremely hard to keep me from drinking too much. It was a long night you know."

"Yeah, that's what brothers do. Andrew is just a bit more protective than most. You have told me a few funny stories about New Year parties in Scotland."

"When we walked into Robbie's place, Charlie had arrived in front of us. He was gorgeous, so handsome and someone taller than me. At that time, I was the tallest in the class at school. Looking back, I remember Charlie's eyes from that night, so dark yet so soft at the same time. He was laughing and joking, and everyone wanted to talk to him. He had been working away, something to do with the police, and no one had seen him for months, so everyone wanted to catch up with him. But he looked at me, then left everyone else and came to talk to me. I didn't know anyone, just Robbie and his girlfriend and Andrew, of course. I couldn't believe this guy who everyone was making so much fuss of wanted to talk to me. He brought me a drink and led me off into a quiet spot and we sat on the floor talking for ages. We talked about music and books and talked and talked. He kept fetching me another drink, I didn't notice anything wrong. We sat shoulder to shoulder on the floor and kept leaning into each other. Then he moved the hair off my face and was leaning in to kiss me when I suddenly felt I was going to throw up and made a run for it."

"So uncool friend."

"Uncool is not the word! I was so fudging sick, it was awful. Andrew was going mad and screaming at Charlie, even Robbie was shouting at him about my age, and he looked shocked and upset. He kept repeating he didn't know."

"To be fair, when I met you at eighteen, you looked a lot older. Those clothes your mother bought for you were so formal I guess, and you being so tall."

"I'm sure he was horrified. We decided he must have been adding vodka or something to my drinks too, so even if I was older, he was being underhand."

"Are you sure?" India thought about the question for a while.

"Well, no, not certain, but it made sense. Robbie was so mad at him, I know they stayed friends though. He has been at a few other New Year parties, but we never speak. Sometimes I catch him glaring at me, though. I guess I was disappointed because he seemed so nice. We were getting along so well, and I was convinced he was about to kiss me. Now every time I see him in the press, he has a different girl on his arm, sometimes two. Maybe my vomiting saved me from something worse."

"That complicates things then. What's the plan?" Typical Katie. Always practical.

"Ring Robbie and see what he thinks. Get Charlie's number and pass it on to Philip, and that's my job done. I might have to type up a resume for him, which should be easy for me. I know when he went to Yorkshire, who he hangs out with on the team and when his best season was."

"Are they letting you loose with a camera yet?" Katie asked hopefully.

"No, I think Philip Bentley keeps me around for my mother's address book. He 'admires' her. Which makes me feel sick whenever he says it. If this wasn't my dream job, that fact alone is enough to make me walk away from it."

"India, being creative is important, you know. It's something you do so naturally. I wish you would find a way to add it into your life, maybe join a camera club or something?"

"So, you keep saying." India was sure she could never be as creative as Katie.

"Promise me you will look at your job and your time outside of work and look to the future."

"Now you sound like my mother, 'You are not getting any younger, India'."

"Oh dear, I certainly don't want to be like your mother or replace her. Shall I let you finish your soup and make those calls? The sooner they are over, the sooner you can get on with enjoying the rest of your life." Katie laughed.

"Thanks, Katie, I think you can expect to be hearing from me a lot this week."

"Well, that is what friends are for, catch you later," and she ended the call, leaving India staring into her soup. She pulled out her notepad and made a list of things she needed to do. Eating her soup, she checked the latest news on Charlie Robertson.

Chapter 3

Charlie Robertson paced the floor of the kitchen in the house he used to share with his teammate. He was glad to have it to himself, even if it didn't help with his current situation. He went over and over the phone call he had last night. Twenty-four hours later, and he still had not found a solution. He looked at his watch and tried to work out how much time it would take him to drive to Scotland and back. Did he have enough fuel and how long would he have when he got there? What would he say or do when he arrived?

Charlie picked up his keys and strode towards the door. He could think on the way. With his coat on and the door open it hit him, the one thing he did know, she wouldn't be pleased to see him there in the middle of the week. He closed the door and put down his keys.

Walking aimlessly around the downstairs rooms with no purpose to his wandering other than to help him sift through all the possibilities, he felt lost.

Finally, Charlie sank into the chair in the corner. He dreaded doing this, but he needed help, and Robbie Anderson was the only person he could call. How he hated being so far away from his mum. Leeds was closer than many of the other county cricket teams he could have chosen, still, 160 miles from Hawick was a long way when she was so ill. Sighing, he reluctantly pulled up the number for the friend who had always stood by him. Even when he was a foolish teenager, he had only seen Robbie mad with him once and he had deserved it; he was even madder with himself that New Year.

"Hello Charlie, what can I do for you, I thought you were down in Yorkshire for all the pre-season stuff you have to do now you are getting older." Charlie's mouth curved at his friend's teasing.

"Yep, I'm in Leeds, which is why I need a favour." Once he was on the call, he stood up from the chair and began to pace around again.

"OK, I'm listening."

"It's my Mum." Charlie stalled. The next part was hard to say.

"Emma said she had seen her in the corridor at the hospital last week, and it looked like she was on her way to oncology. What can I do?" Of course, Robbie knew, he forgot how small the town was.

"Yeah, sadly you are right, cancer. I can't say I understand, but I want to know she is getting the best care. She has only got me since my dad took off. I'm stuck in Leeds, and I need this job; it is all I ever wanted to do. It doesn't pay much yet. Hopefully, I'll be moving up next year. To be honest mate, it's a stretch to keep the two houses going."

"I know she was always there for you but hang on Charlie boy. I see your face in the news most weeks coming out of a club and all those reports about your gambling, is that why you're short of cash?"

"If only it was that simple Robbie, if only it was that simple. Please don't believe everything you read about me."

"So, what can I help with? If you have called to ask me for the cash, you picked the wrong friend."

"No, not money, could you call round my Mum's and see what she needs, I keep asking her, but she won't tell me. And..."

"Yesss?" Robbie was waiting for what else he could do.

"I was wondering if you might ask Emma. You're a great mate and all that, just I thought Emma might know what other help I can get her, what is available, what I can pay for."

"Well, if she doesn't, she'll know someone who does. Don't worry mate, Emma will help, I'm sure. Anything else we can do?"

"Yeah, if you think of a way I can earn some cash this season, let me know. The team has made lots of promises for next year, I don't think Mum can wait that long though."

"Sure, I will Charlie, no idea what though unless you want to play Rugby through the winter. Isn't that your agent's job, though?" Robbie chuckled.

"Thanks, mate, yeah, I need a new agent."

"No worries, now what have they got you doing to get your old body fit for the new season?"

The two old friends swapped stories of how they had to warm up for longer these days and talked about adventures from the past. Charlie resisted the urge to ask Robbie how India was doing. He decided to leave an update on her until a later call. Robbie promised to phone when he had spoken to his mum.

Robbie was right about his agent. He had not been helpful for the last two years. Charlie hated change, so had done nothing about it. Now the agent had retired, he needed to find himself a new one. He could try talking to the coach in the morning and see if he could get some time to go up to see his mum if he explained the situation. Unfortunately, Charlie wasn't confident about his place in the squad. Whatever anyone said, there was always some younger player looking for a break, prepared to work on low wages for the honour of playing for Yorkshire. How safe was his spot in the team?

Despite the photos in the news of him coming out of clubs with girls and the reports of him being seen in casinos, he knew how many of those were versions of the truth. It suited some people for him to be in those papers, in those photographs.

Having talked to Robbie and not asking about India made him think of her again. She was never far from his thoughts. He wondered if she saw those images and the women in them and if she did, what she thought of him now. She must already have a low opinion of him. How could he have been so stupid? Simple, she stole his breath as soon as he set eyes on her, so tall and sophisticated. They had talked for hours. She was not a giggly teenager, wearing friendship bracelets. She was a beautiful lady in a silk evening dress how could she be so young and why had no one thought to tell him?

Sitting on the floor, their backs against the wall, talking about so many things. Someone had been playing Stevie Wonder, it always made him think of her. How could the most wonderful woman he had ever met be just seventeen? Well, she was not so young now, how old was she? He has seen her since, at Robbie's, mainly at New Year and every year she looked more perfect. So why hadn't he talked to her again? Why hadn't she talked to him? He had caught her looking at him, that is certain, so he was sure she had an incredibly low opinion of him. What did he care, there were plenty of women who were very keen to be with him?

Putting down his drink, he made a decision. Showered and changed, smelling every inch of the professional player, he picked up the keys to his sleek black Porsche and went to find one of those women. If you have an itch, then scratch it.

Chapter 4

India looked at her phone, who to ring first? She loved Robbie, but what would he think when she asked for Charlie's number. Her mother would be mad that India had not answered her calls, or that she had been cut off this morning. She looked down at her paper to see she had been doodling.

Charlie Whisky Romeo

What a stupid nickname, but then that was cricket. Laughing to herself she imagined what her mother would think of Charlie. Her brother had agreed not to share what had happened with their parents, and that was because he felt it was partly his fault for getting distracted by some girl with awfully long blonde hair. India could not even imagine Maria Barrington Jones' face if ever Charlie Robertson was in the same room as her, let alone if he were with her daughter. Not that she had any intention of that happening again. She had thought he was a sweet, intelligent guy who happened to be good looking. Now she knew he was an arrogant charmer who considered all the women in the world were there for his amusement.

She would call her mother first and get that out of the way. Pouring herself another glass of wine, she decided on a plan. She would say she couldn't do that date, simple. Picking up her phone, she started to pace. She hated lying, yet sadly she felt the need for some defence where her mother was concerned. Her mother answered on the second ring.

"India! Whatever is wrong with you. I have been asking your father to drive down there and see if you were alright. I have been trying to reach you since we were cut off this morning."

Typical of her mother, she could not believe that India would end a call or that being at work might make it difficult to answer personal calls during the day.

"I rang Philip myself to see if he could tell me anything." India's heart stopped for a moment; horrified that her mother would reach out to her boss. Bang goes her idea of saying she was still at the office or that the event clashed with something for work. Her Mum would simply call her boss and ask for her to be excused.

"Philip was playing golf somewhere; all he could do was assure me you had been fine this morning even if you had been a little quiet." Could this get any more embarrassing? Well, obviously it could. "He asked me if I knew some cricketer from Yorkshire, said you knew him. I couldn't think of anyone we would know who that could be."

"It is one of Robbie's friends, Andrew and I met him once, up at a New Year party I think."

"So, have you got his contact details? Do we know his parents?"

"I'm sure we don't know his parents. I will phone Robbie after this to see if he thinks he would work for this project and if so, get his number. I don't want to hand Philip the number of someone who isn't going to be right for our client."

"When do you think you will be coming home, dear? I thought you went there to explore the social scene, but you never seem to go out."

"I came here to learn the business, Mum; any social life is a bonus."

"Well, that is why I wanted to talk to you, darling. Janet Coombes was telling me her son, is finding it hard to find the right sort of girl to take to his next work event. Seems they have quite a few. This one is black tie dear, and well I know that some girls these days do not know how to behave when fast food is not involved. It is on Saturday the 17th. Would you like me to send you a gown down?"

"I haven't said I'm going yet, Mother!"

"Why wouldn't you go? You need to get real about your future darling, you do not want to be working the rest of your life."

"Can I ask which of Janet's charming sons we are talking about?"

"Don't worry dear, the Coombes are a very modern family, they are leaving both boys an equal sum."

"MOTHER! That is not what I mean. I hope you know that." Snapping was not the answer, but India couldn't help herself.

"Unfortunately, I do. As you asked, it is Michael Coombes who is working in London. The older boy, like Andrew, is working for his father and living close to his parents. Thank goodness he didn't feel the need to run off to London."

"Mum! This is not some sort of gap year, where I'm going to come home to marry someone to provide for me. I want a partnership with anyone I find to live with." India was angry.

"I can assure you, my dear, that I contribute an awful lot to my marriage." She bit back.

India sighed. It was true. In her way, Maria Barrington Jones was very much focused on her marriage and making sure the family lifestyle fitted what was expected of William Barrington Jones, but that was not how she wanted to live her life. They had vastly different views on marriage.

"OK, let me check on some dates I have coming up. I will let you know as soon as I can."

"Oh!"

"I have to go and sort out this cricketer for Philip. I will have to work up a proposal for the client after I have spoken to Robbie. I will speak to you tomorrow." With that, she ended the call.

She arched her back and stretched out her arms. She took the time to make a cup of tea before picking up her phone to call Robbie.

"Well, hello cousin! To what do I owe this honour?" laughed Robbie.

"Excuse me?"

"Well, it isn't often you ring me India, just wondering why today?"

"I call you more often than you call me Robbie Anderson! In fact, I am not sure you have ever called me." India joked.

"Yeah, but I'm a bloke, India, you can't be expecting me to make social calls."

"True and yes, I do want something." She admitted.

"OK cousin, fire away. It seems to be my night for being asked favours."

"Are you in touch with Charlie Robertson?" Robbie paused, taken aback.

"India Barrington Jones, that is the first time I've ever heard you mention his name! I understand the first time you met was an event you may not remember based on how much you drank that night. I've seen the way you look at him, so I'm guessing you remember something. So why tonight?"

"At work today we were going through professional sportsmen who could be asked to do some promotion work for a new account we have picked up and Charlie's name came up as one option."

"Who would throw out Charlie's name? I wouldn't think he would be the first choice for that swish London company you work for?" Robbie knew it must have been India.

"True, the others on the team were looking at Chelsea Footballers," she laughed, "but the campaign is from April to September and the budget isn't that big, which turned the spotlight on Cricket. The only cricket team they had an image for was Yorkshire."

"Well, Charlie does manage to be seen in the press." He conceded reluctantly.

"And he is photogenic." India bit her lip. Why had she said that?

"So, you have been looking at him. If the budget is low, is there any money in this?"

"I think so, probably not enough to attract a big star. Would he be insulted by that?"

"Maybe you need to find a better way to say it," he chuckled. "I happen to know he could be interested in earning some extra cash, in all honesty, you might be exactly what he needs."

"When did you last speak to him? Do you have up-to-date contact information for him?

"I spoke to him less than an hour ago. He rang me to go check on his mum, she has cancer. He is stuck in Leeds for pre-season training at the moment."

"Oh, that is awful. I know there was only him and his mum for a lot of years, didn't his dad leave them when he was eight?"

"Well, you did remember a lot from that night, then. Or have you spoken to him since?"

"No, we haven't spoken since that first New Year."

"He honestly didn't know how young you were India, you know, he isn't like that."

"Robbie, he was putting vodka in my drinks."

"You asked for Martini. He didn't realise you meant straight out of the vermouth bottle. Some people do drink vodka Martini, you know."

"Look, that was years ago. Do you think this is something he will want to do?"

"I don't know. Tell me more about it.?"

"It is a gym kit that fits in your case. I've only seen one photo at this point. I don't know the budget, I do know it is tight. Philip Bentley seems to think there will be other work to come from this company for us, so maybe there will be work for Charlie too."

"It doesn't sound terrible. I guess you will need to talk to Charlie when you have the details. I can text over his number, and I think we may have an address for him in Leeds."

"Robbie? Do you know why he needs money? I don't want to recommend someone who has a 'problem' to my boss."

"India, he is a good guy. Trust me, give him a chance. He has been a good mate to me and right now I know he needs help."

"OK, text me what you have, and I will work up a profile."

"A profile? Don't be using all the gossip column rubbish about him India. He is more than that."

"I know, the trouble is I'm not certain if the gossip column stuff will help or not."

"Can't you work that out when you are in the meeting, start with images and his stats, then either play up or down the gossip bit." Now India was getting uncomfortable, she wriggled on her chair.

"I wasn't planning on doing anything other than handing over his details. I think Malcolm wants to run with this launch and to be honest, I'm not convinced I want to see him."

"Oh India," Robbie paused "You may not have asked me about Charlie, but he asks about you. It's time to forget that one mistake." Yes, she needed to cut this call short.

"Sorry, I'd better go now and get this report sorted. If you can text me the contact details. Does he have an agent I should get in touch with instead?"

"Just ring him India, it's time to grow up." And Robbie was gone.

With two people telling her to grow up in one night, maybe it was time to rethink. Go to that dinner with Michael Coombes, and perhaps speak to Charlie again. There was no one else in her life. Michael and Charlie were not who she was looking to settle down with, but perhaps if she went out, she might meet the man she was looking for. The man who could make her feel safe and would let her be the person she wanted to be. The question is who or what did she want to be?

Chapter 5

India Barrington Jones looked at herself in the mirror of the washroom at Bentley & Bentley. This morning she arrived in plenty of time to be ready for the meeting. She had dressed modestly. Simple clothes under her favourite red coat and neat low-heeled court shoes. Today was the day she was going to show everyone how grown-up she could be. On her desk was a well-prepared profile on C. W. Robertson. The statistics of his career, some background from his life in Hawick. Some carefully trimmed press cuttings and some of her favourite photographs of the cheeky Scot. Smoothing her long dark hair in place, she left the clinical bathroom and made her way to the meeting, collecting her file and notepad and checking her phone for last-minute changes.

Alice and Malcolm were in the conference room already and were sharing something they seemed to find funny. As soon as India walked in, they stopped and straightened their faces.

"Good morning." They each muttered a reply and juggled the files in front of them. India decided they had been preparing lists of alternatives all night, judging by how thick the pile was. Philip Bentley followed her into the room. He was ready for golf and was plainly hoping to be on the course very soon.

"Tell me you have this guy's contact details India." Philip looked unusually anxious.

"Yes, I have his address, email and phone number." India's reply was calm.

"Wonderful, because I saw the client, Joe Cookson yesterday at my club, so we had a brief chat. Apparently, he is from Yorkshire, so the idea of a cricket player appealed to him. Do you think we could arrange some tickets for him as part of this? Sounds like he still has family up there and taking a group to cricket is something that might impress his father-in-law."

India smiled, although the dream team looked far from happy.

"I'm playing golf with him this morning, so hit me up with all the details, and then let's discuss how we move forward with this. I need a plan in place to suggest to them over lunch when his wife, Matilda joins us."

Handing out copies of the profile she had created for Charlie, she asked Philip for any details she would need.

"I believe the Cooksons would love to see this pan out as a six-month project. I think one shoot a month for the glossies and maybe a few social events and match days."

"Well, if they are from Yorkshire, they will be cricket fans so they would enjoy that."

Malcolm coughed, "Does, coming from Yorkshire, make them cricket fans?" he seemed amazed that India could presume that.

"Yorkshire, it is a very diverse county, cricket is one thing that unites them, that and any competition between Yorkshire and Lancashire." India bit her lip.

"Really? OK," Alice looked shocked.

"Yes. The Roses game is at the end of July. Maybe we could work that into the programme. The Cooksons are likely to be interested in that."

"Do you know India, I think you have some great ideas there," Philip looked at his watch, "Is there any chance that you could type that up and make a tentative call to your friend to see if he is interested in taking this further before I leave the office at 10:30?"

"I thought Alice wanted to work on this project with Malcolm. I think they have a few alternatives to look at." India was often generous like this, unlike the two now staring at her from across the table. They looked confused, still they began to open their files.

"Great. So, any other Yorkshire Cricketers in there?"

"No," they said together.

"Any Yorkshire tennis players?" They gave a nervous laugh and said no again. India sighed. She felt certain they thought Yorkshire could not possibly produce tennis players. India opened her mouth to list a few names, then closed it without saying a word. Robbie had said Charlie needed this job, so she was going to help by making sure he had a good chance at it.

"In that case, after the conversation I had with Joe, we are good with this Robertson guy. Can you sound him out, Alice?"

Alice looked nervously at Malcolm, and it was him that spoke for her. "I think India should run with this; it will allow her to show us if she can get one of these people, she says she knows." He smirked at India, then turn to smile sweetly at Philip.

"I'm certain I didn't say he was a personal friend, I know of him, he is, after all, a professional athlete."

"A brilliant idea Malcolm let's see what you can do India. Contact him or his agent now and then we can see if this is at all possible before I see Joe on the first tee."

India was unsure what Alice and Malcolm were trying to do. Usually, they fought to take the lead on every project, leaving her with the run around jobs. Whatever it was, she had no choice but to agree to what Philip had asked, and she collected her files to leave the room. Alice and Malcolm scurried out first, which left her with Philip.

"Did your mother get hold of you yesterday? She sounded worried."

"Yes, I rang her last night. I'm sorry she bothered you."

"She didn't bother me. I like your mum, and mums do worry. I hope if you have any problems, you feel you can turn to me. I mean it India, anytime."

"Thanks." India slipped out of the room to catch Alice and Malcolm in a huddle, whispering behind their hands. What were they up to? If she wanted to work in this field, she would need to ring people she had never met to approach them about projects. So why did this one seem so hard? Because she had met Mr Romeo and because deep down his face or even his name stirred something in the seventeen-year-old India that was still buried inside her. That lopsided grin was enough to make her toes curl up and for her to feel the need to squeeze her thighs together. How ridiculous. Time to grow up India. Now she was saying it to herself.

She slipped back into the conference room and picked up the landline. She did not want witnesses to this call, nor did she want Charlie to have her mobile number. Looking at her watch, it was a little before 9 am and she wondered what he would be doing at this time.

It rang twice before Charlie answered, trying to catch his breath. What had she interrupted? India paused for a split second to wonder if he would know who she was. Then she remembered Robbie had said that Charlie had been asking about her when they spoke.

"Good morning. This is India Barrington Jones. I hope I haven't called at a bad time. I'm calling from Bentley & Bentley in London, and we have a client who would like to work with you to promote a new product they are about to launch. I was wondering if you would be interested and if I needed to speak to you or your agent." She rattled out nervously.

At the other end of the line, the breathing had slowed and was now less pronounced.

"Good morning, India, how lovely to hear your voice again. I've just arrived at the training centre; I ran here, hence being out of breath."

"Oh, sorry."

28

"Whilst I'd love to chat, I need to get inside, ready for the first session at nine. Could I ring you back, say, at eleven? Give me your number."

"That isn't a problem, I will call you. Do I take it you might be interested? We are meeting with our clients today and we'd love to tell them you are a strong possibility before they look at other people instead."

"I'm happy to talk to you later, India." His voice was deep and sounded rougher than she remembered. India blushed. It felt like his voice was rumbling through her entire body.

"That sounds wonderful. I will talk to you at 11 o'clock then."

She ended the call and walked down to Mr Bentley's corner office.

"I spoke to Mr Robertson, he was going into a training session, so I arranged to speak to him again at 11 o'clock. He didn't say no, and he did seem keen to talk."

"I must admit I would have liked more before I talk to Joe, at least this way I can tell him it's a possibility and get a better idea of what they want from the campaign. If this goes ahead, we are going to need him down here to talk face to face and meet the clients. Can you work towards getting him to come down for a meeting and try to find out what he wants from the deal?"

"Of course." *This means spending more time talking to him.*

India left to go back to her desk and opened her computer. She had found the Yorkshire fixture list that might give her some ideas of when he would be available. Then she realised she had to ring her mum and say yes to that event with Michael and get her to send an evening dress. She looked across the modern open plan office and to her relief, Alice and Malcolm looked like they were getting ready to leave for a break. The rain was lashing noisily against the window, and she wondered why they were bothering to go out for coffee today and how Philip was going to play golf. It would give her time to call her mother in peace.

29

India rearranged everything on her desk. She pulled up a year planner on her computer and started to fill in each of the Yorkshire fixtures. Eventually, she was alone and decided to get the phone call to her mother out of the way.

"Good morning, mum."

"Hello darling, how are you?"

"I'm fine. I called to say I can go to that dinner with Michael. Could you let him know and would you please send me a dress, perhaps my red one?"

"Yes, I can do that. I expect he will telephone you to sort the details himself. Are you sure about the red dress, darling? It is not very new; Michael may have seen it before?"

"I don't think that matters Mum, I like it, it fits me and is very respectable."

"I will get it off to you today. I'm seeing Michael's mother this afternoon so I can get that sorted. I'm so glad you took time out to ring me before I had to face her."

India checked the time on the rose gold and steel Hamilton watch her father had given her for her last birthday. It still wasn't time to call Charlie. For so long she had wanted to do more on a project; she liked photography, and she enjoyed styling the shoots and so far, she hadn't been allowed to show how good she could be at that. How ironic that this was a project they asked her to do more, and it was the one project she wanted to distance herself from.

Charlie had sounded keen to speak to her. His accent and deep voice had stirred something within her. This might be a real chance to show people what she could do with this. She pulled out the fixture list again and tried to create a plan for the photoshoots. Philip had left to meet up with the Cooksons when Jayne came to speak to her. She announced she was going out on an errand for Philip and that she had diverted her phone to India's, so she was not to leave the office until Jayne returned.

India was annoyed at the way Jayne announced it, without discussing it with her. Deep down India knew she would never have been able to say no to Jayne anyway, but that was not the point. Alone on their floor, it suddenly felt a little creepy. The entire day so far felt off. She had never known them all to go out and leave her and usually, Alice or Malcolm organised models and shoots.

India was feeling defiant. She found a music app on her phone and plugging in one earpiece she listened to music. It would help her cope with the silence. Quickly making a drink in the kitchen, she was back at her desk and researching more ideas when Stevie Wonder started playing. It took her back to that first New Year Party. She wondered what Charlie thought of her. The call had been brief, she thought he sounded interested. She hoped he wasn't angry with her.

Maybe he thought I should have told him I was seventeen? He always scowls at me whenever we are in the same room, and we haven't exchanged a word since the moment I was sick.

She needed to 'proceed with care', as they say. *This time last week I would have been over the moon to be asked to do this. It feels off. That and the fact that it is Charlie Robertson. That's the part that is making me so uncomfortable.*

This is an opportunity to help Robbie's friend. I have plenty of ideas to make this work that I can share with the team. I want to show them I am capable of more than making coffee. So yes first, talk to Charlie and see if I can persuade him to do this.

Chapter 6.

Charlie looked at his phone, still, only 10:30 am. He couldn't remember the last time he had got showered and changed so fast. All that meant was he now had 30 minutes to wait for her call. Six years was a long time, so another 30 minutes wouldn't kill him, would it? He was sure his heart had stopped when Robbie had texted him to say he had given his number to India and for him to expect a call about a job and it still didn't seem to work properly.

Last night he had been sitting at the bar in Alex's club and he was probably going home with the redhead who had her tongue in his ear when his phone vibrated in his pocket. Seeing Robbie's name, he was concerned it might be about his mother. He was not sure which he had been more pleased to read, India's name, or that Robbie had somehow found him a job.

He looked at the redhead Alex had sent over to cheer him up, and it felt so wrong. How could he speak to India when she called if he had taken this girl home?

His heart had stopped again when his phone rang as he was finishing his run that morning. He had pushed extra hard today. His chest was struggling to bring in any air, was that from the run or from speaking to her?

Charlie wondered if he had time to ring Robbie before she rang back and if Robbie would be at work. He tried a text instead.

CWR: Do you know what India wants to talk to me about?

RJA: She rang last night for your number, something about a PR job that might suit you.

CWR: Thanks, mate.

RJA: It is the first time she has ever mentioned your name. I hope it works out.

RJA: The job.

CWR: Thanks.

Charlie stared at his phone. Still only 10:45. Where should he be when she calls? He wandered down the corridor and found an empty physio-therapy room. Having perched on the edge of the table, he started browsing through his phone, and he saw last night's photos.

CHARLIE WHISKEY ROMEO LEAVES CLUB

EARLY AND ALONE.

Boy, he couldn't win. He thought one of the staff at the club rang the press whenever he was in. Hell, he would not be surprised if Alex rang them himself. Most of the club owners liked to see him in their place, and they made sure he had an enjoyable time. He liked Alex though, so he didn't know why he minded so much today.

He checked Twitter and Facebook next, then his Google alerts. Why was he doing this to himself today? It was time to find a new agent, perhaps one who could help with his PR and social media. He could start by talking to Woody, who always seemed to have his head screwed on and he was his team captain.

When the call finally came, Charlie nearly dropped his phone. Damn, she is still calling from a landline.

"Hello?"

"Hello, it's India, is that you Charlie?" Six years slipped silently away, and he felt he was sitting on the floor with her, shoulder to shoulder, watching the New Year fireworks through Robbie's back window.

"Hello, India."

There was a silence that stretched between them, and together they said. "How are you?"

Charlie laughed and repeated his question. Her voice sounded so unsure.

"I'm fine. I have been asked to call by my boss, Philip Bentley. From Bentley & Bentley. Sorry, I don't know how to start. This is usually someone else's job."

He was right. She was feeling unsure. He could live with that.

"So why did your boss ask you to call me India? I'm guessing it wasn't to see how I was?"

"Well…"

Charlie sighed, his heart stuttered, and he wished he could steady her nerves by touching her arm. Unfortunately, she was in London, and he was in Leeds. He instinctively softened his voice and tried again to help her.

"Robbie mentioned a job?"

"Yes, we have a new client that we are looking to put together a six-month launch project for Gym Away. Basically, it is a gym you carry in your suitcase. The idea was to select a professional sports person to be photographed using the gym or taking it out of his case."

"So why me?" he asked, there was some hesitation. What was she not telling him?

"The project is to run from April to September, which made the team look at Cricket rather than Football or Rugby. The company owners are from Yorkshire, so your team seemed an obvious choice."

"As I said, why me?"

"Can I be honest?" her nerves were showing again.

"I wish you would!" Eek, he hoped that didn't sound aggressive. There was another long pause, and he wondered what the problem was.

"Someone from my department produced a photograph of the team in the meeting and I saw you and said your name without thinking."

Wow. He was right, she did think about him. Was that good or bad? Now it was his turn to pause.

"I've had time to think about this project and I believe you would be a good match. We all know how photogenic you are, you made the papers again today." He still didn't reply, so India kept talking. "They haven't given me an opportunity like this before, I haven't been told to contact people and to get them in for a meeting. That is all I'm asking for at this stage Charlie, come down and meet my boss and possibly the people from the company. Look at the product and hopefully, by then we will have a firm idea of what they are expecting."

"So, you want me to come to London for this meeting?"

"Yes, come and have a chat, let's see if we can work this project to help both you and our client."

"What about you?"

"Well, of course, Bentley & Bentley hope to work on other products for them, so if this goes well the firm expects to extend the contract." India was choosing her words carefully, Charlie shook his head.

"No India, what about you? Will you be at this meeting? What will you get out of me doing this?"

"Honestly, Charlie, I don't know, if you could agree to the meeting, that would help me. We would send you a train ticket and put you up at a hotel."

"OK." What else could he say? For her, he would go to the meeting.

"Thank you." India gushed, suddenly excited at his agreement. "I was looking at dates would you be able to come down for Monday 19th March? I would need to confirm that with my boss and the company, he is seeing them now so maybe I should ask, are there any dates I should avoid?"

"Were you thinking weekdays? It's hard for me to take time off during pre-season training and I'm trying to see my Mum as many weekends as I can. How much time would this take?"

"The business part of it can be as little as an hour, maybe two, however, I think this client will want to get to know you. I'm sorry Charlie I haven't been here long. I'm still feeling my way. Fudge, that doesn't sound professional, does it? Shouldn't I be faking it till I make it?"

"I value your honesty India, I can't say I know any better myself, I left these things to my agent, and they did a great job by avoiding this altogether."

"Robbie said you need a new agent; did you sack them?"

"No, I should have done, and now they have retired."

India blew out a breath. "OK, so can I tell my boss you are interested to know more about the product and the offer, that in principle you would be happy to look at a six-month contract with monthly photoshoots to be fitted in around your team commitments? I get the impression they would like to attend some matches too. Do you have access to tickets, or would Bentley & Bentley need to source those?" India was talking fast again.

"Yes, tell them you have persuaded me to listen to what they want and that I would look at a six-month contract. Can we leave it at that for now? Would that be enough India?"

"Yeah, thanks, she was relieved to be able to report back that she had got this far.

"So, I can expect to hear from you again soon? If you give me an email address, I can send you the fixture list." Charlie wanted to know he could contact her now instead of having to talk to Robbie.

"I have the fixture list in front of me. I don't know who will be in touch with you next. For now, I'll send you my email and other numbers that could be useful."

"OK." He wasn't sure what he had agreed to, but it felt like a start.

"I'd better get the good news to my boss; he is meeting the client this morning."

"Bye then." He said bye still he didn't want to hang up.

"Bye."

And just like that, they had started to talk again. Charlie wasn't certain how it had gone. It didn't feel too awkward, but he felt India had hardly relaxed during the whole ten minutes. Was that because of the work situation, or was it because of him? Their time talking before had been so relaxed, so natural. Could they ever get back to that connection?

Had he agreed to find out more because he needed to find extra money to help his mum? OR had he done it to connect with India again? Was it wrong that by saying yes this morning, he could do both? It did sound like it might help India in her latest job, too.

He had so many questions he wanted to ask her, to understand her hopes and dreams. The night they had met, she was fighting against her mother's plan for her life. The trip to Scotland had been her brother giving her and her mother time away from each other. He wondered how they got on now. From what Robbie had said, there was little chance that her mother had changed her mind and he sincerely hoped India was still the strong, independent girl he had met that night.

Charlie looked at himself in the mirror on the sidewall of the small therapy room. She had said he was photogenic, so she liked how he looked then. He wanted more than anything to talk to her again like they did that first night. He could only hope he did not mess it up this time, and he left the room to find Woody and ask his advice about agents and doing PR work.

Chapter 7

As India came out of the conference room, she saw Alice and Malcolm taking off their coats and settling back down from their break. India got ready to call Philip. As her hand moved towards the phone, it rang.

"Bentley & Bentley. How can I help you?" she used the words she had heard Jayne use many times each day.

"Are you OK Jayne?"

India recognised Philip Bentley's voice, so quickly explained she was covering the calls whilst Jayne had stepped out. Going on to explain that Charlie Robertson was happy to listen to their proposal. Philip was very relieved, as the Cooksons were already keen to push forward with a Yorkshire cricketer. She asked him who would be setting up the meeting with everyone so she could pass on his details. This created a long pause in which Philip made some quiet, thinking type noises, and India wondered why. Eventually, he answered her question.

"Listen India, normally I would have Jayne organising the meeting and maybe Alice or Malcolm working with the clients. It seems Jayne is a little stretched at the moment and I'm wondering if it would work for one person to take overall charge of the entire project. For that to work, I need you to meet the client. I'm going to send my driver back to collect you and bring you down to the golf course to speak to the clients with me over lunch. I think Matilda Cookson would enjoy some female input. Pull together everything you have. The car will be there in thirty minutes."

"Are you sure? That won't give me time to get much together for a professional presentation."

"I think they might prefer something a little more human than the normal set of slides."

"We certainly do!" said a male voice in the background, which India presumed was Joe Cookson.

"OK, Mr Bentley, I'll do what I can."

At that point, Jayne walked down the corridor. She heard India say 'Mr Bentley' and hurried the last few steps holding her hand out for the phone.

"Jayne is here now sir; would you like to speak to her?"

"NO! I need to go finish this game with Joe, see you soon India." And with that, he ended the call.

Jayne glared down her long nose at India.

"What did Mr Bentley want?"

"He wanted to speak to me about Charlie Robertson as he is with the client. They are keen to move forward, and Charlie has agreed to talk further." India was trying to sound in control, but that glare made her quake inside. She hoped it didn't show outside.

"So, does he want me to set up all the meetings? If so, you better give me the details for this cricketer."

"I have emailed you all his contact details this morning, possibly whilst you were in with Philip. He wants me to set up the meetings. He has asked me to meet the client today to go over some ideas with them about the project."

"So, we need to set up the conference room. You better go wash all the cups and make sure that the coffee machine is ready to go. What time are they coming?"

"The client is with Philip now. He is sending Josh to pick me up in about 30 minutes. I better get on it, so I have something to show them when I get there."

Jayne looked at India, stunned into silence. Philip had never sent the car for her; she had never joined him at the golf club. What was it about this girl? She had not seen Philip flirt with her like he usually did with the interns; he was different with this one. Well, never mind she would not be here long. If she were taking charge of this job, how many ways were there for her to mess this up? Jayne resolved to sit back and watch this one get her fingers burnt.

Unsure what else to say, India settled back at her desk and collected everything she could think of. All of Charlie's details and her ideas for the product launch were on the notebook app on her phone. She quickly created another Pinterest board to go with the one she had been using to collect images of Charlie for some time. Using it to pin some ideas she had for set dressing, like suitcases and towels.

In the washroom, she did what she could with her make-up, even adding a sweep of blush to bring some warmth to her face. Looking down at her clothes, her stomach dropped. The extremely basic black pencil skirt and a simple button through white blouse had seemed like a clever idea this morning. Fortunately, she had come to work in her red coat, but she felt she needed to be wearing a little more colour for lunch at the historic London Scottish Golf Club.

She pulled her pashmina out to see if she could arrange it to wear over her white shirt. With some clever use of pins, she was able to drape it across her shoulders. Next, taking out the ponytail she wore to work, she brushed her long dark hair down her back. She dug deep into the bottom of her tote bag and found a pair of striking red and black earrings that Katie had made for her. Now she might feel comfortable walking into the Victorian clubhouse.

Back at her desk, she nervously repacked her bag and put on her coat. India's change of look attracted the attention of Alice and Malcolm across the room. They exchanged a few words and eventually, Alice said: "OK you look nice India, off to meet someone special?"

"Just off for lunch."

"Lunch? It isn't even 12 o'clock yet, don't forget you only have 30 minutes." Smirked Malcolm.

India was tempted to say they had both been out for nearly an hour for coffee, but she didn't.

"I'll be a little longer than 30 minutes. I'm meeting a client, so Philip won't mind." She knew she had probably been unfair not to explain what was happening, still, she didn't think it was her job to tell them what Philip had said.

Jayne was clearly unhappy about her going, making a point of telling her to keep her mobile phone on, so she was reachable. Going on to add that she would have to catch up on her jobs when she got back in the afternoon. India could not help but wonder if that meant Jayne would have to do some of Philip's errands herself today. Swallowing hard, she set off down the stairs to wait by the glass front doors for the car.

The deep blue Bentley was visible in the traffic long before it pulled up to the curb, so India was outside waiting when the car came to a halt. India opened the passengers' door and slipped in next to Josh, the driver.

"Morning Little Girl." India grinned back at him. Josh was so tall he was one of the few people who could call her 'little'. As the person sent on errands and who sorted out some of the things that Jayne 'didn't have time to do', she spoke to Josh often. If he were giving her a lift to do an errand for Philip, she would always sit in the front with him, and he was probably the only person she felt comfortable with at Bentley & Bentley.

"So, lunch at the Golf Club today. Not picking up his suit from the tailors?"

India blew out a long breath.

"Yes, and with clients too, to talk about a new project. I have to say I am pretty nervous, Josh. I didn't come dressed for lunch at The Club."

"You are looking gorgeous, Little Girl, you always do. What did Old Iron Knickers have to say about this trip?"

"She didn't actually use any words, mind you, her body language spoke volumes."

Josh manoeuvred the car through the London traffic, taking the bridge to make their way to Wimbledon, south of the river from their Earls Court offices.

"What do you say to her about me?" India peered at his face to watch his response.

Josh laughed "You are joking. Do you think Old Iron Knickers sits in the front and chats with me? If I'm required to take her anywhere, she expects me to park up and open the backdoor for her. It doesn't matter how busy the traffic is, she would never jump in like you. Even Philip sits in the front sometimes."

"I can imagine." India liked Philip Bentley.

"As far as I know she has never been asked to have lunch either, which I'm sure didn't go down well, especially as she sees herself as the next Mrs Bentley."

India laughed "Seriously?"

"To be fair to Jayne though, I think Philip does rather keep her hopes up."

"No, surely not?" India was shocked at this idea.

"Look, I might be wrong, please don't say anything to anyone else."

"I think you are wrong, but who would I tell?"

"Here we are. I'll drop you at the clubhouse and then go to park up. Probably see you later. I can't see Philip letting you make your own way back from here."

"Oh, Josh, I forgot to be nervous talking to you. Now all those nerves are back. What am I doing here?"

"You're going to lunch with the client so you can share all your fabulous ideas for their project. You will charm them both, with your smile and your ideas. You're a natural India. Go do it."

India pulled down the visor and looked in the mirror. She adjusted her pashmina and touched up her lip gloss. With a deep breath, she opened the car door and walked towards the clubhouse door. Philip spotted her from the bar as she walked in. He waved her over to join them. Philip introduced Joe and Matilda Cookson to India. Matilda looked a little younger than Joe and was incredibly pleased to see India.

"Call me Tilly, I think we may have met before. I think my dad knows your dad. Don't you live in that sweet house near Hurst's Bridge?"

"Who is your father?" India was curious. People did remember the Barrington Jones name.

"Maxwell Sykes, my parents still live near Harrogate. That is why we are so keen on your idea to have a Yorkshire Cricketer. Philip tells us you have found one who is interested."

"Yes, I spoke to Charlie Robertson this morning, and he was happy to talk further when we have a better understanding of what we need from him."

"India, my dear, let's get these lovely people sat down for lunch before you tell them everything." Philip smiled at her and together they led Joe and Tilly from the bar to the beautiful dining room with its oak panels and large French windows overlooking the course. Philip and Joe had changed after their round of golf and Tilly was looking very elegant in a woollen grey dress and green leather knee-length boots.

India sat next to Tilly and admired her boots. As Tilly leaned down to stroke them, India spotted the beautiful bracelet she was wearing. It had incredibly ornate gold work which created heart-shaped settings for emeralds. The green stones were obviously chosen to match her eyes.

"I love your bracelet. Wherever did you buy that?"

"It was a gift from Joe." India smiled. That was what she wanted to hear.

Philip organised the drinks and the food as India asked Joe if he had enjoyed the golf. It turned out he was a member here too. That is how he and Philip had met. Tilly grabbed India's arm and told her she was pleased that she had joined them. She had told Philip she expected to be outnumbered. India suddenly felt more comfortable and decided that is why Philip had invited her, for Tilly.

The dining room at this historic golf course was part of a Victorian building: the panelled walls gave it a traditional feel and the menu matched. Philip suggested they try a sharing platter based on cheeses and hams, which seemed to suit everyone. The men enjoyed that with beer, the ladies opted for soft drinks. Such a simple choice did not take long to arrive, and baskets of bread and long wooden platters soon filled the centre of the table, along with butter, pickles, and grapes. India soon warmed to the Cooksons, especially Tilly, who was so easy to talk to. She asked as many questions as she could, which meant she didn't have to offer too many of her thoughts at this point. It was good to meet a client herself. When she was in team meetings, she always felt like she didn't have enough information. The company was a new part of something Joe's family had been doing for years, and this was the first time Tilly and Joe had worked together. They were visibly excited. Tilly plainly had ideas about branding, so India talked to her about props for the shoots that would be helpful to support the brand image; like buying some nice towels.

As they enjoyed a coffee with some mints, an email bounced in from Charlie. It asked if it would be possible to meet on Friday 16th as he had some time out from training. Seeing his name on her phone was not the same as hearing his voice, but it did still have a physical effect on her body, and Tilly noticed how much she was smiling as she examined her phone.

"Oh, something made our girl smile, a boyfriend perhaps?" she teased. Philip frowned at India. Worried that he thought she was taking private messages whilst sitting with a client, she quickly spoke to reassure them.

"No, I don't have a boyfriend. This is work. Actually, it is Charlie Robertson asking if Friday 16th would work for you to meet him and for him to hear about the offer."

Joe spoke first "We can do that can't we Tilly? You want to do some shopping when I come down for the event that Saturday. If we come a day early then you can have some extra time to shop."

"Oh, that would be great. Would you and I be able to go shopping together for props India?" Everyone smiled. The men were relieved Tilly had someone to talk to, whilst India and Tilly were happy that they could decide together what to buy for the shoots.

"Tell him yes, India, and we can sort the travel details when we get back to the office. Then we can arrange a meeting time to suit." Philip seemed to want to take control again.

India wrote a brief email to Charlie to tell him that the date would be fine with the client and that she would be in touch with travel arrangements tomorrow. India and Tilly exchanged numbers and emails and with their heads together over phones, India shared her idea boards on Pinterest and some images of Charlie.

"India, why is this board named Charlie Whisky Romeo?" Tilly asked quietly whilst Philip and Joe were engrossed in sharing a story with another golfer about a dog walker that they had all encountered around the 9th tee. India blushed scarlet. She thought she had changed the name of that board before she left the office. She explained to Tilly that cricket was full of nicknames, and everyone was known by both initials. As Charlie was never keen to share what the W stood for in his name, his teammates had given the Scottish player the middle name whisky. Coming from north of the border, he was partial to a dram. It seemed to fit.

"OK, so why Romeo?"

"I think it's from the phonetic alphabet, so CWR would be Charlie Whisky Romeo. Maybe you can ask him when you meet."

"I thought it might be because he appears to be a bit of a lady's man. Do people still say that?"

Joe's ears pricked up. "What do you mean?"

"Most times he is in the newspapers, he is with some woman, the man is certainly very attractive."

"But don't we want to appeal to men not women?" Philip was scowling again, and she thought she had never seen his face show so many moods in such a brief time. India smiled.

"Joe, that is a lovely bracelet your wife is wearing. Where did you buy it?"

Tilly laughed out loud. "Oh, Babe, I think she is trying to tell you, that although men are most probably the ones using the Gym Away, they are not necessarily the only ones buying it. And she is right, men are difficult to buy presents for. Gym Away is at a competitive price point for someone to buy it as a gift, especially if that gift will give her man the body of someone like Charlie Robertson."

"The gift market might be something we focus on for the next campaign, say from September to December," suggested India, and instantly Philip was smiling again.

It was time to leave and Tilly Cookson hugged India as they said goodbye and they agreed to organise meeting Charlie the next day.

Philip and India waved the Cooksons off in their smart BMW coupe as Josh pulled the car up for them. This time, India joined Philip in the back of the car.

As they pulled away from the golf club onto the common, Philip was quiet. It made India nervous. She had been surprised by how much she had enjoyed having lunch with the client, but she pulled out her phone to make some notes based on the things she had learned. Philip looked annoyed.

"Is this you texting your friends on my time, young lady?"

India showed him her phone. "No, no, this is my notes app. I'm jotting down some of the things we picked up today, like their brand colours. You know, things to help the team plan the shoot."

"India, I told you earlier you are going to be doing all this. So tomorrow, can you sort out the trains and accommodation for the cricketer and liaise with Tilly about them joining us? I'll get Jayne to organise a company card you can use to charge all that. Use the standard project costs spreadsheet to record it all."

"OKKK" India knew that is what he had said, but she wasn't confident he meant it.

"Now, don't you live south of the river?"

"Yes, I do, off Putney High Street, near the bridge."

"Good, we will drop you off. That way you can get straight on to this project. Now India, we need to talk about this project and what I have seen over lunch."

India's nerves were back again. She had no idea what he was going to say. He started with the positives.

"Well done on asking all those questions. You showed interest in both the product and the client. As you saw, this is very personal to them and so understanding their likes and dislikes is important."

India started to relax, unfortunately, Philip was not finished.

"You do need to be careful about how you behave with the client. Whilst you should be friendly, they are not your friends. I also have to say the same about this cricketer. We need to keep him on board and being friendly with him will help, please don't be getting too involved with this young man. You still have a job to do."

"Of course." India was shocked he felt the need to say that.

"Tell me how you know him?"

"As I have been saying, I don't know him. I met him once 6 years ago at a New Year party, but he is a good friend of my cousin, Robbie. I met him at Robbie's house, and we talked. I was seventeen, and he was a professional cricketer, so yes, I noticed him. I was a silly young schoolgirl. He has been at New Year parties since then, but I haven't spoken to him until I rang him about this job. I was able to get his contact details from my cousin last night."

"You have never been a silly young girl, India. What does your mother think of him?"

"Mum has never met him. Robbie is a cousin on dad's side. She never comes to Scotland with us. His mum is my dad's sister, my Aunt Patricia. Mum uses her as an example of what could happen to me if I don't behave like a lady. She didn't quite get the old 'settle down, get married and have children' in the approved order."

"I see. Well, the best advice I can give you India is, to behave as if your mother is in the room, possibly close enough to hear what you are saying. I'm fairly sure that way you won't go far wrong."

"Of course, Philip, this job is important to me, I will always do my best."

"I know India. That is why I trust you."

Chapter 8

The next morning India bounced into Bentley & Bentley to find a large box on her desk from Hurst's Bridge. She was excited, having been up late last night working on her ideas for the project.

She had found trains from Leeds and a hotel for Charlie to stay at in Earls Court quite near the office. It was one she knew Jayne preferred to use. She had been in touch with Tilly and arranged for them to arrive at the office an hour after Charlie. Tilly had agreed to send India some product samples before the end of the week.

With no idea how her mum had got the dress there so fast, she lifted her parcel onto the floor and fired up her computer. Emailing copies of all the meetings to Philip and Jayne, and at the last minute, she included Alice and Malcolm.

Alice looked up from her desk and smiled a sickly smile at India. "OK Thank you for sorting those meetings for me." India was puzzled, before she could ask Alice what she meant, Jayne came into the open office and announced that Philip would like to see her in his office now. It felt like she wanted to say NOW really loud, but she said it quietly, which made it feel even more menacing. The bounce was gone from India's step as she knocked on the door to Philip's office.

Philip only looked up from his desk to offer her a weak smile. "Change of plan India, Jayne and Alice are going to run their usual roles on this project and you can go back to doing your normal tasks."

"I thought Jayne was too busy?" the wind left India's lungs, she wasn't expecting that.

Philip looked through a pile of papers on his desk and muttered: "So did I."

India felt like the air had been let out of her body like someone had pricked the balloon of her confidence. Unsure what else to say, she walked back to the open office to find on her desk a list from Jayne of errands she needed to do. Mechanically she put on her coat and started to organise her bag and think about which order to do the jobs in. Alice and Malcolm were smirking together in the corner.

"Skipping out of work again India, didn't you do enough of that yesterday?" laughed Malcolm. India turned and smiled at him saying nothing. She couldn't understand what had just happened. When Philip dropped her off yesterday, this project was all hers. She worked until after midnight, sourcing props and trying to work out a plan that would work around the Yorkshire fixture list. Now she had a list of jobs that needed to be done around London. She needed to collect some dresses from a designer and take them to a photographer ready for a shoot tomorrow. There were other props for tomorrow's shoot, and so she decided the photographer was the last place she needed to stop. As she opened the large front door, Josh was parked in front of the building, and he sprang out to open the rear door for her.

Still, shell-shocked from what happened upstairs, India simply stared at him.

"Are you OK India? Philip sent a text saying you were having a rough day and I should help you with the errands for today."

Still confused, India thrust the list at him, closed the rear door and got in the front seat with him. "Help me work out which way we do this; my brain is fried!"

"Did you get some sad news? Is someone ill?"

"Josh, I honestly don't know what happened."

"So, tell me about it, does it have anything to do with Old Iron Knickers?"

"No idea! Yesterday, Philip asked me to take over the entire project for that new client. That is why we met them at the golf club. I thought it went well and I thought Philip was happy with how it was going, from what he said on the way back. Now I'm sitting here wondering what changed his mind. Do you think the client has said they want someone with more experience?"

Josh opened his mouth to respond, but India was thinking again. "That doesn't make sense, because I was arranging things with Tilly last night and she seemed very keen. Maybe it was Charlie?"

"Charlie who?" Josh was looking at India for more clues.

"Charlie Robertson, the Yorkshire cricketer we are trying to sign, perhaps he has said 'not with India'."

"Why would he say that?" Josh looked amused.

"This isn't funny Josh, I felt this was my big chance." India was still lost at the news.

"No seriously, why would he say, 'not with India'?"

"We have history." India studied the list again.

"Really!" Josh was surprised India didn't seem like the girl to have a history with anyone.

"It's a long story."

"Well, looking at this list, it looks like we have all day, especially if we hit some bad traffic." A naughty grin hit Josh's face. "Philip doesn't need me back today. He said I could go home once I ran you round a few places. I don't think he knows how long this list is. Why don't we start by picking up the man's suit, that's the closest, and you can tell me your long story as we take our time doing these jobs?"

India started at the beginning and told Josh all about meeting Charlie at seventeen. The times they had seen each other since but not spoken and about blurting out his name at the meeting. She told Josh how she felt when she heard his voice again. India was grateful Josh had taken over the list and told India what she needed to do every time the car stopped. They were making amazing progress and the back of the car was full of things to take to the studio for tomorrow's shoot and a few personal errands for Philip. At 12:15, Josh pulled the car over and parked up. He pulled out his phone and called Philip.

"Mr Bentley, I'm sorry, the traffic has been terrible so far today. There was a lot more on that list than I thought you meant; we have only done seven stops so far."

"Yes, sir I said seven. There are still a few things to pick up, then we need to get over to the studios south of the river."

"Sir, I need to stop and get my lunch; I have to take breaks."

"No sir, she has been very quiet all morning."

"I will sir, leave it with me." And with that Josh ended the call to their boss.

"I tell you India the root of this problem is Old Iron Knickers. Philip had no idea how long that list was, and SHE didn't know that Philip was sending me to drive you."

"That is crazy!" shouted India, glancing into the back of the car "how could I have done all this, collected all these things and carried them to the photographers? I mean these shops and studios close at five o'clock at the latest. I couldn't have done it."

"I guess that is why you were pulled off this project."

"So I could do these jobs today?"

"No, because Jayne wants to be the one helping Philip and dealing with the talent. You went to lunch with her precious Philip yesterday. After you got out of the car, he rang her to ask her to arrange a company bank card for you and judging by his face she went mental, so he explained you needed it to do this new project and I'm fairly sure she put the phone down on him. Then she rang back to see what time you would be in the office, as there was a list of jobs for you to do that you hadn't started yet. I'm guessing she didn't like being told we'd already dropped you at home."

"Fudge! Josh this list would have been impossible without your help."

"Sweetheart, when I run her around, she sits in the back and doesn't get out at most places, I'm the one nipping into the shops and dry cleaners."

"Why does Philip allow it? He must know."

"I have my theories. Anyway, I think Philip is feeling guilty. He told me to stop for lunch and make sure you had some too and charge it to him. So that is what we are going to do now. We are going into this café and Philip is going to buy us both lunch."

Josh was a wonderful companion. They chose an all-day breakfast in a café, where he seemed to know everyone. They laughed and joked; he entertained her with stories of the people who had done her job before, the loud ones, the mousy ones, and the way-out strange ones. Ones who sat in the back, who sat in the front, who drove their own cars, those who preferred to walk, and the one with a tricycle.

"How many years have you been here and how many people have had my job?"

"Seven years and I think about fifteen people. No one lasted longer than a year, one only lasted three days, six months is about the norm. Most were pretty young girls who seem to leave suddenly. I think only two were guys."

As they were getting back to the car, India's phone rang. She held it up to Josh so he could see it was Jayne. They jumped into the car and Josh started the engine.

"Hello Jayne," India answered the call once the engine was running.

"I know, the traffic has been awful."

"I was going there next."

"I know it was at the beginning of the list, but you didn't say that it had to be picked up early?"

"I thought it…"

"I'm sorry and yes, I'll apologise to Deanna when I get there, and I'll ensure she knows it is my fault."

"If the traffic allows, we should be there in twenty minutes. I'll ring now myself and explain." India ended the call.

"It seems she is upset that I didn't do the list in the order she gave me. It seems she promised Deanna first pick up."

"If we had done the list in the order she gave you, we wouldn't have got to the studio today at all."

"I know! I'm going to ring Deanna and apologise now."

Josh pulled out into traffic, and she called Deanna. It wasn't long before India was laughing as she chatted to the designer, who admitted she asked for an early pick-up because she had another dress that she needed to get to the photographers. Nick had promised to squeeze it in whilst he had some other models in this afternoon as a favour. She knew India would probably help her with that.

At Deanna's workroom, the girls hugged each other and laughed. India explained what had happened and showed Deanna the list.

"The old witch, I wouldn't have dared asked her, but she said she was sending you yesterday, what happened are you OK?"

"Yeah! I'm fine, well no, not really," and again India shared her story. How she believed she finally had a project and about her lunch with Philip and the client and hinted about Charlie Robertson. Deanna gave India the dress she'd called to collect, then went to fetch the other dress for her to leave with Nick, the photographer, to do when he could. India sighed when she saw the dress. It was a midnight blue, very beaded and with a plunging back. Deanna saw the look on her friend's face and held the dress up to her.

"Tell him it needs to be a tallish size 12." She looked hopefully at India. "Unless you can do it whilst you are there?"

"Of course, I can't!"

Deanna helped India to the car with the dresses. When she saw how many things were on the back seat, she laughed at the treasure hunt she had been on.

"Don't laugh. She wasn't aware I had the car. I was supposed to do all this on the Tube."

"No way!" Deanna was shaking her head, she wanted to laugh but it wasn't funny.

"Josh says I'm being punished for the lunch with Philip yesterday."

"Makes sense to me." Deanna waved them off and they made their way to the last stop, over the bridge in Putney. Nick, the photographer, sent his assistant out to help them in with everything.

"What do you want to do now, shall I drop you here or take you back to the office?"

"Crazy as it seems. After yesterday I feel I should go back to the office to prove a point. I left a parcel there from my mum too, so now I have to get that back home on the Tube."

"As I said, Philip doesn't want me tonight. How about I take you back to the office, you work a little past your time, then come out with your parcel and I'll drive you home."

"Josh, I can't ask you to do that, don't you want to get home."

"I can't think of anything I would rather do, India. Look, I'll park around the corner. None of them will know."

"Thank you, Josh." India's smile was starting to get back to normal. Josh was pleased he could help.

Chapter 9

Charlie stepped off the train at King's Cross after he had spent the two-hour journey down from Leeds, mulling over what he would say to India. He wanted to agree to this project if it helped her; he hoped it would clear the air between them. He didn't want to take this job if it was going to make things difficult between them. Yes, he needed the money, well his mum needed this money, still, he would say no if he thought this caused a bigger problem between himself and India. She had made it sound like she wanted him to do this, from what Robbie said this could be her big break. But how much time would it take up, he needed to spend all his spare time with his mum?

He hated making decisions, and the ones that involved India Barrington Jones seemed more difficult. He didn't understand why such a young girl had affected him so physically. Charlie would not deny he liked women, and women liked him. He was used to his body reacting to a beautiful woman, that was simply a natural response, there was just something special about her. Even the brief phone calls they had exchanged had hit him deep inside.

Things had been off the last few calls; he had asked her if she could meet him from the train to help him find his way to the offices. She had sounded sad that she couldn't, and it felt like she was unsure how involved she would be in this project. India had told him a driver would collect him and he should go to the station reception to meet him. Even sending him a snapshot of the driver, obviously from her phone, and telling him the driver's name was Josh. Judging by the smile she had captured on his face; Josh thought India was beautiful too.

Finding Josh was easier than he expected it would be. He sounded pleasant enough; he helped Charlie with his suitcases and pointed out they had an hour to do a 30-minute journey, so if Charlie needed anything before they got there, they had time to stop. Charlie didn't want to wait to see her any longer. Josh explained if he left his bags in the car, he would take them to his hotel and deliver them to his room and that he would take him there after the meeting was over. On the way to the office, Charlie chatted to Josh and in the same guarded way he used with Robbie when he asked about India. That generated a smile in Josh, and Charlie thought Josh must be interested in her. Who was he kidding? Of course, she will have attracted a lot of attention since she moved to London.

"India has been having a tough time, she was told this was her project. The clients loved her, she got you on board and then she was pulled and since then they have given her the most impossible jobs to do. I have helped when I can. Although I'm not sure anyone can protect her from a certain someone."

"You might need to explain some of that. Why was she taken off this project, did she do something wrong?"

"No! Quite the opposite. My theory is as soon as anyone in her job, starts to show promise, they are made to feel or look stupid. Impossible tasks are piled on, and in the end, they leave. They have picked India out for special attention, still, she seriously doesn't want to give up. I get the impression her family thinks she flakes easily."

Charlie sat back in his seat; he didn't like the sound of that at all. Perhaps he should refuse to work on this, but how would that help India?

"How is she taking it? Is it bringing out the fight in her?"

"Sometimes, other days though, she looks like she may have given up. It is a shame because she has more talent in her little finger than the rest of them put together. India is great with people, and she has so many ideas. People will do anything for her, whereas Old Iron Knickers gets things done because businesses want to work with Bentley &

Bentley. To be honest, I think Philip Bentley took her off your project to protect her. I wish it was enough."

"What is he like?" Charlie was curious about what he was getting into.

"Philip Bentley is the best boss I ever had; he likes India and I know it impressed him how well she handled these clients."

"Thank you, I don't suppose you have met them as well?"

"Only a couple of times, and before you ask, I think they are OK too. They come over as no-nonsense folk."

"Thank you, that helps."

The car pulled up outside an impressive building where Bentley & Bentley occupied the top floor. Josh opened the door for him and with a deep breath, he looked Charlie square in the eyes.

"India is a good kid, she feels things you see, it is part of who she is. She cares for everyone even though some of them are horrible to her. I don't know what your plans are, but I'm asking you not to hurt her."

Charlie could only nod at the driver. He was finally here; he had seen her 3 months ago at Robbie's and they had several brief chats on the phone over the last week. Still, he was nervous about seeing her for what somehow felt like the first time in six years. He originally believed they would work together on this job, and he wasn't sure if it would be easier or not to do this now India would not be part of it. *Be honest Charlie you haven't had one consistent thought through any of this. Just get up there and go with your gut.*

As Charlie walked down the corridor, his eyes found her immediately. She was turned away from him and was talking to an older woman with a stern face. India's shoulders were hunched, her long dark hair in a sleek ponytail down her back. He knew the smart linen suit she was wearing would be immaculate. In contrast, the other woman wore high heels and a flowered dress that plunged at the neckline. She was trying to look down at India, and that was not easy.

"If Mr Robertson is here Josh must be back. Make sure he has this list of things to pick up. I would send you, however for some reason Mr Bentley wants you to stay in the office whilst our visitors are here."

"He still has to take Charlie's cases to The Marriot and then collect the Cooksons."

The tall woman raised an eyebrow and pushed the piece of paper at India, who took it and turned to come down the corridor towards him.

His heart dropped. He expected to feel something when he saw her. Usually, she was in party mode, and this was work, yet it still felt wrong. She looked so down and deflated. India offered him a weak smile and a quiet 'Hi' as she passed him. He reached for her arm; they were alone in the corridor, so he stopped her, searching her eyes for a clue. He was not sure what, he didn't enjoy the way seeing her like this felt in his body too. She looked sad and that made him sad too.

"India?"

"Charlie, it's good to see you." It was the quiet answer that scared Charlie.

He snorted, "You could try telling your face that."

India sighed and almost laughed at him and then found a smile. He knew she had better smiles than that.

"I need to give this to Josh, though I don't think he can do all this," she said, shaking her head. "Then I'll be back up and I'll organise a coffee."

"Josh seems like a nice bloke; tell him we can take my cases when he takes me to the hotel if it helps."

"He is and thank you, I will." Smiling, she left him, and Charlie speculated about how much India liked Josh too. *Stop thinking about India and focus on this job.*

The older woman introduced herself as Jayne, Mr Bentley's Personal Assistant, and sat him in a small conference room saying someone would bring him coffee. He stood up looking at the view across London and then took in the room. Although it was superbly finished it lacked any personality like most offices. The door opened and India's face popped around. She was smiling now, which made Charlie smile back.

"Jayne asked me to make you a coffee, but I thought I would check if you would prefer tea. I can make a pot of tea if you would like?"

"Yes please, can you join me?"

"Officially no, but if you keep me talking, it would be rude for me to walk out." Not waiting for a reply, she left him, returning quickly with a neat tray of tea, a cup and saucer and a small plate of shortbread biscuits.

"So, Mr Robertson how would you like your tea?" *Oh, she was playing the keep it professional game.* She was at work, he could do that. He wasn't sure he liked her calling him Mr Robertson, and he was very sure he was not calling her Miss Barrington Jones, ever.

"Thank you, milk and one sugar, please." If they were playing the professional game, he had better keep his questions professional, too. From the way India's blue eyes kept flicking to the door, he guessed she was expecting someone else to join them at any point.

"I hear if I do agree to this project, you won't be working with me on it. Is that correct?"

"Does that mean you haven't decided to do it yet?" the sad expression had crept back in, and Charlie felt cruel.

"I assumed that was why I was here today, to find out what the project needs from me and how much they are prepared to pay."

"Yes, I guess so." He hated how weak her voice was.

"I haven't even seen the product yet, and what about the client?"

"The product is great, and the clients are lovely." And she explained to him all about Joe and Tilly's journey, their backgrounds working in different family businesses and how this was their first product for their own company. She explained that whilst it was a new company and the budget was limited, they did have the backing of the main companies. She assured him this could be the start of something bigger.

Charlie relaxed and so did India, and he began to believe they could go back to communicating properly, that they could be friends and share real conversations. Suddenly, not just India's face, but her entire body changed when the door opened, and two other people walked in the door. Charlie didn't like them the moment he saw them. Maybe it was the way they sneered at India and maybe it was because of the way her body responded to them, but maybe it was because he realised that their appearance meant India would be leaving the room.

"This is where you have been hiding. You better go and organise coffees before Mr Bentley comes through, then get back to your desk."

"I'm sorry. I kept her. I was asking questions about the project that I didn't seem to have yet. Could I have tea again instead of coffee?"

"Of course." She dipped out of the room swapping a secretive smile with him.

Charlie sat still and studied the two intruders in the room. They did not speak to him and were busy setting up a projector from a laptop and looking for something they could not seem to find. They exchanged whispers with each other but didn't glance over or speak to him. When India returned with a larger tray, he stood to hold the door and then take the heavy tray from her. Again, she gave him a little smile. That tiny smile was worth so much. He caught sight of the other two pretending to be busy, yet all the time watching her.

"India! Where on earth did you put the Gym Away kit? I thought I told you to get it ready for the presentation. How can we show it to Mr Robertson when you haven't done your job yet again?"

India held her head up, he noticed she was different with these two than that Jayne woman he had seen her talking to earlier. This was all remarkably interesting. India opened her mouth to speak but before she got one word out, a tall man in his late 40s walked into the room. He was smartly dressed in a suit and tie. Unmistakably, he was the person in charge wherever he went.

"I have the kit because I asked India for it last night." Turning to Charlie, he introduced himself. "I'm Philip Bentley. I am so glad you agreed to meet us today."

"India persuaded me I needed to hear more Mr Bentley; she is the reason I came down to talk to you." It could not hurt to use her name, surely.

"Call me Philip. Now let's see what we can sort out before the clients arrive."

Philip Bentley sat down next to Charlie, whilst India poured drinks for them all. The other two shuffled to the front of the room and started up a set of slides that introduced themselves and the product to Charlie.

"You can go now, India." Said the small chubby guy that Charlie had disliked instantly. Having been dismissed India quietly left, taking with her a piece of Charlie.

From watching some very uninspiring slides, he now knew nothing new. India had given him more details. He learnt they were called Alice and Malcolm and that they did not understand the product. He could not work out why they were using slides to tell him their names or show him a product that was in the room. It was making him feel sleepy after his early start to catch the train that morning.

Malcolm eventually turned off the torture of the slides and turned to Philip and Charlie. "Any questions?"

"Thank you, Malcolm." Philip was stifling a yawn too. "What more can we tell you, Charlie?"

"The first thing I need to know is what you expect from me?"

Alice and Malcolm looked at each other, puzzled, then looked to Philip. So, Philip spoke.

"I'm sure the clients would love you as a full-time model for them, Charlie, however, we understand you have a busy timetable. For the price they are going to offer you; we could suggest that you do one professional photoshoot for them each month. That should take an hour, although we should allow for two or three. Something always seems to happen at a shoot. The client has also shown an interest in some match day time, bringing clients to meet you and possibly a few photos, you know the sort of thing."

Charlie had seen his teammates doing meet and greets on match days. It probably wasn't him, but if the money were good, he would have to say yes. He needed to get things sorted for his mum.

"The clients, Joe and Matilda Cookson, will be here in about 20 minutes so we can talk about money then. Shall you and I go stretch our legs for 5 minutes?"

"I like that idea." Charlie felt more comfortable outside than in a London office. He also thought Philip Bentley seemed like a good guy and maybe on his own, he could be honest.

Charlie and Philip Bentley fastened up their coats and headed for the front door of the building. They said little until they were out of the building.

"Tell me, Charlie, what are you thinking at this moment? Are you ready to do this?"

"On the train, I was thinking this would be fun and if the money is OK, I would be extremely interested. After that 'presentation' I'm not so sure. Would I be working with that Malcolm guy?"

"Alice is the one likely to be at the shoots with you, picking out clothes and helping the photographer understand what we need."

"Oh."

"I have to say, Charlie, that 'oh' didn't sound too positive."

"What happened to India? When she spoke to me about this project, she seemed full of ideas, and she seemed to have a good grip on the product and the clients."

"India is a brilliant and charming young lady, if you were only doing this to get close to her, I would want to ask you to reconsider."

"Good heavens no! Yes, India might have convinced me to consider this, but I assure you there is nothing between us. She was just seventeen when we met, so there couldn't be anything between us."

"I appreciate what you mean. When I met her, she was ten and riding a rather fat little pony, so it is hard to consider her as anything other than my friend's little girl. Rather a shame!"

Charlie looked hard at Philip Bentley, not sure why he hated that last sentence. It was an expression that caused Philip to do some fast explaining.

"I usually rather enjoy flirting a little in the office, oh quite harmless stuff you realise, with India though, it never seems right, and of course, you have met Alice. I'm fairly sure she wouldn't understand I meant it to be fun."

Although Charlie was still frowning.

"So back to you. Before I introduce you to my client, what do you need to know?"

"To be perfectly honest, Mr Bentley, it rather depends on the cash involved. I'll admit that having seen those two this morning, I would much prefer to be working with India, simply because we talk the same language."

"Yes, I have a sinking feeling that the client might feel the same way. Matilda, she likes to be called Tilly, by the way, you should wait for her to tell you that. Yes, Tilly rather took to our India, and I think she talks the Cookson's language too. Now let's talk money."

Philip and Charlie turn the corner and walked back to the office. As they walked, Philip told him about the money on offer, how he would be paid after each shoot, with a bonus at the end of the project. He also suggested that if this went well, there could be other shoots in the future. The pair were nodding and laughing when India heard them coming down the corridor, and so did Jayne. The older woman came out of her office to tell Philip that Josh was on his way with the Cooksons and asked him if he wanted her to arrange coffees in the conference room.

Chapter 10

"We will have this next part in my office," and turning to India he said, "Could you organise a tray of drinks, my dear? You know what we all like."

India smiled; Jayne was wrong-footed there. She knew Jayne would only ask her to make the drinks anyway but wanted to be praised for having passed on the instructions. In fact, that is what Jayne did all day, bully other people to get jobs done on her timetable, which often was nothing like the real one. As the water heated for the drinks, India replayed in her head all the complaints she had heard, from the designers, make-up artists, and photographers that week.

With the new tray ready, she carried it into the corridor to head for Philip's office as the Cooksons arrived.

"You and your tray are a sight for sore eyes," chirped Joe Cookson as he held open the door for her. Charlie sprang out of his chair and lifted the heavy tray as she directed him to the side table. India poured the coffees. Tilly had removed her coat and came over to hug India.

"Can we go looking for props together tomorrow, sweetie?" India was lost for words. Now she was off the project, she didn't think Alice would want her picking towels. Philip was on the phone and excused himself from the room. That gave India time to explain to Tilly.

"I'm not working directly on this launch anymore; Alice will be taking over." Charlie scoffed and then proceeded to cough to cover the noise.

"I don't understand. The reason we agreed to this was because of you, bringing in Charlie and your ideas that fitted so well with mine. Babe, did you know about this?"

"No sweetheart, I didn't. Philip never mentioned it to me, then I guess it wasn't clear that she was working with us. Maybe Alice will have brilliant suggestions too."

"I presume we can hear what she says. Did we sign anything yet?"

"No, we would do that today provided they secured Mr Robertson."

All eyes moved to Charlie. "I'm here because India sold me on the idea. I met Alice earlier she says OK and So a lot, and if she knows which end of a cricket bat to hold, I would be highly surprised. Then we can't all have played for the first XI, can we India?"

India blushed. "Look, I shouldn't be part of this conversation. As the junior, my opinion doesn't count. I should go. Sorry. Hopefully, it will work out for all of you." And with that, she slipped out of the room.

Three faces watched her go, before they could speak, Philip Bentley walked back into his office. Matilda Cookson closed her mouth into a straight line, folded her arms across her chest, and sent Joe and Charlie a warning glare. Now Charlie could see the hint of red in her chestnut hair and the green eyes reflected in the emeralds she wore around her neck. He seemed to get the message that the plan was to sit quietly and let Philip do the talking.

Philip started by introducing everyone, and they had all agreed that they preferred to be called Charlie, Joe, and Tilly. Philip started by saying he had discussed fees with Charlie and that he was ready to go ahead so they could get straight to the contracts. Charlie looked at Tilly, and she was ready to take the lead.

"Charlie was telling us you made some changes to the team. That India has been replaced by someone called Alice, did you say, Charlie?" *Oh, clever don't drop India in it. He could play this game.*

"Oh, yes," said Philip "Alice has much more experience than India and I'm sure you will like her ideas for each of the shoots."

"Lovely, when can I hear them?"

"How about we get her in after we sign these contracts?"

"No, Philip, if there are some changes, then I think we should meet Alice and see what her thoughts are for the launch. We came to an experienced company like Bentley & Bentley for the benefit of that experience and now I'm wondering why we didn't meet Alice in the first place." Tilly glanced at everyone in the room before continuing. "I have to say it was India that sold me on Bentley & Bentley, the questions she asked, her knowledge of the market and who our buyers would be. We liked her thoughts about props and the way she included us in the planning. If Alice has the experience, then maybe she can be a wonderful addition to the project." Tilly sat back in her chair; her words sounded as if she was open-minded, her body language said otherwise.

Charlie was rather enjoying this. At that moment, he had his answer. This would be so much more interesting with India on the team. He was already liking the Cooksons, and Josh had been right; they were no-nonsense people.

Philip left the room to arrange for them to meet Alice in the conference room.

"Why is he moving us to the conference room?" Joe asked the other two.

"I think Alice is unable to introduce herself unless she has access to her slide deck. This morning she was in the same room as me for ten minutes, but this guy made the introduction using the slides." Offered Charlie.

"What are your thoughts, Charlie? If you have met her? We rather like the idea of using you, so unless you are signing, we won't be signing; will we Tilly?"

"No Charlie and no India, and we will be thinking again." Tilly was feeling defiant and crossed her arms again.

"Possibly we can get India and Alice?" suggested Joe. "Let's give the girl a chance."

Philip returned and ushered them into the conference room. This time Jayne brought in coffee and no tea. Alice stood at the front, fiddling with a laptop. The coffee in Charlie's cup looked a weird colour, and he decided not to try it. Joe took a drink and spat his out back into his cup and looked at Charlie. Tilly had a strange look in her eyes as she considered her coffee. "Oh hell!" Joe muttered to Charlie, "keep your head down mate."

Charlie had no trouble sitting back in his chair and watching Tilly take over the show. They were the customer, and he was the "talent" as Alice had described him earlier.

"Alice, it is lovely to meet you at last and I can't wait to listen to your ideas for Gym Away and our launch project."

"OK. Thank you, let me show you how I see this launch going as we take your ICA on a journey with Mr Robertson in each shoot."

Alice showed them a series of settings and talked about what they would use in each shoot.

April was a beach, possibly in the south of France.

May was Charlie on a motorbike.

June was a sports car.

July was playing tennis.

August was playing cricket.

September was back on a beach somewhere else in Europe.

It was Joe's turn to play the game. "I have to hand it to you, Philip, I wasn't expecting anything that exotic on the budget we gave you, you have done well."

"I'm rather wondering how I can get to the beach destination in the two hours Philip said I would need to give you." Charlie bit his lip.

69

"I have a couple of questions?" began Tilly. "Where is the product in each of these shoots, I can see Charlie could exercise on the beach if he could get there given his timetable? What about on the motorbike and the sports car?"

"So, Malcolm suggested your ICA would aspire to own those." Alice drawled out.

"Malcolm?"

"Someone else on the team," Alice said, looking at her laptop.

"When I was speaking to India about this project, and the complications involved, she was working with Charlie's fixture list. How did you manage to overcome those issues? How did you get him to agree to the dates?"

"OK, so we usually send the model the dates and they make themselves available." Explained Alice.

"Alice, if you and Malcolm could join me in my office with your budget sheets, I'll ask India to make some decent coffee."

"OK, India isn't here. Jayne sent her out to pick up a dress from Deanna and take it to Nick."

By now steam was coming out of his ears as he strode towards the door.

Looking at the rest of the group, he began to apologise. Tilly stopped him. "I'll make the drinks, point me to the kettle. Philip, I have to say I'm extremely disappointed with everything we heard today. I hope you can fix this because we were hoping to move forward."

Whilst Philip, Jayne, Malcolm, and Alice were in the corner office, the others huddled in the break room and finally enjoying a decent cup of coffee.

"Charlie, I'm sorry, this is no reflection on you and if we move, we will ask them to contact you. India seemed to have it all planned out, how we could make this look good on a tight budget."

"I'm rather relieved; I didn't understand half that stuff, I mean what is this ICA?

"I think that was Alice trying to sound clever, ICA is a way of referring to the ideal client."

"Those scenes seriously aren't me. I'm not on a beach very often, I do like sports cars, but I never rode a motorbike, and I haven't played tennis since I was 14. Why pay me if you don't want me to be myself?"

"Precisely, if we simply wanted some good-looking guy on a motorbike, we could hire a model." agreed Joe.

"So, we insist on India?" asked Tilly.

"I would love to work with India. It would be far more fun. I even like the challenge of us doing this on a tight budget. To be honest I have no idea how India feels. There is a lot of office politics going on here and I think her life could be difficult if she is back on this project."

"I see. I don't want to push for India if she doesn't want it. We can simply walk away. You guys hold the fort, I'll slip to the toilet and phone her."

Charlie and Joe sat down with the coffees and the conversation turned to Yorkshire's chances this year and which matches they should come to. When Tilly returned, there was still no sign of Philip Bentley.

"You were right. She wasn't keen on working on this because she feels they won't like it. I told her that was OK, we would walk away and find someone else in that case. Eventually, she agreed she would try. We must do what we can to ensure she doesn't suffer though."

Joe looked at his watch, "Tilly babe, we should be on our way, we have an hour to be across town."

"Then what do we do babe?" Tilly sounded desperate to resolve the way forward.

"What about we give them until Monday morning to create a better proposal in line with the budget? I get the feeling that Alice thought she could add on extra expenses as they came up and we would be committed via the contract for six months. I'll go knock on the door and tell Philip what we have decided. This is not what was presented to us, so I have no problem walking away if we need to."

With Joe gone, Tilly stared at Charlie. "I'm sorry we dragged you down here for this."

"I'm pleased to see someone standing up to them. India looked so dejected this morning when I arrived, and Josh said things have been hard for her."

"Look, give me your number. I'll talk to India and do my best to protect her as much as possible. I'll find her a job in a heartbeat if she wants to walk. Maybe she will tell me what the problem is."

"Thank you, if I can help, please ask" He gave her his mobile number and his email.

Tilly hugged Charlie goodbye and produced a Gym Away kit from her bag and passed it to him. "I think you are still going to need this. Joe especially wants to take my dad to a match; he is always trying to make him happy. I'm not sure that will ever happen, but perhaps a ticket to the Roses Match might be a good start."

Joe came out with a copy of the contract to study, and they disappeared, leaving Charlie in the break room. He pulled out his phone and texted India.

CWR: Where are you? When will you be back?

India: A couple of hours. What is happening?

CWR: Tilly and Joe have left, and the rest are in Philip's office. I don't know what to do.

India: How rude? Did you get a drink?

CWR: Yeah, Tilly made it.

India: LOL

CWR: Any chance we can talk tonight, with them looking like they are going to walk away I don't know when I'll see you.

India: At New Year silly.

CWR: I think we need to chat before then.

India: I know but

CWR: I'm setting off for the hotel Would you call me later?

India: Sure.

Philip Bentley came in and sat down next to Charlie. "What can I say. There is no point in you signing a contract if the client walks away. We are going to be re-presenting to the Cooksons on Monday. Let me take you out to dinner tomorrow night. I can extend your hotel suite until Monday."

"I can't stay that long, but I will let you take me out for dinner if you tell me this. Why was India removed from this project?"

"That, my boy, is complicated."

Chapter 11

"India, where are you?"

"I've picked up the dress from Deanna, and I'm going back on the tube to get to Nick's. It could take me a long time to get back. Is it OK if I go straight home from Nick's?"

"No, it is not alright, why aren't you in the office like I asked."

"Jayne told me this needed to be done today."

"It does. Nick is shooting that tomorrow. I'm wondering why you and not her?"

"I'm afraid you will need to ask Jayne that. So, do you want me to take the dress to Nick?"

"Damn it, YES! Be here in the morning by 9 am."

India's heart sank. Tomorrow was the dinner with Michael Coombes, and she had a full morning of pampering planned, haircut, nails, the works. "Sir, I have appointments booked for tomorrow."

"Do I sound like I care about your social life, India? This is a mess, and we have until Monday morning to sort it out."

"Yes, sir."

"Deliver the dress India and go home. But nine am tomorrow we need a solution to this."

"Yes, Sir."

When India walked through the door at Nick's studio, he was sitting alone in the half-light sipping coffee and flicking through the day's proofs. He was about to tease her about being late again, one look at her face told him today was not the day for that. Nick knew why she was often late. Jayne had an amazing reputation for getting the impossible done on a tight time scale, but that was never down to herself doing these things. Instead, he walked to the coffeepot and offered her one.

"Sit yourself down and tell me all about it." Whilst Nick unpacked the dress from Deanna, India sank into the comfy chair in Nick's office space and let it all out.

"Why do you stay there, India? They treat you so badly, no one else stays. Why are you fighting it so hard? Why not move on like everyone else they tread on?"

"My mother got me this job after I lost my previous two jobs. They were both actually temporary from the start, but that doesn't stop my family from sniping. They have never lost jobs, then my mother has never worked and my father and brother work for the family firm. They have never been at the bottom of the ladder in their lives. They have only ever lived in Hurst's Bridge, where my grandfather's name gets them the best table in a restaurant and served quickly, anywhere they go. If I 'lose another job' my mother expects me to go home so she can find me a husband and I never have to work again!"

"That is a lot to consider."

"Oh, it gets better. My mother pushed me into going out to dinner tomorrow at the Ritz Carlton with the son of her best friend of the moment. She has sent me a new dress, as the ones I have aren't suitable for this event! So, tomorrow morning I was booked in for the works, hair, nails etc so I didn't let her down. If I'm honest, it was for my self-confidence, meeting a lot of new people down here. NOW! Because the client has refused to sign the contract because they liked my ideas and not the ones they saw today. Philip says we all must go to the office tomorrow and sort this out. Getting my haircut might be important to me, but it doesn't sound important enough to him."

Nick's eyes gleamed as he stood looking at the dress Deanna had sent over. Then looked at India. "How long do you think it will take tomorrow?"

"It depends how quickly they listen to me?" she said with a cheeky grin. Nick raised an eyebrow, so she continued, "I had the project planned on budget, that fits with both Charlie's work commitments and his personality, for a week. I know the clients will love it because I took the time to get to know them. The client rang me today and said they would sign if I would come back. I hate to sound big-headed, but I had this and the only thing that has lost us the contract is the team not even looking at my plans."

"Could you be back in Putney for say 2 pm?"

"Yes, but I won't be able to move all my appointments to later in the day, so I'll go as I am."

"Cinderella! You shall go to the ball!"

"OK, Nick explain,"

"Well, if you would do Deanna and me a small favour, just a little one."

"Nick, explain!"

"Here, slip this dress on for me." And he handed her the dress she had delivered. India stared at him and then looked down at her suit that had started the day looking smart.

Nick softened his voice. "Do it for me India and I'll explain."

As India changed behind the screen in Nick's studio, he explained he was shooting some dresses from Deanna for Bentley & Bentley, Jayne had demanded he submitted by Monday. Deanna needed some promotion shots of her own. His first thought had been to use the models from tomorrow's shoot, but then he realised that if Jayne saw he had used the same models for both shoots, Deanna and himself would find it hard to get work with them again. If he used a different model and a different backdrop, then nothing could be said. If India would come over and model some dresses tomorrow afternoon, she would get the makeover she was looking forward to so much.

The dress fitted beautifully and looked stunning with India's colouring. India was still uncertain, and she told Nick that she couldn't promise him what time she might be there.

"The offer stands India. Call me before 1:30 pm and let me know and I'll hold the team back to do the shoot."

India promised to call and let him know. Walking back home, she picked up a takeaway and a bottle of wine from the shop beneath her flat. If life didn't change, she might have to move, living over a shop that sold wines and spirits could be dangerous.

Back home, India poured a glass of wine and kicked off her shoes. Checked her messages and found one from her mum, asking her to call. *Not today, Mum, please not today!* India knew it would be about tomorrow night and what could she tell her mum about having to work in the morning.

She wolfed down her meal, not realising how hungry she had been, and got settled down with her wine glass and the bottle to call Katie.

A good chat with her friend where she could download and talk through the best approach for what to do at work did her the world of good. Katie even helped her decide what to wear for the dinner with Michael Coombes.

India ended the call with Katie with a better idea of what was possible tomorrow if only she could stand up for herself. First, she had to call her mum back. She had rung to let her know that India's dad had heard Bentley & Bentley were not doing well and jobs were going to be cut. She felt certain that India would be coming home soon and wanted her to get back before the social season got going after Easter. It was the last thing India needed to hear and was one more thing for her to consider.

India indulged in a long bath, candles, and chocolate, but put the top back on the wine and drank some sparkling water in her favourite glass with ice and lemon. After her bath, she pulled out her thinking book. It was an enormous book with blank pages she used to pour out her problems and find solutions.

As she was getting into bed, she found a text from Charlie she had missed.

CWR: I thought you were going to call.

India: Sorry it has been a rough day, trying to work out what to do.

CWR: Yeah, I got that. Meet me for breakfast?

India: Sorry, got to go to work.

CWR: Nothing sorted yet then.

India: Nope! I'm deeply sorry, Charlie, for dragging you down here when there might not be a job. I'll try to sort this tomorrow. I wish I could be confident I can do that.

CWR: Don't do this for me India. Do what is right for you long term.

India: I have no idea what that is right now.

CWR: Philip is taking me to dinner tomorrow night. Other than that, I'm free until I get a train back, I haven't picked a time yet.

India: Tomorrow is out. When I know what is happening, I'll text you.

CWR: When I say talk, I need you in the same room India. Please.

India: I know. I'll get in touch somehow tomorrow.

Chapter 12

With nothing resolved before she went to bed, she spent a night weighing up the alternatives, who would benefit and who would not from each choice she could make. She was sound asleep when her alarm went off and she started to go through the motions of getting ready for work; she pulled out a suit she liked to wear then put it back. It was Saturday, no clients in the office. Defiant, she pulled on a comfortable pair of jeans and a long, oversized, V-necked jumper.

The Tube journey was a challenge again, so when she walked into Bentley & Bentley, she was the last to arrive. She still hadn't decided what she was going to do today. Hand over her ideas to the team or walk out and resign were just two of the options she had been playing with. Resigning felt like the coward's way out, and she didn't want to treat Philip like that, nor did she want to let Tilly down and it certainly wouldn't get Charlie the job he needed.

Trying to stay calm, she hung up her coat and went to the break room, as she was positive it would be her job to make the drinks. She could hear Alice and Malcolm doing their normal stage whisper, which she was not sure if she was meant to hear or not. She could definitely hear her name being mentioned and the words, budgets, team player, and her name again. Although she couldn't hear every word, she was certain that neither Alice nor Malcolm would take the blame for yesterday's disaster. She was starting to bristle and feel defensive. Surely Philip would not let that go? He knew she had presented well to the client, and he had copies of all the emails she had sent to everyone on the team.

When Jayne shouted to her to bring drinks into the conference room, she had them all ready to go. She put down the tray and pulled her tablet out of her bag. Although India sat quietly, inside she was in turmoil. She still didn't know what was going to happen.

Philip started the meeting. He went around the table and asked each person in turn. He said carefully that each person would have time to speak, and they should all wait their turn.

Malcolm started by saying his involvement had been finding the professionals to suggest and that India was the one who had picked out Charlie Robertson.

Alice said she had worked on six shoots when asked, although she had only had a week to produce her slide set. It hadn't been easy because India hadn't shared any information with her. She explained the budget was totally unworkable and not what we were used to at Bentley & Bentley, inferring that the company was best off without them as customers.

Jayne agreed they weren't Bentley & Bentley customers and if they didn't have the budget for our type of shoot, we should let them walk away now.

Philip was very tight-lipped when he looked at India to have her turn. He looked tired and angry, but India had finally had enough. She wasn't the only one who needed to grow up.

She set her tablet to project to the screen using the Wi-Fi.

"First, I have copied every single one of you into all my emails. You have all had the fixture list, and my notes on the client and the client's likes and dislikes. My notes on why Charlie was a good fit for them. I also sent my ideas about how we could hold down the costs of the shoots so that we could still make the same margin for Bentley & Bentley as we would a big budget project." She flicked through the emails they had all had to prove her point.

"The Cooksons may have set up a new company, however, they both are part of big families which hold multi-million-pound assets. This small project is a foot in the door for us to get work from all of those companies and we need it."

Philip went red, and the rest stared at her, she didn't stop. "The way technology is evolving; the way social media is evolving is a threat to companies like this. Jobs aren't coming through as they have done, and we can't sit back and think we don't have to change too. I put together a perfectly good plan with the client and I prepared them to sign that contract yesterday. What made them walk out?" Silence.

"They didn't walk out because I was out of the office doing another rush job that if we had started in suitable time could have been fitted in by Josh in half the time it took me yesterday and then maybe the client wouldn't have been left making their own coffee because no one else can use the coffee machine." India paused to look at the others in the room. Still silence.

"They were told that Alice had more experience than me, which I admit she does. Then they were presented with six shoots that would create some glorious images that would be way over budget and wouldn't even show the product." More silence. Alice opened her mouth and looked at Malcolm and said nothing. Malcolm squirmed in his chair, and Philip went red.

"Joe and Matilda Cookson are good, honest, hard-working people. They are our clients of the future, but they will mean some challenging work for us. If you want to keep chasing the big corporations that will sign anything and take your word on what the budget should be, never questioning overspend because you are not spending their money, go ahead but it is a diminishing pool, so you need to up your game."

"The question is, Philip, what are you going to do about it?" Philip looked shocked. He was used to bringing in the clients and handing things over to the team. He took them to lunch or dinner and persuaded them to stay with Bentley & Bentley or he brought in friends from the various clubs he went to each day.

"If you check my emails, you will find my suggested dates and shoot ideas that will fit around both Charlie and the client. I didn't have the luxury of a week sitting at my desk picking out dream locations and plush sports cars. I produced what the client wanted because I asked questions and did my research. I am happy to present that again to the client and I will listen to any changes you think might help. What I will no longer do is come here each day to be bullied and belittled. You are always talking about 'the team' Philip, when have we ever been a team?"

Philip looked at his watch. It was 9:45, and the solution was in front of him. He had known that Jayne and her jealousy were the reason the youngest members of his staff never stayed long. He never flirted with India, but he had taken her to lunch and that is when all the problems started. That is when he had pulled India from the project, despite everything he had seen her do with the client. It was now up to him to decide what they do next. Was India correct it was time for the company to change? He needed to think. She was right about the lack of clients and the bank was not happy.

He sent them all back to their desks to create new presentations for Monday morning, which they were to email to him by 4 pm on Sunday. Monday morning, he would ask one person to present their ideas to Tilly and Joe. They should stay as long as they needed to do the job and then they could go home.

Back in the open-plan office, India turned on her computer and opened the design suite to create some slides. Across the room, Alice and Malcolm weren't talking to each other. They were each focused on creating their presentations, in competition with each other for the first time. Realising this was not the place for her to work and quite possibly slides were not the option for Joe and Tilly, she thought about going home. Philip had already left, so she packed her bag and left, too. At least she could still help Deanna and Nick.

She went back to her flat, laid down on her bed with her eyes closed and tried to visualise the results from the shoots she had originally planned. That is what Joe would need to see, magazine pages, not slides. If only she had more time.

She sent Nick a text to say she was free, so he asked her to come straight over to his studio. India had a wonderful time modelling for Nick. Getting her hair and makeup done was such a bonus when she was going to be meeting Michael Coombes. When she shared her ideas with Nick, he agreed a magazine layout would work well. If only they had more time. He offered her the use of his large-format printer if she needed it.

Chapter 13

Charlie woke up alone in the room at his hotel. He went down to breakfast and picked up several newspapers to browse through. He wondered who they would photograph up in Leeds this weekend with him down in London. He couldn't help thinking about India after seeing her yesterday. She looked so beautiful yet so sombre.

Back in his room, he thought he should call his mum, instead, he checked in with Robbie first.

"Hey Robbie, how are things? Did you see my Mum?" He was nervously pacing the room.

"Hello mate, yeah, I did. She said you were in London this weekend, something about a job. I guess it is that thing with India. How did it go?"

"Yeah, I would love to tell you it was a great success but to be honest I don't know. India has been pulled from the job and this girl Alice who has 'more experience' than India is now leading the project! It didn't go down well with the clients, and they walked away without signing the contracts."

"God! I'm sorry, it sounded like just what you needed."

"The project India described was, and I get the impression the clients liked it. The new girl had this fancy plan where I was laid on a beach in the south of France."

"Sounds good. What's wrong with that?"

"Yeah, sounds good, but the plan India was talking about, had me walking out of my life on the road to take photos for an hour, maybe two. A trip to the south of France is going to take a lot more time than two hours and sounds like it was way out of their budget."

"What is the product like?" Robbie was looking for the positives.

"Looks good. I'm going to have a play with it this afternoon and then I'm out to dinner with Philip, India's boss. Tilly and Joe, the owners, seem pretty normal and I got the impression yesterday, that if they walk away from Bentley & Bentley, I'll still get a call to be involved."

"What about India?"

"That was the worst bit mate, she looked so down, it made me sad. She was being pushed around and treated like a dogsbody. It was hard to watch, I wanted to get her out of there, except they had sent her off on some errands across London." The tight feeling was back in his stomach.

"That doesn't sound like our girl, she has more spirit than that."

"Not yesterday, she didn't. I tried to meet up with her today, but they are making her go into work this morning to sort it."

"Is it saveable?"

"I don't know, I'm hoping I can talk to her boss tonight; I'm going to try, anyway."

"Good."

"How was my mum?" He was pacing again, worried about what Robbie would tell him.

"She seems to be doing well, from what Emma tells me she could be like, going through this, but she doesn't seem very happy."

"Why? What was wrong?" Charlie stood rearranging the items out on the desk. Making straight lines.

"This is hard to tell you, Charlie, because I know how hard you worked for this."

"Tell me what, Robbie? Just tell me. Please."

"That big house. I don't think it is making her happy. It's like she can't relax."

"I bought that house so she could relax."

"I guess she misses her friends, too. She lived in the old house for a long time."

"Yes, I suppose she did."

"Look, why don't you talk to her when you see her next. I'm not sure she will tell you and I'm sure she is grateful for everything you do. I know at the end of the day, you simply want her to be happy."

"I can try, I'll be up there next weekend."

"Good. Come and see us and let's see what Emma can find out about additional support for her."

"Thanks, Robbie, I'll be in touch."

"Take care of India."

"I'll do my best." Charlie had no idea what he could do.

At lunchtime he took a walk around a small park, thinking about India and if she was still at work. He couldn't understand it. Talking to the driver on the way to his hotel, he seemed to think the biggest issue was Jayne. Charlie didn't know much, but she didn't make great coffee and certainly didn't think to offer tea.

He found it hard seeing India look so downhearted. He loved how quickly she organised a cup of tea then talked about work, so they could have some time together. He thought back to that first night. Their first chat sat side by side. He always wondered what would have happened if she was older, if she hadn't thrown up. If only he had been more careful, asking her what she wanted to drink.

When he was back in his hotel, he decided to call her.

"India, it's me, Charlie."

"Hi Charlie, how are you enjoying London?"

"Not much fun on my own. How did it go at work today?"

"Hard to say really. Philip gave us all time to say what we thought, then told us to create a presentation to email to him on Sunday night. He will decide who will present on Monday morning. He said we could go as soon as we finished."

"So how long did you stay?"

"I left 10 minutes after him," she chuckled. Charlie was pleased to hear her laugh.

"OK, why?"

"Well, I don't want to change what I already presented to Tilly and Joe, and I'm quite sure they won't want to look at slides. If I had more time and a budget, I would do a mock-up of a magazine, but as I don't have time for that…"

"Will you have time to meet me tomorrow before I go back?"

"That would be great. You are out with Philip tonight, aren't you?"

"Yes."

"How about your hotel in the morning, say 10 o'clock?"

"Sounds like a plan." Charlie was so relieved he let out a long breath.

"Great, I have to go now, I'm doing a favour for a friend."

"See you tomorrow."

Charlie's mood had lifted. Finally, he had a time to meet India away from work so they could sort out the past and that might mean there was a future. He pulled out the Gym Away kit Tilly gave him. There was still a slim chance he would be working with them in some way with this thing, so he decided to learn all he could about it. Maybe he could help Tilly and Joe, even if India couldn't.

Chapter 14

India got out of the Uber and made her way to the entrance. She was a little annoyed that she was arriving alone. After today, she was ready to get back in a cab and go home if Michael Coombes wasn't around to take her into the dinner. Yet there he was, shivering in his evening suit at the top of the steps. He moved forward to claim her straight away, telling her how wonderful she looked and sweeping her off to the ballroom with a hand gently in the small of her back. He directed her over towards the bar to join some of his friends. She was suddenly pleased she was wearing the new dress her mother had sent with her old red one. Whilst it clung to her curves it had no plunging neckline or expanses of skin and she felt more comfortable amongst this group of young men without too much flesh on display.

India smiled and nodded to each of the people he introduced her to. The men each presented their companions to both India and Michael, in a way that made her believe they were all new friendships for the evening. Only one pair acted like a couple.

India stood next to a girl who said her name was Tiff. She looked like she was struggling to stand on the tall silver heels she was wearing.

"I love your shoes; I wish I could wear something like that."

"Thanks, India, I like your dress, very classy, isn't it?"

As the group of men moved, the crowd opened up, and she caught a glimpse of a kilt. It made her chest go tight. She had looked at his back so often at Robbie's. His height, the width of his shoulders, the way his blonde hair licked at his collar, but it was the kilt that sealed the identification. He was wearing the hunting version of the Robertson

Tartan. Then she realised he was talking to Philip Bentley. She knew he was taking him to dinner, no one had mentioned where.

"Excuse me, I have spotted my boss, I better go and say hello."

Michael simply nodded and carried on talking to Tiff's date, Jake. He hadn't spoken to her since they had joined the group. Tiff was the only one who replied. "I wouldn't speak to my manager. Then he wouldn't be here."

India took a deep breath and sighed it out, draining the tension in her body by shaking her hands. She smoothed down her dress as she walked towards them. Philip didn't make her feel like this, even after this morning's meeting. The tension was about speaking to Charlie in his kilt just as he was that first New Year.

"Good evening, Philip."

"India, we were just talking about you."

India blushed and if she wasn't wrong, so did Charlie, who was looking into his drink.

"Really?" She questioned. It was then he stopped studying the amber contents of his glass and looked into her eyes again.

India didn't know what to think. She had never stood up to Philip like she did today, and Monday morning would be interesting, she wasn't going to shrink away now.

"I was explaining that it wasn't your role to lead a project like this."

"I got the impression from Joe and Tilly that they liked the energy she had, and her ideas were so refreshing." Charlie smiled at her.

Philip changed the subject. "You look beautiful tonight India, who are you here with?"

"Michael Coombes, do you know him?"

"No, I don't think I do, I thought you told Tilly no boyfriends?"

"That is still true. Mum asked me to do this. Remember that day she needed to talk to me so urgently she called you?" India bit her lip – maybe this wasn't the time to mention that to Philip. "Well, I believe we are sitting down soon, so I better go back to the group."

During dinner, Michael barely spoke to India. He was too busy talking to his friends. He did keep trying to top up her glass and squeeze her leg, his hand travelling up her thigh. India kept stopping his hand from travelling too far whilst trying to get a conversation going with Tiff, who had moved to sit next to India.

"Phew, I'm glad you are here India. Jake isn't talking to me, just his mates."

"Yes, it's the same here. Have you known Jake long?"

"He has been coming to the café where I work for over a year and he is always flirting with me, though this is the first time he has taken me out."

India smiled and whispered "I'm here because my Mum asked me to come with Michael. It's no wonder they have trouble finding dates if this is how they treat them." Both girls giggled and tried to find some common ground. They didn't watch the same TV programmes or read the same magazines, they did both read romance books and had read some of the same authors and they both rather liked Henry Cavill.

"Do you think Henry would be so inattentive if he had invited us to a grand dinner?" mused India.

"No, I'm quite sure he wouldn't. I'm sure he would include you in the conversation even if he was squeezing my hand whilst he was doing it." Laughed Tiff.

They giggled together and looked at the dates they had come with. After dessert was served, the boys moved back towards the bar, allowing Tiff and India to escape to the toilet together.

"I've enjoyed talking to you, Tiff, but I think I'll get an early taxi home. I've had a big day already and I'm meeting someone for coffee in the morning."

Music had started to play in the ballroom and the two girls stayed outside the door to finish their chat.

"I know what you mean. I've been working in the café from 8 until 5 today. My feet are killing me, and this isn't what I expected when he said, 'come to dinner with me'."

India chuckled, "I'm unsure what I expected, but after my day, I have had enough."

"What was your day like?"

"I had a nice spa morning planned haircut, nails, the works ready for this, then everything went wrong at work yesterday and my boss made us all go in this morning. Which meant I had to cancel it all. Rather glad I didn't waste my money now." India tossed her hair back over her shoulder.

"Is that the same boss you went to say hello to earlier?"

"The same man, yes."

"As I said, I wouldn't talk to my manager when I was out."

"You see, I stood up to him this morning. I think tonight I was trying to prove I wasn't sorry and hold my head up." India threw back her shoulder as if to reinforce the feeling.

"And your hair looks stunning considering you missed your spa session." Tiff was looking closely at India's hair as it tumbled around her shoulders.

"Well, that was this afternoon. I helped a friend out by modelling a couple of dresses for her and a photographer we both know, so he organised the make-over done for that and tonight. Two birds, one stone."

"Wow you have been busy, is that what you do for a job India, are you a model?"

"No, I work in PR, but we do a lot of jobs for designers and they in turn work for us, and I meet lots of photographers too."

"I bet that is fun. No wonder you are tired. And did you say you have something in the morning too?"

"Yeah, coffee with Charlie before he goes back to Leeds."

"Who is Charlie?"

"Actually, he is the guy in the kilt who was talking to my boss earlier."

"Is he incredibly tall with blonde hair and model looks?"

"Well, yes."

"So, is he the one who has Michael by the throat?"

India turned to look into the room in the same direction as Tiff. Charlie did indeed have him by the collar. He was red in the face and was shouting at Michael. She wasted no time running up to them and grabbing Charlie's arm.

"NEVER TALK LIKE THAT ABOUT ANY WOMAN!"

Looking down at India he lowered his voice and said: "Keep your sticky hands off India and if I ever hear you have done anything to upset her, don't bother looking for your friends because I'll be there with all mine."

Phones were flashing, and India could see tomorrow's papers now. She hissed in Charlie's ear. "Put him down, Charlie. He isn't worth it. I was about to leave anyway because I have an important meeting in the morning."

Charlie had loosened his grip on Michael, and he had pulled away.

"Charlie, I would prefer you were at the meeting and not locked up somewhere."

He dropped his shoulders and started to walk quietly towards the door and stopped. India collected her jacket and bag then walked out without a word to Michael and joined Charlie at the door.

"Where is Philip?" India was feverishly looking around for her boss and holding her breath.

"He left straight after the meal." She exhaled.

"So, he didn't see that?"

"No. Look India, I can explain…"

"Let's get out of here first, Charlie."

Today was India's day for taking charge. Instead of calling a cab, she started to walk towards Charlie's hotel. The walk would do them good, she thought. For a while, they walked in silence. It wasn't a painful silence; it was just each of them resetting ready to have a real conversation. Eventually, Charlie started to speak.

"India. I'm sorry."

"What are you sorry for, Charlie?"

"Everything," he whispered. India chuckled and leaned sideways to nudge him. He kept talking. "For not realising how old you were when we met, for giving you so much to drink, you were ill. For not speaking since that night. For the way you have been treated at the office, for how sad you seem. Everything."

"Charlie, I'm pretty sure you can't be blamed for all of that." Charlie was certain he could.

"Oh, I can, and I can explain it all too!"

"How are you to blame for work?"

"Do you think you would have said my name if you hadn't been so sick that first time we met?"

"Probably not."

"How did this morning go, by the way?

"As I said earlier, we were informed we had until 4 pm on Sunday to submit our new presentation to Philip by email."

"How did that go?" his voice was softer now, and it helped India relax. She pulled an Eek face. "I sat in that room with Alice and Malcolm and thought I can't do this in here, after what they had done and said. Then I looked at my proposal and although there is always something you can tidy; I thought the basic plan was good given your fixtures."

"Yeah, my life pretty much revolves around that fixture list."

"And then I thought the last thing Tilly and Joe will want on Monday is another slide show, so why create one?"

"Have you decided what you will do?"

"I'm not sure it matters, but if I had the time and resources that Alice had to prepare for this, I would produce some magazine mock-ups."

"Alright, what do you need to do that?"

"Well, longer than the 18 hours I have?"

"18 hours if you don't sleep, and what else?"

"Photographs of Gym Away, photographs of you, and you with the product. And well shots of you unpacking it in a hotel room, maybe some interviews with you and with Joe or Tilly, possibly even some shots of them too, they are a stunning couple."

"So basically, you need me and the product in a hotel room to take some photos?"

"Well, yes."

"India, my hotel is a few metres over there. I have the Gym Away in my room. How good is the camera on your phone?"

"I like the way you are thinking, but I can't ask you to do that now, you must be tired."

94

"India, I, unlike you, have had a quiet day, and after tackling that worm, it will be a while before I'm ready to sleep."

They had stopped close to the hotel and had turned to face each other. India realised she hadn't even asked what had caused Charlie to take hold of Michael and threaten him in that way. She had been so fed up with Michael and his friends, anyway; she had already decided she was leaving to go home. Looking up into those brown eyes so deep, she thought she could get completely lost in there. Charlie's eyes crinkled into a smile as he reached out his arms to grip her hips and pulled her towards him.

Chapter 15

Holding her close, he looked down and held her gaze as he spoke softly "India, I said I'm sorry for everything, I'm not sorry I got hold of that guy."

"You might be when the papers hit tomorrow. We should do some damage control for that."

"What do you mean?" the sparkle was gone from his eyes.

"We can put out the story that you were standing up for a colleague. What did he do anyway?"

"I wasn't speaking out just for you but for women in general. I heard him saying some things I won't repeat here about what he was going to do when he took you home." India's face went red. Charlie knew in his heart that it was because India had been the subject of the boasting that he made him lose his temper. Saying he was standing up for all women was his way of hiding how deeply it had hit him, hearing her discussed that way.

"Cheeky Fudging Drip, I was about to leave without him. Thank you, Charlie, I'm pretty sure he won't have learnt a lesson though." She smiled up at him. "Oh, talking of damage control, I'd better message my mum and tell her before the other side gets in with their version of the story. Thinking about it I should send it to my dad instead."

"Look, we are back at the hotel. I know you have had a long day, but would you like to come up and we could try some of this 'damage control' and have a cup of tea? We could see if we can get some photographs to help you with your mock-up tomorrow. Say 'Yes', India."

Her eyes met his and her smile widened, "Yes, India." He laughed and hugged her closer. Pulling apart, he took her hand and led her to the room that she had booked for him.

Although the suite wasn't huge, it had a separate living area to his bedroom and a bathroom off the hallway. The living area had a small sofa and one easy chair beside an immense picture window looking out over the park. On the other side of the room, there was a dining table and chairs. All very neutral colours.

Charlie made tea whilst India was busy on her phone. She had kicked off her shoes and was sitting on the sofa with her feet curled up. First, she messaged her dad and explained to him what had happened. She asked him not to say anything to the Coombes unless they brought the subject up. He needed to know that she would not be seeing Michael Coombes again, and she hoped he wouldn't be welcome at the house. She told her dad that Charlie had been standing up for her as she was out of the room when Michael was making the comments. She was careful to tell him about Michael's behaviour before that.

Charlie brought over two cups of tea and between them, they composed a "statement" about what had taken place that evening. India contacted a friend on the Evening News and told him what had happened. She explained she didn't want to embarrass the son of her mum's friend, however, if they were offered the photos, could they include the statement? He hummed and hawed a bit, saying that would kill the story, and so India offered him a possible story about Charlie teaming up with the Cooksons. He was keen to get as many exclusives from India as he could, and he was a good friend. When he read the statement, he didn't hesitate and was soon asking India if she was alright.

"Wow, you're on a roll, girl!" Charlie exclaimed. It struck India how she was in Charlie Robertson's hotel room, and she felt comfortable. She was enjoying being with him, and that old connection was back.

"I think finally standing up this morning and saying what I have wanted to say for so long, has helped me feel good about myself."

"I'm glad I'm not looking at yesterday's version of India, I didn't like that look, seeing her so sad made me feel the same." They sat next to each other on the sofa and India's hand was so close to his bare knee he longed for her to touch him. Charlie reached out a hand to her face and smiled a sad smile. India jumped up from the sofa, leaving Charlie with his hand in mid-air.

"Hey, do you know what Tilly and Joe were doing tonight?"

"Going to see a show, I think. Why?" Charlie's eyebrows pulled close in puzzlement.

"I was wondering if it was too late to message them. What do you think?"

"What if I message them?"

"We are both trying to keep a job Charlie, yours could be already saved if you don't blow it."

"By being in the papers for 'fighting'?" the corners of his mouth dropped.

"I'm pretty sure Tilly and Joe will be fine about that if we tell them what happened."

"I take it you are thinking more damage control then?" he smiled the soft smile that melted her heart.

"I was going to see if I can get them on board to take some photographs tomorrow."

"Good idea, but is that cheating? Won't your teammates be upset that you have talked to the client?" India threw out her arms, palms upwards. Why didn't people get it?

"Not talking to the client is where they went wrong in the first place. People buy from people."

"That way Tilly and Joe are more likely to buy from Bentley & Bentley because they like you?"

"And people are more likely to buy from Gym Away if they like them."

"Clever, still let me send the text. I'm a bloke, they won't think anything about me texting so late."

"Go on then. Have you got your Gym Away? I can get some shots of that whilst we wait?"

Charlie pulled the Gym Away from his case, passing it to India. He sent a message to Tilly and took their cups away to rinse them before putting them back neatly in place. He settled next to India whilst she took the first few shots, and she showed him the results on her phone.

"I could do with more light?" Her eyes roamed the room for something to light up the space.

Charlie fetched a lamp from the bedroom. India was grateful. "That should work, but it would be easier tomorrow with more light. What time is your train?"

"I had two picked out, one about ten o'clock if I couldn't see you or four o'clock if I could persuade you to talk to me." India smiled then laughed softly, "I know we needed to talk, and I'm so glad we have." Charlie's smile reflected her own.

"It is funny I knew we had to talk, and I imagined it would be awkward. I thought we would be unpicking the details of that night and yet here, we are moved on without really speaking about it."

"I guess today's situation makes what happened at a party six years ago seem pretty irrelevant, doesn't it? Charlie, I'm glad we are back to talking." India straightened herself up and looked at Charlie in his evening jacket and kilt.

"Can I take some photos of you?" Charlie nodded his reply and stood up.

"Sit back down, for now, I want to try some headshots from different angles first and you are so much taller than me." India pulled out a chair from the dining table and placed it in a space so she could move all around it. Then fiddled with the lamp. She took several shots from varying directions, liking a few and leaving the rest to delete later.

"Can you do some chest exercises with the bands?"

"Yes, do I need to change?"

"Have you got any gym type clothes with you, like a vest and shorts?"

"No." he laughed. "I have some track pants and a sweatshirt?"

"How do you feel about keeping on the kilt and taking off your shirt?" Charlie raised an eyebrow and smiled. He took off his jacket and slowly unbuttoned his shirt. He was looking at India, but she looked away.

"I'll look for the right surface to stand you in front of whilst you get ready."

Without an audience, Charlie was quickly stripped to the waist and connecting two of the bands to make one stronger resistance band. India decided a textured concrete wall was a good background if they moved a small table. Charlie's phone beeped with a response from Tilly. They sat down on the sofa again, and Charlie typed as India watched.

Tilly C: Just back at the hotel, is everything OK?

CWR: I'm with India, is it OK to call?

Tilly C: Are you both OK? Yes, Call. I want to talk to India.

Charlie pressed the call button, and Tilly answered instantly.

"Hey Tilly, did you have a fun time tonight?"

"Charlie Robertson, you didn't call to ask me about the show, pass the phone to India!" He chuckled and pushed his phone towards India. She sat back on the sofa and picked up her feet.

"Hi, Tilly." India's stomach clenched. *Can I ask this?*

"Hello India, tell me where you are and why you're with Charlie? I thought you had some date tonight, which is why you said you wouldn't come to the show with Joe and me." India wriggled in her spot.

"I was. I went to a dinner thing with the son of one of my mum's friends. It wasn't going well. Charlie was at the same event with Philip. When I was in the loo, he overheard my date mouthing off about me and whilst he was explaining why he shouldn't talk like that about women, well he got hold of Michael's collar to emphasise his point. Lots of phones came out and it might hit the papers. I wanted you to know why it had happened."

"Are you both OK?"

"Yes."

"Did Charlie hit him?"

"No." India was shaking her head; this could have been a lot worse.

"That's OK then. Back to my questions. Where are you now?"

"We are at Charlie's hotel."

"In his room?" *Here we go again.*

"Yes, But…"

"I knew it!" Tilly exclaimed. India huffed. Why had she let Tilly think this was more than it could ever be?

"Tilly, I hate to disappoint you, but nothing is happening between Charlie and myself. It couldn't."

"So, what are you doing?"

"This morning Philip had us all come into work to discuss your project."

"How did that go?"

"Let's say I might be looking for a job soon because I'm afraid I told them all what I thought. It feels good to have said it though and I don't regret doing it."

"I don't get it. Why are you with Charlie in his hotel room; when you keep telling me there can be nothing between you?"

"After he rescued me from that slime ball, Michael, we were walking, trying to calm down and reset. The subject turned to what Philip had asked us to do this morning. I was telling Charlie that if I had the time and the resources, I would prefer to do a magazine mock-up. I'm not sure if you realise yet, but Charlie is competitive. He kept asking why, and what did I need? I explained I needed photos and interviews, so here I am in his hotel room, taking some photos on my phone. Tomorrow I can try again with a camera and maybe get some shots outside in the park well certainly in a better light."

"India, that is amazing, although I feel I need to say something. On Monday, if Bentley & Bentley can't offer what we want, we will walk away, and we will probably ask Charlie to be part of a project with another firm. Any ideas you share with us now, are bound to leak into that. Will you be OK with that?"

"Tilly, of course, I so want this to work for you and Joe, and Charlie too."

"Good! So, what can we do to help?"

"I hate to ask, would you like to join us tomorrow? I think you and Joe should be part of the story. If I could get some photos of you and do some interview type questions, we could do mock-up interviews with the three of you."

"Joe is never keen on photographs, but we will be there, and we will do what we can."

"Great, which hotel shall we use?"

"Are you taking photos at Charlie's now?"

"I am. He was in his kilt, so I have him stripped to the waist and he is going to do chest exercises with the bands. He is getting warmed up."

"Oh my, send some of those photos, will you? Why didn't you mention kilts before?"

"I only thought of it tonight. I mean, the first time I met him he was in a kilt. I'm not sure why I forgot."

"OK, so our hotel, what time tomorrow?"

"10, 10:30 I need to get back and create the mock-up once I have the images and the words. It would be for a couple of hours at the most."

"That's fine. Get here when you can between 10 and 10:30. I went shopping for 'on-brand' towels today too and some kit that fits Joe. Hopefully, it will be OK on Charlie."

"Brilliant. See you tomorrow."

India ended the call and passed the phone back to Charlie. He had been busy trying out different moves with the resistance bands.

"Are you OK with meeting them with me in the morning?"

"Of course. What else am I going to do? The girl I wanted to meet for coffee will be working." He chuckled.

"OK let's see if we can get some shots that will work for this mock-up."

India directed Charlie, in the same way Nick had directed her that afternoon. Charlie was well aware of his body and could break down movement into small steps so she could get the light to bounce and highlight the shapes on his upper body. The blues and greens of his kilt provided superb contrast between the lower and upper half of his body. India was soon lost in playing with the light and the muscles she was now studying in detail. Suddenly the light picked out a speck of blue cotton just below his left nipple, and she reached out to remove it without thinking. Shocked, Charlie grabbed her wrist, and she looked up once more into those brown eyes. His hands dropped to her hips and pulled her to him.

"India, I'm glad we have found our way back. You look so beautiful tonight." He murmured into her neck as his lips brushed her hair. India's body sank into his in response. But within seconds, she was pulling away and putting her things back in her bag.

"India?"

"Charlie, we can't do that. You know we can't. This is a job, and we need to stay professional. My mother is going to be beside herself about Michael Coombes, you know how she will respond to you." Shocked and hurt, Charlie stared at his hands and India slipped away to go home.

Charlie could not forget how she felt in his arms tonight. He longed to smell the crisp apple fragrance of her hair again and hold her to him, to keep her safe from the people that seemed to fill her life in London. He couldn't understand why they didn't treasure her more. Unable to sleep, he took a shower and remembered those last moments of India in his arms. He found the relief he needed there, as he leaned into the tiles and wondered how he would survive six months of working with India Barrington Jones.

In the back of her taxi, India replayed the last 48 hours. Seeing Charlie again had been a quite different experience. She was glad they could now talk like friends, and she was excited to be working on this project with him. Looking at his body through the camera on her phone had shown her how right he was for the sort of images she envisaged for the Gym Away launch.

Being in his arms tonight had felt so comfortable for those few seconds she had let herself enjoy it. It was because it felt so special that she had to make sure it didn't happen again. She knew only too well how many women he had been seen with each year. None of them seemed to last long at all. She was determined she would keep this job now and she would not be bullied by the others. When Philip saw her work for this, he would have no choice but to recognise her skills, even her skills with the camera might become more valued.

It was well into Sunday when she got back to her flat. India slipped quietly into her bed and despite the chaos that filled her brain, this time she fell fast asleep.

Chapter 16

India checked her camera bag had all the little extras she liked to keep in there, including a spare battery, double-sided tape, safety pins and clips. They had all come in useful on shoots. Nick was particularly careful to teach her these simple tricks each time she worked with him.

Happy she had everything she might need, she pulled on her duffle coat and walked over to Nick's studio where her taxi would pick her up. She knocked on the door but then stepped in to find him in his office area. For once, she was pleased that he worked most days.

"Hi, Nick."

"Morning Beautiful. I'm editing your shoot from yesterday. Deanna has seen them, and she is over the moon. She wants you to have that dark blue dress."

"Oh, I couldn't."

"I think she is hoping you will do some tagging on Instagram. She knows your followers keep growing."

"Thank you for helping me today."

"Sure, the lights are over here ready for you."

"Thanks again, of course. If Bentley & Bentley get the job, I want you for the shoots. This mock-up is to secure it."

Nick smiled "I know that Beautiful, the printer is over here if I'm not here when you come back. It works off Bluetooth so you should have no problems connecting."

"I'm to submit using email by 4 pm tonight, but I won't need the printed copy until Monday morning."

"Have you got some help today?"

"Yeah, Charlie Robertson, he is the Yorkshire batsman we are hoping to use to showcase the Gym Away, oh and the clients."

"The clients are helping you write your bid?"

"Well, yes."

"Why?"

"Why not?"

Nick shrugged smiling and gave her a spare key so she could drop off the lights or use his printer if he wasn't there.

"I was thinking it might be useful if you have a key, you are dropping props off here most days."

"If you're sure? Then great. As soon as my taxi gets here, I'm off." India was anxious to get started.

"Want to see how beautiful you looked yesterday?" Nick asked, bumping her shoulder.

India pushed him away. "As opposed to how rough I look today?"

Nick surveyed her dressed-for-action clothes. With her almost black hair braided down her back she wore yoga pants and a sweat top, she was still attractive. Being tall helped but there was more to it with India. Some are beautiful from the inside out. He worked with many stunning models, few had the inner radiance that India had, and not for the first time, he thought about asking her out. He pulled her by the hand into his office to show her the photos from yesterday.

"I can send you some of these for your Instagram if you remember to tag."

"I always tag, and you know it."

"I do, and that is why we all love you. Well, one of the reasons." He genuinely did like India. She was one of the good people. Always wanting to help others.

Nick helped her into the taxi with her bags and the lights wishing her good luck for getting the mock-up done in the time she had. Charlie was waiting for her outside with his case.

"I've checked out. I can go straight to King's Cross from Joe's hotel." It hit India that he was going back to Leeds. If Bentley & Bentley didn't clinch the job, or if she wasn't given the lead for the project, she might not see him till the next party at Robbie's.

"What is with that face of yours, India?"

"I was thinking if I can't make this work, I won't see you again until New Year."

"Silly girl, stop hiding at that side of the taxi. Come over here and have a hug." India looked at Charlie, afraid to move. She couldn't get involved with this man who had so many women in his life, still part of her ached to feel his arms around her. Charlie extended his arm across the back of the seat.

"Come on sweetheart, I thought we were friends again." Oh, he means as a friend, of course, what else could he mean. I'm just a silly young girl who threw up the first time we met. She slid over and let his arm rest gently over her shoulders. He smelled of mint and some cologne she couldn't place.

"That's better. Now, what is all this rubbish about you not winning that launch? Aren't we on our way to see the client?"

"I guess Joe and Tilly like my ideas, but Philip might not approve of what I send him, then I think they will walk away. I'm sorry Charlie, I know you need the extra money."

"And if this project doesn't happen with Bentley & Bentley, I could still get the job, so thank you for getting me to meet them. We can still see each other, we are friends, right?"

"Yes, but you are in Leeds."

"India, it is two hours on the train, less if you are in Hurst's Bridge. Now let's focus on you winning this launch. Show me what you have on your timetable."

India gave him a breakdown of her ideas for the shoots and the Meet & Greet dates she had in mind.

"How do you feel about the Hawick shoot, I thought it would give you time to get home and illustrate more depth to who you are? Robbie will help with that, won't he?"

"Of course. He would do it for you, if not for me. That cousin of yours has a soft spot for you. You have worked so hard on this India." And he hugged her closer. It felt good, maybe too good, so she pulled away slightly.

"Charlie, about last night, you do understand that if we are working on this, we can't be together?"

"I get it India. I'm just pleased we are talking. When we met, we talked so much and now it is great to have your friendship, I don't want to spoil that again."

By the time the taxi arrived at the boutique hotel, India felt they were going to be fine. Tilly and Joe were waiting for them, and they had the newspapers. India was relieved that there were no reports from the night before. Whilst she dug through her bag, Joe and Charlie looked at the Gym Away and were busy swapping ideas. Tilly rang down for a tray of tea and toast to fuel their morning.

India stood up with her camera in her hand and explained, "I want to get this done in two hours so I can work on processing the images and the words. Then tomorrow you will see what your product could look like in a magazine."

"Tilly says you want some photos of me and her too? Is that right?" Joe was uncomfortable.

"Yes, big glossy photographs of a professional athlete will look good in the adverts we buy. Plus, we can submit some interviews with each of you too."

"OK, you're the expert."

"Think of it this way, Joe. If I show you what it could look like tomorrow, you can decide if you want to do that more easily. I think you will find editorial pieces are quite effective in terms of getting sales."

"Do I have to pay extra for editorial pieces?"

"You may pay us to prepare them, but you won't pay the publication. However, we will have more success getting editorial coverage in a magazine we are paying for adverts in."

"Do you want to see what I bought for props?" Tilly seemed excited to share them.

"Of course," and whilst the boys went back to looking at the Gym Away, India and Tilly inspected the towels and gym kits she had found.

"I like that I get to buy these myself. I can control the cost, splurge if I feel it will be worth it or save when I can see an offer." Tilly's excitement was bubbling over.

India passed the clothes to Charlie and asked him to go try them on whilst she tried different photos of the Gym Away kit packed in a case on the bed. Charlie was eating toast so pushed the last of the slice into his mouth, overfilling it and then licked his fingers. India scowled at him. Was he trying to tempt her deliberately?

He took the clothes and disappeared into the bathroom to get changed. Tilly gave India a long look, then said.

"So, what gives with you two? You keep saying nothing is happening between you but believe me from where I'm standing, the sparks are definitely flying."

"Really?" India knew she felt something, she had hoped others wouldn't see it.

"Yes, really, and from the photos you sent me of him in that kilt, I want to say why on earth not?"

"Well, there is one good reason. He is hot, and he has any number of beautiful women ready to drop everything and do what he wants up in Leeds."

"Have you looked in a mirror recently? You are gorgeous, even today in your casual gear, you look amazing, but it is more than looks India, you are beautiful inside and out. You care about people."

"Yeah, usually I care too much and end up hurt when guys move on to the next girl they meet. You've seen him, Tilly, I would be devastated to think I had lost him, at least this way, we are friends, and he doesn't want to spoil that."

Tilly started to argue when Charlie came back into the room and that conversation was over, although India got the idea that Tilly hadn't given up. The top was rather loose on Charlie and wouldn't show off his chest in the same way as she had seen last night. India had spotted a suitable space with plenty of light to get some upper body shots again. With the cunning use of some clips out of sight, she took some beautiful shots of him in the vest and shorts.

Whilst Charlie changed again, India talked to Joe and asked him to help her understand more about Gym Away, its features and benefits, and how it differed from anything else on the market. After a while, she took them all outside to a park to get more shots of all three of them. Throughout, she was talking, asking questions about them, their company, and the product.

The two hours flew by, and India had enough to do a mock-up. There would be plenty of time to perfect the ideas if her proposal were given the go-ahead.

"Time for me to go process all this material. I have plenty to send to Philip tonight."

Tilly was the first to hug her, but Joe gave her a pretty big one too, which left Charlie. He held both her hands and India thought she saw a small tear in his eye. He pulled her into his arms and clung on. "I'm so pleased I found you again. Please don't stop talking to me. Promise whatever happens tomorrow, we can talk soon."

"I promise." India had tears in her own eyes now and was glad when Tilly gave her another hug.

They all helped to pile her into her taxi, complete with sandwiches to keep her going until her deadline.

Chapter 17

As the taxi pulled away, she looked through the photos on both her camera and her phone and deleted the ones she didn't want. It would help them upload quicker.

Katie's face lit up her screen as a call came through.

"Hi, Katie. You picked a good time, I'm on my way home, and when I get there, I have to work."

"India, I work seven days a week, but I work for myself and take a time-out when I need it. You work silly hours five days, why are you working today?"

India re-lived the last few days with her friend. She told her all about standing up and speaking out on Saturday, which got a cheer from Katie. Then she had to tell her about Michael fudging Coombes and his behaviour the previous night, and again Katie cheered when she heard about Charlie grabbing him by the throat.

She told her about her morning and what she was going home to do.

"Charlie and I have been to meet the clients and get more photographs and some words for this mock-up."

"Oh, listen to you 'Charlie and I'. What is happening with you two then?"

"Nothing he has hugged me a bit too long twice, and I made it clear that we can't be together, and he said he understood. I didn't want us to go back to not speaking."

"So how does that feel?"

"Between you and me it feels fudging horrible."

"India! It must be bad if you have the fudge out. Why can't you swear like the rest of us?"

"Well, it does Katie. I like him I always have. I understand all the reasons we shouldn't have a relationship, but there is something easy about being with him. When he hugs me, I could stay there all day. It's like coming home."

"Be very careful little one, I know how much you love every stray cat you meet, this one could do serious damage and not just to your heart."

"I know. I truly do know and understand all that. I'm telling you because you're the only person I can say this out loud to, my body wants to melt into his body. My head knows all the reasons that can't happen, but the rest of my body hasn't caught up yet."

"Be strong. When does he go back to Leeds?"

"His train is at four."

"That should help then."

"Yeah, hey Katie, the taxi is pulling up at the flat. I need to focus on the work now. I'll send you some images when it is done."

There is something about a deadline that focuses the mind. That is certainly how it felt to India. As soon as she got through her door, she started up her laptop and set her camera to download. Whilst the computer and the camera talked to each other, she popped the kettle on and made some peppermint tea and pulled out the food that Tilly had given her.

Talking to Katie had reminded her of a similar piece she did for her jewellery last year. No one from Bentley & Bentley had seen it, and that would save her time. She opened the old document and started by changing the brand colours on the template. Next, she selected various pictures and edited them to fit the layout grid she had used. She focused on cropping the images to suit the spaces she had and didn't get drawn into using filters at this stage.

At the last minute, she decided she needed to add 4 slides to explain why they should do this launch with Bentley & Bentley. As much as these were her ideas, it was the contacts in the trade that would make or break this proposal; getting the right space in magazines at decent prices and being able to book the best photographers.

India would have loved to work on this longer and she hoped she had done enough to convince Philip to use her ideas to show the clients. She wanted this to be a Bentley & Bentley project and if she was honest with herself, she wanted her boss to acknowledge her worth in the company.

At 3:50 pm she pressed send with a note to say she would bring a print version to share with the client tomorrow morning. She waited for a read receipt and then threw on her coat to go round to Nick's studio, grabbing a box of fudge as she walked out the door.

She was so happy to find Nick still working in his office. She offered him some fudge.

"Thanks. How has it gone?" he asked, helping her put the lights back in the storage space. "You know, I could have helped you with the layout."

"I was so short of time I used an old one I had. I guess we could tweak it before we print it?" India opened up the files and showed them to Nick.

"Well, Beautiful, I don't think we need to mess with this at all." Whilst they waited for the printer to work its magic on glossy paper, India told Nick more about the project and let him look at the photographs on her phone. She knew Nick was a great creative, so she talked him through her plans. Nick took his time to examine each of the images.

"Wow, India, he will be a dream to work with. Look at those angles. How tall is he?"

"6ft 3 That's tall for a batsman. Looks good, doesn't he?"

The printing finished, Nick helped India crop it to size and fold it. He found a box to help her keep it flat and safe for the next morning. Nick insisted she take the blue dress from Deanna when she left to go home.

By the time India was back home, exhaustion hit her. She filled a bath and selected some music to relax to. The water system was old, and the bath took some time to fill, so she carefully picked out an outfit for the next day. She wanted to be on top form for this presentation. Laying in the water, she tried to decide what she was going to do if Philip chose Alice or Malcolm. Surely, they had upped their game, and so perhaps one of them might have produced something better than her. If she could see Philip had made a good decision for the client, maybe she would stay.

One thing she was determined about was, not being bullied any longer. She knew it was her job to do most of the running around. She accepted that but at some point, it had all gotten out of hand. After her bath, she tried to settle to relax and when her phone buzzed, she was sure it would be her parents. Unusually, it was her father.

"Are you OK dear?"

"I'm fine Dad." India's face held a tight smile.

"I was sad to read your text, but I wasn't shocked." It was a difficult call, though India was glad her dad had taken the time to ring. They had a chat about the last few days.

"So, an eventful weekend, then. Were there any fun bits?"

"Well, I did some modelling for a friend yesterday, which was a great help. I had missed the hairdressers and things when Philip made us go into work on Saturday. If I had known Michael was going to be so obnoxious, I could have stayed home and worked on my presentation instead. I had a wonderful morning working on it with Charlie and the clients today. The extra time would have been good though."

"So, when are we going to see you home again? What about Easter? You know your Mum loves an excuse for a big roast dinner with you and your brother."

"I don't know. It depends on tomorrow morning. To be honest, work has been a struggle the last few weeks."

"Just because you have to work a few extra hours is not a reason to leave another job India."

"I know Dad." Whatever energy India had left, disappeared with those last words. She knew he worked hard and sometimes put in long hours, like Andrew, her brother did. They both had a wife at home who made sure their lives ran smoothly. India was all alone here in her flat and physically tired most of the time. She felt certain she couldn't be like her mother and not work at all, then when she looked at how hard Andrew's wife worked to hold down a job and run the house, she didn't think she could do that either.

Taking herself to bed, she resolved to take each day as it came for now. First, she had to get through Monday morning.

Chapter 18

India stepped into Bentley& Bentley with a tight hold on the box holding her mock-ups. As she hung up her coat, she noted that Alice and Malcolm had both taken the time to look good today, too. India smiled weakly at them both, sadly she saw no response at all. Instead, they were talking quietly between themselves. So, she sat down at her computer and checked her emails. She found a message from Deanna, thanking her for Saturday and saying please do it again soon. Nick copied her into the proofs of images that he had been working on for Bentley & Bentley over the weekend.

She heard giggles from the other side of the room and glanced up to see Malcolm showing Alice something in the morning papers. Even from where she was sitting, she could see it was an image of Charlie kissing a girl outside of a nightclub. Well, he didn't waste much time, did he? Thank goodness she had put up resistance to his charms. How dare he be so critical of Michael when he evidently intended to do something similar to the girl in his arms in that picture? Were all men the same?

Jayne strode into their area rather over-dressed for Monday morning.

"Mr Bentley's office in 5 minutes; India, make the coffee," she barked out in her succinct way. Her rich auburn hair was not in its usual tight bun instead it was tumbling down her back.

Here we go again, my return to doing the fudging jobs. India was unsure what the answer was. From what Josh said, they had someone in this post all the time he was working here, and they had all been treated the same. The job was not the opportunity to learn that she had been led to believe it was. With fewer clients coming in, there wasn't a chance of another junior joining to share the jobs. Alice and Malcolm were comfortable in their posts, so comfortable they were possibly the reason work wasn't coming in. India suspected they were trying to cherry-pick which clients Bentley & Bentley took on.

Still, she made the coffee and whilst she was there; she prepared the tray for when Joe and Tilly arrived. Nerves were making her uncomfortable and doing something useful in the kitchen helped her to control those butterflies that she was certain would escape her stomach very soon. She carried the first tray into the corner office and went back to collect a couple of copies of her mock-up and her thumb drive, which held her slides.

Alice and Malcolm were already in the room, and if India was nervous, so were they. Malcolm was visibly sweating, and Alice kept folding her hands. Jayne followed India into the office, clutching her shorthand notepad. She wasn't usually part of these meetings, but nothing was usual about today.

Philip Bentley sat at his desk; his head bowed to his steepled fingers. He had on a dark navy suit with a crisp white shirt and a striped tie. His slightly greying hair slicked carefully back at the temples. He raised his eyes and studied the three people who had each submitted a presentation the previous evening. A sideways glance at Jayne made him shiver. He knew she would expect him to ask Malcolm to take the lead on this project. She created such a fuss in the first place about him asking India that day he had invited her to meet the clients. He was confused about what to do on this one.

Malcolm's presentation was fresh, and he appeared to have taken more notice of the information that India had provided. Philip still felt that he was stretching the costings. If there hadn't been such a mess on Friday, he could have probably persuaded young Joe to up the budget, but he wouldn't buy it now.

Alice, on the other hand, had this time been ruled by the money constraints, which had led to a lacklustre set of ideas that focused on the cricket angle.

His friend's daughter, India Barrington Jones, had yet again surprised him. He felt sure that after her outburst on Saturday she would simply present a tidied-up version of the idea she had already shared. Jayne had let him know she left very shortly after him. Why not? after all, the clients certainly loved it. The mock-up she produced was inspired. It showed the client exactly what to expect without sleep-inducing slides. The suggestions were practical and doable within the tight budget and presented in a clear and visible way. She obviously had the support of Joe and Matilda Cookson, in addition to Charlie Robertson, as they were all in the photographs she used. It was remarkable how much she had achieved over the weekend. Philip was also pleased she had taken the time to reassure the client that spending money using Bentley & Bentley would be a sensible investment.

Philip pondered the way forward. If he gave the project to India, the others would feel disrespected, and, of course, Jayne would be angry with him again. He started by thanking them for working over the weekend and announced that if the Cooksons signed the contract today, they could all take an extra day's holiday. He went on to talk about the positives of each presentation.

Philip then asked them all for their comments on each other's proposal. It was hard to say who was most surprised when Alice and Malcolm both spoke positively about India's mock-up. India, of course, found pleasant things to feedback about each of their projects.

Malcolm started to speak again, and India clutched the sides of the old wooden chair she was sitting in.

"One look at India's layout tells me one important thing, the client is obviously on board with her ideas. As she kindly told us all on Saturday, this is a new kind of client, that will mean demanding work that she is ready for. She clearly knows the locations like Headingley and Hawick much better than anyone else in the company. I think I speak for both Alice and myself when I say, she should take the lead on this one."

Philip began to relax. Jayne still wouldn't be happy that she would be missing someone she could boss around, but this way she couldn't place all the blame on him and suggest it was because 'he fancied India'.

Alice agreed with Malcolm. "OK India believes so much is possible within the budget; I think it will be a wonderful experience for her. That is if she thinks she can handle a loose cannon like Charlie Robertson."

India realised why she was being handed the project. Neither Malcolm nor Alice wanted to work with Charlie. It wouldn't be the same as working with one of the usual models, which they mainly left to whichever photographer they used. No, Charlie would require more delicate but firm handling. They probably didn't fancy a trip north of the border to Hawick, and she was certain that neither would like the idea of Scarborough in August for the cricket festival.

Philip took a deep breath and said the words India felt she needed to hear. "I don't doubt that India is the person on the team who is best suited to this project. As we can see from her mock-up, she already has the client on board. I feel that their hostility on Friday was in some part due to them being surprised that India was no longer taking the lead, for which I'll take responsibility. India, do you think you would be able to take on the launch?" When she agreed, Philip gave out the jobs for the rest of the morning. He asked Jayne to organise some of those small little cakes that always seemed to woo the clients, and Alice to organise the drinks. Malcolm was asked to help India prepare to present at 10 am.

India was rather blown away at how smoothly that had all gone. Now she couldn't wait to see Joe and Tilly. She was so excited she needed to nip to the toilet. She could hear Jayne ranting to Alice in the tiny office kitchen.

"I hope Lady Muck doesn't think she is going to get away with not pulling her weight around here. I can't believe I am expected to fetch cakes for her!"

121

"OK, shouldn't you be out collecting them?" a confused Alice asked.

"No, I'm having them delivered."

Having stopped to listen, India realised she had heard enough and quickened her pace to get to the toilet and back.

Josh was collecting the Cooksons from their hotel and bringing them to the office for the meeting. Philip was laying out the red carpet. Like India, he realised they were the key to working with the rest of the family. By the time Josh delivered them, Bentley & Bentley was ready for Joe and Matilda Cookson.

Philip Bentley, looking as smart as ever, greeted them and ushered them into the conference room where Malcolm, Alice and India were waiting for them. Joe was stoic and had made up his mind he was prepared to walk away this morning if the deal was not right for their product. Tilly was anxious, she wanted this to work so much; she scanned the room for clues, searching faces for answers but when she spotted India's mock-up out on the table, she visibly relaxed. When Tilly relaxed, Joe became less tense too and Philip thought there was still a chance. Tilly looked at India as her face lit with excitement, India fought the urge to grin back and instead offered a professional smile.

As the Cooksons settled down in their seats, Alice began fussing with coffee and the delicious little cakes that Jayne had arranged. Philip stood at the front of the room, commanding attention, and began the meeting.

"Welcome back to Bentley & Bentley. We have listened to what you said on Friday and over the weekend the team has been working together." Tilly choked on the cake she was nibbling and reached for her coffee and Joe stroked her back. India bit her lip and looked down to study her shoes.

"We believe India should be the person to work with you most closely on, what will, of course, be a project the entire team will contribute to. She will be at all the shoots and handle the talent." Tilly winked at India at the words 'handle the talent'. How could India get Tilly to understand her job was important to her? That nothing could happen between her and Charlie if she ever wanted to speak to her parents again?

"I'm going to ask India to give you a flavour of what Bentley & Bentley would like to do to help you with the launch of Gym Away. India will also be the one to explain what a difference working with Bentley & Bentley will mean to your launch." Joe and Tilly had picked up the mock-up and were examining the photographs of themselves. India stood up and moved to the front of the room. Sliding her hands down her thighs, she smoothed down her skirt and straightened her blouse. The presence of her colleagues made her more uncomfortable than seeing the clients. She took her time and smiled softly at each one of them before she spoke.

She explained her discussions with the proposed photographer Nick, and Charlie Robertson, about the shots that would emphasise the best points of Gym Away. She also explained which dates she proposed that took advantage of Charlie Robertson's locations for matches. India took the time to remind them about Charlie's commitment to Yorkshire County Cricket and how that came first. She was confident that although some dates or locations might need to change, Charlie was committed to the project and would ensure they had enough access to fulfil the project. With careful planning, they should avoid any problems. Turning to her slides, she explained the benefits of working with Bentley & Bentley.

Joe looked at his watch. "Philip, thank you for this and you can tell Tilly and I are on board with working with India and Charlie. We had great fun working on this mock-up yesterday. If the contract is the same as you showed me on Friday, I'll sign it now. It would be wonderful if we could sit down and talk to India in more detail today before we return home."

"Most certainly. If you want to step into my office, we can sort all that out. Would you like to meet India after her lunch break?"

"If we can take her away now, I can assure you, Tilly will ensure she is well fed?"

Philip looked at India, who nodded. Joe and Philip moved off to sign the necessary paperwork. Tilly got up and hugged India as Alice and Malcolm shuffled out of the room. "I can't wait to get you out of this place," she whispered in India's ear.

India left Bentley & Bentley with Tilly and Joe.

"So how did it go before we arrived?"

"It all went remarkably smoothly. Even Malcolm agreed I should take the lead."

"I was nervous for you, were you nervous?" Tilly looked like she was running on adrenalin and was talking extremely fast.

"Funnily enough, I realised I was more nervous about presenting in front of them than in front of you."

"I'll take that as a compliment," laughed Joe, and he squeezed Tilly's hand. "What about you Babe?"

"The four of us working for those two hours yesterday was such fun. I think we worked well together. We had such a wonderful time with Charlie after you left."

Chapter 19

India looked at the list on her desk. She was working from home and getting ready for the first shoot. Although she had lots of calls to make, she still had a bag to pack to take to the match the next day. She started by calling the clients.

"Hello, Tilly. I wanted to let you know your parcel arrived with the props and talk to you about any ideas you had for tomorrow."

"Hi India, great to hear from you. I wish I could come with you tomorrow, but Taunton is even further from here. I think we will wait until you are further up north."

"That makes sense. I'm glad that Nick wanted to drive."

"Tell me about Nick, you sound as though you spend a lot of time with him."

"Tilly, are you trying to find me a boyfriend again?"

"I just want everyone to be as happy as Joe and me, now answer the question, what is he like?"

"He is tall, about six-foot, dark hair, cute face about 35, I guess."

"And how do you feel about older guys?"

"As you pointed out, Nick is someone I see a lot, FOR WORK, and as you know I don't think work is the place for finding dates."

"Is that your only excuse for not dating Charlie?"

"That is one reason! Now, anything you want me to get Nick to shoot tomorrow."

"You said you got the sweatshirt?"

"Yes, it all arrived at the office yesterday. Would you like him to wear it?"

"Yes, take that and a towel, that should bring the right sort of colours in."

"Great, that was on my packing list already."

"Listen, Joe is calling so I better get going. Have a wonderful time and call me if you have any questions. I'll be at the office, though I'm not in any meetings, so you won't disturb me."

"Thanks, Tilly, Goodbye."

India ticked that phone call off her list and packed the sweatshirt with the towel into her tote bag, ready for the morning. Looking at her watch, she decided it wasn't too late to call her boss to remind him she was going down to Taunton tomorrow. Philip was pleased to speak with her and reminded her it would be a long day and she should finish early today. India thanked him knowing she would work on this well into the evening, but she would take the time out to make a few calls after dinner.

India was going through her notes of the interview she had with Charlie, ready to use with this month's professional photographs. Seeing him tomorrow would give her a chance to check any answers and ask extra questions if she needed to. This would be seeing Charlie again in a large group. She would have Nick with her, and she presumed some other players would be around too. In some ways that made her feel safe, nothing could happen beyond talking.

Now everyone was on board with India leading this project, the ideas came flooding in. The drive down to Taunton for the first shoot was long. Even longer than she expected with traffic building up on the M3. Driving down with Nick had helped, but he had been asking a lot of questions and seemed interested in how she knew Charlie Robertson. As much as she liked and trusted Nick, it didn't feel right to tell him about that first New Year party, so she was vague, saying he was a friend of her cousin in Scotland.

India had debated what to wear. It was a shoot where grass was involved, so she was in jeans and good trainers. As she would hopefully meet some of Charlie's friends, she had been careful to choose a pretty top that tied at the neck and had taken extra care with her hair and make-up. Getting out of the car, both she and Nick took time to unbend and stretch before collecting their bags from the back. Nick was loaded up with his favourite camera and a selection of lenses whilst India carried the props from Tilly.

It was the first day of the four-day match in Somerset and rain had prevented any play before they arrived. Charlie was hanging around the door, waiting for them. He looked pleased to see India and gave her a massive hug, lifting her off the ground.

"Missed you, my angel" came that soft Scottish lilt that took India back to their first meeting. She softened in his arms until they both remembered where they were and that they were being studied by Nick and Ben Woods, who had followed Charlie out.

"Is this a new girlfriend, then Romeo?" Ben teased. He wasn't as tall as Charlie, but he was well built with strawberry blonde hair. Quite cute in a rugged sort of way.

"As you well know, this is India. She is Robbie Anderson's cousin."

"Hello Ben, this is Nick who is here to take photographs of Romeo without a girl for a change."

"Now where is the fun in that? Sure you couldn't be in a few? How will people recognise him?"

"It's the fresh look I'm working on for him."

"Yes, I'm rather worried about which type of men she is trying to attract."

"Charlie, behave yourself, or I could be looking for another Yorkshire cricketer." That tickled Ben, who couldn't resist teasing Charlie more.

"We have plenty of them inside, step through this door, young lady." And he took India's hand and pulled her into the clubhouse. Nick was grinning away at the back of the group as Ben led India around, introducing her to all the Yorkshire players, telling them she was looking for a Yorkshire cricketer to replace Romeo. His brother Dan took up the teasing, going even further than Ben had done. He stripped off his top and came to take her hand from Ben.

"Brother, you are married. I think this is a job for a single guy, and maybe someone born in Malton will be a lot better for her than someone from North of the border. He doesn't even have the right accent." He pulled India away from Charlie and Nick and carried on with a sales pitch.

"Now look at this torso, I have muscle on my muscles why on earth didn't you come straight to me instead of that old Romeo." Daniel did have a wonderful chest, but his arms and legs threw his body out of proportion. He looked like a blonder and stretched out version of his brother.

"Daniel Woods, this has been fun, but I'm here to do a job. If you will excuse me, I need to get back to Romeo, I mean Charlie and my photographer."

"Ha! She called you Romeo too. How long has she known you?" laughed Dan.

"Long enough," was all Charlie said. India noted he wasn't keen on his friends knowing the full story either. It was hard to decide if that was a good or a bad thing.

"Come and have a look at the locker room and see if that will work for a few shots, then I thought if it stops raining, we could try outside?"

Nick and India followed Charlie down the corridor to the team's dressing room. Nick got out his light meter and was striding around trying to get some idea of the best locations to use. India handed Charlie a sweatshirt to wear. She had been worried about taking photographs when his teammates were about, she was delighted he seemed rather relaxed. He had been grinning throughout that silliness with Ben and Daniel Woods. In fact, he was smiling quite a lot. Although India liked the look in the locker room, Nick was complaining that the light was hardly good enough. The rain had briefly stopped, so they went outside.

By the time they had taken as many shots as Nick thought he could, it was announced that there would be no play that day and the team were being bundled onto the coach.

"Come back to the hotel and meet the guys some more, it will be fun."

"I would love to, Charlie, but I think Nick wants to get on the road. It took us over four hours to get here and well, I'm sure he would rather be at his studio processing today's photographs than messing around with the likes of Daniel Woods."

"He isn't that bad, the others are a lot more mature."

"Not this time, Charlie."

Chapter 20

With all his kit packed meticulously for the match, Charlie set off south down the M1. On the drive, he had plenty of time to reflect on how he felt about the Gym Away launch. It gave him money to pay for the extra things at his mum's that Emma had suggested. It wasn't just having help with the physical things such as changing the bed often; it helped by providing company for her, having someone in the house every day, making sure she ate a healthy meal and got some gentle exercise. Charlie wished he could be the one there looking after her, sadly he wasn't.

He hadn't thought he would like this job, surprisingly he was actually enjoying it. He liked both Joe and Tilly, and of course, India was a whole different story.

Charlie had met Nick at Taunton, and he was shocked at how he felt seeing India react to another man. It was hard to say if they were in a relationship, they appeared to work well together. Perhaps Nick was why she had been adamant there could be nothing between them. She was right, of course. Not only was she in London and remarkably busy with her job, but he was rarely in one place. Although he lived close to the Headingley Stadium, matches could be anywhere, even the "home" ones. Robbie had also gone to great lengths to make him understand how her family would react to anything between them. Robbie's mum Patricia had been distanced from the family when she married his father. Her brother – India's dad - had been the only one to stay in touch, but they would never be welcome back in Hurst's Bridge. India, Andrew, and their cousins had access to the family trust, Robbie and his sister had no such help.

Following the instructions India had sent him, he pulled his car up outside NW Photography. It was a white painted wooden front to a railway arch workshop. Driving down a day earlier than the team to pull in this session was a simple idea that let him have some time in the studio for India. He could join the rest of his teammates at the hotel tomorrow. She had planned his shoots in great detail around his match days, after her trip to Taunton, she had realised how little she could control those.

When he walked into the building, he found Nick and India rolling around laughing uncontrollably on a bed-like structure on the ground. India's long hair tousled in such a way it made him wonder what she looked like in a morning.

"Sorry if I'm interrupting anything." It came out in a more disapproving tone than he had intended. India jumped up, blushing, and pulled down her sweatshirt to cover the inch of tempting tanned flesh that had become exposed.

"We were getting the bed ready as a base for a flat lay with your suitcase when 'someone' suggested it would look more believable if it looked like it had been slept in." She did a mock disapproving stare at Nick, who was still laid out on the mattress, waving his arms and legs about as if he were making a snow angel.

"It wasn't me who was trying to decide how active Charlie was in bed, young lady!" India blushed and walked over to the kitchen area. Over her shoulder, she asked Charlie if he wanted tea or coffee.

"I would love tea please India." He loved saying her name. Was that wrong?

"Nick?"

"Need you ask? Coffee for me please, Beautiful." With India busy, Nick talked to Charlie.

"Rough drive?"

"Yeah." Better to blame the journey than confess what he had just seen had changed his mood.

"Have you got your cricket gear with you?"

"I have my match day bag still in the car. Do you want to use it?"

"It would give me a distinctive look." Charlie reluctantly handed over his precious match day bag. Nick sensed he was nervous. "It's OK, I'll be careful and put everything back."

Charlie frowned; his response was terse. "I'll pack it myself. It's part of my routine."

"OK, I can do the flat lays with your kit and stuff whilst you enjoy your tea and decompress a little." His smile and his accommodating nature didn't help Charlie's mood right now. He wanted to hate Nick for being someone India could be with.

When India walked in with the drinks, he felt like an extra light had been switched on. Her face was aglow. Somehow everything felt better.

"It is wonderful to have you here Charlie away from all the madness." Not quite sure which 'madness' she meant. He acknowledged that it felt good to be here with her and without the rest of the world. Even with Nick here, it was great seeing her again.

Smiling he asked, "how long will this take?"

"I booked Nick until 5 pm, but if you have enough before then, he will stop. He always stops when he isn't getting what he needs from the subject. That is why I enjoy working with him so much. Towards the end of the day, nerves can get frayed, so Nick calls a halt and starts the editing process."

"Does that mean we could get a meal and catch up tonight? The team doesn't arrive until early afternoon tomorrow. I don't want to be hanging around on my own till then."

"Sure. I think Nick would like that." That wasn't exactly what Charlie had meant. *I guess that confirms the idea that they are a couple.*

"If you two already have plans, I don't want to play gooseberry…"

"Don't be silly, Charlie." She smiled and went off to help Nick select props for the layouts on the 'bed'. India chatted with Charlie whilst helping Nick set up each shot. He was clicking away, and she seemed to know what he needed.

Suddenly, Nick stopped what he was doing and looked at his watch. Then looking straight at Charlie, he asked: "Shall we get a few topless shots in before we break for food?"

"Whatever works." Nick laughed at this response. "Most models I work with don't even want a drink of water before we shoot their abs."

India checked on a clipboard she had been sharing with Nick. "If you brought your kilt, we could use that and a bare chest like the night at your hotel."

"Do I want to know about that?" asked Nick. Charlie walked away to get changed. India could explain if she felt she wanted to.

They were talking quietly when he walked back into the room carrying two kilts. "Sorry I brought both kilts, but I forgot the rest of the stuff like my hose. It is going to look stupid with sports socks." Nick screwed up his eyebrows as if trying to picture that. India's eyes lit up.

"Just the hunting tartan kilt." It was Charlie's turn to look puzzled.

"I mean barefoot and bare chest." When Charlie came back out wearing the blue and green tartan kilt, India couldn't stop staring at his feet. Charlie blushed and started to ask her what was so fascinating about his feet when Nick cut in.

"Beautiful, go grab some oil for this chest. You will need to get a fresh bottle. I'll take a few shots without it."

India came back with a fresh bottle of baby oil and a spray that looked like the one his granddad used in his greenhouse. The thought of India applying baby oil to any part of his body made him pleased he had tight cricket briefs on under his kilt. He had anticipated he might need something to hide how he felt about her, even he hadn't thought about oil, and now he did think about it… oh boy. *And I am getting paid for this.*

Nick looked up from his camera "Oh the spray, so you want the sweaty look? Yes makes sense, these shots without anything on are great anyway. If we get a few more lights coming down on an angle more towards his abs, I can get more shadow to define them without the oil."

The excitement dropped from Charlie's stomach. He wasn't as keen on the spray. "Tell me, what's in the spray?"

"Just water and glycerine, and Nick adds a little lavender oil to help you relax."

"Let me get a few more with the sweaty look then."

Nick was very precise in his instructions to Charlie. Look down, now lift your eyes to look at my left shoulder, lower your chin a little more. The noises he was making suggested to Charlie that he liked what he was getting. He tried hard to focus on Nick rather than look at India.

India had him swap to a pair of shorts to do some movements with the wheel from the kit. Nick continued to shout instructions for her to pass props or move lights, and she seemed to know what he meant each time with simply one or two words.

It was only when Charlie's stomach began to rumble did the process stop as Nick announced "Lunchtime." India picked up her bag and saying this was on expenses, she left to fetch them food. Charlie pulled on his jeans and a sweatshirt leaving his feet bare for now.

Back in the studio, Nick invited him to look at the images from Taunton. As Charlie followed Nick into his office, he stopped in the doorway, as he was hit by the large print of India on Nick's wall. She was wearing a long dress in the darkest blue; it was beaded and looked expensive, very expensive in fact. Charlie was unable to take his eyes off her face. Her hair was swept up in the same way it had been at the eventful dinner. Nick looked back at Charlie.

"Now you know why I call her Beautiful. She was having a real rough time back then, they had taken her off your project, and that hurt her. Jayne was jerking her around even more than normal. She was under pressure to rewrite the pitch when the clients liked the one she had already done. Even then India, being who she is, still gave me three hours to help Deanna. She is beautiful inside and out."

"She certainly is."

"Have you known her long?"

"We met a while ago." If there was something between her and Nick, he didn't want to be the one to tell him what happened.

"So, you have a history?"

"Her cousin is one of my best friends."

India walked back in before he had to explain further, and started to lay out bread, cheese, ham, and pickles. There was sparkling apple juice she must have picked up in Taunton plus crisps and pork pies.

"Charlie it's great working with you, mate. Proper food and a sense of humour, an impressive body that you have amazing control over. Maybe I'll start to specialise in cricketers."

"Thanks, Nick." As they ate, Charlie watched the others carefully for clues, looking for something more between them. When Nick reached over and wiped some pickle from the side of India's mouth, he thought he had his answer. It was the first time they had touched in nearly two hours, but the softness in her eyes when he did it made Charlie's heart stop.

Nick's voice broke the tension. "OK India, what do we need to do this afternoon? Shall we try some outside in the park?".

India seemed to agree. "Good idea. What about some with the dumbbell? And maybe some jogging." She consulted her list of exercises from Joe and added, "How about side bends?"

"What do you want me to wear?" India got up and started looking through his case. Charlie's brain started to panic. *Shit, did I leave those condoms in my case? Please don't let her find condoms in my case.* He watched her rummaging in his bag and he couldn't help but get up and tidy everything neatly back into its place.

This was torture – Being there with India was exactly where he wanted to be. Knowing he couldn't be in a relationship with her and seeing her close to Nick was tearing him apart.

Chapter 21

Going to the park was a great idea. Out of the tight space of the studio, Charlie felt much lighter, and this was where he was at home, and he started his normal warm-up set.

Nick asked him to run up and down for a while, taking photos of him as he came towards him and away from him. Then he found a background he liked and had Charlie do side bends with the dumbbell. Nick was moving in and out, finding the light he wanted. India stood behind him holding Nick's bags and hers whilst clutching Charlie's coat to her chest. What a shame he wasn't still inside his coat. It was early May, and the temperature had dropped. She was walking backwards, watching Charlie, calling out ideas and trying to step out of Nick's way.

Charlie spotted her approaching the concrete strip that was raised around the edge of the grass. He shouted to her to be careful, but it was too late. Dropping the dumbbells, he ran to her. Nick walked over and stood behind Charlie as he crouched at her side.

"Are you OK, Beautiful?" India was slow to reply, a little shocked at what had happened and trying to work out why she was on the ground. Charlie picked her up, holding her to his chest, he carried her over to a wooden bench.

"Where does it hurt, angel?" the Scottish lilt in his voice softening as it did whenever he held her.

"My right ankle and the back of my head."

"You hit the concrete hard. You may have a concussion," Charlie said, looking closely into her eyes. Nick scratched his chin. Charlie continued, "Ice is what you need on both the foot and the head. Reduce the swelling now."

"I'm sure it will be fine," she said. "Sorry no dinner out for me tonight."

"Of course, you should stay awake for some time. I think it's six hours and not to be alone in case of concussion."

"Is there anyone who can stay with you Beautiful, if we get you home?" It surprised Charlie that he might leave her, but Nick continued "I have a night shoot on the South Coast, though I could go in a cab with you now."

"I have my car. I'll take her, and I can stay if it helps."

"Brilliant, mate." Nick looked pleased, but India tried to object. "I shall be fine, and a taxi would be better. There is nowhere for you to park near my flat, anyway." Nick recognised the set in India's chin.

"Let me ring whoever is going to sit with you. When I know you have company, I'll let this drop." India was stuck. She didn't want to be alone with Charlie, well she would LOVE to be alone with him, even though she knew she shouldn't. However, her head was hurting and as she tried to stand up to prove she was okay, she couldn't put any weight on her right ankle. She had no one to ask to stay with her. Stella, her cousin, was due down soon to live in the flat below hers, but on this particular Wednesday night in May, she couldn't think of anyone else to call. The shock was setting in and as she began to shake, Nick took charge. He pulled out his phone for a taxi to take them to the studio. India was wrapped in both Nick and Charlie's jackets as she sat down on the bench. Charlie put his arm around her shoulders, pulling her close to keep her warm.

"Mack is going to come and collect us. We can go back to my place and park your car inside the gates. You can leave it there as long as you need. India has a key. You can sort your bags and then Mack can take you both to India's. I'll get Mack to pick up a meal for you later. India, any worries, just go to A and E. Don't be brave."

"Don't worry, I have been on concussion watch a few times with teammates. I won't say I'm an expert, I can say I'll watch her closely."

"I bet you will," Nick said quietly, still Charlie heard it. Mack arrived and when India was struggling to stand, Charlie picked her up and carried her to the car. Charlie lifted her so gently into the back seat then slid in with her, putting his arm around her shoulders. He was whispering into her hair. "Don't worry, angel. I'll look after you." Nick sat in the front and explained everything to Mack, who was nodding in agreement. Nick picked up one of Mack's cards and passed it to Charlie. "India probably has Mack's number, but if you need him tonight, just ring him and it will go onto my account. If Mack can't get to you, he will send a car to you, you can trust him."

"Thanks." Charlie couldn't fault the mature way Nick had taken charge. He tried to figure out how old he was.

In no time at all, they were pulling up in front of a row of shops on a corner. India had been silent and stayed in the car whilst they got organised at the studio. Mack held the door open as Charlie helped India out of the car. She passed her key to Mack who unlocked the door between two shops. India began to speak a little more.

"I'm two floors up." India tried to walk up the stairs, it was soon clear that was not a great idea. Charlie picked her up. Mack checked that lasagne would be okay for later and that six o'clock was a suitable time. Unable to think too hard, Charlie and India both agreed.

"You can leave your bags here; the other flats are empty." Gratefully he put down his bags and then very carefully, he carried her upstairs, her arms around his neck. She was able to unlock the door and Charlie carried her through the flat, past a bedroom and a bathroom, sitting her down delicately on the sofa near the window. He sat down next to her for a while and then he got up to get some ice and put the kettle on.

"You don't have enough ice." He used what he found to make a compress for her ankle.

"I don't normally need much. I think the wine shop sells bags of it. Maybe you could buy some from there."

"Great," he said, applying the compress to her ankle. "You need this raised too." He pulled a small table over and slipped a cushion on it before placing India's foot gently on the improvised stool.

"How do you feel? Want a pillow?"

"Please, there is extra bedding in that cupboard for the sofa bed." Charlie pulled out a pillow and a quilt.

"I'll make the drinks, then I'll go in search of more ice. I can get my bag at the same time." Once he was convinced she was comfortable, and she had a cup of tea, he went downstairs, taking her keys. In the wine shop below her flat, he found both bags of ice and some chocolate (purely medicinal, of course). He checked the shops nearby and found a tiny orchid in a small white pot and what he was particularly hoping to find, a crepe bandage for her ankle. Nick had taken charge earlier, now it was his turn. Letting himself back in, he took his treasures up to the woman who had caused such a stir in his life.

When India saw the chocolate with the ice, she smiled. And when he produced the bandage and the tiny orchid, Charlie thought he saw a small tear in her eye.

"How cold is that ankle? Can I have a look at it? We should maybe leave strapping it until the morning unless you feel the need for the support now?"

"Yes, OK, take a look." Charlie carefully peeled back her sock with his other hand supporting her calf. The bruising was starting to appear, but there wasn't much swelling.

"Now, what about your head? Can you see OK? Do you feel sick?"

"It hurts, I'm fine. Perhaps you could help me get to the bathroom?"

"Sure. What about a bath? We have about 40 minutes until Mack brings that lasagne."

"Hmm, that sounds like a lovely idea. I think the shock is easing now, I still feel cold for some reason. A nice hot soak will help me warm up and relax. It might be interesting doing it though."

"I'm happy to help."

"I'm sure you are."

"Let's do this then. Tell me what to do."

"Help me to my bedroom and then go and run the water." Charlie picked her up and carried her. Having her arms around his neck felt good, more than good, but sitting on her bed made his jeans feel tighter. India directed him to find some pyjamas she could wear after the bath. He took her to the bathroom and finished running the water as she sat on the toilet lid.

"Got any Epsom salts or lavender oil?"

"Yeah." India pointed to her stash of bath products, and he created the perfect bath. Charlie gently helped her over to the bath, took off her socks, and left her.

"You relax now, shout when you are ready." He sat waiting for a while, he was watching the clock. He washed up their cups and some pots she had left at breakfast. Finally, he tidied her tiny kitchen area. Charlie liked things neat. He looked at his phone again. Six o'clock was coming up and so he checked on India.

"Great timing, help me back to the sofa." He lifted her once more.

"Feeling better?"

"Much better." No sooner was she sat down, than the door buzzer sounded, Charlie ran downstairs to get the food from Mack. He pulled out his wallet, and Mack stopped him.

"NO. My mum sent this, she loves India." Charlie carried the box Mack had given him upstairs.

"Apparently, this is from Mack's Mum." Opening the box, he found a large lasagne which looked homemade, some garlic bread and a small bunch of tulips.

Charlie put the flowers in water then served the food. Eating helped them both feel much better. They drank water, Charlie having announced wine was not a good idea for India tonight.

"I know you are feeling tired, but you need to stay awake a few hours longer. When I have done this before we usually played cards."

"I don't have any cards."

"I have some in my case, any card games you want to play?"

"You carry cards?"

"Yeah, there is a lot of time to fill in cricket, waiting to bat, or the rain to stop. What do you want to play? What's your favourite game?"

"I bet yours is strip poker?"

"Not when I'm playing with Woody. How about cribbage? Have you got paper to score?" Cribbage was a brilliant choice. The scores fluctuated, and despite his competitive spirit, Charlie made sure she won. She needed to have her spirits lifted. They talked and laughed, and Charlie told her stories about him and Robbie growing up. At nine-thirty Nick rang India to see how she was. Asking to speak to Charlie, he asked if she was fit to be left. Charlie told him he intended to stay if she would let him.

Charlie made them one more drink, then carried her to bed. India had reluctantly agreed to let him sleep on the sofa bed in the lounge. As he carried her to her room her arms encircled his neck and her body fell into his. Charlie felt a strong pull to protect this girl, this woman, this angel. He set her carefully on the bed and helped her find everything she needed and put it close by. He had to fight the urge to tidy the drawers at the side of her bed but the biggest urge he had to fight was climbing in bed beside her.

"Goodnight angel, sleep well. Shout me if you need me." And he lightly kissed the top of her head, taking in the crisp apple smell of her shampoo. He had reached the door when she spoke to stop him.

"Charlie, would you mind stopping with me for a while. I know you've had a long day, but I think I could use the company." She bit her lip wondering why she had asked, was she secretly hoping for Romeo to climb into bed with her, for this to be her night with him?

"Of course." He smiled at her, inside he was fighting a battle to sit next to her on a bed, the gentle scents of apple and lavender filling his brain and not touch her. Instead, he sat up on the other side of the bed from her and he asked her about things he had heard from Nick and Josh, about the way she was treated at work. India started to cry, and he could fight it no more. He pulled her into his arms and held her close. He felt terrible for upsetting her. He simply wanted to understand what was happening at Bentley & Bentley and how much was down to him. The last thing he wanted was for India to be upset. He kissed her hair again lingering even longer this time.

"Now my angel, you aren't going to be able to walk on that tomorrow. How will you get to work? Will you get Mack to take you?"

"I think I'm going to ring Philip and work from home. This is a work-related injury," she laughed. "As long as I bypass Jayne and phone Philip on his mobile, everything should be fine." India fell asleep in Charlie's arms. He wanted to protect her from the fall, from Jayne, and anything else that could hurt her. He summoned all his resolve and left her bed to sleep alone on the sofa.

Chapter 22

Charlie was, as always, awake early and made some tea, taking her a cup through to the bedroom.

They spent the whole glorious day together in her flat. Charlie was enjoying being her protector. India was trying to work and make the most of Charlie being there she worked on the details of the coming shoots. Every time she asked one more question his smile got wider. He loved her attention to detail and the way she liked to plan everything and come up with backup plans. The rained-off day at Taunton was possibly making her more intent on having alternatives as all the other shoots were planned for outdoors. Watching her face as she worked was hypnotising him and he had to stop himself from staring at her mouth which seemed to be the barometer of her moods.

In his turn, Charlie was planning for what she would need when he left. He strapped her ankle, and by lunchtime, she could hobble about.

"What did you have planned for tomorrow? Can you stay at home again?" He felt so responsible for her. Knowing he would be leaving her was hard. He had put his phone on silent so she wouldn't know how many messages he was getting to find out where he was.

"I have work to do, Philip said it was fine to do it here," she said softly. "When do you need to be at the hotel to meet the rest?"

"No particular time, the team bus was due to arrive at about three o'clock. I guess I should get there at about nine o'clock to stop Woody from panicking. He has already texted me twice today. You have me for a couple of hours. What do you want me to do?"

Charlie spent the time doing what he could to see that India wouldn't have to move far. When it came time to leave, he just didn't want to go. He told himself it was because she was still hurting, even he didn't believe it. He stood with his bag by the door, as she supported herself against the wall. Charlie walked slowly over to her and pushed the hair back out of her eyes before pulling her to him, in what he hoped looked like a friendly hug. He was trying to keep it light, it was getting harder every time they parted. India leaned into him when he hugged her, and this time she didn't pull away. The day in her small flat had been so easy. They seemed to fit together, not just in the hug, but in every sense of the word.

"I can come back after play tomorrow if you need me."

"Thanks, Nick is going to call around and my cousin is arriving on Saturday, so I won't be on my own very much."

Feeling like he had been dismissed, Charlie kissed the top of her head and left.

FRIDAY 5 PM

CWR: How are you doing?

India: Fine. You?

CWR: Finished for today, the surface was rubbish. My whites are more green than white.

India: I see Ben isn't playing. Who will open the batting with you?

CWR: Zach, and they made Ryan captain, he feels crap tonight.

India: They did score a few runs.

CWR: Fancy joining me and some of the lads for a drink.

India: My ankle is better, but I think that might be too much.

CWR: Want me to come over?

India: No go out with your friends.

CWR: What about tomorrow?

India: Nick is going to call tomorrow, and my cousin Stella is moving in sometime this weekend.

CWR: OK if you are sure.

FRIDAY 9 PM

CWR: Are you in bed yet or do you need my help?

India: Where are you?

CWR: In my hotel room, trying to find a film to watch.

India: Didn't you go out with the team?

CWR: Nope. So did you get to bed OK?

India: Just going to have a bath, then climb in bed to watch a film.

CWR: What film?

India: Man from Uncle, I like Henry Cavill.

CWR: Want to watch it together?

India: Don't think that is a great idea Charlie, you know that.

CWR: I'm just missing you.

India: Missing me?

CWR: Yes, being at your place was fun, I liked being useful.

India: It was good to have some help. I'll see you soon, Charlie.

CWR: Good night my angel, I'll watch the film here so if you want to talk when it is on you can ring me.

FRIDAY 11:45 pm

CWR: I liked the bit on the water.

India: You mean when Solo is eating in the van.

CWR: Yes but nice film. Thanks

India: Good Night Charlie.

SATURDAY 5:30 PM

India: I have the proofs from Wednesday. They look good.

CWR: Are you drooling over my bare feet again?

India: I'm not sure drool is the right word.

CWR: Did you get enough then?

India: Sure, it will give me something to work on at home on Monday.

CWR: I like that news.

India: Sorry to see today wasn't better for you.

CWR: I was out there for 3 minutes.

India: Not good

CWR: It is a long time since I was out for 0.

India: What happened?

CWR: Zach misunderstood, and I got run out.

India: Will Ben be back for the next match.

CWR: I hope so. Do you want me to come over?

India: Sorry I'm tired after Nick was here.

CWR: As long as you are OK.

India: Stella arrives tomorrow that should be fun.

SATURDAY 9 pm

CWR: Goodnight, call me if you want anything.

India: Goodnight Charlie

SUNDAY 7 pm

CWR: You OK?

India: Yes My cousin has arrived. My uncle brought her here and all her stuff. So much stuff.

CWR: I hope you weren't carrying anything.

India: No, they are being strict about my ankle. It wasn't easy sitting watching.

CWR: You are tired then?

India: So tired.

CWR: Good night India

India: Good Night Charlie x

Why did I put a kiss, what do I do about that now? I always put a kiss, but he doesn't know that.

MONDAY 9 am

CWR: Morning Sleep OK?

India: Yes having Stella downstairs helped I think.

CWR: So, you working on photos today?

India: Writing words mainly

CWR: I'm driving home today.

CWR: Will you stay at mine when you come to Leeds.

India: Hotel is booked for me & Nick.

CWR: If you change your mind here is where to find me.

Charlie sent a link to an online map. India couldn't resist the urge to click through and see where he lived.

Chapter 23

India stood on Charlie's doorstep. Her hands clenched at her sides. She had stopped crying now, and she refused to cry anymore. This whole situation was crazy and with Philip, her boss, away in the Caribbean, it could be a few days before she would be able to sort the mess out. Her taxi was waiting at the curb, and she prayed Charlie would be home and would save her once again. He had asked her to stay with him. She only hoped the offer still stood. As his front door opened, another taxi pulled up behind hers. Tilly and Joe Cookson got out and Tilly ran towards her.

"You changed your mind! I'm so pleased." India was completely lost now. The tears she had been shedding had left their mark and Tilly saw this wasn't the usual happy India. She pulled her through the door past a very stunned Charlie. Joe was paying both taxis and bringing in their cases. Tilly led India down a short hallway with a typical Victorian tiled floor, past a staircase, to a large space at the back of the house that had been extended to what some would call a Great room. It was a kitchen, dining room, and lounge all in one and very modern for the age of the building it was in. If India felt more composed, she would have noted how well thought out it was. But after Tilly's big hug, she was hovering between tears and anger.

She was aware of Joe and Charlie muttering in the hallway and Tilly putting on the kettle in Charlie's kitchen.

"I don't know what the problem is India, but we can solve whatever it is." Tilly crossed her fingers, hoping that the issue was something they could all sort.

"I didn't know you were going to be here." India's words were quiet and in some ways in the distance, as though she were talking to someone else.

"Tea first, then we eat those bacon sandwiches that Charlie promised me. I'm glad you decided to stay here too." Charlie was bringing her suitcase into the room, and he shook his head at Tilly.

"Tea! Exactly what we need, Joe is taking your cases up to your room Tilly, now my angel, are you going to stay with us after all?"

"I didn't know they were coming," India whispered. Tilly and Charlie exchanged worried looks. She jerked her chin to Charlie to tell him to take over the tea making, and she came over and pulled India into a chair.

"Explain it to me, from the beginning."

"Sorry, I keep swinging from getting so angry I could cry or just plain crying, seeing you here was the final straw."

"You said you didn't know we would be here. Surely you got my message or Charlie told you when he invited you to stay here with us?" India looked from Tilly to Charlie and back.

"Nope, Charlie suggested I stayed with him. It didn't seem like a good idea and Philip wouldn't approve. Which is why I don't understand it at all. It is crazy. Nothing makes sense."

Joe walked into the room and looked at Tilly wondering if this was one of those days she wanted him to leave her whilst a friend had a good cry. He never minded leaving, still, he wouldn't go in case he was needed. Tilly took control. India was still making no sense, she felt she would get further without the boys. As Charlie came over with the teas, she started.

"What happened to that bacon sandwich you promised, Charlie?"

"I was waiting until you got here. I was going to fetch them whilst you and Joe were settling in."

"Sounds like you are fetching enough for four. Take Joe to help you carry them." Looking relieved to be escaping, they left through a door, into a courtyard at the back and out through a side gate.

"Now why are you so upset and angry?" Tilly's arm was around India's shoulders.

"This is my first overnight assignment. Philip went through everything with me. Mainly because he wanted to make sure of what I was spending. Then when they checked my ticket on the train, it was void and my card wouldn't work to pay for a new one. I presumed it was the onboard connection and paid for my fare and the penalty with what cash I had. That left me with no money for a taxi, so I walked from the station to my hotel. Once I got there, my room hadn't been held because again there was a problem with my business debit card. I couldn't get another room because I had nothing to pay for it with me." India sighed and fought back the tears, she hated to cry about something like this, but it had been an early start and she wasn't sleeping too well. With a deep breath, she continued.

"Charlie had invited me to stay here, and I said no. If he had mentioned you being here, I might have considered it. Don't look at me like that. Charlie is called Romeo for a reason, you know. I didn't want to be in the position of him giving me a goodnight hug and me not being able to pull away this time." Tilly raised an eyebrow in question but said nothing.

"Philip has been clear that I have to maintain a professional relationship with the 'talent'. I'm not sure what he would say about me being here, or that I had somehow messed up the train ticket and a hotel booking, and I know my mother certainly wouldn't understand.

"When I saw you were here, it made me wonder. What if someone had done this on purpose? Philip is away in the Caribbean, so I can't contact him for help. If you were here and I didn't make it, then maybe that would get me in trouble at work."

"Who would do that?"

"It had to be someone who knew what my plans were."

"Or someone who could cancel your card."

"JAYNE!" they said in unison as Charlie and Joe came back through the door clutching brown paper bags that smelt divine. The four sat down around the table and shared out the bacon sandwiches, which were huge breadcakes with lots of tomato and fried mushrooms and of course some delicious bacon. Eating them was a messy process as the contents seemed to spill out from all sides. There was lots of tea in an enormous pot too. India couldn't remember the last time she'd enjoyed a meal so much.

Tilly and India told the others what they had worked out so far. Tilly told them she had left a message with Jayne that they would arrive today so they could see more of the shoot for themselves tomorrow. India suddenly remembered that Nick would arrive in the morning, going straight to the ground, but his hotel room wouldn't be there either. She picked up her phone to ring him and was shocked when his friend answered.

"Where is Nick?"

"He's in the shower. We've been surfing. Looks like we picked a great weekend."

"Weekend? He is supposed to be in Leeds with me tomorrow!" Nick took over the call.

"Is that you, India? When you emailed to cancel, I took the opportunity of a rare weekend off to get away and grab some waves. Where are you?"

"I'm in Leeds expecting you!"

"I don't understand?"

"I think I'm beginning to; can you reply to that email and say you are going to bill Bentley & Bentley for the late cancellation?"

"It's OK I'm glad to have a weekend off, to be honest."

"Nick, I didn't cancel the booking and I need to get to the bottom of this. I'll pop around to the Studio on Tuesday and see if we can work this out. In the meantime, can you forward that email to me?"

"Of course."

Sandwiches finished, Charlie offered them chocolate teacakes wrapped in distinctive red and gold foil as Joe pulled it all together.

"Let me get this straight. We think someone, possibly Jayne, has cancelled your card, therefore, cancelling your train ticket and your hotel, knowing you wouldn't discover that until you were on the train to Leeds. When was the first stop?"

"Doncaster, I could have got off there and phoned my parents, but that is the last thing I wanted to do. Fortunately, I had enough cash to pay my fare. At that point, I didn't realise it was my card that was the issue."

"So, then you discovered you had no hotel either and now somehow they have cancelled the photographer."

"Yes, they used my works email, and for once I hadn't been texting him to remind him of the ideas we had. That was probably because for the last two days I was kept remarkably busy with other jobs."

"And you didn't get the message that we would be here."

"Yep! I'm guessing this was to make you as angry as you were after Alice's presentation, and then you would walk away from using Bentley & Bentley. She isn't very keen on you either, but she just wants me gone. Philip is away for three weeks, so he wouldn't be around to smooth any ruffled feathers. I'm thinking she hoped you would blow up and I would resign all before Philip got back." Tilly grinned and that made everyone else around the table grin.

"Oh dear, she really should learn to judge people's character. What do you think, Babe?"

"I think we have got such impressive results from the work India has done so far; we wouldn't walk away from this after one cock-up. As we know who has caused the problem, we can let Philip know we are upset, and why. I think we pay for any expenses this weekend and then we withhold that amount from this month's payment. And I say we make this month's articles and adverts the best so far."

"Without Nick?" India's head dropped into her hands. "I didn't even bring my camera."

Charlie got up and left the room, Joe followed him as Tilly moved around the table to sit next to India. "I know it all looks impossible right now, India, but I know if anyone can do this, you can. You have somewhere to stay, and you have the three of us on board. No one blames you, as you might guess. We all want to show that woman, just what people like us are capable of. That is what this is about, isn't it? She doesn't think you belong at Bentley & Bentley, and she doesn't think we are good enough to be customers too." India looked at Tilly, open-mouthed. She had heard Jayne say she didn't think the Cooksons were the sort of client they wanted; she hadn't realised that she also felt the same about her.

"You realise it's often the northern accent. Some people will judge either your intelligence or your suitability by the way that you talk." India knew her mother certainly did. Even though she was from the northern counties herself, her mother's accent was impeccable. Tilly was right. She probably didn't approve of Charlie because she wasn't able to bully him like she could the regular models they used. In fact, yes, quite simply, the four of them were not people she could bully to do everything on her timescale. Plus, Philip liked all of them and Jayne seemed to like to keep Philip to herself. More determined than ever, India took a deep breath and realised how lucky she was that she had such a great relationship with the other three. And as Charlie and Joe came back into the room, she told them all that. "I'm so glad to have the three of you here or this could have been a real disaster."

Charlie passed her a camera. It was miles better than her own and the sort she had always wished she had. "Here, take this. I got it as a 'man of the match' prize last season. I used it once. I know you could do so much more with it than I can."

"If that isn't good enough, we can go buy you one this afternoon." offered Joe.

"I need to think, and I need to try out this camera. Maybe a walk to shake down those sandwiches will help. Could I stay here tonight?"

"Of course, you'll have to share a bathroom with Zach though, he'll be here this afternoon." India laughed, she had been worried about being alone with Charlie in his house. That obviously wasn't going to be a problem. She put on her coat and refused the offer of some company from the others; she had some processing to do. She took her phone and the camera then followed Charlie's directions to the park.

Once she was out and away from the house, she called Katie. After she had downloaded the story so far, she stopped and waited for Katie's response.

"The Bastards, the dirty rotten bastards. I hope you are going to show them just what you are made of India Barrington Jones. Now is the time to think like your parents, like your brother, and most of all this is the time to show them what a brilliant eye you have. Did you take your camera with you?"

"No, I was trying to save weight, not carrying too much coming up on the train. Charlie has lent me a great-looking camera. I'm off up to some park to try it out."

"Wait, where are you?"

"Headingley?"

"I know that! Where in Headingley?"

"Well, I've left Ash Road where Charlie lives and now I'm on St Ann's Road I think, I can see the park coming up."

"That Park is at the edge of the University Campus where Jon is."

"Your brother? That Jon?"

"Yes, that Jon, if you need any more help, I can call him."

"I think we've got it covered."

"I'm going to ring him so he knows you are around and might ring and I'm going to text you his number just in case."

"Thanks, Katie, I don't want to bother him. I'm sure it is all sorted."

"Jon will be mad if he finds out later. Look, he has always liked you and yes you are far too old for him, but hey the guy likes you, so if you need help, please call him." India thanked Katie for listening and for suggesting Jon, and she said goodbye. She was on the edge of the park and could see the big halls of residence of the university across the rolling grass. There were squirrels and birds everywhere amongst the trees and running over open, grassy sections. She had plenty to try the camera out on. People were playing tennis and there were a few joggers. India tried out shots of moving people and was amazed at what she could capture by adjusting a few settings. Katie was right, what would her family do? Her father would be carefully recording the costs and checking contracts. Andrew would be looking to find alternative ways to do the shoot and her mother, well, she would be hitting up her address book and planning a party. She was completely lost in thought when two young men stopped running in front of her, trying to get their breath.

"Hey India, Katie said you were here!"

"Jonathon! How on earth did you find me?"

"It wasn't hard, a woman, not a student in this part of the park with a camera. Plus, you are the tallest girl I know and have the most amazing hair. This is my mate Adam, we were about to go for a run anyway, so we decided to look for you to make it more interesting."

"Nice to meet you, India. Did you find somewhere to stay? We could always sneak you into halls for tonight?"

"Nice to meet you too, Adam, but that won't be necessary. I'm staying at Charlie Robertson's house."

"You are joking?" Adam mocked staggering back, he was shocked.

"Adam is a big cricket fan. He is so annoyed he didn't get tickets for the international against Pakistan tomorrow."

"Maybe we have a spare. Our client is staying at Charlie's with me. Do you want me to ask?"

"Let's walk you back and you can tell me the full story. Katie was fuming and Adam was itching to get out for a run so I don't know what went wrong, other than you might need to ring me, which I kinda hope you do. I like the idea of rescuing you, India."

They walked to Charlie's house, and India told them her tale. The more times she repeated it, the more it made sense. She hadn't thought to ask for a key, so when they arrived, she rang the bell again and Charlie answered.

"I let you out for less than an hour and you come back with two young men!" Charlie looked amused but India wasn't sure, she explained and introduced Jonathon and Adam. Charlie invited them in, and the kettle went on again. "Zach has arrived, and he is upstairs, putting his bags in the room next to yours. Please use the lock on the door to your bedroom!" Jon and Adam exchanged excited looks, and before they could say anything, Zach Mitchell, the Australian opening batsman for Yorkshire, bounced into the room.

"Alright, mate! What are we doing now and what are we doing tonight?" his grin widened as he took in the other people and Charlie introduced everyone.

Chapter 24

"Have you remembered I have my sponsors staying this weekend?"

"Of course, I did, all the more reason to entertain them, Charlie boy."

"I need to be in the papers for all the right reasons, and India here will be the first one to tell me how important that is for my career." India smiled at Charlie. At last, the message was getting through. In some ways Zach was right, they needed to make sure that Tilly and Joe had an enjoyable time. But Charlie was onto it too, he'd been plotting this all week, although the bonus of India being here would make it even more interesting.

"Zach, I have a simple day planned. You and I are going to hit the nets with some other guys from the team. Then I was planning on getting some pizzas in for tonight. If you and the guys want to head into town, after that I understand."

"Well, that sounds like a good plan mate, no match until Wednesday means we can have a relaxed time in the nets today, it is Saturday after all."

"Yes, I want to take Joe down there. He might enjoy watching us. The Woods Brothers will be coming too and perhaps we could drum up a few more." Zach turned to Adam and Jon.

"Are either of you cricket players?" Adam and John looked at each other excitedly. "We certainly are."

"So, fancy bowling a few balls to some batsmen who need a bit of extra practise?"

Ideas were forming in India's head. If she could get the students and a few other players to try out the Gym Away, she could add some interesting comments to this month's magazine submissions.

"You know I'm here to take photos of Charlie with the Gym Away and if any of you guys fancy trying out the equipment later and maybe letting me take some photos, but certainly giving me your thoughts then I'll organise pizza and beer for anyone who would join in."

Charlie laughed "Hey girl, this is my party! Are you already tired of taking photographs of me? You're now inviting any number of men into my house and offering them booze as a bribe."

"I'm sorry, Charlie, do you mind? You will still get paid for this month."

"I think it is a great idea, we can bring some of the guys back from the training session."

"Where are Tilly and Joe?" India was still planning.

"They went shopping. No idea what for though."

"So, let's sort out a plan, what time are you guys going to the training centre, and what and when are we going to eat."

"Nets are from 2 till 4 o'clock, I really want to take Joe."

"Let me text Tilly and see when they will be back and talk to her about food too."

"That sounds great." Charlie was relieved to be handing some of this over to her.

"We'll go back to uni now and meet you at the training centre?" Jon was looking for reassurance that this was actually happening.

"Why don't you bring another two along, as long as they know what they are doing – what about some women players? You have a great women's team up there."

"We can ask around." Jon and Adam left with huge grins, looking at their phones and throwing out girls' names. India heard Adam telling Jon that he had a great sister, and it made her wonder why she hadn't thought of the student connection before.

India and Charlie spent a few minutes on their phones. In which time Tilly and Joe were on their way back picking up food for lunch and Charlie had more bodies for the afternoon session. He also ordered 15 pizzas from a wonderful little Italian restaurant around the corner. Zach had organised beer and some soft drinks.

When Tilly and Joe arrived, Joe also carried in two large cheesecakes from the taxi. Charlie pulled out bags of crisps and some fruit.

"Keep your eyes off the cheesecakes, they are for after the pizzas. How many people are we expecting?" Tilly looked excited about this shift in focus.

"The five of us," said Charlie, motioning around the table, "and another 10 it depends how Jon gets on drumming up other students."

"India, I have to say you keep managing to not only make this fun but something that feeds the product development. I'm so glad Philip pulled you in on this, and I think he is right, your address book makes you doubly valuable. So, tell me, how did you go for a walk and come back with two student cricketers?"

"That one is simple. I rang my friend, Katie. She is always the one I ring when I need to think aloud. I was downloading everything that had happened this morning when she reminded me that her brother lived around the corner, too. I told her it was fine, but she called Jon anyway. He found me when he was out for a run." Zach laughed; he had been sitting strangely quiet all through lunch so far, now his Aussie accent boomed out.

"You should have seen Charlie's face when you turned up with two blokes. He had been pacing all the time as he does, you know. Well, he does he paces when he is nervous. Anyway, when the doorbell rang, he rushed to the door, but when he saw those young guys it was like someone hit him in the face with a frying pan." Zach was rolling and holding his sides with laughing. Although Tilly and Joe were trying so hard to hide it, they were laughing too. Charlie blushed and stormed out of the room and India sat open-mouthed.

Zach shook his head "I'm only telling it like it is." Tilly couldn't speak so it was Joe who said, "Oh we know, it's just these two who are still in denial."

Zach and Charlie organised their bats and somehow the men got changed and left to go hit some balls, leaving Tilly and India to prepare for their return. They wanted a straightforward way to record as many people's thoughts as possible in the time and still have a party atmosphere. They opted to create an online survey that they could use again. They started a list of other people they might ask to review Gym Away in the coming weeks. Tilly emailed the questions for Joe to check whilst he was waiting for his turn in the nets. He sent a couple of minor changes. Now they had ten great questions to ask everyone who came for Beer and Pizza.

They had a brilliant time, the cricketers were already in a great mood from their two-hour net session. India was pleased to see both Ben and Dan Woods as she knew Daniel was a lot calmer when Ben was there. Joe focused on getting people to answer the online questions. Charlie and Tilly played host, passing around food and encouraging them to help themselves whilst India took hundreds of photos. Zach was, of course, in charge of entertainment and made sure everyone joined in.

At nine o'clock everyone except Tilly and India set off for town. India's head was spinning and not from the alcohol. She lost count of how many times Charlie had touched her during the Pizza and Beer session. Moving her around when she had her eye in the viewfinder, touching her arm when he asked if she needed another beer and generally being very hands-on. The way he kept calling her 'my angel', it was his name for her. She was trying to decide if it was just her he was being touchy with, or if he was the same with Tilly and even the students. She wanted to ask Tilly but was fighting that idea in case it encouraged Tilly anymore.

"So, Charlie was very touchy-feely tonight?" It sounded like a question from Tilly and India was relieved that it wasn't only her that thought he had been touchy.

"I'm so glad you said that. I thought it might be just me he was being hands-on with."

"Oh, it was only with you. It was so obvious. Joe and I were trying to decide why tonight. Joe thinks it was because he was more relaxed and had been drinking. My theory is it was because the other guys were here, especially that tall thin one. Is his name Daniel?"

"Oh yes, Dan, he is so wicked, isn't he? He kept touching me too, from what I have seen he is like that with everyone."

"Yes, I think you are right. He has a wicked grin, and he was very hands-on with all the girls, but I think that is why Charlie was touching you and calling you 'my angel'."

"Men! What can you do?"

"Hope they come home fairly sober?"

"The morning should be fun getting them up, and down to the stadium for the match. At least no one has to drive."

The girls had settled down in the small lounge with a bottle of wine, as they looked through the images India had captured and worked out which ones to delete and which to upload. India poured another glass of wine whilst Tilly built up the open fire. Being outside the capital wasn't all bad. Charlie's house with five bedrooms, so close to shops, it wouldn't be something she could afford in London. She thought about life in Hurst's Bridge and how predictable it was. Life here was more interesting, here with Charlie, and before she knew it, she was imagining living with Charlie in his lovely Victorian detached house, cooking together in the Great room. Being able to walk into the town centre and be there in minutes – Leeds, even had the big stores.

India and Tilly went to bed well before they expected the boys back from the jaunt into town. After the long day she had faced since leaving her flat before 6 am, India was soon asleep. She was woken by crashing in the bathroom next door at around 2 am, which she presumed was Zach back with the others. Breakfast was going to be fun.

The next morning, Tilly and India enjoyed a quiet breakfast of cereal and toast with their usual big pot of tea. Tilly had popped out for the papers, and they drank more tea and enjoyed the Sunday papers spread out in Charlie's Great room. India managed to check for images of Charlie when Tilly was busy in the kitchen area. There were a couple of photographs of the entire group, and they seemed to have collected a few more girls with them. Still not understanding why it bothered her so much, India closed the page quickly and turned to the fashion pages where she saw a piece on Deanna's designs, and they had used one photo of her. Charlie had walked in and was reading over her shoulder.

"I see you made the papers this morning angel, I do love that photo." He flashed India his phone to show it was now his screen saver. *Nick is such a lucky boy.*

"You still made a couple of pages last night."

Tilly looked over at them both excitedly. "Oh, was Joe in the photos, he thought he had been caught in one."

"Yes, he is." and with that, she passed Tilly the papers and went back to her room to get ready for the day.

The match wasn't as exciting as she had hoped. She did manage to take some photographs of some rising stars for England playing with some of the older semi-retired squad. It had been a development game, but Tilly and Joe enjoyed themselves, and that is what counted most.

After the match, everyone else set off back home. India had to wait until Monday morning to catch her train to King's Cross, so she was staying one more night at Charlie's, this time alone. She hugged everyone goodbye, especially Tilly but also Zach. The tall Australian lifted her from her feet and held her close and whispered in her ear.

"It's been smashing to meet you, at last. Now you be careful down there in the big city. You get back here to Yorkshire where you belong as soon as."

The house seemed very empty when they were alone, but their friendship was blossoming again. They spent a comfortable night bickering in front of the TV and eating a lasagne he had pulled out of the freezer. They avoided drinking any alcohol, and India was amused when he went down into the cellar below the great room and returned with some cans of Irn Bru, his favourite soft drink from Scotland.

She wanted to catch an early train, so she had a bath and slipped into bed. The two bedrooms on the top floor fitted in the eaves of the roof and made them feel very cosy. She was cuddled down, curled up with her back to the door when she felt her bed dip as someone sat on the edge. She could smell it was Charlie, and even if he hadn't been the only other person in the house that night, she would have still known it was him.

"Are you awake, my angel?" That lilt to his voice again was resonating with the way her body was vibrating in response to him.

"Why?"

"I want to ask you a question?"

"And it can't wait till morning?"

"Maybe it could, but I would have lost my courage by then." With a sigh, India turned over, then sat up and opened her eyes. Charlie sat beside her on the bed, just like in her flat, with his legs stretched out next to hers. He looked so vulnerable. She wanted to hug him like he had hugged her that night after her fall.

"OK Charlie, what do you want to ask me?"

"When you were hugging Jon goodbye today, you said Nick wasn't your boyfriend. Have you really broken up with him?" India shook her head and tried to work out what Charlie was saying. "I'm sorry, can you ask me that again?"

"Have you broken up with Nick?"

"NO!"

"Oh, OK then." And he started to get up from her bed. India reached out and grabbed his forearm, noticing straight away how thick and sinewy it was.

"Charlie, I haven't broken up with Nick because I'm NOT, nor have I ever gone out with him." Her eyes searched his, trying to process what he was thinking.

"But I thought… when I was at his studio… I mean seeing you together… you have a key to his studio. He came to your flat when you hurt your ankle. He took care of you."

"Nick and I work together – a lot. I used to live around the corner from there and when I moved to the new place, I stored some of my boxes there. I often drop off things and pick up things from the studio. Me having a key means he doesn't have to wait for me, it is convenient for WORK! Does that answer your question?"

"When we go to Hawick, will Nick be there?" He sounded so insecure.

"No, we are going more for social media shots. We will use the kilt shots we got in the studio for the glossy pages."

"Will you drive up with me?" his voice pleading for some time with her, alone in his car.

"Yes, Charlie." India's heart ached. *Why was he so vulnerable tonight?* She squeezed his hand.

"Will you come and meet my mum?" His tone had lifted.

"You are staying with her, aren't you?"

"Yes, but I want her to meet you." The pleading was back.

"Why?" She was curious as to why it was so important.

"So, she knows who I'm talking about."

"OK, Charlie - now goodnight." Charlie stood and then bending down to stroke the hair from her face, he dipped down closer and kissed her lips so gently but not so innocently.

"Sweet dreams," and he left the room as quietly as he had entered it. India touched her burning lips. *This trip to Scotland is going to be fun.*

Chapter 25

India was back on the train, heading for Leeds. She was trying to relax, knowing that a couple of days in Hawick were likely to be busy, as any day she spent with Charlie was. Except, of course, in her flat when she had hurt her ankle and her last night at his house. Some of the time they were together was peaceful, like real friends when you don't even need to speak. She knew Tilly had a theory that Charlie struggled when there were other men in the room, she couldn't decide if that was true.

In Hawick, they would be back where it all started. She was going to be staying with Robbie and Emma whilst Charlie was with his mum. Emma had invited everyone over for Sunday lunch so she could catch up with all the others in the family, too. She pulled out her kindle and had settled to read her book when they came to inspect tickets. India's heart was in her mouth. She had been issued with a new bank card and although she was told there would be no further problems, she had come with extra cash and her own cards this time, just in case. One more week and Philip would be back in the country, then maybe she could relax more.

It was hard for the office to interfere when they were staying with the family on this trip. Charlie was going to meet her at Leeds station, and they would drive up together from there. He also had the camera she used two weeks earlier. Nick was impressed with the photographs she had taken and had given her a few tips to help with this set of images. Relieved that her ticket was OK this time, she settled again and checked her phone, finding a message from Robbie.

Robbie: What time will you get here?

India: Hard to say. My train gets into Leeds at 12:13 I guess it depends on traffic and if he wants to stop.

Robbie: I don't think he usually stops – but he might with you.

India: Do you need me to text when we are close?

Robbie: That would be cool. Emma is working so I'm in charge of dinner.

Stepping onto the platform and out of the busy station, India headed for the pick-up point where Charlie had dropped her two weeks ago. She wasn't standing there long before Charlie's sleek Black Edition Porsche pulled up for her. She pushed her bag in the back and jumped into the passenger seat. Charlie smiled at her with his cheeky grin and reached over to squeeze her hand.

"Just checking you are real."

"Hello to you too, Charlie."

"So next stop Scotland?" His grin was infectious, and she returned it with a grin of her own.

"Oh. Yes!"

"Gretna Green?" India froze. *Why would he say that? Was he trying to be funny?*

"Why would you say that?" She snapped.

"I'm thinking I'll have to marry you to get you to sleep with me."

"Why would you say that?" she growled now.

"I guess, all these people who wouldn't be happy about us being together, would back off if we got married."

"I didn't think you were the marrying kind, Charlie."

"Neither did I." India was shocked, not as much as Charlie himself.

"Well, I hate to disappoint you, but I think we should give that a miss today."

"OK. I want you to meet my mum first, anyway," and the grin was back, and India relaxed.

Being in the car with Charlie felt a bit like being a couple. Sitting side by side, they talked and talked the way she could only imagine doing with him. Driving toward Hawick was running towards her happy place, seeing the side of her family where she didn't feel she needed to prove herself. It was a world where the usual pressure of the name Barrington Jones wasn't a ball and chain holding her in one spot.

"You've gone quiet. What are you thinking about?"

"How free coming up here felt because there were no expectations. Everyone is simply pleased you came."

"I think that is wonderful and sad at the same time." He looked sideways at her and squeezed her hand once more. India smiled back at him. This wasn't a day for feeling down.

"It makes this a place of escape, though."

"Do you think you will see that sexy cricketer you met there before?"

"I usually do whether I want to or not."

"India, I want to say, I'm sorry you were sick, but I'm so glad I met you and I'm pleased we have this chance to get to know each other again. If there could be some way, this could go further, I would want this without question. I just want you to be happy." India shifted in her seat and stared at him, before she could voice her thoughts though, Charlie continued. "I know we can't be together, still it doesn't stop me from wanting it." Her thoughts were lodged in her throat. She couldn't begin to share the things that were going around her head, but she was angry with him for spoiling the journey and the easy conversation that they had been sharing. She reached out and turned on the radio, and then twisted her shoulders away from him to look out of the window. Charlie felt an icy blast down that side of his body.

When they arrived at Robbie's, the chill hadn't thawed. They walked in silence to the door. Charlie stopped and turning towards her, took both her hands in his, staring deep into her eyes, searching for the woman he loved. "I'm sorry. Can you forgive me? Please don't let it spoil this weekend."

What me? Spoil the weekend? It was him! In her head, she replayed what he had said. Looking back into his eyes until she came to the part that had stopped the conversation. He was right, all Charlie had done was be honest about how he felt. Why was she so angry with him for that? From everything Tilly had been saying, from the questions about Nick, it all pointed to the fact he might want to be more than friends. It was a good job she wasn't interested in him. Robbie opened the door to welcome them in. Charlie dropped her hands and walked to his car to retrieve her case from the back.

India smiled at Robbie, but when he didn't smile back, she knew he had seen them. "Not now Robbie, not now."

Chapter 26

The atmosphere at Robbie's had been strained. They all spoke but the normal relaxed feel wasn't there. India was still not comfortable again with Charlie. Robbie was snapping, clearly upset, possibly with both of them, and Charlie didn't know what to say to make it better with either of them. India was glad to escape to visit Charlie's mum before dinner.

She was confused when Charlie parked his car on the drive of a pleasant, detached house in Wilton. "I thought your mum lived around the corner from Robbie's mum."

"She did. I wanted her to have a nice home when I finally started making money."

"Does she miss her friends?"

"Have you been talking to Robbie?"

"No, he told me he has been going to see your mum, and that she had cancer. She must miss you."

"I know I miss her, but what can I do about that? If I moved her to Leeds, she would be even more isolated, and I'm not there that much myself. I can't get a professional cricket job up here." India saw the sadness in his face, his whole body. No wonder he was looking so vulnerable, and suddenly she felt guilty for her behaviour in the car earlier. It must have been difficult driving up and not knowing what changes he would see this time. She remembered how he looked when he asked her if she would come and meet his mum with him. India couldn't imagine how she would feel if it were her mother. She knew that his bond with his mum was extraordinarily strong. When they first met, he couldn't understand her relationship with her family at all. She offered him a smile and reached for his hand.

"I see what you mean and why you try to come home as often as you can." Charlie sighed and smiled back at her. "So, anything I should know before we go in?"

"Yes, I think she thinks you are my girlfriend." Charlie jumped out of the car and walked purposefully towards the door.

"What!" India ran after him. "Charlie Robertson! Explain!"

"She doesn't have long. She just wants to see me settled, so when she assumed we were together, I didn't put her right. When you meet her, you'll understand?" The door opened and Mrs Robertson stood waiting for them. "This isn't over, Charlie," she hissed.

"I know." He grabbed her hand and took her to say hello to his mum. "It is an hour of your time India, please I'll explain. I realise I should have explained earlier, but I have no idea where to start with mum."

Watching Charlie with his mum was like watching most adults she knew, put them in a room with their mother and suddenly they are fifteen again. Elizabeth Robertson must have lost a lot of weight with her illness, her clothes were hanging loose about a tiny body. India volunteered to make them all a drink whilst Elizabeth showed Charlie some jobs she wanted him to do. He did a few trivial things and put the rest off until his next visit, which surprised India. As they sat and chatted over the tea, she realised that Elizabeth didn't always hear what Charlie or she said. It was hard to decide if it was through choice or if her hearing was failing. After less than an hour, she was looking tired, and Charlie helped her settle down for a nap as India washed up. One of the nurses would be in to help her eat and see her to bed.

Charlie took India back to Robbie's. They had arranged to pick up a takeaway for them all to save Robbie cooking dinner. As they got into the Porsche, Charlie looked drained.

"Every time I see her, she looks to have slipped further into this damn disease. At some point this weekend, I must convince her that the hospice is the next step, and we have to prepare for that."

"Is that why you were putting off some jobs."

"YES!" He spat out, frustrated by the situation.

"Charlie, I am so sorry. I understand that won't be easy. Is her hearing failing?"

"Yes, that's part of the problem." India looked out the window, finally spotting the Chinese Takeaway shop.

"Do you think taking in dinner will thaw Robbie out and help him talk to us?"

"Robbie is a good bloke, he'll be fine when he knows we aren't going to rock the family boat. I'm more worried about you, angel."

"Me?"

"Yeah! You. I tried to be honest with you before we got here and you sulked for 50 miles, then the frosty reception from your cousin. Now you have met my mother, who wonderful as she is, lives in her own version of the world, so she assumed any friend who is a girl is my girlfriend."

"Oh Charlie, if it were just you and me, there would be no problem. I love spending time with you and sometimes my body doesn't remember why we can't be together, so I think I understand what you have been saying. But we've got a job to do."

"I get it India and I'm really grateful for the work. It is making it easier to help mum and has certainly lifted my money worries."

"Charlie let's focus on getting this done and staying friends. Sadly, everyone has an opinion on our relationship but if we don't let anyone else into this, into us, then we can define it how we like. We don't need to give it a name."

"Sounds like a plan."

Emma was home from work when they arrived. Over dinner, the conversation revolved around Elizabeth Robertson and the best way to care for her over the coming months. No one mentioned how much or how little time she had left. Robbie seemed to have forgotten to be cross about her and Charlie, or perhaps he could see India was doing what she could to support him.

India helped Emma create a list for Charlie of things he should do. The shoot tomorrow was in the afternoon and at the fabled rugby club, which meant Charlie could enjoy some time with his mum in the morning. Emma and India offered to go shopping for her, buy some clothes and nice toiletries to help the move feel more like a holiday. Emma had suggested that Charlie talked to his mum about it being a break where she could be looked after more carefully, whilst he got on with some jobs that needed doing around the house. When Charlie left to head back to his mum, he hugged them all, telling them how much he appreciated their help. India could see the glisten in his eyes and when she hugged him, she held on that little bit longer. Rubbing his back and giving him an extra squeeze, she hoped it would be enough for this vulnerable boy in a giant's body to get through the next day or so.

After their shopping trip, Emma dropped her in the car park outside the clubhouse. A small crowd had congregated and there was lots of banter amongst the group, which turned out to be all lads who had been at school with Robbie and Charlie. They were all dressed in an assortment of rugby shirts which had India thinking about colours and photographs. Whilst India spoke to Robbie about how to get the most out of the session for her, Charlie collected the shopping and talked to Emma.

As the men ran out onto the rugby field, they were throwing the ball between them. Still laughing and joking about school days, India snapped away. It was wonderful to watch the stress of the past 24 hours roll away from Charlie's shoulders and see him back to being a teenager in a good way this time. India lost count of the number of shots she took, but she was sure she had some great ones of Robbie and Charlie's faces, enjoying running free with a ball. After about an hour, they retired to the clubroom and Charlie showed his friends the Gym Away and let them try it out. It was a similar process to the beer and pizza session in Leeds. Charlie bought everyone a drink, including her. India sat to the side, Robbie slipped into the chair next to her, looking over her shoulder.

"Did you get what you need?"

"Yes, and it looks like Charlie got what he needed too."

Robbie was puzzled. "What do you mean?"

"This is the most relaxed I've seen him since this started. I hadn't realised how much he was struggling until this trip. I knew his mum was ill, but it is hard for me to appreciate what that means in practical terms."

"Do you understand why I'm worried about him now?"

"I get it.".

They all parted, Charlie to spend more time with his mum and start to discuss the hospice stay and show her the new clothes. Robbie took Emma to a fundraiser at the hospital. India was happy to curl up at Robbie's house and check on the content she picked up today. She knew Sunday would be intense, and she was ready to just breathe. After a while, the book on her kindle was calling to her so she retired to bed. Robbie's dog followed her and took up sentry duty at the top of the stairs. As soon as she turned out the light, her phone buzzed with a text from Charlie.

CWR: Thank you for today.

India: How is your Mum?

CWR: Asleep I took her for a drive to look at the river.

India: How are you?

CWR: I'm tired too.

India: And me lol I guess we have had a busy day … or 2.

CWR: Are you looking forward to tomorrow?

India: I should be looking forward to a Sunday dinner. It isn't something I cook living alone. I think it is all the mums being there making me a little nervous. I haven't seen my Aunt Patricia in a while.

CWR: It will be fine. Now go to sleep Goodnight my angel – get some rest.

India: Goodnight Romeo.

Chapter 27

On Sunday morning Emma wanted to sleep late, so Robbie and India took his dog for a walk. It was a terrific way to catch up and talk.

"Tell me about Charlie, is the girlfriend thing honestly just for his mum?"

"What do you think?"

"I know you both tell me that nothing is happening, and both have agreed that nothing can happen. I see you sit apart, but there is something there. I guess there always has been on his side. He has always asked about you, carefully trying to not sound too invested – then last night Emma was fascinated with how you react to him."

"I can hand on my heart say nothing has happened between us."

"Nothing?"

"Well, a couple of goodbye hugs, a single simple goodnight kiss, more a peck than a kiss."

"Didn't he help you when you hurt your ankle?"

"Yes, he did, and he stayed the night and slept on the sofa. I have stayed at his house, so there were times when something could happen, but it didn't."

"OK, new question. Do you want something to happen?"

"I think he does."

"That wasn't the question." India looked away, her eyes following the dog as he snuffled in the bottom of the hedge.

"If I weren't India Barrington Jones, if I thought my parents would accept him. If I wasn't working in London, if we weren't working together. Then I admit he is attractive, he is so attractive he doesn't need to try. Women throw themselves at him, so even without my job and my family, I'm not sure I could trust him not to break my heart. Robbie, you know as much as I do why it's a bad idea."

"Oh yes, India it wouldn't be a good idea but for someone you say never has to try, he looks to be trying hard for you."

"Robbie, what can I say? I have been clear from the beginning why we can't be together."

"Do you regret suggesting him for this project?"

"No," shaking her head firmly "No I don't. It means Charlie and I can talk now. It means he can help his mum with money. Even this farce of her thinking I'm his girlfriend, if it helps her believe he will be fine when she is gone, I can't regret that."

"And will you be there for him when something happens to his mum?" India stopped, turning to Robbie. She fixed him squarely in the eyes.

"I don't believe you, Robert Anderson. Stop. And. THINK. Every question you asked me this morning, you should have known the answer to all of them."

"God, India, I'm sorry. I love you both, these last few weeks have been so hard for me. I listen to him talking about you. Although he usually agrees you shouldn't be together, that is because somehow, he believes he isn't good enough for you and he doesn't want you to split with your family like my mum had to do. Maybe you should speak to her this afternoon."

"She realises I'm not his girlfriend, doesn't she? she gets why?"

"She talks to Charlie's mum a lot, so more than anyone she knows how important it is for her to believe he will be OK when she dies."

"She might not die!"

"India, we all die. Emma tells me she won't see another Christmas."

"Are you sure?"

"Very. She needs to go into the hospice, but she has been fighting it until your visit."

"OH!"

"Emma has a place ready for her and Charlie will come back next week and take her in."

"He didn't say it would be that soon." India felt lost that he hadn't shared that with her.

"He doesn't find it easy. I think you know his story, it made them close. I guess that's why he doesn't want to take you from your family."

"Robbie, I'm sorry you are in the middle of this, and I can assure you that neither of us taking this situation lightly. The thing we are both determined to do is stay friends and to stay talking to each other because we could literally talk 24/7. I know we will always be friends and we would never intend to hurt each other."

"I'm glad. Come on, let's go help Emma with this meal. With three mothers coming, she will be a nervous wreck."

"I'm nervous, and I'm not even cooking."

The meal was wonderful, a nice big juicy joint, plenty of vegetables, two big jugs of gravy and all the trimmings. Something India hadn't seen for a while. The atmosphere was a little strained, especially around Elizabeth Robertson. She hardly ate and seemed to miss the important bits about every conversation. Everyone was pleased that she had been there, including her. There were some embarrassed faces when she had moved India up from girlfriend to someone who was going to marry her son any day, and how that would make them all one family. Although there was some relief when Charlie took her off home, most people were sad that she would be moving to the hospice so soon.

When Emma left for work at the hospital and Robbie took Emma's mum home India was left to tidy up with her Aunt Patricia. When

Patricia smiled at India, she felt she was about to get another lecture about Charlie Robertson.

"Please don't say anything – I've heard it all." India focused on the pan she was washing.

"Oh, have you indeed? And do you think that will stop me? Tell me, how are my brother and his wife?"

"As far as I know, they are much the same as always. I haven't seen them since Christmas, although Mum calls all the time. Look, this isn't what you think. Mrs Robertson doesn't hear very well, and she assumes that if I'm Charlie's friend I'm his girlfriend."

"Elizabeth has selective hearing. She's been doing it for years. She is very well aware of what is happening with you and Charlie, but don't be cross she hasn't got long. Seeing Charlie settled with you would be much better than seeing that rubbish in the papers."

"Oh!"

"Look India, there will always be plenty of people who will have an opinion on anything you do. It doesn't matter if it's how you cut your hair, what sort of shoes you wear or who you choose to have children with. With each of those decisions, you will never find a solution that everyone in your life will like. So, my advice is always to decide the option that will make you happy."

"Really? Look at what happened when you married."

"And do you think I have ever regretted marrying Robert?"

"I always felt bad for you, but now when I look at your life, you always look happy."

"Do you know, I think they did me a favour?"

"I don't understand?"

"Do you think I would be this happy if I still had to see your mother? Or behave like a Barrington Jones is expected to behave? If I had to feel their disapproval every time I saw them?"

"I hadn't thought about that."

"Tell me India, do you know how you feel about him? If you switch off all those 'you should' voices. The ones that say you should be with him and the ones that say you shouldn't."

"Honestly, I truly have no idea how I really feel. I'm glad we are doing this project together. I'm happier now we are talking, and I hope we can remain friends, because I do feel some connection to him."

"Well, I guess time will tell. Stay talking but try to shut out all those other voices so that you can hear what your heart is telling you. India, you are an intelligent woman. I suggest you forget the word should – find a way to do what makes you feel the way you want to feel."

Chapter 28

India was pleased that Nick was going to the Roses match at Old Trafford. She had never been so nervous. Joe and Tilly Cookson had begun to see some success with Gym Away, and today they were hosting a corporate event on the second day of the match. They had included buyers from potential stockists, including a larger department store chain and one of the shopping channels. She had a feeling both Joe and Tilly were more eager to impress Tilly's father. They had also invited Philip Bentley, Joe's brothers and more importantly for India, her brother, and her parents. Workwise she just had to make sure Nick recorded the images they needed for upcoming press pieces, adverts, and promotional material. In India's mind, you could never have too many photos.

There were lots of opinions on how she should get from her flat in London to the match at Old Trafford. Charlie, of course, thought she should drive over with him from Leeds. Andrew, her brother, believed India should visit the family and arrive with them. She decided to follow her aunt's advice and forget all the 'shoulds' and do what worked best for her. Nick was setting off from Putney. Going on the train with him was by far the simplest. She didn't have to worry about saying the wrong thing to her parents, or things getting more complicated with Charlie, although she wanted to let him talk about his mum.

On the train Nick quizzed her on what to expect, he had noticed something different about her. She eventually confessed to being worried as her family would be there, but she didn't share the confusion she had over her feelings for Charlie. India had been so convinced it couldn't happen, she hadn't let them out, and now after talking to Patricia, she was beginning to wonder what if? She had told herself this wasn't the day to explore that more, today was the day to do her job to the best of her ability.

In the taxi from the station, her phone started to buzz with texts.

CWR: I'm not on the team sheet. My shoulder is playing up. It means I can be there more for T & J. Can you tell them?

India: OK I hope you aren't in too much pain. Remember, my family will be there.

CWR: As if I could forget.

ANDREW: I don't know if this is good or bad news. Mum isn't with us, but Grandad is meeting us there.

India: Thanks, can you make sure Dad knows I'll be working today? Both Philip and the client will be there.

India started to relax. The taxi was pulling up outside the venue with plenty of time to spare PLUS, she wouldn't have to deal with her mum. This was still going to be a long day. She could relax a little knowing she had already gotten over her biggest issue.

Nick and India carried their bags into the room to be greeted by Joe and Tilly. Joe hugged her, then Tilly held on when she hugged India.

"I'm so pleased there will be a friendly face here, well I'm sure everyone will have their best faces on, but I know you are on my side and then if things start shifting your magical brain will make it a bonus instead of a problem."

"This is Nick, our fabulous photographer. I have talked to Nick about the photographs I want for the project however if there is anything you want, tell me and we will try to fit it in."

"Thank you," Tilly said with a sigh and held India's hand.

"I have some updates for you. Charlie is injured, so he won't be playing however that means he can be in here with all your guests for more of the day. I had a message from my brother to say my mother isn't coming so my grandfather is going to join them."

"Brilliant, that will impress my dad if nothing else," grinned Tilly.

Nick started to take some shots of the setup of the room. There was a buffet table currently set up with teas and coffees and some tempting Danish pastries. Tilly had the table dressed with napkins in brand colours and on the end of the table was a large pedestal fruit bowl full of green apples mixed with stress balls in the shape of cricket balls with the Gym Away logo on them. Across the other side, there was a layout of the product. Tilly had been highly creative with fabrics and the pop-up banners and boards that India had designed. Seeing her work on display made India a little more excited to see Philip's reaction. And just maybe she wanted her father to realise how hard she worked.

"I hope Philip likes my work," she said softly, glancing out the large windows where the umpires were examining the wicket.

"It will be interesting what he has to say about the mess the last time we saw you." Grunted Joe, his whole body changing at the memory.

"Babe – will that cause a problem for India?" Tilly looked from Joe to India, concerned not to create any more problems for her friend.

"I have no idea. Please don't mention me crying or anything unprofessional. Today I would be grateful if you don't say a word that suggests something between Charlie and me. Philip has made it clear that shouldn't happen, and my parents would be sure to try to stop us from working together. Both Charlie and I need this job."

Tilly and Joe assured her they would be careful. It didn't prevent India from worrying, so she threw herself into the job, working with Nick to find the best angles for the images they needed. When Charlie arrived, Nick spoke to him about getting out onto the side of the pitch, and then he started taking shots of Charlie in his Yorkshire blazer. India stood near them, lost in watching the arrival of the guests.

She froze when she spotted Philip walking up to Joe. It looked like he was asking questions about the display. She saw that change in Joe's body that suggested he was getting upset again. Philip was staring at India, and he didn't seem pleased.

The room was filling up, but she was able to greet her father and brother when they arrived. Taking the time to ask after her mother and tell them to pass on her love when they got back. Andrew's eyes were flitting around, and she guessed he was looking for Charlie. She could still see Philip glaring at her, and she decided she couldn't stand that all day, so she went over to speak to him.

"Good morning, Philip, have you had time to look at the display yet?"

"Are we talking about that set of cheap-looking unprofessional photographs over there or are we talking about the display you are making of yourself?" He spat the words out at India's face and then looked away, clearly incredibly angry. India gasped; she had never seen him like this. "Why would you be so unprofessional as to tell the client about the mix-up? How could you do that?"

"I didn't go running to tell them what had happened. I turned to Charlie for somewhere to be whilst I got things sorted. They arrived as I was explaining to him." Behind Philip, India could see her father starting to pay attention to who she was talking to, and he raised one eyebrow. He would want to know what had happened. "I'm sorry I panicked."

"Well, you shouldn't panic, my dear." India shook her head. She knew panicking wasn't the answer, it didn't last long, and she took action that pleased the client. Before she could say any more Charlie walked over to stand next to her, she felt certain he was about to put his arm around her and make things worse, thankfully no arm came. Instead, his soft Scottish voice spoke quietly to Philip.

"I think the clients were happy with what she managed to do – I'm interested, Mr Bentley what would you have done in the circumstances? Obviously, you wouldn't have panicked but I would like to know what you would have done in her situation."

"Well, I would have…."

"Now, before you get started with your answer, let's be clear what the situation was, so you can put yourself in her place. You are a 23-year-old girl who earns a small salary. Your boss insists you book a first-class ticket on the express train to Leeds, first stop Doncaster. The guard tells you your ticket is invalid, and you must buy another one. With the penalty fees, that ticket costs £278. Your business card is defunct, your hotel room is cancelled, and you have just paid out the entire content of your bank account to cover the train ticket. What would you do? Who would you call?" Philip didn't answer.

"I already said she could stay with me as I live so close to the stadium, but because she was concerned with what you would think, she declined. When she tried to contact the photographer to let him know not to go to the hotel, she discovered he had been cancelled and was away in Cornwall. Unfortunately, we were all there when she rang Nick so not something she could hide."

Philip was looking more uncomfortable still he started to speak. "But she was the one who emailed him to cancel the shoot."

By now India's father had moved over to listen to what was being said, and Andrew joined them. Charlie was shocked at Philip's response. "If you believe that you are a bigger fool than I thought you were. Now back to what India did do. She asked for some time and left the house to sort it, so she wasn't in front of me or the clients. Within the hour she arrived with some local Phys Ed students, a camera and a plan." Philip was looking uncomfortable.

"Philip, I'm sorry; if there was something else I could have done, I just didn't know what it was. It was Saturday, I couldn't ring the office, I have no authority at the bank. I might have been able to get a hotel, though that wouldn't have solved the 'no photographer' problem. If I had been given the message that the clients were going to be at

Charlie's that day, again, I wouldn't have turned up there." India's chin was out now. "So, if you are upset with me, Philip, I'm sorry." Philip looked at the audience who had gathered around him, including Nick, who had walked over with his camera.

"India, this isn't the place to discuss this." Philip was snarling under his breath.

"No, you are quite right. I have a client to look after, but that didn't stop you from starting this conversation."

"Now excuse me, Nick, Charlie, and I are here to do a job, so if you will excuse us, we are going to do what I came here for. I did what I thought was best at the time. Now time for you all to enjoy this game." Tilly picked that moment to grab India's elbow. "Sorry gentlemen, I need you, India." And she pulled India into the ladies' washroom.

"My God! I'm sorry I asked Joe not to get you in trouble. Philip put him on the spot, I know Joe was only trying to defend you." India blew out a long breath. "I'm not sure what I was supposed to do differently."

"What has been said about it at work?"

"They are all denying it. Jayne even said I did it myself to throw myself at Charlie."

Tilly snorted and her hand came up to cover her mouth. "Now I have heard it all. What does Philip really think?"

"To be honest, I don't think he knows what to think. I guess he was hoping to ignore it until Joe spoke to him. Right, I'm going to go do my job. Wish me luck."

"Charlie sprang to your defence...." India stopped her before she could go on.

"Tilly, I'm sorry I asked you not to do that. Will you please stop suggesting something is going on between Charlie and myself, especially today with my boss and my family here. I need this job and

I don't want to lose my family." India turned on her heel and left Tilly looking into the mirror.

As she re-entered the room, she saw her brother was watching her closely. Her grandfather had arrived now, the cricket had started, Charlie was talking with some guests and Nick was taking photos of people chatting to him. There was lots of banter about who would win, Yorkshire or Lancashire. Tilly introduced India to her father Maxwell Sykes, who was speaking with William Barrington Jones and her brother Andrew.

Maxwell Sykes was complimentary about India's work, not just the project but her photography too. He complimented her on the intimacy she created in her shots. That word caused Andrew's eyebrows to raise, but then he knew how she and Charlie met. Mr Sykes asked to meet Charlie who was talking quietly to Joe, so Tilly called him over. Charlie recognised India's brother. They had the same dark, almost black hair and amazing blue eyes, so he was careful not to touch India and he avoided even looking at her. Andrew was watching everything closely, and when Tilly and her family moved off to talk to some other guests, he cornered her on her own.

"Really India! How are you working with that bastard?"

"Philip isn't that bad."

"Don't play games with me, India, you know I mean Charlie Robertson."

"Charlie Robertson is the 'talent' on one project. I only have to spend a couple of hours a month with him, and Nick is there for most of that time, sometimes Tilly and Joe too. The clients love him, and he has done wonders for the product. I'm just doing my job." She excused herself and went back to Nick.

At this point, Nick understood why she was sticking so close. Bentley & Bentley gave him a lot of work, so he wanted today to go great too. It was rare for Philip Bentley to be anywhere near a shoot, so even Nick could feel his hands starting to sweat a little. With tension rising, he suggested they went out to the side of the pitch with Charlie to make the most of the venue. Nick had his hand on India's back as he steered her out of the room behind Charlie. There was a collective sigh when they got outside.

"I was worried about my mum, now I'm just worried about Philip."

"I've seen him looking at you, Beautiful, he is doing the same to me and Charlie if that makes you feel any better."

"I'm not sure it does, we are five months into this six-month project, and I don't see the Cooksons giving Bentley & Bentley any more work and that will not go down well."

"I thought they were happy?"

"They are with the three of us, but if they move PR companies, they can still use Charlie and you, I guess I'm expendable."

Charlie and Nick both put an arm around India and hugged. It was a show of solidarity, not sexual, she told herself. But then she could feel Charlie's thumb gently rubbing circles on her shoulder and her body said, 'what if Patricia is right?'.

When the break came for lunch, Zach was still in, having scored 54 runs, sadly no one could stay with him, that was Charlie's job. And it was obvious he was being missed. Poor Dan Woods was out for 0 in 2 minutes and even India knew how devastated he would be. Charlie excused himself to go and see the team, so Nick and India returned to the room to get something to eat themselves. It had been a long day and Nick had long, hollow legs.

India caught her father talking to his dad, looking at the display. They were looking at the photographs India took in Hawick. "Is that Robert? Have I been a fool, William?"

"She is still your daughter Dad; she hasn't changed, and Robbie is a great lad." India wanted to say something, she had always felt guilty that she received a lot of support from her grandparents whereas Robbie and his sister got none. She opened her mouth to speak then closed it again, not knowing what to do or say.

"Ah, India, how are you? And how is Stella settling into her flat?"

"I'm fine, Granddad, and Stella is Stella, so full of energy. She starts her job next week, so maybe that will slow her down a little."

"I doubt it. They tell me they will have finished work on the flat soon, so your grandmother and I'll be down to check it all out."

"I shall look forward to that."

"Now tell me about this job. A day out at the cricket doesn't look like they are taxing you too much?"

"Most of the work was done before the day for this one, Granddad. I'm mainly here to supervise Nick, the photographer and support the clients."

"Today is a day you should be looking for new clients, isn't it?"

"I guess so, but I think that is what Philip is here for."

"Dear girl, if you want to spend the rest of your life running around after the likes of Philip Bentley, whilst he spends his days playing golf or watching cricket, you are not the granddaughter I thought you were." Her grandfather was smiling at her. Her father had a quite different look on his face.

"From what I have seen today, he doesn't seem very happy."

"Dad, this isn't the place for this discussion, but yes, things are getting more difficult. However, as you will be the first to tell me, I still have a job to do with this client and I'm going to do it to the best of my ability." She walked away, not before hearing her grandfather.

"There she is, my feisty granddaughter."

India had just found Tilly and Joe again as the cricketers returned to the pitch after lunch. Charlie came back to the room and with him, Daniel Woods. India couldn't help but smile. Of all Charlie's teammates, Dan was the most incorrigible. Maybe Charlie was using Dan to make himself look like a sensible option. He was taller than Charlie and had incredibly long limbs. When he saw India, he bounded over to her and gave her a huge hug, wrapping his long arms around her, lifting her from the ground.

"Here she is, the girl with the smile that will make all my troubles dissolve." Far too many eyes watched this, including her boss and her family. "Shit India, Charlie warned me to behave as well," he whispered into her ear, and he put her down. He then proceeded to hug and lift both Tilly and Joe for good measure and did a little eek face to India. "I can't stay but there are too many long faces in there for even me to ignore, so Charlie said I could come and see you."

"It is nice to see you too, Dan." Joe had a soft spot for him.

"When are you guys coming back to Headingley, I hope it's before the next Roses match?"

"Probably not, but we are coming to Scarborough."

"Tell me you are there for the whole festival, then I'll have two lovely ladies to dance with." India was the first to let him down.

"I'll just be there for the day."

"It is a long way for one day, India." Tilly looked concerned. "Joe, I think we need to look at that. It will be the last shoot too. I'm so going to miss you, India."

"I take it that means you aren't thinking of using Bentley & Bentley again?"

"Oops, I didn't mean that, though now you have asked. I think it is doubtful."

"Please don't say anything to Philip yet."

"Of course, it has nothing to do with you, India. In fact, I wish you would come and work for us. Will you please think about it?" India looked around the room.

"Not now, Tilly, not now. Dan, come and meet my family, then they might forgive you for that hug." She led Daniel Woods off to meet her family, and she wondered if she, too, was trying to make Charlie look like a safe option. It made her chuckle.

Her grandfather was keen to tease Dan about his performance, however, Dan had the perfect response, in India's eyes, anyway. "Yeah! It was a poor show, but I wasn't the only one who didn't score a run, even if I was the quickest at getting out. No, we are all really missing Charlie out there today. He isn't the guy to score big numbers, although he can do that when they let him. He is the calm out there; it's his job to keep running when we should and stand our ground when we need to stay. Like a lot of quiet people, you only realise how much they do when they are gone." And with that, he walked away to leave her family looking at India.

"I didn't know he could be that deep," said a shocked Andrew.

"He hides it well," chuckled India.

Eventually, the second day of play was coming to a close. Yorkshire looked set to win and they could use the points to drive them up the results table. Zach Williams had scored well in each inning, but it had been a struggle. India wondered if he missed having Charlie at the other end of the wicket, as Dan had said. India and Nick set off early to catch a fast train back to King's Cross. As they sank into the seats in first class with a coffee, India finally relaxed. It had been a long day and now there was only Scarborough left for her to navigate through.

Chapter 29

India settled once again into a first-class seat, leaving King's Cross. Today she was alone and needed to change trains at York. Joe and Tilly asked her to go for the whole four days of the festival and were sending her the day before, so she had time to recover from the travel. The weekend added another hour to the train journey, yet somehow everything seemed more relaxed. She'd worried about packing enough clothes for six days at the British seaside, especially when there was a rather elaborate sponsor's dinner to attend, too. Last weekend her grandparents came down to stay in the flat and her grandmother had taken Stella and herself shopping. Consequently, she had a few new items to bring with her.

To India, it seemed like there had been a shift in her family since the Roses match. Her father rang her to ask about the situation at Bentley & Bentley. He hadn't said so, but she thought he was beginning to get a little worried about her working there, maybe he was just concerned she was in London.

Over dinner, her grandparents asked her and Stella what seemed like a hundred questions about their plans. Stella, newly arrived in the city, was full of big ideas, unlike India, whose enthusiasm was fading. Her grandfather had been correct when he had said she couldn't stay doing what she was doing forever. Her grandma asked about Charlie, which led to talking about Robbie. India thought she saw some regret in her grandma's eyes, but she wasn't certain.

Her train got into Scarborough at 12:15, and she couldn't check into the hotel until 4 pm so she checked her luggage at the station. It would be fun to explore the town, but not if she were lugging around her biggest case and a large holdall. She found a lovely bar for lunch, enjoyed a fabulous sandwich and a glass of beer. Stepping out into the sunshine, she had a spring in her step.

The sea air had that effect on her and even though it was a work trip, it felt very holiday like; she slung her bag across her body and taking a deep breath; she tried to decide what to do next; go look at the sea or wander round more shops. She still had three hours before she could check-in. The hotel was overlooking the beach, so she decided, for now, to browse the shops and make her way towards the station in time to collect her bags.

India was on an emotional roller coaster. This was the last of the sessions for Gym Away. Possibly the last time she would see Charlie, still, this was a full week away from the bickering at Bentley & Bentley. She had managed to keep Charlie out of the press and there had been no recent reports of him with scantily clad women or coming out of a casino. The clients were happy with her work. She was on top of the world until as suddenly as someone emptying a bucket; the sky emptied so much rain onto her, she looked like she had just walked out of the sea. Her clothes were stuck to her body, and the hair she had carefully curled that morning was hanging down and clinging to her face. She froze, wondering what she could possibly do for the next three hours. The craziness of the situation made her think about buying a swimming costume, so she set off towards a department store she had passed earlier. To add to her plight, she stepped into a puddle and now her feet were drenched, too. With the rain driving into her face, she put her head down and tried to avoid as many puddles as she could, although it all felt pointless now. Rounding a corner, she bumped into a wall of muscle. Everyone muttered sorry, including India, and then she caught a familiar smell and looked up to see Charlie with Zach and both Woods brothers.

"Crikey, India mate, you look like you have been walkabout in the rainy season. Where are you off to in such a hurry?" it was Zach who had hold of her shoulders.

"I thought a swimming costume might be a clever idea, so I was off to buy one." That made them all laugh. Daniel was the first to respond.

"Now that sounds like a wonderful thing to do on a wet Saturday on the Yorkshire coast. Need any help?"

"Actually, I was only doing it until I could get into my hotel. It's a long time until 4 pm."

"We are already checked in. I guess it is a perk of being in the Yorkshire team. We were off back to the hotel, come with us, and wait for your room there." Ben Woods was used to organising the team and had hold of India's elbow and was turning her in their direction. Dan playfully hit his brother for spoiling the fun, and Zach seemed pleased with the idea. India glanced at Charlie, who so far hadn't said a word. He just shrugged at her, so she set off for the hotel, accompanied by four tanned men who looked like they were ready to take on the world. It was still raining heavily and as India tried to step around another puddle, she bounced into Charlie. He took her arm to help her the rest of the way back to the Victorian hotel that had been dominating the coast for so long.

"You are soaked India. We need to get you dry."

"I was saying a prayer, hoping my hotel room has a bath because I could really, really do with one after this."

"My room has a spa bath?" offered Dan. Ben hit his brother.

"Shut up brother, all our rooms have a bath."

When they came to a rather busy road, India had lost all hope of not getting any wetter when traffic passed. She stood almost dazed at the side of the road. These four men were leading her to somewhere safe, she hoped, somewhere dry. Charlie slipped her hand into his. *Like when my father helped me cross the road. But my father never stroked my palm with his thumb like that.*

Once across the road, he held on to her. The gentle rhythmic stroke of her hand with his thumb was hypnotic, and India's daze deepened.

At last, they stood facing the hotel with cars streaming past them. India was beyond caring. She was ready to dive into the traffic just to get out of the rain that was driving into her face and dripping down her neck. India had never seen rain like it, it continued to come straight down and as the wind came off the sea the rain seemed to dance in ribbons. She longed to watch it from the safety of her room.

"Don't worry mate, we will soon have you inside and we can order some tea, I know you like tea, don't you girl?" Zach was trying to pull her out of the daze. Dan tried teasing her with more offers of the use of his bath and Captain Ben was encouraging from the other side. Charlie simply held on to her hand and stroked her knuckles. He squeezed her hand to let her know he was still there.

At the heavy glass doors of the hotel, Zach held them open for the whole group. "I'll order that tea."

"I think we need to get her dry. She can use my room and I'll order tea from room service." Charlie had finally broken his silence.

The other three didn't reply or object. India stopped and stared at Charlie. "Angel, be sensible for once. No one is going to know now, are they?" He was staring at his teammates. Ben answered for the three of them.

"It is a case of needs must India. You can trust Charlie to look after you. I'm not sure I could say the same for the Aussie wonder or my brother. I'm not even sure I would trust myself to take you to my bedroom. No, you go with Charlie."

Still holding her hand, Charlie led her up a grand staircase that split into two. He pulled out an old-fashioned room key. Charlie opened the door into a dated but spectacular room. It was dominated by large sash windows that looked out onto the sea. He had to coax India into the room; she was standing fixed to the ground in the corridor. His hand in the small of her back he helped her through the door. "Here Angel, sit down and let's take your coat off." Charlie set to work, he talked incessantly. "I'll go start the bath, then ring for some tea. Would you like something to eat with your tea?" Although India shook her head when he rang down he asked for a selection of cakes to be added to the tray. Then he went back into the bathroom and poured oil into the water. "How hot do you like your bath?" The familiar Scottish accent once again helping India to relax a little more. She still hadn't spoken. Charlie seemed to think he needed to speak for them both.

"I've put in some lavender oil. My mother makes me carry it for cuts and stuff. I think she believes it cures anything. It will help you relax. I'll get a clean towel out of the wardrobe. Now let me see what dry clothes I can lend you. If we hang your clothes on the towel rail, they will dry once you are out of this bath." India was still incredibly quiet in his room, so he kept talking, "Where is your case, my angel?"

At last, she found her voice, "It's in a left luggage space near the station," and as if to prove what she said, she pulled the ticket out of her handbag. "That's good then. Come now, I think this bath is about ready, time for you to get in it. You will soon warm up then."

Charlie came out and holding her hand he led her to the bathroom. It took her breath away. Again, it was dated, but it was much grander than anything she had ever seen in a hotel before. The bath was large and there was plenty of room for two. India blushed at the thought. Charlie helped her take off her clothes, peeling them off her body where they clung like a frigid second skin. Once she was down to her bra and pants, he went back into his room. When he left, she felt the absence more than she felt the cold, it woke her up instantly from the daze she had been in.

Charlie had taken her wet clothes with him. As she removed her bra and pants, she put those onto the heated towel rail to dry. Stepping into the bath, she looked around at the room that had Charlie stamped all over it. His razor sat by the mirror next to a hairbrush. To the side was an open brown leather bag containing all his toiletries. They were neatly arranged, standing upright in tight rows.

Sitting down in the steaming water brought warmth to her cold, wet body. She thought she might stay there for the night. India could hear Charlie talking quietly in the room. She presumed he was on his phone. She heard two people come to the door: one must be the tea, but she was unsure what the other might be. Finding the dial, she set off the bubbles in the spa bath. This had to be the best bath she had taken in a long time. Maybe because she needed it so much. Josh and Nick had teased her to be ready to get wet if she came to the Yorkshire coast, but today the weather had been incredible.

When she finally stepped out of the bubbles, she wrapped herself in the indulgent fluffy towel that Charlie had put out for her. Her flimsy knickers were dry on the hot radiator, although her bra would take longer. She inspected the pile of clothes Charlie had left for her and picked up a cricket jumper; it was the traditional white V-necked style, with two rows of colour around the neck. India held it up to her body. It was going to drown her, but it would do until she could get her case and holdall. She inspected the sweatpants, she was sure they would be far too long, she wondered if she could roll up the legs then she looked up into the mirror, she realised the bottom of the jumper was well down her thighs and she didn't need trousers to sit in Charlie's room and drink tea.

She opened the door and took a tentative step into the main part of Charlie's room. She found him sat on the floor with a cup of tea. He had changed into dry clothes, but his hair was still damp. He had his back against the wall, watching the storm out at sea. When he saw her in just his jumper, his heart stopped for just a moment. A broad smile hit his lips.

"Better?" The sight of her legs below his jumper extending his smile to his eyes.

"Better!" she affirmed.

"Come sit with me and enjoy this lovely Yorkshire tea they brought us." Sitting next to Charlie on the floor reminded her so much of when they first met, it felt like something friends would do. Charlie's ankles were crossed, and he seemed relaxed.

"Do you spend a lot of time sat on the floor with women you meet?"

"Only with you." His grin lit up the room.

"Seriously?"

"Yeah! I sit on the floor a lot, but you are the only girl who would join me."

"Oh, Charlie." She felt sad that others didn't appreciate this simple side of him.

"It's OK. If I have you, I don't need anybody else, now do I?" He reached his arm around her shoulder and pulled her closer to him. "And before you start to lecture me, I know I don't really have you, but you don't control my dreams."

India's brain was bouncing with all the reasons this wasn't a clever idea but sitting there on the floor with Charlie's arm around her shoulders felt so right as if she had finally come home to where she belonged. They chatted away about their journeys to get to Scarborough. Charlie was doing most of the talking, telling her about why he liked playing at the seaside ground, some of the histories of the festival and the hotel. They sat there so long India felt her legs and her bottom beginning to seize up. Charlie stood up and ordered more tea to go with the cakes they still had to eat. India walked over to one of the tall sash windows. They were old, and the glass was loose, she could feel the cold rolling off them. Charlie had the heating turned up in the room though, and she felt safe staring out to the waves. It was hard to believe it was still raining so heavily, making her pleased she had been rescued by the four men. Charlie came and stood behind her, his hands on her waist and his chin on her head.

"Are you glad you aren't out there?" he whispered into her ear.

"I am. Thank you for rescuing me."

"My pleasure." He sighed as his mouth dropped to where her neck met her shoulder, and he gave her the briefest of kisses. They both froze. A line had been crossed, what was to happen next was very much up to India. She reached one hand back and gripped the back of his thigh, just below the tight swelling of his bum. The gentle squeeze of her hand was all the encouragement he needed to go back to light kisses on her neck. India arched her spine and threw back her head onto his shoulder. She moaned quietly, her eyes closed, enjoying every touch of his lips onto her bare skin. She surrendered to the internal battle, going with the physical pull she felt toward his body. As she leaned into him, India no longer cared for right or wrong or simply what was sensible. Finally, she turned away from watching the sea into his arms as they wrapped around her waist and pulled her flush to his taut chest. There was no hiding his desire as it pressed into her soft stomach through his own cricket jumper. India thought she could stay there forever.

A loud insistent knock on the door stopped all that, as they sprang apart, looking embarrassed at what had started to happen. Charlie answered his door to find Dan and Ben with a key for India. The other three men had arranged an early check-in and fetched her things. Charlie explained he had given Ben her ticket and lent the brothers his car so they could collect her bags whilst Zach had been left to charm the reception staff. Her bags were now safely in her room, and she had no reason to camp out with Charlie in his jumper.

Ben handed the key to India. "You want to eat with us tonight or do you have other plans?" India looked at her watch "I don't know. I have work to do. Where were you thinking of going?"

"We have several events we have to go to this week, part of the festival, you know, but tonight is a free night. The match starts tomorrow so nothing crazy. I booked a table for 10 of us at a fish bar on the front, but a couple of the guys have bailed out, so if you would like to come with us you are welcome."

"Hmmm, I'm not sure."

"Don't stress it, India. We will be meeting downstairs at 7 o'clock. Join us if you want to." And with that, he left India in Charlie's room. The silence was uncomfortable. She didn't know what to do or say now the spell had been broken. She started to collect together her wet clothes; her eyes fixed downwards. Charlie tried to talk to her but was so unsure what to say. He reached out a hand and took hold of her arm. She stopped immediately and turned to search his face. Words were no longer enough. He pulled her into his arms, stroking her hair as he kissed her forehead.

"There is no rush, India. We can take this one step at a time; I do hope you will keep taking steps with me. Come out to dinner tonight. The guys will be there so you will be safe."

"Charlie, thank you for today. I don't know what to say. I'm not sure I'm ready to take this further."

"You had me fooled there."

"I am sorry, I need to go to my room and get on with that work." She stepped away and walked towards the door.

"I hope you do come and join us tonight, don't be alone."

"I'll see." Was all she could say as she left.

Chapter 30

As India entered the reception area of the hotel, she had no problem finding the people she was looking for. A group of professional cricketers was hard to miss. Zach had been joined by Garry Bayliss, an equally tall Australian, although Garry was a bowler to Zach's batting skills. He was taller than the rest of the group, with longish shaggy blonde hair and the biggest brown eyes a girl could get lost in.

"So, this is the famous India Zach rescued today. Smashing to talk to you, eventually."

"Yeah, mate. She was a drowned rat, but it was a team effort. I can't claim all the credit."

"So do you belong to some guy, or is there still hope for me or Zach?" Belonging to some guy was not something India aimed for but after her afternoon with Charlie, she didn't exactly feel free to offer herself to Garry or Zach. Her eyes flicked to Charlie. He was watching closely, when he saw her eyes hit his, he looked away. Was he regretting this afternoon already? "I'm a hard girl to please," she said, with a challenge in her eyes.

"Let's go see if Ben is right about fish and chips in this town. Come this way, Pretty Girl." Zach led the way to the hotel entrance and held open the heavy glass doors for the whole group. Ben seemed to be in charge, and he led the way off to the right of the hotel and down a set of steps. The stairs led the way to the beachfront. They were steep and irregular, which made India look carefully before setting off down them. Garry grabbed her arm to make sure she made each step.

"Here, let me help you. I counted these bad boys on the way up this afternoon and there are 153 of them." India smiled, grateful for the help, still not daring to look at Charlie.

At the bottom of the steps, India looked back up at the way back to the hotel. Charlie came over and whispered in her ear. "Look what's next door, you can take a ride up when we come back, so don't be worrying and you won't be needing any help from either of those two." India smiled and relaxed as she took in the Victorian lift back up to street level. The effect of his breath on her neck gave her goosebumps and Garry turned to look at the two of them. He started to grin.

"Hey Pretty Girl, are you going to sit next to me so you can translate the menu for me?"

"I'm sure Ben will have it all in place, I wouldn't worry." Garry was enjoying playing with her. "Yeah! But he isn't as pretty as you, and he sure doesn't smell as sweet." He grabbed her hand and pulled her down the front, along the side of the beach. The area was full of people, and India was rather pleased to be holding on to someone. India was tall at 5 ft 11in, yet in this group, she felt quite small. It wasn't a long walk to the restaurant. Ben was still leading the way, and he opened the door and set off up the stairs to the main seating area. A table was waiting for them in front of a window overlooking the beachfront, where India could see the lifeboat station. The guys made a fun attempt to be the one sat next to her, which resulted in Garry sitting on her left and Dan Woods sitting on her right. India took one look at the menu and chose 'the special', which included bread and butter and a pot of tea. Ben decided all the guys would have the same, but with giant-sized fish and large chips. Dan, Garry, and Zach decided they would have a beer with theirs, although they were happy to have tea, too.

Charlie sat opposite her, and his eyes burned into her face as Dan and Garry competed for her attention. As their meal arrived, Zach asked Ben to explain about the meal they were about to have and Dan, who was also from 20 miles down the road too, took over. "Fish and Chips are always popular at any seaside town in the UK but here in Yorkshire they use dripping to fry in, which adds flavour."

"I had forgotten just how good it was eating fish and chips here." India licked her lips, tasting the salt and vinegar she had made sure her meal was well covered with. The bread and butter and the tea all added to the feast. This was something she had done with her brother and her father, it was not something her mother approved of, so it had been a rare treat. William Barrington Jones loved to spend days out with his children, but his busy life meant it didn't get to happen often, especially when you added in the social life his wife organised to help his business. "There is something about eating near the sea that helps things taste special." Charlie was watching her closely and the lip-licking was having an effect on him, he couldn't explain.

The meal was more than enough for India, but all the guys except Charlie added on a real pudding with custard to their meal. India was thinking of all the kiosks selling ice cream and doughnuts on the front, amongst the arcades. Charlie must have read her thoughts.

"I think, what you actually want, now you are at the seaside, is an ice cream."

"How did you know?" Their connection sparked across the table as she looked at Charlie.

"Because that is what I want. The point is, do you want me to buy you one?" India looked round the table. Garry was the one to speak out.

"Mate, you let me do all this work on the girl and then take her away just as we are getting ready to leave."

"Garry, I keep telling you that you need to learn better timing." Charlie stood up and held out his hand to India. She stood up to join him. "How much do I need to pay?"

"I've got it," Charlie said, throwing some notes on the table next to Ben.

Daniel stood up to help India with her coat. "Do you really want to go anywhere with this guy?"

"I have known this guy six years, Dan. Can you imagine how many women I have seen him in the papers within that time and now he works for me. I can assure you that you're not going to be missing out because nothing will ever happen between me and Charlie Whiskey Romeo." The table burst out laughing and pointing at Charlie. Zach was holding his sides, and Garry was close to doing the same. India pulled her camera out of her bag. "Come on Charlie, let's see what we can do with all these lights."

"You don't want photos of us all enjoying a meal together?"

"Not unless you are passing Gym Away around at the same time. Have you forgotten this is my job, getting photos of Charlie and others with the Gym Away is paying for my train and the hotel? This is my last shoot with this guy. I need to file as many images as I can." Dan sat down with a thump. "Your last shoot? Does that mean it is our last chance to convince you to give one of us a chance?"

"Come on, Dan, cheer up. She was never going to pick you, mate, not when she could choose Garry or Me! So, India, do you want to wait and get that ice cream with me?" Zach looked up at her grinning.

"Not tonight, I'm going to see what I can get with all the touristy lights on the arcades. Then I'm going to let him buy me ice cream." They were interrupted by a member of staff who asked if they could get a group photo for their social media. India stood back and let the staff take photos of the boys. Her camera was in her hand, so she took a group shot for herself, to remember the time six fit cricketers were fighting over her. Well five, as Ben Woods was married, and he stayed out of the banter and so did Charlie actually, plus Ryan was engaged and just being playful. So, the three men then. As she checked the image of six good-looking guys on her screen, she realised she was more saddened by the fact Charlie wasn't trying than she was boosted by the three that were.

With photographs over, Charlie and India slipped silently out of the door at the bottom of the stairs. Daylight was fading and the lights of the buildings were shining more brightly than when they arrived.

"What do you want to do first? BOSS." India had never heard him use that voice. Was he upset with what she had said earlier? She decided it was best not to acknowledge the change and let him see her speech had been to throw the other boys off from thinking anything was happening between them. After the attention he had given her neck that afternoon, she was hopeful of things progressing further. Even if they did, she didn't want everyone to know, not whilst it could still create problems with her job.

"Let's try getting some shots with you at the railings with the lights behind you." India picked out a spot where the lights in the background would work with the Gym Away brand colours. She asked Charlie to turn at different angles as she moved in front of him, adjusting the setting in her camera to get different effects. Eventually, she was happy and decided they could take a break. "Come on Charlie, I think I need to buy you the ice cream as you bought my dinner."

"Of course, I bought your dinner. I wouldn't let one of those guys pay for your meal. I'm not sure what all that posturing and trying to impress you was for. It's so hard knowing I can't have you but seeing you with one of those guys would be more than I could cope with, India." He turned away from her and headed away from the ice cream stand straight in front of them.

"Where are you going?"

"Come on, you want a great ice cream, don't you?" He reached out and took her hand. Pulling her back down towards the harbour, then up a road going off on their left, which rose steeply up towards the town centre. As they rounded another corner, India saw why they had come that bit further. This ice cream shop was like a 50s diner.

"Inside or out? What would you like?"

"I was thinking a sugar cone when we started out but now we have done some work, maybe we deserve something more." They went inside and found a table by a window that looked down towards the harbour. Over a couple of sundaes, the tension of earlier was fading away. They were back to two friends who could talk non-stop. Charlie asked India about what was next for her, they were about to finish this project and she had now been with Bentley & Bentley for 10 months. "What do you see yourself doing next India?"

"What do you mean?"

"I know when we started this, you said that you didn't want to leave the job after 4 months. I'm hoping you aren't thinking of living the rest of your life in a one-bed apartment in London chasing around for that crazy woman. I see you when you pick up the camera India. You start to glow, it makes me think it is something you need to do more of."

"I don't know Charlie, yes I love using your camera and I want to buy one just like it."

"No, India, that camera is yours. You keep it. It isn't something I would choose for myself, I would rather see it in your hands."

"Charlie, that is fabulous, thank you. What can I do to thank you?"

"You can use it. Use the camera to feed your creativity India, please don't use it to make more money for Bentley & Bentley though, you are more than that place."

"Thank you, I guess I have been focusing on finishing this project for Tilly and Joe before I have let myself think about 'what next'. I'm due some time off and no holidays planned so I think I'm going to go home and spend some time with my family."

"Really?"

"Yeah, I think I have been making decisions based on what I thought my parents wanted when I was 18. When we were at the Roses match, I thought I saw a different side of my father and I know he was upset about that night with Michael Coombes. Maybe I do need to think about what other things I could do."

"I guess that's good. You ready to head back?"

"It's darker now. Can we try a few more shots on the way back?"

"It has been a long day, India. Would you mind if I say no? I want to walk my friend to the hotel and forget about work. I wish you would switch off too." India was a little taken aback it was the first time he had ever said no to her over photos, and he used the 'friend' word again, and yet this afternoon, before Ben had knocked on his door, they were about to move so far away from being friends. Maybe he was having second thoughts. She hoped he didn't regret the moment they had together. Her body was confused. She wanted to throw her arms around him and thank him for saving her from the rain, for giving her the camera and for getting her out of the restaurant with three men all trying pretty hard to impress her.

"Of course." She said no more. She paid the bill and put on her coat. Charlie was quiet. India knew he wouldn't be happy with her paying, but he knew it was important to her, so he didn't fight it. The mood had shifted as they stepped outside and rounded a bend back toward the way they came. They walked a small distance apart. A silence had settled between them. India was not comfortable at all. She looked at Charlie, his face was set, and he wasn't looking pleased either. When they turned the corner onto the main stretch of the front, the sun was setting on the horizon. The crowds had increased and so had the noise. It was Saturday night, mid-August, the height of the summer season. Families were mixed with groups of friends laughing and joking. The pavements were full, and the larger groups made it harder to walk in a straight line and the space between them got wider. India thought she might lose Charlie in the crowd. She got left behind, unable to catch up with him. When he realised he had lost her, he came back and wrapped his arm around her waist.

"You are far too precious to lose in this crowd, my angel." India instantly felt like the emotional distance between them had been closed with the physical distance. She looked at him and smiled. This felt so much better. What was she going to do after this week when they had no reason to be together? She had grown used to his texts to lift her day, to planning her month around when she was going to see him. All she could do was focus on the now. Charlie looked down at her and saw her smile. He pulled her closer hugging her into his side. She didn't want this to end.

Charlie must have felt the same. He pulled her across the road to the side of the beach, leaning on the railings, looking down across the sand, where only a glimmer of redness sat on the horizon.

"Want to walk on the beach?" India just nodded, not wanting to speak and spoil the moment. Charlie took her hand and led her to the steps down onto the sand itself. That friendship, that feeling of being home, was back, and they walked on, not chatting this time, but squeezing each other's hands from time to time and swapping looks.

Before they realised it, they had gone too far and were approaching the Spa. With a deep breath, Charlie led India off the beach and up onto the footpath. They carried on past the hotel to the tramway that would take them back up to street level. They were alone in the lift cage and Charlie sat by her side, holding her hand on his strong thigh. It was another moment India wanted to capture forever.

Although India wasn't ready for the day to end, she knew Charlie started a four-day match the next morning and so when he walked her to her room, she knew this was goodnight. Charlie pulled her into his arms and kissed her forehead. "Goodnight Angel."

"Goodnight Charlie. Thank you again for today."

"You are very welcome." He slipped silently away to his room.

India prepared for the next day at the North Marine Road ground, making sure her phone and her camera both had fully charged batteries and her bag was ready to go. When she finally slipped into her bed, her phone buzzed over on the desk where it was charging. She got back out of bed to check the message.

CWR: I'll be going down to the ground with others at about 8 am. Do you want to come with us or are you going to follow later?

India: Not much I can do at 8 am I guess I can come down later as it is so close. Thanks for asking.

CWR: See you tomorrow Sleep tight.

India: Goodnight.

The days of working with Charlie were ticking away. Tomorrow she would get to watch him play for the first time. The butterflies were back, and India's lips were curved up as she fell to sleep.

Chapter 31

After a substantial breakfast looking out at the waves in the expansive hotel dining room, India decided to walk up to the ground. She set off up the road enjoying the sea air, and the soft sunshine lifted her mood. It was twelve hours since Charlie had left her outside her door, and she had spent that time processing what had happened lately. Even as she slept, her brain was considering the possibilities. As Patricia had said, everyone had an opinion about her job and more importantly, about Charlie, and they were all part of her deliberations.

When she walked through the iron gates, the holiday atmosphere of the cricket festival overwhelmed her. People were sitting in stripy deck chairs around the boundary and a beautiful white marquee was surrounded by more deck chairs and covered in colourful bunting.

Yorkshire had gone in to bat first and Charlie was still working away, supporting the other batsmen at the crease. Zach was out and was sat nursing his wrist. He greeted India in his usual jovial tone. "India! Mate, come and sit with me. Any good at sprained wrists?"

"Is that ice you have on it?"

"Yeah, our Physio is AWOL, but their guy said to ice it, what do you think?"

"Oh, you mean with all my medical training, I can tell you more than they can?"

"I don't know, you seem to have done wonders for Charlie's game. I thought maybe you could do the same for mine." His grin was infectious, so she smiled at him, though she had no idea what he meant when it came to 'Charlie's game'. Garry sauntered over and sat down next to India, pretending to be looking after Zach. "Zacho, what you going to do tonight, mate, with no right hand?"

211

"I'll just have to lift a few pints with my left hand."

"You know that I wasn't talking about drinking, but I won't embarrass India. If you are lucky, she might help you out." The banter last night was getting a bit out of control, and India decided the time had come to set some boundaries.

"Guys, I love hanging out with you and I'll always be grateful you helped me out yesterday, so if I can help you I will. Just so we are clear: I'm not looking to get physical with any one of you."

"Bugger India, did I go too far again? I haven't quite got used to the British sense of humour. I'll learn though. Say if you hear me saying something that a girl would object to, you kick me, you would be doing a guy a favour." It impressed India how quickly he had apologised, and she realised it was one of those topics where some people might be OK to joke about it and others weren't.

"Garry, to make life more complicated for you, different girls will object to different things at different times of the day. Your comment just now might have been less of an issue after a few beers in the evening, but at 10:30 on a Sunday morning over tea; not so much."

"India, that means you need to spend more time helping me understand all that. What are you doing today?"

"I'm here to get more photos of Charlie, mainly friendly stuff for social media, over the next few months. I think I'll grab a few snaps now whilst he is still batting. Goodness, is that the score?"

"Yeah, Zacho took a blow to his wrist in the second over and well, I'm bowler, how can you expect me to last long against that spinner they are using. Charlie is the only one who seems to be doing OK."

"Now Ryan is in with him, hopefully, they can settle down and get a few more runs on the scoreboard before lunch."

"I hope you are right, Zach. I'll try not to distract him." India stood up and moved to the front of the stand and took over a hundred shots of Charlie batting. She was looking at his style and thinking it was far more traditional than the flamboyant Ryan, who was using his bat to knock as many balls as he possibly could past the boundary. Watching Charlie use his body for what he had trained so hard for was mesmerising. Even under all that padding and his helmet, she could see his body flexing. Her camera had dropped down by her thighs as she stared at him jogging between the wickets.

India thought Charlie had spotted her, so she retreated into the seats. She sat with Zach and Garry and waved to Ben and Dan Woods. Looking up from her notebook, she saw Ben getting fidgety, and he finally came over to talk to Zach about his wrist. He needed to know exactly who would be able to take the field when Worcester came in to bat. Ben talked in hushed tones to Zack and Garry about what would happen at the changeover. He also asked them for anything to pass on to the batsmen who were still to go in. Dan joined the gang and bounced down next to India, His long legs struggling to fit between the rows of seats.

"India, can I have a plaster?" She was puzzled why he had asked her.

"Sorry Dan I don't have a plaster, I'm confused why you thought I did."

"Well, I just thought as you are with Charlie you would be as organised as him, he always has plasters in his bag."

"I'm not "with" Charlie, just get one out of his bag if he has them, he won't mind." They all stopped talking and looked at her. The silence was deafening, India looked from one face to another, but no one spoke. Eventually, Dan broke the silence.

"Well, it's obvious you aren't with Romeo! If you think it is OK for anyone to touch his bag. Even wearing my helmet and two boxes I wouldn't dare do that!" Dan stalked off and everyone went back to their conversations. India returned to watching the players out on the field.

By the lunch interval, Charlie and Ryan had built up a 75-run partnership. The mood amongst the Yorkshire squad was subdued. Although this was a home ground for them, they only played a couple of matches here each year. India heard Ben tell the team they would all be eating together at the hotel tonight, and he expected them to retire early. Charlie glanced over to India, but they didn't get to talk to each other. They were surrounded by the rest of the lads, and somehow talking was something they did in private.

On the fourth ball after lunch, Charlie was run out for 65 when Ryan was being a little optimistic about a ball he had pushed towards extra cover. India was considering ordering some tea when Charlie found her.

"India, come join me in the marquee. We can get you a special treat to go with your tea there. I want this to be like a holiday for you, so let's find some deck chairs too."

"That sounds like a fantastic idea, Charlie, but will you be okay over there?"

"Yeah. Someone like Garry or Zach might struggle. These guys aren't interested in me."

Charlie guided India over to the member's marquee, where he found her a chair overlooking the game, and he ordered tea and cakes for them both. As she waited, India picked up one of the newspapers from the table.

"Were you reading the paper when I was batting?"

"No, I was taking photographs until I thought I might be putting you off so then I sat back down again."

"I hear you put Garry in his place this morning."

"News travels fast!"

"Yes, in this little world it does." As India turned another page, she gasped. There, in full colour, was a photograph of Charlie Robertson in a bar, with a redhead on his knee. The girl had her mouth clamped over his ear, and Charlie's hands were holding her hips. Charlie looked over her shoulder. "Oh my God! I'm gonna kill Alex."

"Charlie, you told me you were going to be more careful."

"India, that photograph is months old. I was totally sober, and I had been in the club for about 10 minutes. I had just received bad news about my mum. I admit I had gone there expecting to get blasted and maybe leave with someone like that. I took a seat at the bar and the owner, Alex, passed me my favourite single malt and I poured out my woes. He sent the redhead over, as soon as she sat down, she had her tongue in my ear. It was weird. But that is when Robbie sent me a text to tell me you would be calling me. I left almost immediately without finishing my drink. That was the same night they posted photos of me leaving the club alone, suggesting I had lost my touch. I have that photo on my phone if you want to compare it. I kept it to remind me I can't win whatever I do. The papers feel the need to portray me as some sort of Playboy. The very next day you rang, and honestly, I haven't been with a woman since."

"But ..."

"You may have seen more photos, but honestly India, I haven't even kissed anyone since that phone call."

"Honestly?"

"I talked to Alex; I thought he may be responsible for a lot of the photographs. He was always very generous to me, and I think it helped him raise the profile of his club if players like me hung out there. I didn't realise what that was doing to my mother and my reputation at Yorkshire. Yes, the fans liked it, I'm not sure about the selectors. Do you think this will cause problems with Joe and Tilly?"

"One old photograph? No, I don't think so. You do need to be careful now. Now is the time to be looking for more sponsorship deals. Did you sort out an agent?"

"No, I've been distracted. I keep blaming everything on mum's illness. What will I do when she's not there to blame anymore?" Charlie's eyes fell to the grass around their feet. India looked at the way his hair kissed the neck of his shirt, and she felt a pain in her chest. How could she have forgotten how ill his mother was? She searched for something to say in response, but before she could find the words, Charlie spoke again.

"Damn! It is looking like I need to get ready to go out to field."

Once Yorkshire were all safely out fielding, India decided to walk back. If she set off now, she could take the coastal route. Going round the headland would take much longer than her walk there that morning, but the sun was shining, and she wanted to play with the camera. She would start by checking out the North Beach with its surfers and families enjoying the wide stretches of sand. Then get a few treats along South Beach before retiring to the peace of a hotel room.

She picked up her phone to leave Charlie a text, it was out of battery. Zach saw her collecting her things from the player's area.

"You look like you're leaving us."

"I am, will you tell Charlie I'm walking back down the coast road, my phone died?"

"It could rain again."

"Well, at least tonight I can get into my own room."

"Be careful, beautiful girl. You have a lot of people on that field who care about you."

Reaching the beach, India was disappointed the tide was quite high. It didn't look like she could walk along the sand for long, but she couldn't resist taking off her sandals and pushing her toes into the sand. She closed her eyes and inhaled the ozone rich sea air, relaxing further with each breath. Out in the waves, a dozen or so surfers were making the most of the swell. She tried to capture their movement in the waves with Charlie's camera, it was harder than she expected. The sun was still bright, and she searched in her huge tote bag for her sunglasses, but she didn't find them. It was nothing new.

Once in the South Beach area, she was lost in how many choices she had for things to eat. The fish shops still smelt the most tempting. Her mouth was watering all the time she stood waiting for the girl to serve her food. With a traditional wooden fork clutched in her hand, she covered the food in salt and vinegar before finding a bench overlooking the harbour to enjoy her meal. A rather cheeky seagull landed on the railing in front of her, eyeing her chips, and India shooed him away.

She walked the last 400 yards or so back to the hotel past the arcades and stopped at a machine out on the pavement. Written in a red elaborate font were the words **The Great Zoltán Speaks**. It professed to read your palm and with all the turmoil in her head about what to do next, India couldn't resist giving this one a try. She found the coins needed and put her hand into the space. The figure inside the glass went through a series of jerky movements then stopped abruptly. A cream card flew out of another slot.

You are exceedingly creative.

You will be happy when you find the

people who will understand and support you.

India slipped the card into her pocket and walked pensively towards the hotel. It sounded like something Katie would say to her. In the lift back up to street level, her head filled with the image of being in there with Charlie, her hand on his thigh. Watching him move today had held her focus. His body was so in tune with the job he was doing. The memory of the warmth of his arms around her and the sense of being home when he held her was confusing her brain again.

In her room, she kicked off her sandals and hung her coat on an old brass hook on the door. Her first job was to plug in her phone to see what she had missed. Whilst it charged, she opened her laptop to check her emails. It being Sunday, she wasn't expecting anyone to be working other than her. How wrong could she be? There was an email from Philip with the word urgent as the subject. The message itself was a terse note about the photographs of Charlie in today's papers. Asking her what she thought she was doing. If the Gym Away people didn't renew their contract with Bentley & Bentley, it was undoubtedly India's fault.

She dropped back onto her bed. Replaying it, the joy in her heart slipped away, leaving her with an overwhelming feeling of helplessness. There was nothing she could have done about the photograph, and it wasn't something she was answerable for. Even if it had been taken since the project started, she couldn't be held responsible for Charlie's behaviour. Except she was the one who had mentioned his name and then told Philip she believed he was a good fit for the client. Damn, was Philip right? Had she been unprofessional when she recommended Charlie because Robbie said he needed the work? Had she proposed him so she could see him again?

Chapter 32

A buzz from her phone stopped her destructive thoughts.

CWR: Are you back yet?

India: Just

CWR: I have your sunglasses can I bring them to your room?

India: Sure Thanks

India looked down at her clothes and checked herself in the mirror. Her hair was looking a mess from the wind and salt air on her walk, so she quickly brushed it. As she cleaned her teeth, she questioned why and wondered if it had anything to do with last night's kiss. Within minutes, Charlie was knocking on the door to her room.

"Thank you for rescuing me yet again. I'm pathetic needing help two days running."

"I'm kinda enjoying it." That cheeky grin was showing itself, but India couldn't enjoy it. It simply reminded her how unprofessional she had been. Charlie couldn't fail to notice the change in her mood.

"OK. What is wrong?"

"Just a work thing." Charlie studied her face. *Why was she being so evasive? A work thing she didn't want to share.* He hoped it had nothing to do with him. "Does it have anything to do with that photo in the Sunday Mirror today?"

India slumped down on her bed. "Yes, I'm afraid it does."

"India, I need to understand, explain." She pointed to her laptop, where the email was still open. Charlie read it quietly, his body was showing his reaction to it all too clearly.

"That is ridiculous!"

"That is my job."

"Do you reckon Joe and Tilly will be bothered?"

"Probably not that much, but I guess they have already had enough of Bentley & Bentley."

"I think we should talk to them. They weren't pleased about what happened to you at the Roses match. I'm sure they will want to help if they can."

"That isn't a very professional way of working, Charlie, which is exactly what Philip was complaining about at Old Trafford."

"I'll ring them then." Before India could stop him, Charlie had called Joe, and he had answered.

"Hey, Joe, I called to apologise about today's photo in that rag. I wanted you to understand it was an old photograph taken before I signed for you guys. I have no idea why it was printed today."

"Tilly said it was an old one from the length of your hair. She was insistent it was pre-season. Don't worry about it mate, I'll check tomorrow to see what it has done to sales though. Just out of interest, you understand. How is the Yorkshire coast, are you and India enjoying it?"

"If you had asked me before India saw that photo, I would say yes. Now looking at her face I can't possibly be happy when she isn't."

"You did tell her how old it is?"

"I have explained it and I think she understood, but her boss has waded in yet again and is blaming her for it."

"Hang on, Tilly is asking me too many questions. I'm going to put you on speakerphone. Is India there?"

"Yeah, I'll put you on speaker too."

Tilly was openly annoyed. "Just tell me what he has said."

India read out the email. "Shit." said Joe and Tilly simultaneously.

"You aren't going to renew the contract, are you?" whispered India, almost to herself.

"Sorry India, no we are not, it has nothing to do with you and everything to do with the rest of the company." offered Joe, and Tilly went further.

"India, we love your ideas and Charlie is a great fit for us, but we don't need Bentley & Bentley to use Charlie. When you pitched, you talked about all the connections they had and how it would fast forward the project for the launch. We simply hate the way they have behaved and the invoice for extra expenses we got on Friday was the final straw."

"EXTRA Expenses? That's fudging ridiculous."

"Yes, we got an invoice on Friday listing extra expenses for this last shoot. It was my idea for you to stay longer at the hotel to finish this off. We were ready to pay for the extra nights' hotel and your time, we didn't expect to be paying another £1,000 on top of that." Joe sounded annoyed, and India was at a loss to explain why there would be so much.

"I don't understand, what extra expenses? The train ticket price is the same, and it was made clear to me that I couldn't charge for meals over the hotel breakfast that comes with the room fee. I have even been walking to the ground and back, so I didn't have to pay for taxis."

Tilly was getting agitated now. "You were told what?"

"It was explained my hotel and breakfast had been paid for by Bentley & Bentley and nothing else. Other meals were like a normal workday, and I couldn't claim for them, and Jayne specifically mentioned taxis."

"Wait till I speak to him tomorrow morning."

"Oh, no please don't. I'm in enough trouble already. If he thinks I spoke to you about this, that would be a breach of trust and I could be instantly dismissed. Even telling him we talked about the photograph will cause problems. He says I'm too friendly with you." Charlie was getting frustrated.

"That is rubbish India, you are simply talking to your friends."

"No Charlie mate, I get it," said Joe. "If she worked for me and was telling John Lewis stuff like this, I would sack her, think about it if you were in the pub tonight and talked to the opposition about Zach's wrist. But that doesn't mean we can't use the information."

"Joe's right, what we can do is make Philip Bentley understand we are not concerned about what was in the paper and ask for details of the expenses."

At last, India was thinking strategically. "OK, so you need to do this in writing and copy me in, so Philip knows that I'm aware of your thoughts."

Between them, they composed an email for the next day that asked for a breakdown of the extra £1,000 and mentioned them being OK about the photo. Joe wanted to wait until the morning so he could gauge the effect on sales if any. Charlie needed to make a statement.

"Can I just say, since that first conversation, I haven't been drunk, nor have I been with a woman? That call woke me up to what I was doing to my mum, to my career, and any chance I had of a woman wanting to settle down with me. I spoke to Alex at the club about the photos, but I am going to call him again."

"How is the match going?"

"Not so good. The captain wants us all back, pulling together and we are eating as a team tonight to prove that solidarity. That means I better get there."

"Great, I'll copy you both into the email tomorrow. I'll not mention this chat or even hint at the fact we have spoken in any communication with him. India, I value your honesty and I sincerely hope we can work together again. I'm sorry that will not be at Bentley & Bentley."

As the call was ended India stood with her eyes closed, trying desperately hard to compose herself. He stepped up to her quietly and softly, put his hands up to cup her face, his thumbs stroking her cheek and ears.

"I'm going to kiss you, and I want you to be here, in the now, with me. Stop worrying about work and all that rubbish you can't control. None of that is your fault." He dipped his head and touched his lips to hers, tasting the salt and vinegar from her meal. His tongue slipped gently in to touch her tongue and tasted the minty freshness in there. India stood still. She did not reject his kiss, but she didn't join in either. She just stood and enjoyed the caress of his mouth on hers. Charlie's arms dropped to wrap around her and draw her into him. When the firmness of his body pressed into her own softness, she began to melt and return the kiss. Slowly at first, moving only her tongue to dance with his. Very soon she was returning his kiss with her whole body. Her hands went to his waist and pulled him even closer to her as if she could meld the two bodies into one being.

Charlie guided her towards the bed. She knew where they were going, but her body still jerked as the back of her legs hit the mattress.

"What are we doing?" she questioned quietly.

"Not as much as I really want to, but we will forget everything and everyone else. We are going to enjoy each other for a little while before I must leave. And tomorrow you and I are going to do this properly. I think we have both waited far too long. We are adults who are both single, we don't need anyone else's permission to do this."

"My job? Your job even?"

"India, I want nothing more than to announce to the world you are mine. I want to tell the rest of the team to keep their hands off my girl," he growled.

"We can't do that, not now anyway. Charlie. We can't let them know about us."

"OK, if that is what it takes, now kiss me again." He laid down on the bed next to her and pulled her back into his embrace. His lips travelled up her neck to her jaw in tiny tender kisses until at last, they found her mouth. She was ready to return the kisses, and the passionate dance of their tongues started again. India was lost. She had forgotten all the reasons she should not be doing this very thing. Somehow her soul needed this, and it demanded more from this man who had haunted her daydreams for so long. Six years of passionate dreams had her fingers exploring his chest and his broad shoulders, enjoying each dip and hollow of his defined muscles. Charlie's hands returned the same respect, touching her body through her clothes, reaching round to feel the weight of her breasts.

The kissing paused as they both gasped for breath, and Charlie groaned into her neck as his hand slid lower. Again, India's body answered to his. Her hips pushed forward onto his palm, and she reached down to touch the hardness behind his jeans. Charlie's fingers gripped her wrist and looked into her eyes. "India, no, not like this when I have to run away and join the team. We have waited this long. We can wait another day." India froze, rejected after she had finally let down the barriers. "No India don't look like that. Let me do this for you, let me give you this time. Tomorrow we can both enjoy so much more." Before she could respond, he kissed her with the same passion, the same need he had before, and she responded. He returned to undressing her as he slowly lowered the zip and slid her jeans down her slim thighs. Pulling them off took a bit more force, and they both giggled as he struggled to pull them from her ankles. "Now where was I?" he chuckled before joining her on the bed, his lips finding hers instantly, their tongues back to their own intimacy. He held the hem of her T-shirt, lifting it over her head smoothly, tossing it on top of her jeans. He stared at her body, exposed to him for the first time. He had often imagined her beneath him in her underwear and it was always in matching black as she wore today. The last six months had been torture, and his brain flicked through the memories that stood out as he looked down and studied her. The night she hurt her ankle, her standing on his doorstep, the night he had sat on her bed in Leeds, her dressed in his cricket jumper.

"I have waited for this so long and I was wise to wait, to leave other women alone because this, just this, is worth all that." India squirmed on the bed. To have someone examine her in such detail was new and this was Charlie. What was going to happen? He lifted his eyes to her eyes and held her gaze. His eyes firmly fixed on hers, he calmly climbed back over her body. He lowered his lips to hers, finding the passion and the dance, he explored her more. He rubbed her nipple and his other hand lowered to press on her need through her panties. Charlie's mouth left hers to kiss down to her jaw and on down her neck as he released her bra. Her breasts finally free, pushed up to find his lips as they descended to her aroused buds, gently teasing her more. He pushed down her panties until she was naked. His mouth and both hands now exploring every inch of her.

With two hands softly caressing the swell of her bottom, he lifted her to meet his mouth, so sweet on her wetness. Licking delicately, lapping at her. India gripped the duvet on the bed, her fists tensing and releasing as the sensation in her core intensified. He reached to cup her breast, pinching at the already pebbled nipple.

"Charlie please." She groaned, her fingers now gripping his hair, her body arching upwards to meet his mouth, his tongue, her undoing. The tendons in her legs tensed, and her toes dug into the sheets as she arched more.

"Let go, India, let me give you this." As a wave of contraction rolled through her core, the muscles in her legs and arms stiffened. She dropped back, relaxing into the soft mattress. Charlie crawled up the bed and gave her a final kiss. "Thank you, my sweet angel," he sighed and pulled her naked body into his fully clothed one. Every nerve in her body on full alert. She could recognise the softness of his shirt, in contrast to the roughness of his jeans that held his stiff arousal.

He looked at his watch. "India, my precious darling, you have no idea how hard it is to move, but I must go and meet the team. I hope I can appear convincingly humble when we are getting bollocked by Ben tonight." India rolled away from him, burying her head in her pillow. What had she done? She didn't want him to leave, yet she had known he couldn't stay from the moment he arrived. "Just go Charlie, don't make this any harder, but thank you for this and please Charlie, this is between us." She rose from the bed and headed for the bathroom.

"Of course." He reluctantly agreed as his eyes fell on her clothes he had dropped to the floor. He carefully folded her clothes and laid them neatly at the end of the bed then left the room whilst she was still in the bathroom.

Chapter 33

Hearing the door close behind him, she looked up into the bathroom mirror, her hair a mess again. India stood with her fingers lightly touching her lips. She could still taste him there. Had she finally stepped over that line?

She filled the bath and stepped in for a long soak. When the water was cold, she reluctantly got out and slipped on a favourite pair of comfy PJs. As she was combing her hair, there was a knock at her door. She wasn't expecting anyone, so was surprised to find a room service trolley.

"Mr Robertson asked me to bring this for you." The porter lifted the tray and carried it across to the table by her window and put it down. The tray looked beautiful, and they had taken care to present everything very carefully. A tiny silver vase with a single rose held up a handwritten card. There was a bottle of her favourite fizzy water, a small bottle of wine, sandwiches, with a nice salad, plus a small box of chocolate truffles. The note was from Charlie.

Darling girl,

I so wish I was with you now.

I hope this keeps you filled until I can take over.

Love always Charlie x

India blushed and thanked the porter as she closed the door behind him. She couldn't contain herself anymore, and she had to share this with her closest friend before she burst. She snapped a photo and sent it to Katie in a text. It was time for a good old-fashioned girl chat. Take all those things going around her head and lay them out and get a second opinion.

She took a few more photos and stored the note carefully away in the pocket of her suitcase. She was pouring herself a drink when a message bounced back.

KT: Are you alone? It is time you did some explaining. Ring me if you can.

India settled in the easy chair near the window and next to the table. She called her friend, who answered in seconds.

"India Barrington Jones, I'm your best friend, and we haven't spoken in two days tell me everything. Where are you? Why are you alone? What have I missed?"

"Phew, where to start. No problems with the train this time. I got into Scarborough four hours before I could check into my hotel, so I parked my cases and went off to discover the town."

"Wait, is this your first visit?"

"We came when we were children, but not as a grown-up. I wanted to explore artists and chic clothes shops."

"So, all is good, well it looks it but…"

India told Katie all about getting wet and being rescued by the guys from the team, about the bath in Charlie's room and wearing his cricket jumper. She added how much fun the others were, possibly to distract Katie from how she was starting to think differently about Charlie.

Katie was interested to hear about the photograph in the paper today and how old it was.

"How does that make you feel? Knowing that photos turn up when he hasn't been anywhere for six months?"

"It makes me realise that I judged on those images in the past. I'm angry for him too. He has been trying hard for his mum and this job. Images like that will affect his chance of getting a sponsor deal after this one. He said something today about how is any woman going to want to settle down with him when that is happening."

"Oooohh! So, he is considering settling down? Who is that with?"

"How would I know?"

"India, if another woman is on the scene, why would he be the one sharing his bath and his jumpers? The other guys were offering."

"OK. I admit he claims he wants there to be something between us. He says he is prepared to do that in private as he sees that is so important to me. But am I being played? Is he saying what he thinks I want to hear; Am I a challenge that once he has conquered it, he will be on to another?"

"You said you were going to proceed with caution. If you have sex and he moves on, you will know you were right."

"I would like to be certain."

"India, it has been six months, and this is your last photo shoot. You have been cautious and now the time is running out. Of course, if you aren't attracted to him?"

"I'm so attracted to him it is unreal. This is new to me. When he touched me, my whole body lit up like one of those pinball machines they have here."

"Then go for it."

"My family though? What about them?"

"If this is a one-night or a four-night thing and it doesn't progress past your stay in Yorkshire, they need never know. If it goes on beyond that then you can work it out. The fact you are thinking about how they will react tells me that you do want this to go on further. Are you seeing Happily Ever After with this guy?"

"I'm confused. Perhaps the projecting forward is my head's way of telling my treacherous body that this shouldn't happen."

"India, that could simply be your body telling you it is time to let it explore sex again. How long has it been?"

"Not since Dave."

"And when you were having sex with Dave, did you ever wonder what your mum would say?"

"No, but with Charlie, my brother already has an opinion."

"So why was he in your hotel room tonight?" India told Katie about the email from Philip and the phone call to Joe and Tilly.

"See there he is protecting you again. Now about Bentley & Bentley? How much longer are you going to stay there?"

"I'm not planning to leave but staying gets harder every day."

"Time for me to go, so my advice, if you want it, is to make some plans about your job, just don't make plans with Charlie. Enjoy some Yorkshire holiday sex. Who knows what your future holds?" India laughed and told her about the Great Zoltán and the card that told her to find the people to support her being creative.

"That, my friend, is splendid advice, and there is no reason you can't enjoy wonderful sex whilst you are looking. Be safe though."

"Yes, Mum." They collapsed in giggles on either end of the phone. It was usually India telling Katie to be safe.

India settled with Netflix on her laptop and enjoyed the food on the tray. Until her phone buzzed.

CWR: Been sent to our rooms! I feel 14.

India: You should have played better today then.

CWR: Zach getting hurt threw us. We should be bigger than one player.

India: How is he?

CWR: Can I ring you?

India: Sure

India's phone rang and she picked it up immediately. What a wonderful way to end the day sitting on her bed talking to Charlie.

"Thank you for sending the food, it was very thoughtful."

"I'm 'thoughtful' about you all the time, India. I'm ready to do more than 'think' about you."

"So how is Zach? Will he be able to play tomorrow?" India wanted to move to a safer subject.

"We are hoping to rest him and have him back to open the batting. That means he has to spend some time out in the field but definitely not bowling."

"Did Ben talk to you about playing without him? Is it a possibility you should be ready for it?"

"It's true we missed Zach, but for the whole batting side to collapse the way it did. My instructions are to stabilise the hitters during the second innings. That is pretty much my role anyway. I need to show that's what I can do tomorrow."

"It's a good job you're getting an early night. It's rather early though will you be able to sleep?

"I'm guessing it isn't the only thing that's bringing out the fourteen-year-old. Some action in a certain lady's bedroom tonight has got my body reacting like a fourteen-year-old. I'm busy playing tents in this bed."

"Charlie Robertson! I don't believe you are saying that to me."

"India my angel, I would do more than talk about it if you were down here."

"Yes, well, you're having an early night, young man, and I'm tucked up in my own room. I'll see you in the morning."

"You are coming out to dinner with me tomorrow. It is time we had our first proper date, just me and you. Then I'm going to bring you back to the hotel and do all those things I wanted to do earlier. So, make sure you save some energy for your night with me."

"I won't forget but it does feel strange going on a first date."

"Goodnight my angel, sleep well, because tomorrow you may not get the chance to sleep." He laughed.

"Goodnight Charlie." She giggled in response.

Chapter 34

India arrived at the cricket sometime before lunch. She spotted Zach and talked to him for a little while. Then she walked around the ground, snapping photos of spectators in deck chairs and Charlie out in the field. She caught some action shots of his bowling. Charlie wasn't on the regular bowling squad, but with Zach injured and Worcestershire batting for so long, he was called in for a few overs to rest one of the fast bowlers. She paused with her back to the fabulous wrought-iron gates to the ground, taking more and more photos. A tall man in a dark suit approached her and started talking to her. He introduced himself as Jackson Wilde. He wanted to know what sort of photographs she was taking and why she was taking them. She showed him some of the images on her camera, explaining the project she was working on. As he looked through the images on her camera, he scrolled past the cricket images and ended up looking at some artistic shots she had taken on her walk back to the hotel the day before.

"Would you consider coming to work with me? You have a great eye. I could use someone like you in my company. Come have dinner with me tonight, let's talk about it, I'm sure we could come up with a mutually beneficial arrangement."

"While that all sounds very interesting, I'm afraid I have another commitment tonight."

"Please tell me it isn't another man." He held a hand to his chest and pouted.

"I'm sorry Mr Wilde, we have only just met, so forgive me if I don't trust you enough to give up my job to come work for you or to go out to dinner with you."

"Of course, you don't know me yet, so come have lunch with me now and we can get to know each other."

"Now I might have lunch with you here if that is what you are asking?" He leaned in and put his mouth next to her ear. "Ahh, at last, three times of asking you to come with me, - I would love you to come with me."

India's skin crept up her back. Who was this man and how did she escape him? Why on earth did she insist that Charlie and her were to be kept secret?

"She can't work for you, Wilde! She is going to be working for my daughter and I. Time for lunch India." It was Maxwell Sykes. His hand on the small of her back, he directed her towards the member's marquee.

"That man is a creep. We aren't all like that. Take me, for instance, people say I'm hard. I don't think I'm hard. I work hard myself and I don't like lazy people, who expect a wage every month, but they give nothing of themselves." Maxwell Sykes guided her to a reserved table and ordered two of the lunch specials for them, and a bottle of her favourite fizzy water. How did he know? He was a powerful man used to getting his own way, and she was curious to learn more about him. He was Tilly's father, and so there must be some good in him. Her father and grandfather respected him, and she knew that he had many business interests.

She hadn't said one word to him but had been swept away from the expensively dressed creep who had introduced himself as Jackson Wilde.

"I wasn't expecting to see you here today, Mr Sykes."

"I'm over this way buying a property for the family, somewhere near the sea we can escape to. A holiday home we can share." He poured her a drink and continued.

"About working for Tilly and myself. I spoke with her last night, and she is genuinely concerned about you and your job. She feels responsible for the impossible situation you find yourself in and I know she would like to give you a job working for them full time." India was staring at him, not saying a word. Maxwell Sykes realised his mistake.

"Have I really just done what that creep Wilde was asking you to do? And I didn't even give you a chance to say no. Tilly will kill me. Please accept my apologies and let us enjoy the lovely lunch I just ordered for you as if you were my daughter. The trouble is I remember the ten-year-old India playing in her parents' garden, my daughter raves about your skills all the time so I do feel like I know you very well. Could we start again?"

India finally smiled at him. She did feel like she knew him well enough and certainly trusted him more than the last man who offered her a job.

"Show me the photos you have been taking and tell me your view of your current job."

"Please bear in mind I'm getting to know this camera and I haven't started to delete the images I don't want." India passed him the camera and then tried to decide what more to say.

"My current job? It is hard to know what to tell you without being disloyal to them."

"Tell me what your job description is and how much you are paid."

"Mr Sykes, my father would disown me if I told you my current pitiful salary if we are talking about a job. My job title is PR Assistant, Philip Bentley is a friend of my mother's, she had told him I wanted to work in PR, and he offered me a job. I'm ashamed to say I didn't ask enough questions. I'm the youngest and newest employee there. I make a lot of coffee and run around London collecting and delivering products. At events, I get to do front of house and hand out the printed materials and samples. I've been a paid intern I guess, and this project is the first I've been allowed to help with. Philip asked me to take it on to relieve the pressure elsewhere. After some objections internally, I was pulled, at which point Tilly and Joe looked like they would walk away. Long story short I was back on the project."

"Have you enjoyed doing it?" He watched her face as she replied. It lit up.

"Oh yes, an excellent product, wonderful clients and my own concepts."

"Would you enjoy working for Tilly and Joe full time?"

"That is a hard question, I love Tilly, we have become good friends and I'm not sure working for your friends is a good idea. Would I like to work on more projects for them? Undoubtedly, yes. I might get a job wherever they move to."

"What if they moved to your company?"

"Mr Sykes, I don't have a company."

"Call me Max. You don't have a company YET, but you should think about it."

"I don't have enough experience."

"Yet! But what you do have is possibly a better understanding of the new avenues of marketing via social media. A lot of small start-up companies like Tilly's don't have the money to spend with the Bentley & Bentleys of this world but they do need help and support at an affordable price. If you weren't paying for expensive rents in London and top-class photographers and models, you would be able to keep your costs low and charge less. Think about it, India. Do you know a good accountant to look at figures with you?" They both laughed softly.

"Mr Sykes, I'm quite sure if I tried to discuss this with any of my family, they would all faint. My mother would be packing my bags and taking me home to marry me off to someone 'suitable'. I'm fairly sure I would be the trophy wife creating a home and family and never working again whilst my husband had a string of affairs."

"Is that how you see your parents' marriage?"

"No, my mother runs the family without lifting a finger. She thinks it is terrible I want to work."

"Do you want a family?" It was a tricky question.

"I don't 'not want a family' if that makes sense, but again my mother gives my brother's wife hell because she still hasn't produced an heir. So, let's say not yet." she smiled.

"I see you have a lot to figure out, India, and it sounds like you don't feel able to discuss some of this with your parents. Sadly, I think Matilda is the same. I want to change that. If you would like to discuss possible business ideas with someone, please call me, and when you do, my name is Max, not Mr Sykes." He found a card in his jacket pocket and wrote a mobile number on the back for her. He excused himself from the table and left her to enjoy the cricket from there, whilst he went to talk to more men in suits.

Maxwell Sykes was right. She had a lot of things to think about. She was still clinging to the hope of resolving things at Bentley & Bentley, as she didn't want to retreat home to be a puppet of her mother. If she did leave this job, would she stay in London? Who else would give her a job? She wouldn't get a good reference from Philip Bentley, and how would she explain leaving without badmouthing them?

The sun was shining today, and her sunglasses were on, as she sat in a deckchair, watching the cricket. Yorkshire were still fielding, and Charlie had taken a wicket that was sure to lift his spirits. She was concerned that he would be too tired to go out tonight. She was trying not to build up their "date". She didn't like being disappointed. Her head was telling her to accept that after a full day of cricket and with two more days to play, this probably wasn't a good moment for the first date with someone she wanted to consider a friend. But her body thought otherwise. The anticipation of what she might enjoy later was making her skin tingle and her stomach do somersaults.

After her lunch, she decided to take time out from the cricket and go for a walk on the North Beach. It seemed Worcestershire would be batting all afternoon. She spoke to Zach and asked him to text her if it looked like there would be a changeover. He was excited to get her number and sent her a message before she got out of the ground.

Zach: Missing you beautiful girl. Be safe

India turned to where he was sitting and grinned back at him.

On the beach, she slipped off her sandals and dug her toes into the sand. It was something she always did. Katie would call it grounding. She loved the sea and being close to it helped her reflect. How lucky was Tilly? Her father buying a house to escape to. What an amazing idea, to have your own bolt hole to go to when you needed it. Somewhere on the coast. Maxwell obviously wasn't the hard man Joe felt he was. Some muscle in her heart hoped that Tilly and her dad would get to a place where they could support each other again. She was positive that would not happen in her family. They were all far too judgemental.

She walked down to the sea and watch the frilly edge of the water bubble over her toes. Normally this would clear her brain, but there were far too many issues to resolve in a half-hour walk on the beach. India closed her eyes and took deep steadying breaths. What should she do today? She would do an excellent job for Tilly and Joe. Tonight, she would enjoy a nice 'date' with her friend and hopefully explore being with him physically, as well as the mental connection she had. Her thoughts drifted to the night before, how she felt when he left, squeezing her thighs together she let the memories wash over her.

The sea had its share of surfers today, and the beach was littered with families enjoying the soft Yorkshire summer sunshine. Although there were people wherever she looked, if she focused on deep breathing and the cleansing of the waves, she could find space inside to sort her troubles out. Rather like sorting the junk drawer in her kitchen, finding the area to lay out all the issues she was facing gave her the chance to decide what was important.

It had been six years of mixed emotions about Charlie Robertson. At seventeen, her hormonal heart had locked on to him and believed him to be her soulmate. The total embarrassment of vomiting and being so disappointed had stayed with her for some time, cemented in the comments from Andrew and Robbie. For years she had partly hated him and yet there was still part of her inside drawn inexplicably to him. Since that first phone call about this job, that original connection was back. Charlie was the guy she had sat side by side with that night and shared her soul. Her heart told her this man would not hurt her again. Robbie's reasoning voice said he wouldn't mean to hurt her, but he probably would.

This project was nearly over, and she had much to resolve at work to wrap up this job. Charlie and she would remain friends, but he could break her heart. With Joe and Tilly's job finished, she could leave Bentley & Bentley and return home to Hurst's Bridge as her mother wanted. She knew they would welcome her with open arms, and she loved the place, the people, the town, and her family. What she wasn't ready for was how they would use this to control her life going forward. The way they would have another job failure to remind her of.

Last night with Charlie had been so delicious. Only a few minutes in each other's arms and she wanted to stay there forever. It felt like home. Watching him out fielding today had been torture. She wished nothing more than to hug him and let him hold her close, whispering into her neck with his soft Scottish lilt. Being with Charlie was not something she was ready to share with the rest of the world. She didn't want their opinions. Only Charlie seemed to be in favour of it happening. If they explored this with each other alone until the end of the festival, maybe, just maybe, they would both understand a little better what could be, what was possible, if anything, between them.

She wanted to do that, take this week, hidden within the group of teammates. Let them explore this thing between them, this attraction.

She walked away from the waves and towards North Marine Drive. That is what she would do. She would not make a decision other than to give herself to Charlie until they left here. She would not decide about Bentley & Bentley, Maxwell Sykes' idea, or even her mother's plans until she was back in London. She had seen Joe's email to Philip asking for a breakdown of the extra costs, but she did not doubt that Philip would find some things to add across the six months of the project. She also saw that sales were up again for Gym Away.

Only when this trip was over, and the project signed off would she talk to others. She would listen to them. But only once she was more certain what this pain in her heart was whenever she walked away from Charlie Whiskey Romeo.

Chapter 35

Tonight, many from the team would be attending a dinner in a marquee back at the ground. It made it easier for India and Charlie to have some time without the rest of the circus joining them.

India chose to wear a soft jersey dress that evening. The stretch made it cling to her body, a comfortable yet stylish look. She picked sandals with a wedge heel. Her long hair piled high on her head. She added a pair of copper earrings that Katie made for her birthday. It wasn't about playing it safe, it was about focusing on where things were going with Charlie. She lingered as she turned herself in front of the mirror, checking and re-checking her hair, her lips, her shoes. Charlie being tall, she indulged in wearing heels tonight. With the team for company this week, she packed a few pairs, but all the walking meant she hadn't really indulged so far. Still looking in that full-length mirror, she breathed deeply, her hand resting on her stomach, trying to calm the butterflies.

Why was she so unsettled? They had eaten together plenty of times; he had held her hand and put his arm around her. They had kissed innocently, and then with more passion. Last night he had taken the time to explore her with delicious results. Tonight, was different because of those kisses last night, the way he had touched her, the promises he made. Charlie had made her heart sing for some time yet last night his body spoke to more parts of her, her body's reaction was evolving from the yearning heart of a seventeen-year-old to the passionate responses of a woman.

Her hand drifted up to her lips, delicately touching them, trying to recall the kisses from their stolen moments together. But this felt like a date with her best friend. She valued the relationship with Charlie. They had always had a great connection. Maybe that is why he had stayed so long in her memory.

Charlie had certainly made the effort. He arrived wearing a black shirt, dark jeans, biker boots, and a fine black leather jacket. The leather was butter soft and the shirt looked soft too – India longed to touch him. The smell of the jacket reached her nostrils first and then the spicy citrus cologne he wore filled her head.

The restaurant was close by, so their walk was short. As always now, when they crossed a road, he took her hand. It was summer and the roads were busy all day in the town. He had chosen a small intimate Italian style café set back from the main road. She discovered he had arranged a table at the back where they would not be in full view; she wondered if that was for him or her. India was in no doubt that Charlie cared for her if nothing else. He couldn't seem to stop touching her; his hand on her back when they went through doors, holding her hand when they crossed roads. When he wasn't touching her, he was caressing her with his eyes and now sat at the table, their hands linked. He gently stroked her palm as he looked into her sun-kissed face.

"If only we had met three years ago instead of six, perhaps your brother wouldn't hate me so much."

"Hate is a strong word Charlie, I'm not sure he hates you, not now anyway."

"Are you hungry?"

"Are you rushing to get back?"

"No. No! I just thought..."

"Oh, I'm sorry, Charlie, it has been an exhausting day. You have been stood out for so long, you must be tired. Did you want to give tonight a miss?"

"No, Heavens no. But shall we order the main course and then decide if we want more? Let's not let the small stuff get in the way. We are friends that is a great bonus."

"Sure." The words "want more" bounced around India's brain, and she struggled to focus on the now and not on what was to come.

"What do you fancy; pasta, risotto or steak?"

"Hmm Steak. A nice thick fillet. Medium rare."

"I think I'll join you."

"You've had a long day fielding and bowling. Are we drinking?"

"Tomorrow will be another long day, so no, I won't be, but don't let that stop you."

"OH!" India was still thinking about what was to come later. She didn't want to be out of it – but she was far from relaxed, so she opted for a bottle of Italian beer.

The steak and conversation were good. They talked about the day's play. Charlie had taken two wickets, so that helped the mood. Whilst they ate, Charlie let go of her hand, and then he simply let his eyes work harder. He was attentive, filling her glass, asking if she was too hot, too cold. Having her so close to him physically and not touching her was hard. His teammates weren't here tonight, but he still felt the need to claim her, he wanted to reassure her too; he thought she was nervous about the plans for later.

Charlie wanted to talk about her future. India still wasn't ready for that. She had been thinking about it all afternoon. She didn't feel confident despite her conversation with Maxwell Sykes.

India asked Charlie about his mum.

"I'll go back up on Saturday. She does seem comfortable in the hospice. The staff there are wonderful. It is a sad thing to say, but they are particularly good at letting people die with dignity and as pain-free as possible. I phoned today, and she was asleep. She was asleep when Emma called in, too. I know it is coming, I'm just not ready for it. She is all I have."

India squeezed his hand. She wanted to help and found it hard to imagine being as close as Charlie and Elizabeth Robertson.

They admired the gooey toffee cheesecake, which was tempting, but they were both keen to get moving. Charlie got up to organise the bill. As he approached the host, he was stopped by a woman with huge blonde hair and a very plunging neckline. Her hands were all over him, and India's skin bristled. Charlie was being polite and still trying to move away from her. India was getting upset. The woman had been watching them for a while, so she knew that Charlie was with her. How Rude! The Maître D saved him in the end. It seemed to take some time and when he turned, he held up a white box. She decided to join him so that he wouldn't be accosted again. How wrong could she be? Before they made it out of the small restaurant, two more women asked him for autographs and phones were out these people wanted photographs as well. India was in a difficult position; she had made it clear she didn't want to be identified in any connection with Charlie, so what could she say.

Outside, and finally alone, Charlie seemed embarrassed. "Well, they gave me some cheesecake, but I'm sorry about all that, maybe we shouldn't have come out."

"Is it always like this?" Is this something else to face in her future?

"No, I think the Cricket festival means there are more Cricket fans around than normal."

They enjoyed a peaceful walk. They held hands and swapped glances. Charlie's thumb constantly brushed across her knuckles. He led her towards the cliff, where they stopped to look at the tide rolling in. India shivered as the breeze from the sea hit her. Without a word, Charlie removed his jacket and slipped it around her. Gripping the edges, he pulled India towards him.

"I would like to invite you back to my room."

"I thought we could go back to mine." India bantered back, and they both laughed.

"I have the view of the sea and the spa bath?" She wriggled inside his jacket, wrapped in his spicey cologne.

"Charlie Robertson is that you saying your room is bigger than mine?"

"I have cheesecake." He waved the white box to remind her.

Again, they laughed, and Charlie pulled her into his hard body. His thin shirt left him cold now his nipples were hard and erect. India melted into him, his body, his clothes, his smell. She wanted it all.

"Are you sure about this? Today was rough and you have a long day tomorrow." She tried to be fair with him, but inside she prayed he would say he couldn't wait any longer. Her head pressed into his shoulder as she filled her lungs with his spicy scent in case it had to carry her through another night.

"I don't care, it has to be tonight India, we have waited so long." His breath rushed out in a moan. India tipped her head to one side and the corner of her mouth lifted. Just what she wanted to hear him say. Despite the urgency in each of them, the walk back to the hotel was tantalisingly slow, every step warming their bodies for what was to come.

Chapter 36

In Charlie's room, they still lingered, looking out at the waves crashing on the sea wall. There was an urgency in both of them, yet each of them was too afraid of going faster after all this time. Charlie had a small lamp on the desk, casting shadows and giving out a gentle wash of light. Excitement danced between them. Encircled in each other's arms, the kisses were gentle and persuasive. He kissed the edge of her lips and slowly up to her ear, licking and nibbling at her neck. His hands at the base of her spine, caressing and stroking, still holding her firmly against him.

India's hands were on his shoulders, her fingers reaching up to his ears and hair. Those fingers itched to explore more of him, his thin shirt left nothing to the imagination allowing her to run her hands over the muscles in his back. She explored more, his hair, and his mouth. The mouth that was lighting up every nerve of her body as her mouth waited not too patiently for its turn for the attention of his lips.

"Are you warm enough now, my angel?"

"Sure." India stood and watched as he removed his leather jacket, barely moving. He didn't stop though, looking into her eyes for approval his hands reached for the top button at the front of her dress, India smiled back her consent and waited excitedly as Charlie slowly and carefully undid each button and slid it from her shoulders, leaving her in her favourite blue lace underwear with two tiny bows. Still in her wedge sandals, she was close to his height and their mouths met with force as he once again pulled her body into his.

"More than I could ever dream of," he groaned into her ear as his lips began again to trace their way down her neck. India stepped back and his heart leapt. Had he gone too far? Too fast? But India's unsteady hands were on his shirt buttons as she followed his lead, taking her time to remove it. When she reached down to fumble with the button holding his jeans, his hands reached hers and stopped her. His eyes had been constantly searching hers for clues.

"I have to ask again, my sweet. Are you sure?"

"I'm more than sure, Charlie, my body has wanted this since that day you carried me into my flat."

"Thank God for that. Here let me get these off first." He sat on the bed and tugged off his boots and socks. Wriggling his toes, he looked up at India. "I know you love my feet, so I think I'm safe there. You seem fond of my chest too, judging by the number of photographs you have taken without a shirt. I hope the rest doesn't disappoint." He was half laughing, half-serious. India teased him back, "I can simply focus on the bits I like, I guess."

He stood up and peeled off his jeans, leaving his boxer briefs in place. India gasped; it didn't surprise her how firm his muscles were; she knew how hard he worked to stay fit; it was his job. He seemed so perfect. She was about to see him naked for the first time. She stepped towards him, gently kissing across his shoulders and down his chest. Charlie backed up to the bed and sat on the edge, pulling India down to sit on his lap. His arms reached around her, and with trembling fingers, he unfastened her bra.

Charlie stared at India. It was beyond the fantasies he had tried to keep at bay for so long. Whilst one arm held her safely on his lap, he explored her full breasts. The roughness of his fingertips pulled on her tender white skin, her nipple standing erect and waiting for his attention. Charlie dipped his head to take it in his mouth, his tongue exploring gently and persistently. India sighed, and he let out a breath. His eyes found hers, constantly checking for permission to move forward. Her eyes were closed, still, her soft smile sent him to explore the other nipple. Desperate to not break the spell, he moved slowly. Wanting to maintain the friendship with her, but needing more, needing the physical connection too. This was not just sex for him, and he hoped she understood that.

Gently but firmly, he rolled her onto the bed at his side. She lay on her back, her knees bent, her arms spread wide. She appeared relaxed as he looked down at her. Her eyes fluttered open to see why he had stopped. She recognised the question in his eyes was him once again seeking permission to go further. In answer, she reached down and took off her panties with a teasing smirk. He returned her smile and stood to remove his boxer briefs. It was India's turn to stare. She knew he was well endowed from the shapes that filled his trousers. She had felt him hard against her body the night she arrived in Scarborough. She was in no doubt he was attracted to her as a woman. As he stood erect in front of her now, this was more than she could have imagined. The desire within rose more, India didn't realise that was possible. This sensation was new. It was deep in her core, a need to be with him. Any doubts were swept away.

Charlie crawled onto the bed, moving up her body with gentle, soft kisses. Kisses that triggered her skin to spark. Tiny pecks to the inside of her knees, between her thighs and halting at the apex of her limbs. Licking and opening her up. India's knees fell to the side as he explored the centre of her desire.

They were both aroused more than they had ever experienced before, but they moved on slowly, both petrified to ruin this moment. This was a relationship that had no future, yet they could no longer stay in the friendship they both so much wanted. The primal urge to connect deeper was too strong.

India's back arched from the bed, and Charlie held her hips to keep her under his mouth. Last night had been a wonderful release for her, but tonight, with the promise of more to come, her brain was working overtime. The thought that he would soon be entering her ramped up the excitement that lit up her body, leaving every inch of her skin screaming for his touch. One hand held her still, the other opened her legs more until one finger slowly found its way into her centre. India visibly softened into the mattress, and he smiled, adding another finger, curled inside her to tap rhythmically on her G spot. It was all India needed to enjoy her second orgasm beneath him.

As she twitched and turned with the aftershocks, Charlie climbed higher up her body exploring her, worshipping her breasts. With both hands and his tongue, he treated them both with a reverence that startled India. He was such a tender lover. Climbing more, his lips finally met hers and she sighed, melting into the bed beneath him.

His mouth moved from her lips to her ear and between the kisses, he whispered to her. "Are you ready for this?"

"So ready."

Charlie reached for the condom, and once it was in place, he gripped firmly at the base and held that hardness against the wetness at her core. Sensitive, she felt him move the crown across her, back and forth from her clitoris to her entrance. It was hypnotic, but she could wait no longer.

"Now, Charlie, please let it be now." She pleaded.

Charlie placed the tip of his cock ready to enter her and pushed slowly forward. Stopping and waiting a few times until he sensed she was prepared for all he could give her. He sank into her completely, filling her. He paused and waited for a moment or two for her to adjust to his size. He searched her face constantly, wanting that reassurance that they were together, that she wanted this as much as he did.

His stillness made India open her eyes again. Lost in those deep brown pools, she nodded just once, and he began to move. Withdrawing slowly and returning to fill her again and again. She marvelled at the control he had over his body and hers too.

Charlie changed the pace and the angle he entered her. He was using every ounce of restraint he had to make this special. He wished for this to be the start of a deeper commitment. He wanted to claim her in front of all the team, in front of her family and the rest of the world. He wanted her to be his. As he moved between her legs, he could feel the end coming, and he hoped he could give her one more orgasm.

"Come with me India, come for me, let go." And then he kissed her with a passion that added to her arousal. Her climax pulsed around Charlie, throbbing, and ending his need to wait. The release for him pumped on for several seconds as he stilled and waited before he withdrew from her.

They rolled together in the centre of the bed. Charlie wiped the hair from her face, gently stroking her cheek. This was a new experience for India. Sex before this was often some hurried fumbling explosion that was over quickly. This was deeper.

"You are the most beautiful girl. I don't think I'll ever get enough of you. But you were right, I'm tired."

"Do you want me to go so you can sleep?"

"No, I want to hold you in my arms forever. I would love you to stay. I know we are keeping this quiet for now, but I can't wait to tell the world you are mine. I want to hold you for the rest of time so no one else thinks they can steal you away."

"Charlie?"

"Please stay India."

"How about we set an alarm so I can retreat safely to my room?"

Charlie finally let go of holding her and disposed of the condom. He made a cup of tea and dug out the cake they brought from the restaurant.

India slipped on her panties, then swiped the cricket jumper she had worn that first night.

"That looks better on you than it does on me, but I do prefer you naked."

India laughed, "Says the man who just covered up his interesting bits with his briefs."

They sat in chairs next to his window, watching the waves rock against the seawall. The noise from the water and a good breeze rattled around the old windows.

India tucked up her legs and pulled Charlie's jumper over them, licking her lips. She was openly enjoying the cheesecake.

"Do you have to torture me? Eating like that?"

"You bought it. How do you want me to eat it?"

Charlie stood and took the dessert from her, placing it on the side table. "You can finish that later." He pulled his jumper over her head and then sank to his knees in front of her. Cupping each breast in turn, he tasted, licked, and sucked. "Who needs cheesecake?"

"It might give us a little more energy?"

"Great! Eat it and come back to bed." He left her, gobbled up his cake and emptied his tea. He wiped his mouth and bounced over to the bed.

"Come on, I have waited a long time for tonight."

"We both have!"

"Really? How long have you waited? Not since that first night, surely?"

"Hard to say, but I did feel something that night, something that drew me to you."

"So don't waste any more time," and he held up the covers for her to join him again. They spent another hour slowly and carefully exploring each other, making their connection even stronger.

Eventually, they slept in each other's arms, their legs tangled together. Until the alarm insisted she got up to go back to her own room.

As India dressed to leave him, she sat down on the side of his bed.

"You realise that this has to stay between us Charlie, we can't let anyone know."

"I understand, much as I want to tell the world, I agree that is something we have to do together and at the right moment."

Chapter 37

India made it back to her room without seeing a single soul. Her phone was out of charge again, so she plugged it in and climbed between the sheets. How did it seem so empty being alone in bed? India told herself she was being crazy. One night and she was missing him, fudge it hadn't even been a full night, and still, she missed his arms around her already. What had she done? She had kept her lust for his body at bay for so long, now she felt drawn to him more than ever. What on earth was she going to do? They had all warned her, her brother, Robbie, her boss. Her mother would disown her for sure.

Her brain settled on the problems with her job. She loved working with Tilly and Joe; it let her creative side shine through. Alice and Malcolm were so not like her. They seemed to live in a different world, and they resented her. Jayne, well Jayne was just out to prove to Philip that he couldn't cope without her, and she defended her place at his side like a tiger. She would never be happy with India playing a bigger part at Bentley & Bentley. Which led her nicely to Philip Bentley himself. India respected Philip at first and had been delighted when he asked her to join him for lunch to meet Tilly and Joe. Then when he pulled her off the project, she began to question him. If Alice and Malcolm were lazy, was that because he allowed them to be? At the bottom of her heart, she knew it was time to move on. She wanted to leave to start a new challenge, not to be let go from yet another job. She could hear her father sighing from the thought. Her mother would insist on her going home and what else was there other than to go back to Hurst's Bridge?

She realised the company was in decline and that she was probably at the top of the list to go. Although she was the lowest paid and the hardest working member of the team, if Philip found out she had not listened about Charlie and had gotten involved with him, he would have the perfect excuse to sack her, and it would make getting another job even harder. Philip being friendly with her mother didn't help. He would feel the need to tell her why he couldn't keep India on his staff any longer. There had to be a way to move on to the next stage in her life without returning to Hurst's Bridge and everything that would mean. She loved the small town, but that is what it was, small. Everyone knew everyone. People were friendly yet she had no friends there. Her parents had good intentions, sending her and her brother to private school, but it meant they had no local friends. Andrew had got lucky and fallen in love with a perfectly wonderful local girl, and he had inherited friends through her. What would India do back there?

India hoped to catch a little sleep after her night with Charlie. She tossed and turned worrying about work. There was no need to be at the cricket early but that is where Charlie would be all day. She was unable to stay away; she needed to see him, even if she couldn't touch him.

When she arrived, Yorkshire was still fielding, and Zach was sitting alone with a bigger bandage on his wrist.

"We missed you last night, beautiful girl. How come you didn't come to the festival dinner?"

"I was working." It was a cover in case someone noticed her with Charlie. "Something change with the wrist Zach?"

"It started to swell again and now they think it's broken. Someone is going to take me for an X-ray later. Come sit with me and keep me distracted."

"That I can do."

"So beautiful girl, tell me about you and Romeo. You said you had known him for a long time, but you are young. How old were you when you met?"

"I was just seventeen when we met at my cousin's house. Robbie and Charlie are friends from school."

"AH, seventeen, no wonder the poor guy is confused."

"Yeah, he didn't realise I was that young either."

"Crikey mate, poor guy. Has he been in love with you all that time?"

"Charlie in love with me? Now you are crazy. How long have you known him, Zach?"

"Two seasons, I lived with him for one year. He took me in when I first arrived over here, and he helped me fit in."

"So, tell me how many women you have seen him with in those two years, and then tell me he is in love with me."

"Ha! That is actually my point. I have seen many women draped over him. I have seen him sit next to women. I have even seen him dance with a few. But I have never seen him with anyone the way he is with you. I have never seen him look so protective over a woman either."

"Excuse me?"

"That day in Headingley, when you walked in with those students, he was ready to explode. The whole weekend it was so obvious."

"So, is that your opinion?"

"No mate, the entire team thinks so. Most of them have known him longer than me and Garry."

"So why were you all flirting with me when we were out for fish and chips?"

"Because we knew it would drive him mad. So why aren't you guys together?"

"A few reasons really, this project is my job for a start, and well, my parents wouldn't approve."

"Not approve of Charlie. Why on earth not?"

India opened her mouth to explain, but the team physio appeared, rattling his keys, ready to take Zach to Leeds to get an x-ray and a full set of scans on his injury. He gave India a little hug and brief kiss and whispered, "Look after him India, don't break his heart," and he was gone.

India sat down as her phone buzzed with an incoming call from Tilly. She had missed a few calls from her with the phone playing up, but Tilly hadn't left a message. India answered it as she made her way out of the stand.

"Morning Tilly. Are you almost here?"

"That's why I'm calling. We won't make it today. Joe's mum is ill, and I want to be there for him. I know you can do the job on your own anyway, I just wanted to explain. Hopefully, we will be there tomorrow."

"That would be good. I hope things are OK when you get there. Don't worry about me."

"Thanks."

"Hey, I bumped into your dad yesterday. He rescued me from a weird guy called Jackson Wilde."

"Yeah! Dad says cricket is a great place to network, better than golf. Sounds like a story for tomorrow."

India took herself to the tea tent where she could watch Charlie playing in the centre of the pitch. She spotted more photos of Charlie in a newspaper someone was reading at the next table. When they left the paper behind, she retrieved it to check out the article. The report said Charlie had missed the festival dinner and was seen around Scarborough with several women. It suggested this was the reason the Yorkshire team was doing so badly. The photos included some of the selfies the women had taken at the restaurant. It said Charlie had been seen entering the hotel with two women and had an eyewitness statement. Fortunately, there was no photo of her.

It didn't make sense to India at all. Someone was making things up and all she could think of was Charlie's mum. She stayed at the table and sipped tea. Looking out across the crowd she glanced at a young couple in each other's arms, obviously in love. Watching Charlie jog between the wickets she wondered if they would ever be able to be together in public. Her stomach flipped at the idea. She pulled out her notepad and made a list of images to take, that gave her an excuse for going to his room. She closed her eyes picturing the two of them back there. It had an interesting effect on all her senses. When she looked again the players were coming in for lunch.

With her list (excuses) firmly clutched in her hand, India made her way to the pavilion hoping to speak to Charlie. Why did she doubt him? When he spotted her approach, a broad grin spread across his face as he stood to welcome her.

"Good morning my angel, did you sleep well?"

India blushed. "Mostly."

"I missed you this morning."

After Zach's comments, India wondered if they were fooling anyone at all, still, she carried on the pretence as a vision of her mother talking to Philip Bentley came unbidden into her head.

"Any news of Zach?" Changing the subject seemed like a good idea.

"No, though to be honest, it doesn't sound promising." His body slumped as he acknowledged all the possibilities.

"Oh!"

"He will be fine long-term, but I'm guessing he won't be playing again the rest of the season. That means he is likely to fly back to Australia early and if he does Garry will probably go with him. That would leave a big hole in the squad. Ben Woods is in a mood trying to work it out."

"OH!"

Charlie looked around hurriedly. "Please don't repeat that."

"I understand."

"Where are Joe and Tilly? Aren't they coming over today?"

"Tilly rang, they were off to the hospital to see Joe's Mum. Not sure how serious it is yet."

At that point, Ben came over and whisked him away to talk privately. India felt lost until suddenly Dan Woods and Garry sat down beside her. The two tall blondes were bantering even more than usual, and India decided the team were unsettled, possibly by the situation with Zach and possibly about the score in the match. She simply smiled when she thought she should, all the time wondering what was so important that Ben needed to speak to Charlie about it.

Before long Charlie and Daniel Woods were going off to bat again and India sat bewildered. She was surprised to watch Charlie begin to hit out at the ball, instead of his normal controlled strokes he was now swinging his bat and finding the boundary. The runs were finally starting to mount up for Yorkshire. Dan was grinning from the other side of the crease, and he too hit out.

By 3 o'clock they had created a 60-run partnership and spirits were lifted in the Yorkshire camp when Zach arrived back from the hospital. One look at his face told India it was not good news. As soon as his eyes found India, he walked over and lifted her in the air spinning her around.

"Don't be sad beautiful girl. It just means I'm going home a little earlier than I expected."

"How soon?"

"Maybe next week, it depends on how quickly I can sort things out, flights, my flat, the boring stuff you know."

"That soon?"

The scoreboard took his attention, "Probably, what has been happening whilst I was gone?"

India smiled as Zach realised the score had started to improve.

"Alright! Finally, they let Charlie do some real hitting!"

India smiled softly once again. "Catch you later beautiful. I better go talk to the guys."

As India processed Zach's news over the afternoon, it brought home how fragile Charlie's career was. She knew the team would miss Zach and Garry too if they flew back to Australia together. She was going round in circles when her phone rang. It was Nick.

"Hey there, after last time I decided I better check if the email cancelling me tomorrow actually was from you."

"What?"

"I have an email from you cancelling my trip up to Yorkshire."

"Fudge!" India felt the blood rush to her neck and face and her arms tense as anger washed over her. "Nope! It isn't from me."

"Do you want me to come up and pretend I haven't seen the email?"

"I guess that is the best way to play this. What can anyone say? Who is doing this?"

"Have you been in touch with Josh recently?"

"No, why?"

"He was here picking up some proofs and he asked about you. Had I spoken to you? Would I be seeing you? He was concerned."

"OK. That is somewhere to start, isn't it? I'll try talking to Josh."

Josh's phone went to voicemail. She didn't leave a message as he might be driving Jayne or even Philip Bentley himself. He would see the call and ring back.

The cricketers were coming off the field and the mood was better than it had been since the match started. It was unlikely Yorkshire could win at this point but at least they were playing well now. Charlie came over with the rest of the lads and they all seemed to be in high spirits. Zach was the first to speak.

"We are going out for my leaving party tonight India. Ben has booked a table for us all at the Chinese restaurant on the way back to the hotel. Will you come?

India glanced briefly at Charlie, if she joined them, it would be hard, it was only a meal, she would eat in the hotel and try and sort out what to do about Nick and the job.

"Not this time Zach. I have work to do. You enjoy yourself with your teammates." She was looking at Zach, but she was speaking to Charlie, giving him the same message. Charlie lingered to talk to her, asking her a question about the photos they still needed to take until they were on their own.

"Are you sure? I want to be with you."

"Go Charlie, go for Zach and the team."

"I won't stay late; will you wait in my room for me? I'll be there as soon as I can."

"Hmmm, that sounds like a plan."

Charlie squeezed her hand and ran off to catch up with the rest of the team.

Chapter 38

India took her camera bag and her laptop to Charlie's room. She realised it was probably ridiculous to keep up the pretence, but she felt she needed to. She had squeezed a few overnight things in around her camera. India also knew she would take some photos whilst she was there to help her conscience. And that is where she started, hotel room shots with the product. Part of her brain saying, "See I'm working" and the other laughing and saying, "You aren't kidding anyone".

There was still no response from Josh, but her phone was still playing up and she resorted to emailing Nick about coming up the next day. Between them, they decided to be fair to Joe and Tilly. He would come up and take the photos they were expecting. India promised him "proper" fish and chips and a chance to see the rest of the team again. Nick arranged to get a taxi to the ground directly from the station.

Joe and Tilly confirmed that his mum was already home from the hospital and that they too would meet her at the cricket ground the next day. Everything was falling into place, and although she wasn't confident about the chances of things working out long term for Charlie and her, she felt happy as she turned on the water for Charlie's spa bath.

India took the time to indulge in a long bath and then warmed herself in the extra fluffy towels as she walked into the bedroom. She laid on the bed watching the festive lights around the harbour. The sounds of the amusement arcades mixed with the crashing waves rocked her to sleep.

A crash of thunder woke her, and the rain was driving onto the shore, rattling the glass in the worn window frames. Startled to discover she had dropped off on top of the sheets, still in the towel. She got up to close the curtains to block out the storm and find something to wear to bed. She picked one of Charlie's t-shirts. It was 11:30 and no sign of Charlie. A little unsure, she climbed into the bed but tossed and turned, wondering if she should go.

Uncertainty and anxiety ate into the confidence she had earlier. She turned over and faced the clock on the side table.

00:00

Midnight and he wasn't back. She stared at the clock, it still didn't change. She closed her eyes and reopened them.

00:00

How long was a minute? Well, 60 seconds eventually it clicked over.

00:01

00:02

00:03

This was crazy. She got up and checked her phone, but it was dead. With no idea what to do next, she returned to Charlie's bed and hugged his pillow.

06:35

She must have fallen asleep at some point. The rain had stopped, and the sun was shining straight in from the east-facing window. No sign of Charlie, and India decided she needed to get back to her room.

She hurriedly packed her things and snuck down to the next floor and into the safety of her own room. As she opened the door, she found a note pushed under it.

I'm sorry, I will see you at the ground.

CWR

What the hell?

Her battery was still dead. She had to do something about that today. She fired up her laptop and used the hotel phone to ring her brother. It was early, but Andrew would be up and was her go-to person for anything techy like her phone.

"Where are you? Dad has been trying to call you?"

"Scarborough, but my phone is playing up, that's why I rang."

When she explained what was happening and answered all his questions, like how long it had been doing it and how long she had the phone, an exasperated Andrew pronounced "India just go get a new phone, do it today and call Dad."

India realised she needed to talk to a few people before her father, so she searched online for a phone shop and found one a few yards away that opened at 8:00. Relieved that she had solved one problem, she decided to brave looking for news about Charlie online too.

Her screen filled with images of him out with the team. One stood out from the rest. Charlie was leaving a casino. Each arm was around the waist of a stunning girl, one blonde and one redhead, but both spilling out of low-cut dresses. Charlie was grinning. The headline said it all: ROMEO IS BACK. No wonder she had woken up alone. He had no reason to come to her when he had his choice of two stunning women. Maybe he didn't even have to choose. India felt sick. How could he? *I should have known better than believing he had changed.*

India snapped into business mode. A swift shower to wash off any remnants of Charlie from sleeping in his bed, her hair fastened back tightly and black trousers and blouse. She couldn't face the hotel breakfast and possibly seeing the team. *No wonder he was sorry!*

The first job, sort out her phone. After dropping his room key off at reception, she walked into the phone shop and told the young girl behind the counter what the problem was. She answered lots of questions and 30 minutes later walked out of the shop with a wonderful new phone that looked like it had a great camera and on a cheaper contract.

It was too early to go to the cricket ground, so she got a takeaway breakfast of coffee and a bacon sandwich and sat overlooking the beach under the statue of Queen Victoria. Her new phone started to fill with all the texts and missed calls from yesterday and today. Where to start?

The coffee and bacon smelt wonderful, but her stomach was still clenching with visions of Charlie's latest appearance in the papers. She could tell that the images were from last night. She knew where the casino was as she'd walked past it on her way to the cricket ground. Zach was in the background with the new bandage he got yesterday. Closing her eyes, she held her sandwich close to her chest. The last thing she wanted to do today was go to the cricket and not only see Charlie but Zach and the rest of the crew who would know that Romeo was back, and she was forgotten. So much for Zach thinking she had tamed him. She had no choice though, Tilly and Joe were coming and so was Nick. She had a job to do. Just a couple more days and she would be in London, back in her little flat.

It was nearly 9 o'clock, so she tried Josh.

"Hey, little girl. Are you OK?"

"Why do you ask?" Has he seen this morning's photos?

"Lots of things, but it started because I could hear Jayne talking on Monday no idea who to, she was laughing and I heard the words 'She won't know what has hit her, I'm guessing she won't dare show her face here again.' I can't be certain she was talking about you, but something made me think of you."

"You are probably right. Things have been happening. Nick got another email cancelling him for today. Too late so he would charge Bentley & Bentley, anyway. Leaving me without a photographer in front of the client again. Philip was so angry when it happened last time."

"So, what will you do?"

"Oh, Nick is still coming. What can they say? They can't say I cancelled him?"

"I hate to say this India, but this isn't worth it. I'll miss you, but seriously you have to walk away from it. I've seen her do some stupid stuff in the past, there is no telling what she'll do next."

"I know, I have to finish this job before I make any decisions."

"That I understand. Give my best to Charlie. See you when you get back." India didn't reply. Why did everyone like Charlie? Well, except for her family, that is.

Next, she rang her father and explained about her phone and letting him know she had sorted it. William Barrington Jones sighed.

"India, I worry about you far more than I worry about Andrew dashing off all over everywhere, probably because you are a girl." Her dad had never shown concern before and it surprised India he even noticed she was away from her flat.

"So why did you call Dad?"

"Jackson Wilde told me he saw you having lunch with Maxwell Sykes. He seemed to think you were going to work for him. Is it true?"

India giggled. "Yes, we sat together at the cricket over lunch. He is my client's father. I have not said I will work for him."

"Really India? Maxwell Sykes? He has a reputation of being a hard man."

"Look, Dad, I have to get off and meet the client." It was a lie, but she wasn't ready to talk about moving to Leeds and setting up her own business. She would need a much stronger idea before she exposed it to her dad's scrutiny.

"OK call me later. We still need to talk."

India looked down at her breakfast, now going cold in the early morning breeze. She sighed. *What would my mother think?* A cold realisation hit her. *It's not my mother I'm worried about it's his mother.*

Fudging Heck! Why would he do that to his mother? And why had she let him pretend she was his girlfriend? He didn't care, did he?

India tried to find her positive face. *Today is the final shoot, and Joe will be here with Tilly so I can address any problems they have. Hopefully, Charlie's appearance all over the papers today will only improve sales.*

India could sense herself sitting more upright on the bench and squaring her shoulders. She wasn't happy about the photos, but she couldn't let anyone else know that. She had been a fool to risk her job over him.

India stared out to sea and struggling to focus on the job, she ate the cold bacon sandwich and found some determination, enough to get her to the finish line of this project. All thoughts of moving to Leeds, to work more with Charlie, Joe and Tilly, now gone.

Arriving at the cricket ground, India avoided the player's area. She picked up her new phone and sent a text to Tilly and Nick to let them know where she was. Charlie sent her a text.

CWR: Are you OK? Did you fall asleep? I knocked, but you didn't answer. I'm sorry about the photos.

India: Really? Sorry you got caught?

CWR: It's a long story.

India: You told me you wouldn't be late.

CWR: Got to go. Can we talk later?

India didn't reply. She slid her new phone into her bag and pulled out her notebook. That fudging book was starting to be her anchor. The Cooksons were the first to arrive. Joe was excited to see Charlie hitting out.

"Our boy seems to be having another great day."

India looked down at her notes, not knowing what to say. Tilly saw the hurt look in her eyes.

"Oh India, I'm so sorry." Her arm went around India's shoulders as she sank down next to her. "What is it? Are you in trouble again? Is it the photos?"

"Yes." It was a quiet yes, and Tilly could tell there was more.

"And?" India didn't reply immediately. She kept her eyes on her notebook, eventually, she spoke.

"Nick should be here soon, is there anything you want him to focus on?"

Joe was busy watching Charlie, so hadn't noticed India's mood. He kept talking.

"Well, Charlie is playing well, so definitely some action shots."

Tilly watched India closely as she looked at her lists. Without taking her eyes off the page in front of her, she made her own suggestions.

"Hopefully, I can get a few more interviews before we sign off the project so Nick can get some good shots of you, too. Perhaps watching the cricket or talking to Charlie." The word 'Charlie' was almost a whisper.

"OK India, what is going on?" India looked up at Tilly. She didn't need to speak. Tilly saw her broken heart through her red eyes. Both her arms shot around India as she dispatched Joe to get them all some tea.

"Tell me, girl, what has happened?" India didn't speak.

"Is it the job? Tell me it isn't Jackson Wilde."

"No, it's not Jackson Wilde, although he did try stirring it with my father saying he saw me with your dad."

"I have to say that weirds me out. Thinking of you and him."

"And I do have to do something about my job, but I have no idea what."

"But that is nothing new, India. I haven't seen you like this before."

The crowd erupted as Charlie hit a six. Tilly stood, clapping with the rest. India looked back down at her book.

"Oh my gosh. It's Charlie!"

"Hey, look who I found!" Joe was laughing and juggling three cups of tea. Nick was with him, carrying his camera case and a holdall. Nick dropped his bags and scooped India into his arms.

"Are you OK? Did you get hold of Josh? Has anything been said about me coming today?"

India didn't know where to look or what to say. She shouldn't be having this conversation in front of the client and if she could, where would she start. She was beyond tired. Tears slowly trickled down her face. Her three companions swapped looks. Joe produced a hanky, and Nick held her close as Tilly stroked her back. With a huge intake of breath, India found enough composure to pull away.

"Sorry about that. Yeah. Life is a bit of a bitch isn't it." India pulled away from the group taking a deep breath. Shaking her shoulders, she started to give orders to Nick.

"This match won't last much longer so, get some shots of Charlie at the crease and Tilly and Joe enjoying the cricket, maybe in the deckchairs. Later, can you try to get Charlie talking to Tilly and Joe?" She thrust a list of photographs into his chest and marched off towards the toilets.

"Hang on." Shouted Tilly as she jogged to catch up with India.

"India, tell me to mind my own business. I know I am the customer, but I hope I am your friend too. I hate to think this project has caused you so much pain. I want to help. My dad was asking about you."

"I like you, I genuinely do, but how can I talk to you about all this?"

"Can you just tell me how much of the pain I see in your eyes is due to Charlie?" India turned away without an answer.

"You told me to stop pushing. It's all my fault." Sighed Tilly. "If I hadn't insisted on you being on this project and if I listened to Charlie and to you."

"Tilly, it's not you. Charlie and I... we have history." It was Tilly's turn to be quiet. India pulled out her ponytail and carefully combed her hair, pulling it back tight. It was something she could control and as she did so, she recalled the story from the beginning.

"What has he said about last night?"

"That he is sorry." India showed Tilly the texts from that morning "And then he went out to bat."

"You didn't reply?"

"I didn't know what to say. Do I listen to him explain where he spent last night? Waking up alone this morning hurt dreadfully, but seeing those images fill my screen made me feel physically sick. I just keep thinking, where was he? Who was he with?"

"I don't think he would want to hurt you."

"What was he even doing at the casino? He was going to the meal and then coming back to me. Maybe it was my fault I was trying to keep this quiet, at least till the end of this project."

Tilly closed her eyes. "It is this project. Why did I push so hard? What can I do to help?"

"Stop talking about it! It's time to go do a great job for a brilliant client." Straightening herself up as she looked in the mirror, she tucked in her shirt and tried to find the professional India Barrington Jones.

"And Charlie?"

"It's a good thing I found out now. So, let's do this Tilly. No more being nice to me. Let's do this job."

And that is what they did. Charlie was eventually run out and could take more photos. Yorkshire were all out as Worcestershire won by an innings and 180 runs. The game was over before lunch. Nick and Joe collected Charlie for photos in his kit. Tilly started to organise some lunch for them all, but India made her excuses and left.

Chapter 39

It was noticeably quiet as Charlie drove them to the hotel. Joe and Tilly had squeezed into the tiny back seat of the Porsche. Nick sat in the front.

"I love this car, man." Nick stroked the leather trim. "I couldn't even afford the insurance."

Charlie gave him a tight smile. "Ah, you see it isn't my car."

"It isn't?"

"No, a guy who specialises in second hands sports cars loans them to me for two to six weeks at a time. Then he sells them on. I think he is one of the people making sure my photo is in the paper." Joe and Tilly were listening a little harder now.

Things were beginning to make more sense to Tilly. She had a tough time matching the Charlie she had met to the hard-drinking, gambling womaniser in the papers.

"Is your mum likely to see the photos, Charlie?"

"Sadly not. She is hardly awake these days. I'm going straight up to visit her as soon as the big dinner is out of the way."

Tilly coughed and slid forward in her seat. "Charlie, can I ask about last night?"

Through another tight smile, Charlie looked at Tilly in his rear-view mirror, "Were they a problem for you guys as well? I'm very sorry."

"No, not really, but I don't get it. You sound like you don't want the photos?"

"I've realised the problems they are causing me long term. It is hard for the team to consider me for more coaching duties with that sort of press. Besides, what woman is going to take me seriously when that keeps happening?"

Tilly looked at Joe, but Charlie was parking outside their hotel and they all started to climb out of the car and stretch their legs.

"Guys, you have both done a lot already today. Joe and I would like to pay you to do a few more images whilst we are all still together and then we will take you out to dinner."

"It's been a long week, but I get your point, and this is the last day of photos, so yes. To be honest, I could use the money. If it's OK with Nick that is."

"Sure, I'm here now."

"I need to get my key, then we can go get the shots you want in the bedroom."

Tilly pulled Joe to one side. "I'm going to find India in a while. It is your job to find out what he is doing with India and what his intentions are."

"Really Tilly?"

"Yes, Joe I feel responsible."

"I'll try."

"Shall I call India and see if she is joining us?" Nick asked, still not understanding the situation.

"I think she is avoiding me!" Charlie said sulkily as he opened the door. Stepping inside his room, he could smell her, almost feel her presence. His bed had been made and draped over the end was one of his t-shirts. Picking it up to put away, he realised that India must have borrowed it to sleep in.

He sank onto the bed, clutching the t-shirt. Her scent lingered but she was gone. What had he done? He didn't want to hurt India. But this was for the best. He would only hurt her at some point, anyway.

Tilly looked at him and decided not to wait for Joe. Sitting down next to him, she placed her hand over his. "Charlie, what is happening?"

"This is so hard." He said, pulling a hand down his face. When he looked up, he realised there were three people there in the room who cared for India. All staring at him.

"Last night wasn't what it seemed. Come on, you know what the papers do to me and others." No one responded, so he filled the silence. "Look, it is better that she walks away now. I have to believe that and so should you."

Still no response other than three big sighs. Again, Charlie spoke, getting them all back to work.

"So, what are we doing first and what do you want me wearing?" he started to remove his shirt. Tilly looked away, then leaned in to kiss Joe.

"You guys can handle this without me. I'm going to our room, touch base with the office and finish unpacking. Then dinner about seven?" looking at Nick and Charlie. Charlie busied himself with re arranging the clothes in his case, but Nick responded.

"India promised me 'proper' fish and chips."

"I'll see where she thinks is best." Charlie didn't look up from his bag.

The boys were left to get on. Nick focused on styling images in the Victorian room with all its moulding and large windows. Joe joined in, suggesting different exercises. As Tilly slipped away, Joe's phone buzzed with a text.

TC: I'm going to see India. You see if you can get Charlie to talk.

JC: No, I'm staying out of this and so should you.

TC: But it is my fault.

JC: No, it is not.

TC: Please.

JC: I'll start a conversation, but I'm not pushing it.

As Tilly arrived at India's door, she sent her a text too.

TILLY C: It's me. I'm outside your door let me in

TILLY C: I'm alone. We need to talk about the project.

India reluctantly opened her door, carefully checking the corridor before letting Tilly in. Tilly took one look at India and sat them both down on the bed.

"Tilly, I'm fine, or I will be. I hope this hasn't spoilt the end of the project for you."

"No. Nick has taken an impressive set of images and you are doing extra work here too. Everything you have done has brought more sales. But I'm here as your friend." She tried to get India to look at her as she continued. "I feel guilty because I kept pushing you. I still don't understand. In my head you should be together and that working with us is keeping you apart. I have no idea what he is thinking. From what he said today he has plenty of reasons for not wanting more photos in the papers, his mum for one."

"Did he say how his mum is today? I haven't been able to speak to him." She whispered as she twisted away from Tilly to stare out the window.

"Not really. I get the impression she is 'sleeping' most of the time. It sounds like he will go up to Scotland as soon as he can get away from here."

"The match is over. Why is he waiting?"

"I guess he is committed with us and Nick here."

"Fudge! If I hadn't convinced Nick to come…"

"And something about the dinner tomorrow and seeing another couple of sponsors."

"I guess he will need to find more now this is over."

"Once we are set up with a new PR company, we will be in touch. I guess it will take a few months. Have you considered what my dad suggested about setting up in Leeds?"

"I have," India said with conviction, "but maybe I thought Charlie would be part of that move. To be honest, now I realise the truth of that relationship, making decisions about my career will be simpler."

"Well, that is good. Isn't it?"

"So why don't I feel that? Why do I feel like someone has stepped on my heart? Most of all I'm upset he would end it like that. I thought we were friends. Why leave me waiting in his room? And as you say, why the photos?" Both girls exhaled a long breath. India pulled back her shoulders.

"At least now I know. I can wrap up this project, get back to Bentley & Bentley, and then decide what I want to do. No rush decisions. No man influencing where I will go."

Tilly looked down at her hands. Her voice was clipped. "That sounds very sensible."

"What do you mean by that?" India was feeling defensive.

"Oh, I don't know. Can I just say think about my dad's suggestion? He usually knows what's a good business idea AND PLEASE think very carefully before you move back with your parents?" Tilly was frustrated, she still wanted to see India with Charlie and running her own business up in Leeds. Was she being selfish? Did she just want time with the two of them together and India there to help with their business? Shaking her head, she went on.

"Now dinner? Apparently, you promised Nick 'proper fish and chips.'"

"Would you all hate me if I said I wanted to stay here and work on these interviews?"

"Would we hate you? NO. Would we believe you? NO. Charlie won't mind if you join us."

"It's too soon Tilly. I hope Charlie and I can find that friendship again but not right now. My wounds are too sore."

"I understand. You know my people were against me getting together with Joe. Even Joe wasn't sure. But now? Well, I can't imagine not being with him every day."

Tilly left India with a hug. The conversation with Tilly made sense. This job with them would be over, and she could move on. She wouldn't be seeing Charlie or being teased by his friends. Things at Bentley & Bentley should go back to normal. Yet she still felt in turmoil.

Her new phone buzzed on her desk.

JOSH: Watch out. Heard Jayne talking to Malcolm it sounds like tonight was important.

India: Do you know what?

JOSH: No sorry. Be careful.

India: OK

Chapter 40

Once Tilly had left, India looked back at her laptop. Staring at the screen for what seemed like hours, it was, in fact, twenty minutes. This wasn't working. She was free to make her own plan. Charlie was a guy, and how was she supposed to understand what he was thinking. She could talk to Robbie but that would mean having to admit what had happened between them, and he would be mad at her. He had warned her, hadn't he? Actually, everyone had, including her boss and her brother. If she called Katie, India knew she would say be happy for the time you had with him, now move on.

She abandoned her laptop and took a bath. Her body began to relax in the warm bubbles, and she looked back at those snatched moments with Charlie. How he had cared for her when she hurt her ankle and the way he had stood up to Michael Coombes. The way her body felt when he held her. The way his kisses made her tingle. She even recalled that first New Year leaning into each other on the floor. That instant connection. It came back so easily when he came down to London. When she was in his arms, she felt like he would defend her from all the world but who would save her heart from him.

In an attempt to forget Charlie, she tried to go through the situation with her job. Her position was at risk because Bentley & Bentley were not moving with the times. Would they ever see what she had been trying to tell them about print media and online presence? Did she want to stay in London?

Out of the bath, she wrapped herself in a towel and sprawled out on the bed, totally despondent. India tried to motivate herself to sit up and apply some body lotion, which usually helped her mood. She laid there arguing in her head, to get on with her life, to look after herself, to be the independent woman she always wanted to be. Her body didn't respond. Staring at the ceiling she laid spread-eagled on top of the bed covers. Taking a deep breath, she sat upright when her phone started to ring. The caller display told her it was Robbie. Hell, what did he want?

She hesitated, but the phone kept ringing, so she answered it.

"Is he with you, he isn't answering his phone?"

"Who? Charlie?"

"Yes! of course, Charlie!"

"No, he isn't here. I haven't seen him since I left him at the ground with the client."

"So, you don't know?"

"Know what Robbie?"

"His Mum died today. I wondered how he was taking it. I'm guessing not well. Will you go check on him?"

"Robbie, this is awkward."

"Bloody Hell, India, this isn't a time to be messing about. The guy has lost his only family. All this extra work has been to take care of her. I'm not sure how he'll react. I'm guessing he is looking at the bottom of a glass. He doesn't handle emotions well."

"He was with the client. I can ring them and check he is OK."

"India, Charlie is my best mate. I have been dreading this day. Please find him."

"OK, Robbie, I won't let you or him down. I'll make sure he has someone with him, a teammate or something."

"Call me when you find him."

"OK."

India ended the call and looked at her phone to work out who to ring first. She started with Tilly.

"Hello India, did you change your mind?"

"No, I'm trying to find Charlie. I just found out his mum died today."

"Well, that makes sense then. He got a phone call as we were leaving and cried off. I was under the impression he was staying in the hotel."

"If you see him, stay with him until I can get someone to be with him. I'm going to try Zach next."

"Let us know if you find him."

India's heart was thumping. It sounded like Charlie had got the news about his mum, but how would he react, would he be drinking as Robbie believed?

"Hi, Zach."

"Hey beautiful girl, what can I do for you?"

"Have you seen Charlie? Is he with you?"

No, I'm out with the rest of the team. I presumed he was with you. You guys had a lot to talk about after you locked him out of his room last night."

"I did what?"

"He couldn't get back in his room last night. You must have been dead to the world. He slept in my room."

Fudge! No, fudge with nuts!

"No, I have no idea where he is, and I just heard his mum died today. He shouldn't be alone."

"You're right. I'll head back and see if I can get the rest to check out some of the other bars in case he's out in the town somewhere. Stay in touch, beautiful girl. Don't worry, he will be alright."

India hurriedly pulled on jeans and a jumper. What Zach had said about Charlie sleeping in his room didn't make sense. It made her more nervous. She needed to find him quickly. Grabbing a pair of slip-on shoes, she shoved her door key and her phone into her purse. Taking the lift up one floor to try Charlie's room before she checked out the hotel bars.

As the doors opened, she saw a man with a camera around his neck was leaning on the wall and talking on the phone. The man gave her the creeps, and she was wondering why he was waiting by the lift with his camera. She ducked into an alcove and pulled herself against the wall to listen to what he was saying.

"Malcolm, I have this covered. I couldn't get any photos of him in the bar, but Chelsea is bringing him up here. She already has his door key so if all else fails I can get photos of her leaving his room."

The man listened for a while, then said more. "You haven't paid me for this morning's photos yet. You want sleazy, and I'm giving you sleazy. It won't get any sleazier than these tonight. Chelsea has the girls on display. She looks a right tart."

"Hang on, I can't hear you, son, let me try to get a better signal." He wandered down the hall shouting, "Can you hear me?" over and over.

India peered around the corner, all she could see was the creep with the camera walking away. Then everything happened at once. Nick came up the stairs and was surprised to find India lurking near his room. His eyebrows shot up and he was lost for words. He began to open his door and started to invite India in as the lift door pinged and out tumbled Charlie. He was partially held up by a short woman with bleach blonde hair that India guessed instantly was Chelsea. As the two lurched out of the lift, Chelsea was struggling to keep Charlie moving.

"Quick Nick! help me." Shouted India as she grabbed Charlie.

"Here! He's wiv me."

"Not any more Chelsea, now sod off back where you came from."

The commotion fetched the photographer back. He lifted his camera, but India had not let go of all the anger she had been carrying around all day. She shoved Charlie at Nick, lifting her arm to knock away the camera and grabbing the room key from Chelsea's hand. Nick took

Charlie into his room and came out to help India, it was all over in an instant. The other two ran off down the fire escape.

"I recognise that guy. I can't remember his name though it will come to me. He got into trouble over something to do with using underage girls on shoots. Let's get Charlie sorted, he looks out of it."

Back in Nick's room, Charlie was laid out on the bed. His eyes were closed, and India's heart stopped. He looked so peaceful and yet she knew his heart would be in pieces over his Mum's death. Had he drunk himself into this state or had Chelsea added something to his drink? Nick and India debated what to do. She wanted him checked out by a doctor, but Nick warned it could damage his career. In the end, she called Zach.

"I have found him."

"Well done, beautiful girl. Ya don't sound pleased?" India explained what had happened and asked for his advice on what to do. Zach said he would bring Garry, who was better with these things. He would tell Ben they had found Charlie, and nothing more for now. India told him what room they were in, and he promised to come quickly.

Nick and India worked together to get Charlie's jacket off and his shoes, rolling him into the recovery position in case he threw up. Charlie started to mutter. "I'm sorry." A simple phrase that he kept repeating. Every time he said it, Nick looked sympathetically at India. Eventually, India sat on the edge of the bed and held Charlie's hand. That seemed to calm him down and Nick took to his phone to check out what to do if you had taken Rohypnol. India watched Charlie's face, it changed from restful and looking asleep to frowning, his eyebrows pulled together, and he looked uncomfortable.

"Nick, he is going to vomit." Nick passed her the waste bin and together they got Charlie closer to the edge of the bed. Nick went to get towels as Charlie started to throw up. Her stomach was in knots, but India was quick with the bin. By the time Nick was back with towels and water, he was opening his eyes a little.

Nick spoke to him. "Charlie, that's it son, get it out of your system, it is hopefully still in your stomach so try to be sick." Charlie carried on vomiting, drinking more water, and vomiting. He was still doing that when Zach and Garry arrived.

"That's right, let him get it all up." Zach took over from India, as Nick and her filled the newcomers in with what they thought might have happened. Charlie was starting to appear more awake.

"Relax Mate, you're with friends now." Zach moved over to Charlie and patted his arm. Charlie closed his eyes and was soon asleep again.

"Do we move him? Or keep him here?" India was lost. "Does he need a doctor?"

Garry took a deep breath. "It isn't simple. We might need a doctor, but if we dodge it, he will be grateful. The press would have a field day. It is the same with moving him. If we are seen, or if a doctor is called to his room, then it is bound to turn up in the papers. At this stage in the season when he needs to resign a contract let's hope we can avoid it."

India bent over Charlie. "How are you feeling, do we need to get a doctor?" Charlie's eyes flew open. "No Doctor. I just need you, India. I love you." India closed her eyes.

"So, we watch him here in Nick's bed. Nick can sleep in my room if he needs a break. I presume water will help to flush his system. Anything else we can give him once he finishes throwing up?"

"We need to know what they have given him. If we find that photographer maybe we could persuade him to tell us."

"If I could recall his name, it might be easier... Hang on, my mate Paul had some issues with him, he will remember." Nick pulled out his phone. A quick chat with his friend produced a name and a number. The three guys left to go see if they could find him leaving India to cope with Charlie for a while.

She filled a couple of glasses with water and sat next to him, eventually climbing on the other side of the bed, and stroking his back. India wanted him to be aware she was there. That simple contact with him brought her straight back to go over what had unfolded that week. Charlie had said he loved her. Could she believe that? She knew he was hurting. The death of his mother when he was still down in Yorkshire would have been painful. Had he even started to come to terms with the fact this was the end for her.

Keeping the contact, she pulled out her phone to tell Robbie she had Charlie, and maybe Emma had some advice on what to do.

"Have you found him?" Robbie was quick to ask before she spoke. India took the time to explain carefully what had happened and asked for advice. Emma spoke to her and asked questions. From what they could work out, Emma said it was more likely alcohol than drugs. Whilst they were talking, Charlie rolled over and snuggled up to India. "I'm sorry. Please don't leave me. I love you." His voice was rough, and his words slow.

"Well, I heard that. I'm still thinking we are dealing with alcohol. Should I tell your cousin what he said?"

"We don't need to worry him any more than he is. Besides, it's complicated."

"Love is always complicated India. Don't let that stop you from being together if that is what you want."

"Tonight is not for that discussion. It sounds like the others are back. I will ring in the morning."

"India can I just say… If you think he needs a doctor call one."

The three boys came bundling into the room laughing. "You can relax, beautiful girl. They have been adding vodka to his beer. His body will handle that. But you should have seen that guy's face when he was surrounded by three big guys. I think he will need to change his undercrackers."

"I still think someone should stay with him," India said quietly.

"Sure. Mate, he is going to have a bad headache in the morning."

It was Zach's turn to take charge. "Gazza and I can watch him. You guys get some sleep. But we need to decide who we tell about this?"

"What do you mean?"

"Well, I think it better the team doesn't know. Ben is a great mate, but as captain, he'll be torn and feel he should tell the boss. Dan is daft enough to tell the wrong people by mistake."

"I told my cousin Robbie. He was worried he couldn't get hold of Charlie which is why I was looking for him. I'll let him know not to tell anyone else."

"So other than that, we keep it between us in this room." Zach's face was stern and his voice solemn.

"India, it was that slime ball Malcolm. He was the one who had set this up," grumbled Nick.

"What? I heard him talking to someone called Malcolm. Are you certain?" India's raised voice stirred Charlie. Everyone froze, and he rolled over again.

"Yes, I'm positive, and that business last night too." Nick looked away. He knew how this would hurt India.

"It actually makes sense after what Josh overheard today. Damn. Do we tell Tilly and Joe?" India felt so rattled by this news, her brain was buzzing, so much to take in, even without hearing Charlie say, "I love you."

"Why don't we let Charlie decide that tomorrow." Zach again seemed to be in charge and India in her confused state was happy to have him do that. "Well, we don't need four of us sitting up with him."

"I want to stay," said India, settling down on the other side of the bed again. "Here is my room key Nick, if you want to go get some sleep."

Nick hadn't unpacked, so he picked up his bags and left to use India's room. Zach and Garry decided to split the night between them to support India by looking after their teammate. Garry left for his room after they promised to call if he was needed. Zach settled down in the chair, watching over the ones on the bed. India reached out to touch Charlie again. As soon as she touched his arm, she relaxed, and her breathing returned to normal. It felt so right being here with him. She had no idea what that meant, but she was better knowing he was going to be OK and that she was there with him. Tomorrow she could worry about everything she had heard that night.

"He needs that contact. He's had a rough couple of days. He only wants you to be safe, you know. He hates that you were hurt."

"So why Zach? If he doesn't want to hurt me, why do it?"

"I'm sure he has a reason that makes sense to him, beautiful girl."

"I have no idea what to do now Zach."

"I get that."

"What about you Zach? What are you going to do?"

"I'm flying home earlier than expected and getting to work on a recovery plan."

"Will Garry go with you?"

"I think so."

"Will you be back?"

"I hope to be. Next week I'll park my gear in my old room at Charlie's. He is a great landlord. Why don't you take one of the other rooms?"

"That isn't a brilliant idea. But I like Leeds, I might move there."

"Really? That would be brill."

Charlie started to stir again, and his arm moved around India's waist. She stroked his biceps and followed the movement of his chest, lifting and falling. His steady breathing relaxed India and as the room fell quiet, India too fell asleep. Zach stayed awake and watched the two together until Garry came to relieve him.

When India opened her eyes, the sun was rising slowly over the sea outside of Nick's room. It took her a few moments to remember where she was and why. Across the room, Garry grinned at her. It didn't take her long to decide she preferred not to be there when Charlie woke up. She made her excuses and asked Garry to phone her if she was needed. She left as quietly as possible and went back to her own room on the floor below, where Nick was sleeping. She still had no idea what to do about everything that was falling apart in her life.

Chapter 41

Nick and India sipped weak coffee they made in India's room.

"Well, I wasn't expecting this much excitement when I set off north for the Yorkshire coast."

"What time is your train back?"

"My ticket is flexible; the trains leave at half past the hour. I'm aiming for 9:30 but I can go later if you want to get some breakfast."

"You need to check out."

"All my stuff is here."

"You better make sure Charlie and the gang have left your room."

"India Barrington Jones is that you wanting me to go check on him?"

"That's me trying to be practical."

With that, there was a knock on her door. It was Zach with Nick's key. India invited him in, her stomach was once again in knots. Zach seemed tired, but he was showered and ready for the day ahead.

"How is he?"

"Not brilliant, we moved him to his room and ordered breakfast for there. He needs to be looking OK for tonight's dinner, he has people to meet. Tomorrow morning, he will drive up to Scotland to sort out things up there. They will give him leave for that. He wanted me to thank you both, for all you did last night."

"Tell him that's OK and ask him to get in touch with Robbie. He will be worried, and he'll want to help with the arrangements for his mum."

"Does that mean you won't be talking to him yourself India?" India's eyes fell to the floor, she wasn't used to the Australian being so stern.

287

"We both have a lot to work through," India paused, "it doesn't mean I'll never speak to him again." She stared up straight into Zach's face. "I just think we both need the space. Bentley & Bentley may well have been responsible for what was happening to him. Tell him I'm sorry about that. I'll do what I can to sort that out."

"Will you be at the dance tonight?"

India produced a weak smile. "Yes, I'll be there."

"I like you India. Charlie is a great bloke, and he needs to hear this for himself. You both need to talk to each other." Zach nodded at Nick and left the room.

As the door closed, Nick cleared his throat. "Right, shower and then let's get some breakfast. I'll pick you up back here in thirty minutes." And he, too, left the room. India sat in the chair at her desk, staring off into the distance. Glad that Nick had suggested breakfast.

Turning on the shower, she sent a text to Robbie.

India: He is back in his room You can call him.

Robbie: Thanks India Stay in touch

India: Let me know about the funeral.

She decided to save calling Tilly until later. Standing under the rain head she tried to imagine the water washing away her problems. *Would Philip believe me about Malcolm? And even if he did, what would he do about it? If Malcolm left, there would still be Jayne. Would Philip blame me for the Cooksons not signing another contract? Was it my fault for being so honest with them? Was Maxwell Sykes right about setting up in Leeds, or was he just looking to support Tilly from a distance? Could I do that? What would Dad think?*

India checked her thinking and climbed out of the shower. Although she wasn't looking forward to the conversation. she couldn't put it off any longer, she rang Tilly.

"Is Charlie OK?"

"Yeah. Zach and Garry are looking after him."

"I'm out for a walk with Joe making the most of this sea air." She laughed, "It's almost blowing my wig off. Bracing that's what they call it isn't it?"

"Yes. I'm going to eat breakfast with Nick and then when he has caught his train I'll be back in my room finishing off those pieces we looked at last night. Can we go through them later?"

"Sure, what time?"

"About 12 ish?"

"That works for me".

India made a note on her pad about seeing Tilly at twelve o'clock. She dressed carefully before drying her hair. By the time Nick knocked on her door, she was ready to face the world. They walked quietly to the café on the corner. It was a traditional seaside café, with no frills but an amazing smell of cooking bacon. They chose a booth by the window, sitting opposite each other, their long legs tangling together under the table. Ordering a full English breakfast, Nick followed India's lead and ordered a pot of tea to go with it.

Nick couldn't believe the plate of food that quickly appeared in front of him. He looked up at India with a puzzled expression.

India laughed, "You are in Yorkshire now. Wait until you taste it."

Nick started with the bacon and then tried the sausages. The faces he pulled and the soft moans he was making left India in no doubt that he was enjoying every mouthful. Smiling, she tucked into her own breakfast. As she paused to pour more tea. Nick decided it was time for them to pick through what India did next.

"Are you going to tell Bentley & Bentley to fuck off and come live with me?" He looked straight into her eyes, his face set. India dropped her spoon into her saucer and stared back at him. Nick's mouth broke into a grin at the shock he had created. "You could be my assistant and my lover too."

"Why are you saying that?"

"I want to get you thinking. Let you see there are options."

"Nick!"

"OK let's start with your job. All this rubbish they have put you through. What is stopping you leaving now this project is over?"

"My parents. They see me as a flaky little girl who walks out of a job if it gets a little hard. I need to prove to them I'm serious."

"What about your love life?"

"If you had asked me out 6 months ago, I would have agreed in a heartbeat, you are a great guy."

"But now?"

"Charlie Robertson stole my heart when I was seventeen. Everything that has happened in the last six months has shown how it's important to me that we are friends above anything else. I did start to think, to hope I guess, that we could be more, a lot more. I thought what we had was special. But now I think I had a narrow escape."

"Are you going to this dinner tonight?"

"Yes." It wasn't like India to give one-word answers, so Nick pushed more.

"Why?"

"It's the professional thing to do." Nick watched and waited for India to add more.

"It is a chance to make connections. Tilly and Joe will be there." India told Nick about the conversation with Maxwell Sykes.

"So, you would leave London?"

"It's an option." India popped more bacon into her mouth and watch Nick's face for clues. He wasn't giving anything away today.

"And these parents you are trying so hard to get approval from, what would they think of you moving, would they approve of Charlie?"

India laughed and shook her head. "No."

"Is that why you are not going forward with Charlie?" India offered him a weak smile and told him about Robbie's mum and how she had been cut out of the family. Smiling a little wider, she told Nick about talking to Patricia on the trip to Hawick.

"I think my Grandad is beginning to regret what they did, and I like to think that I'll make my own mind up about Charlie. The last couple of days though, well they make me grateful that my parents don't know about us."

They fell silent again as they finished their breakfast. India was pleased Nick had made her reassess. As they ate she realised that working for herself was something she would love to do, but was she ready? Nervously, she looked across at her companion.

"Nick, can I ask you what's your opinion of Maxwell's idea?" Nick stopped eating and looked at her, focusing all his attention on his answer.

"Working for yourself is simply that, FOR YOURSELF. You can't do it because someone else thinks it's a good idea. There will be challenging work at the beginning and probably right through. You can ask questions about the specifics, but this would have to be something you do for you." They fell silent again.

"Look, I have my train to catch. If you want to talk, if you need a job, well you know where I am. Whatever happens, you have a great future ahead of you. If I can help, I will." They clung to each other as they hugged goodbye, and Nick gave her an extra squeeze. "See you next week. Come to the studio."

Back at the hotel, India had the rest of the day to get ready for the dance and complete all the paperwork for the project with the Cooksons.

She decided to try Josh to see if he could help with the things that Malcolm might have done.

Little Girl: Can you talk?

Her phone buzzed in response.

"Hey, Little Girl. How is Yorkshire?" Josh's voice echoed through the phone, and she realised he was driving and talking hands-free.

"Yorkshire is great, the sun is shining, and the food tastes amazing. Listen, did you hear any more?"

"Sorry, nothing specific Jayne and Malcolm both look like they are up to something. They are having whispered phone calls, and both look so smug. Has anything else happened since Nick's email?"

"Yeah, some photographer has been staging photos of Charlie. Last night they put so much vodka in his beer he couldn't stand. Luckily, I had been looking for him and managed to get him away from them. We think that was Malcolm."

"Will that cause more problems for the guy?"

"No one needs that, but Josh, his mum died yesterday, he was a mess anyway."

"I am sorry. He seemed a nice guy. When are you back?"

"Monday. Look I want to talk to Philip Bentley on Monday about all this, so if you discover anything you think will help, let me know."

"OK. I think Philip is away on Monday though. I drove him to the airport on Tuesday and I pick him up Monday at 8 pm."

"Well, that explains a few things. The last email mess happened when he was away." Whilst she was talking to Josh she had looked up flats to rent in Leeds. *Am I actually considering this?*

"OK, I'll see you when I get back. Thanks for the heads up about Monday morning."

She went back to her notebook and was ticking off tasks when Tilly and Joe arrived. India was starting to flag. She had slept beside Charlie last night, she had been worried about him. It had been a restless sleep, she kept waking up to check he was still breathing. Tilly was worried about her, even Joe was worried. They felt some responsibility for all this. India saw the questions in her eyes.

"Tilly, please don't ask me too many questions. It is quite possible I shouldn't answer them, or can't answer them, or most probably don't want to answer them!" Tilly's mouth opened and closed. Joe spoke.

"I think I'm going to take two beautiful women to lunch. Where do you want to go?" Tilly looked at her friend, "let's try the hotel terrace, the weather is nice, but I don't want to go far."

India packed her notebooks and her phone quietly as Tilly smiled encouragingly at her. Then Tilly spotted India's screen and the list of flats to rent in Leeds. She hugged India.

"You are going to move to Leeds!" It was a statement, not a question.

India shook her head. "I don't know, I guess I'm checking my options."

"But you are thinking about what my dad said. He usually has some clever ideas."

"I have a lot of thinking to do, please Tilly, let it go. I need to decide this myself."

Tilly's eyebrows drew together. "Have you been talking to Charlie?"

"Nooo? Why would you ask that?"

"No idea." Tilly was not very convincing, but India was tired and confused enough.

The three had a lovely lunch on the hotel terrace overlooking the beach. They went through all India's interview questions and when she had everything she needed she headed to her room, leaving the Cooksons to drive up the coast to meet Max and see the house he was thinking of buying.

India put her bag down on the chair and kicked off her shoes. Without meaning to she laid back on the bed and drifted off to sleep. In her dreams, she was lying in a wonderfully lush garden enjoying the sun whilst Charlie was rubbing oil into her shoulders then he was playing with two sweet children, a boy, and a girl, neither very old. India had no idea about children's ages. She hadn't thought about children. In her ear she could hear Charlie's voice from last night, rough and whispering, 'I just want you. I love you'.

A text came in and buzzed her phone, waking she reached for the phone to see the message.

CWR: Can we talk?

India: Is that a good idea?

CWR: Probably not.

Before she could respond again, her phone rang. It was her father.

"Can we talk?" India was a little taken aback. Not only had her father rung her during a workday, but he had also used the same words as Charlie. It took her a few seconds to respond.

"India, are you there, are you alone?"

"Yes Dad, I'm here, and I'm alone. What do you want to talk about?"

"I just had Max Sykes call me about you, India. What is happening?"

"What did he say?"

"That he was with his daughter and that they were all worried about you. He seemed to think it was time for us to talk. What is going on? Do you need help?"

"I have some thinking to do, Dad. This is something I need to work out for myself."

As she finished the call, she looked back at the texts from Charlie.

India: I'll be at the dance tonight. See you there?

CWR: OK

What could they say to each other? She was sad about his mother, but she couldn't begin to understand how he felt. She wasn't as close to her parents, and she had never lost anyone she was close to. What could she do to help without making things more difficult between them?

Chapter 42

India pulled out the dress Deanna had given her. Then she pulled up the photos on Instagram. She wanted to look again at how they did her hair and her makeup, especially her eyes. She couldn't hope to reproduce it, but she wanted to look her best tonight. This would be her goodbye to Tilly and Joe and the Yorkshire team. More importantly, it could be the last time she saw Charlie. Her pride wanted him to remember her looking her best.

Taking extra care over her makeup, she was pleasantly surprised by how close she looked to the photo Nick had taken. Stepping into her silver kitten heels and checking her small bag, she locked her room.

Reluctantly, she made her way towards the Palm Court Ballroom, walking slowly up the wide sweeping staircase. Each step seemed to amplify the butterflies turning somersaults in her stomach. Being dressed up always raised her excitement but she hated goodbyes. Not knowing what was coming next for her made this doubly difficult. As she walked through the grand entrance to the room her fear melted away as her eyes fell on Zach and Garry talking to Joe and Tilly. Tilly wore a scarlet dress that hugged her curves, and she was wearing the emeralds Joe liked to buy her. The men all looked so comfortable in the dinner suits she wondered how they could go so easily from the sportswear she usually saw them into looking so formal. Being tall and well-built must help with the look.

"Look whose here Mate, it is that stunning model old Romeo has on his screen saver." Garry was smiling so hard his blue eyes almost disappeared, but Zach sticking his elbow in his ribs changed that and made Zach wince too. "Go get the lady a drink before you say something else."

Garry passed her a glass from the trays that were circulating. "Is this OK?"

"Sure." India didn't want to make this any more awkward for them all. The five stood and made small talk looking out over the lights that lit the seafront towards the spa further down the coast. The conversations were all safe, but India was nervous when they were called to the tables. On the plan, she was sat between Joe and Charlie, but as she found her seat she was sat between Daniel Woods and Joe Cookson. Charlie was further round the table. One of the umpires arrived at the table and moved Charlie's name even further round so he could sit next to Tilly.

Charlie came to the table carrying a glass of water, hardly surprising after last night. India couldn't help smiling at him wearing his kilt and evening jacket. It was what he was wearing the night she first met him and seeing him in his kilt would always take her back to that night. Charlie looked shocked to see he had been moved again and he now found himself sat straight across from India. They looked at each other for split seconds, they smiled automatically and then checked themselves to look to the person on their left. Dan put his arm across the back of her chair and leaned down to talk in her ear. "Let me pour you some wine." And so, it began. Dan was flirty and attentive, and Joe Cookson kept asking if she was OK. Occasionally she would catch a glimpse of Charlie across the table, sometimes they swapped a small smile. More often if Dan were leaning in or being flirty Charlie would frown. After the main course, Joe Cookson excused himself to go to the bar, Daniel Woods stood up to go to the toilet before he left, he kissed India on the top of the head. "I will be right back." India was now sat alone, and she lifted her head slowly to look at Charlie, he was talking to a player from Worcestershire, and they seemed engrossed in whatever they were discussing. It allowed India to study him more carefully. His dirty blonde hair had lightened across the summer matches and was now looking sun-kissed across the front of his face. The curls framed that face. From the side, she couldn't appreciate his chocolate brown eyes, but she knew they were there and when he finally turned to look back at her she fell headfirst into them. He looked towards her and winked just the briefest of winks and she looked around to see if anyone else had noticed. At that point, Daniel Woods slipped back into his seat and kissed her cheek. Charlie looked away and the moment was gone.

After the meal was cleared away, they brought out jugs of coffee and India heard Charlie ask for tea at the same time as she said it. They looked at each other again. It was India who looked away first this time. Charlie excused himself and went to stand at the bar. India was relieved she didn't have to look at him anymore, or so she thought, because now although he was stood almost out of her line of sight. He was standing at one end of the bar and was just in her peripheral vision. Unable to stop herself, she repeatedly found reasons to turn her head to check he was still there, and he was drinking slowly. Each time she looked she caught him looking at her and each time he turned away.

Joe Cookson touched her arm "He will be OK. He has a lot to get his head around, the last thing he would want is for you to be concerned."

"I just want to hold him and make it stop for him."

"Tonight, with all these eyes on him that wouldn't be wise for either of you."

"I know you are right Joe. That doesn't stop the pull in my chest."

"Give it time India, give it time."

Daniel Woods reached over and took her hand, "Come dance with me." She loved to dance and maybe this would help her relax. Dan obviously loved to dance too, he was singing along to every song and giving the dance everything he had. He was obviously more coordinated than his body shape suggested. India tried to relax and enjoy the music, but it wasn't really happening. She was still hyperaware of Charlie who was currently talking with two older dinner suited gentlemen she didn't recognise. She must have been distracted because she didn't see Zach approach across the dance floor.

"I need a dance with this angel before I go back to the other side of the world." Dan bowed out kissing India's hand as he left. "You can borrow her if you promise to keep her safe."

"I promise." Zach held her right hand in his and slipped his heavily bandaged right hand around her waist. India had no idea what was coming, her eyes searched Zach's serious face.

"It has been wonderful getting to know you and before I go, I wanted to make sure you don't do anything silly." India frowned. "Everything I said about the way that guy feels about you is true."

"How can he still feel like that."

"I was there last night when you sat beside him, it is clear that although you feel hurt you still care deeply for him." India looked away. "And I was there the night before, I saw the way he was suckered into that photo. At the time he said it might take the heat out of people thinking he was with you. He didn't want to do it because of his mum, but they taunted him asking if it was true, he was off the market, he laughed it off to protect you. Then when he couldn't wake you in his room, well he would have slept anywhere not to disturb you or for you to be seen. I'm sorry. He'll be mad I told you. He thinks it's better for you if you walk away from him."

"Fudge!"

She felt the heat of his hand on her back before he touched her, and she closed her eyes as the opening bars of Stevie Wonder stirred her body's memory. India could have used some time to process what Zach had just told her before she had to speak to Charlie again.

"I tried to stay away." He whispered.

"I know."

"I couldn't do it." His mouth next to her ear.

"I know."

"I'm sorry." His head dipped.

"So am I." She couldn't look at him.

Charlie pulled her into his body, as always, India melted not just her body into his, this time, the heart she had tried so hard to protect, melted too. Charlie let his forehead drop to India's as they slowly moved to the song that had been stuck in her head for 6 years.

"I'm sorry about your mum."

"It was on the cards though."

"I'm still sorry you are going through this now and I'm really sorry about all these problems with photos in the papers."

"So, it was you getting your own back, putting vodka in my drink."

"I hope you know that isn't true."

Charlie lifted his forehead from hers a sparkle in his eyes as a small smile lifted the corner of his mouth. "Yeah, I know you wouldn't do that, but you have to admit it was life coming full circle. Who did you tell about that night?"

"Well, my brother and Robbie knew, other than that, just one friend, Katie."

"So, you didn't think the vodka was significant?"

"NO! I seriously hope you don't think I would do that to you... why would I rescue you?"

"I hear you were the one who dealt with me being sick."

"Yeah."

"I also heard I was saying things."

"Yeah."

"India?"

"Yeah?"

"Can we get out of here?"

"Yeah."

India collected her things from the table and Tilly grabbed her arm. "Are you OK?"

"Yes, well I will be, we needed to talk, we have spent too many years avoiding these awkward moments that has to stop." They walked out together down that spectacular staircase.

"If we go outside, will you be warm enough?"

"Yeah," India checked herself for the one-word answers, it was all she had right now. They walked side by side towards the beach, they hadn't spoken, they hadn't touched but the atmosphere between them was electric. Charlie kept looking down at the floor, then looking sideways at her, India was staring straight ahead, she could see him looking at her, not knowing how to respond, she forced herself to look forward at all the lights. As they reached the steps to the beach Charlie let out a long breath and broke the silence.

"Can we walk along the beach?" When India nodded her reply he carried on. "I would like you to hear me out India, please let me say what I have to say, don't stop me, let me get it out."

"OK" she certainly wasn't saying much tonight, perhaps she didn't know what to say, she was still so confused. India slipped off her shoes and he reached out and took her shoes in one hand, the other took her hand rubbing her knuckles. He smiled then started them walking along the beach.

"That night I met you, I felt that connection. When you were sick, when I discovered how old you were! I was lost. I didn't know what to do or say. Each New Year it was painful to be in the same room as you, but I just couldn't stay away. Each year I was drawn back." India looked down, she understood that feeling. "Each year I thought you were a year older, and I still didn't think I could talk to you. I've missed that friend I found that first time."

"When I needed an extra job and Robbie said you were going to be in touch. It felt like you were my angel come to save me. I was so excited and so afraid too. I worried about how we would get over that first meeting. I thought we needed to talk but India, it was like everything that was wrong just rolled away, and we never did speak about it."

"Because we didn't need to Charlie, that connection was still there."

"Was?" India looked away she didn't know the answer. Charlie continued, wondering if he was too late.

"Spending time with you these last few months has been so challenging. When we are together it feels so right to touch you, to hold

301

you. But when I see what it will do to your life, well I don't want to be the reason you lose a job or worse, your family. India I can't do that to you. The night I met you I know you were fighting your mum's image of what your life should be, and I think you are still fighting that same battle, which is why you were at that dance with that awful man. You're still young, you still have time India, go work out who you want to be. Find where you want to be."

"Charlie I …" India didn't have words to give him back, she was trying to sort everything out in her head, and it just wasn't working.

"There is no need to answer me, India. I just want you to know that I never want to hurt you again, maybe down the line you will knock on my door like you did that day."

They walked on down the beach. India tried again "Charlie... I …"

"Hush" and as if to stop her talking he bent his head and kissed her, it was a slow patient kiss. India needed more and when she kissed him back it was more urgent.

"Charlie, I can't do this, I can't say goodbye to you."

"Tomorrow you will be in London, and I'll be in Hawick. I wish I could be with you down there, but you know I can't and a part of me wishes I had you by my side through the funeral, but I know that can't be either. We both must be strong, and I'm hoping when I don't have to watch you dance with another man this pain won't be so hard. I have five matches left this season, I need to focus and so do you."

It was India's turn to kiss him; she didn't want to hear more about how they couldn't be together. This kiss went deeper as their tongue shared that familiar dance. "We have tonight, Charlie, please say we have tonight."

"I don't know India; will that make it harder?"

"I don't know either."

They walked back to the hotel; Charlie's arm slung around her shoulders. They didn't speak, as they clung to those last moments. He squeezed her shoulder and hugged her body into his. At her door, he gently kissed her forehead, taking in her scent for the last time before he turned and walked back to his room.

India undressed in slow motion, packing for the morning as she went along. Eventually, she climbed reluctantly into bed. Turning out the lights she watched the rain hit the window and make magical patterns with the twinkling lights of the street below. Her heart felt heavy, yet the rest of her body was just numb. The last few days and nights had left her exhausted, still, she couldn't sleep. She lay waiting. She had no idea what she was waiting for until there was a soft knock on her door.

Slowly opening the door, she found Charlie in sweatpants and a t-shirt. Leaning on her door frame and looking down he spoke softly.

"It's not tomorrow yet." He lifted his eyes until they reached her, looking for a response. India walked away from the door leaving it open for him to follow her and climbed back into bed. Entranced by the lights she turned her back on him. Charlie moved up behind to spoon her, laying his arm possessively across her waist. India took his hand in hers and their fingers interlocked.

Charlie silently pressed his lips against her shoulder. There was nothing left to say but she could have tonight safe in his arms. Wrapped in his body, his scent, his breath on her neck. Safe.

India turned her head back for them to kiss. She could feel his arousal pressed against her back. The kiss became more urgent, and she lifted her leg to wrap over his legs, pulling him closer to her.

"India?"

"One last time, Charlie please."

"India…"

"Please?"

He could feel the pull to be with her way down at his root. He slowly and gently lifted her t-shirt and lowered his pants. His erection found her core. Slipping home to fill her. His hand massaged her breast, pebbling her nipple. Their bodies rocked together, finding a gentle pace and rhythm. He dropped his hand to her clit, circling it to pull out her orgasm. As her body clenched around him, he continued to rock gently maintaining a pace until she relaxed. He pushed into her over and over again, kissing her neck. His hands touched her searching for a response, remembering every inch of her. His strokes began to lengthen and quicken until with his release her body reacted as one. Contracting and tightening.

As their bodies relaxed. they stayed locked in each other's arms until sleep took them both. When India awoke, she was alone again, and part of her brain wondered if she had been dreaming. She reached across to his pillow caressing it and found his note and the shirt he had been wearing. It was the one she had slept in.

Darling

Don't be mad at me for being a coward. I hate goodbyes.

Let that last time be our goodbye. Be safe my friend.

You know where my door is if you need me.

Charlie.

Chapter 43

Pulling at the sleeves of her jumper as she looked in the mirror, India spent much more time than normal tidying her hair and reapplying her lip gloss. It was Monday morning, and she was prolonging the process; she wasn't keen to start in the open-plan office, knowing what Malcolm had done. She had work to do. Over the weekend, she pulled together the last of Joe and Tilly's interviews. She had also created a set of notes about what had gone wrong over the project; the press entrapment, emails cancelling Nick and not getting messages passed on from the client. She swallowed hard and pull down the sleeves again. A smile pasted on her face and, lifting her chin, she strode bravely into the room.

The fact that Philip was away had her worrying about how the others would behave. Sitting down at her desk, she found one of Jayne's lists. It was full, but she had been working in Yorkshire for the last week. Across the office, Alice nudged Malcolm, who smirked back. India looked down at the yellow paper to work out how she would be able to get around. She was pleased to see Deanna and Nick were on there. She would escape the building for most of the day doing these jobs. Although it was a lengthy list, she was determined to manage it. Jayne marched into the room.

"Good! You found my list. Here are a couple more things," she sneered, handing India a note with three more stops. Although India smiled, she was controlling a laugh. This was now ridiculous. She mentally added this to tomorrow's discussion with Philip Bentley.

"I better be on my way." As she was collecting her coat, she heard Malcolm answer his phone "I can't talk now, Clive. Yes, you will get your money."

Her phone buzzed with a text.

JOSH: I'm guessing you have a long list today

INDIA: Yes & for once I don't mind.

JOSH: Want a lift?

INDIA: Are you sure?

JOSH: Philip isn't back until tonight. It is Bentley & Bentley business.

INDIA: OK

JOSH: Be there in 5

INDIA: I'll get the coffees

It was nearly 10 minutes later when India slid into the passenger seat of the company Bentley. She shared the list with Josh.

"You better phone around and check if Old Iron Knickers has promised anyone an unrealistic time. Then we can hopefully juggle a few stops, but let's start with Deanna. By the time the car pulled up outside Deanna's studio, Josh and India had a plan for that day, including a break for lunch. Josh came in to help India carry the dresses. Deanna hugged India before she spoke. It felt like Deanna was trying to squash her back together.

"How are you?" India looked closely at her friend, wondering what she knew.

"I spoke to Nick yesterday. It's getting silly, isn't it?

"You should see today's list. I plan to talk to Philip tomorrow."

Deanna swapped looks with Josh. "Are you looking after her all day?"

"I am, but Jayne doesn't know that." sniped Josh.

"Then can you please take some extra things to Nick?"

"Of course."

Back in the car, Josh decided to ask India about her trip to Scarborough.

"What made you certain it was Malcolm that was arranging those photos?"

"Nick recognised the guy and got a number and name from another photographer. Two of the cricketers joined him to find the guy. We really needed to know if Charlie had been drugged or something. Poor Charlie was hardly coherent. It was Nick that discovered Malcolm had been paying him. Well, actually I don't think he has paid him yet."

"Why would he spend money doing that?"

"Why indeed."

"So, let's take today's list and do a first-class job. No need to give Old Iron Knickers any excuse." Josh tried to make the day fun. He was telling funny stories and playing upbeat music.

"Right next stop lunch."

"Great." but India's reply was without any enthusiasm and then she fell silent again.

Josh was about to have another attempt to cheer her up when Stevie Wonder came on the radio and a sob escaped India as tears fell down her face. Josh didn't know what to do. India was always so strong. He'd seen her tackle far worst jobs from Jayne. As he parked the car, he reached out and took India's hand.

"What can I do?"

"Nothing. It's all too much."

"India walk away. You don't need this."

"My mum would love that. She will believe anything Philip says."

"Let's get something to eat."

"I'll just stay here."

"How about I buy some sandwiches and we have a picnic in the park."

"Josh, you are wonderful."

"Go get some air. I'll meet you as soon as I've got some food." The park was quiet and eating there was a brilliant idea. Together they talked through what India was going to speak to Philip about.

"Philip is a good bloke. I'm sure he'll be shocked to hear what Malcolm has done."

"I hope you are right." Philip's response at the Roses match was nagging at her brain.

"I'm certain he will sort all that out."

"He can't turn all that back, though, can he? Tilly and Joe won't be back and Charlie..." The tears were back.

"What's the deal with that guy, he seems nice. You sound as if you like him." The tears continued to flow down her face as she listed all the problems.

"I'm in London – He is in Scotland, Leeds and a list of cricket grounds. My parents would disown me. Even my brother hates him... Unless I moved to Leeds and set up my own business."

"Really?"

"It is one of the many things bouncing around my brain."

"No wonder your head is exploding. Well, let's get this finished."

The afternoon sped by, and eventually, they were pulling up outside Nick's studio. Josh and India walked in with arms full of Deanna's dresses. As soon as India's hands were empty, Nick hugged her.

"How is my favourite roommate?"

"She's better than she has been," offered Josh. Nick held her tighter.

"Have you decided to take me up on my offer? Both my offers?" He grinned, wiggling his eyebrows. India giggled.

"Not yet, but tomorrow could be your lucky day."

"Good to know it isn't a firm NO yet."

"Let's get you back to the office before Iron Jayne becomes twitchy."

When India finally got home that evening, she collapsed on the sofa and kicked off her shoes as Stella bounced through her door.

"Grandad and grandma are coming down."

"When?"

"Tonight. They are due any minute, so dinner in their flat at seven. I'm cooking. How did your day go?"

"Don't ask! We don't have time."

"That bad?"

"Pretty normal list from Jayne, and Philip isn't back until tomorrow. So yes."

"Go take a bath and I'll text you. I'm aiming for seven o'clock."

"OK."

Stella adored making a home. Yes, she was great at interiors, she also loved cooking, too. The table was set with a yellow cloth and white daisy-like flowers sat in a vase in the centre. She had made the top-floor flat look much more together. She'd added family photographs and India spotted one she hadn't seen before. It was her grandmother with all her children. Patricia was sat on her knee. Before she had a chance to ask about it, Stella called them to the table. India tried to join the conversation, she was tired and kept drifting off, staring into space. She did love her family, especially her grandparents, but could she live up to their expectations? That photograph of Patricia, so plainly loved, and yet cut off for so long. It seemed so sad that she had to choose.

"We're here for a week, so dinner on Wednesday night. You girls pick." India offered a weak smile.

"India, are you working too hard? You look shattered." Her grandfather sounded cross.

"I had a tough first day back in the office after Scarborough."

"I am so proud of you." On hearing her grandfather's words, India couldn't hold the dam back any longer. Silent tears fell down her face.

"India, darling, what is wrong? I have never seen you cry." Her grandmother's voice was softer. India didn't speak she had cried so much over the last week she couldn't believe she had tears left. Their grandparents looked at Stella.

"It is not my story to tell. I'm going to take India down to her flat." Stella led India downstairs.

"India, they love you."

"They loved Patricia."

"So, is this about Charlie?"

India shrugged. "I can get a new job."

"Oh, India." Stella hugged her as she shed more silent tears. India knew one thing; she couldn't go on like this. She was not used to all this crying.

Chapter 44

The next morning, India was out of the shower and flicking through her wardrobe when there was a knock on her door.

"India it's me. Do you have time to talk?"

"Come in Gran, you can help me decide what to wear."

"Oh Goodie!" This was something that she loved doing with the girls. "So, what are we trying to do? Who do we need to impress? What do we want to say?" India smiled at the way she had said 'we' but what could she share.

"Oh, Gran."

"Just tell me what you can. Let's start with getting dressed for today. Why is it important?"

"I need to talk to my boss, and it isn't going to be an easy conversation."

"Then you need to be put together. Like 'Don't mess with me, my name is Barrington Jones'."

"Yes."

"You still want to look like a young creative, not a corporate clone."

"Yes." Her grandma really did understand. India was relieved to have her input.

"Why don't we take two suits and make one look?" She pulled out a red suit that had a boxy red jacket and a pencil skirt then a black linen trouser suit that had a safari-type jacket. What about these black trousers and the red jacket? Will you be able to keep your jacket on? Is it warm in your office?"

"At this time of year, it is hot."

"OK jacket off, we need a special blouse then, oh and pearls, nothing says Barrington Jones like pearls. I'll fetch some." India giggled then stopped. She loved her grandma. How could she give this up for Charlie?

As India took in her reflection, there was still a sadness hanging over her. But she looked good, and she realised that the first step to having the sort of future she could enjoy was sorting out her job. That alone was enough to make her ready to face the day.

Stepping into the office, the bravado was starting to wane. As she put down her bag, she tried not to see the smirks from the other side of the room when her phone buzzed.

STELLA: Message from Granddad. He and Gran are proud of you. Make today the day you are proud of yourself.

INDIA: Thanks, I think I needed that.

India stood a little taller as she knocked on Philip's door. When she walked in Jayne was just standing up and she was hovering by the door.

"Could I have a word?"

"Of course." Philip said, but Jayne was still lingering.

"Alone." Jayne's eyes narrowed, and her lip curled up as she slowly walked out.

"India, we need to talk about your first project. Tell me how you felt it went. Have the clients signed for your gift idea?"

"I loved having more input on the creative side. The challenge of fitting into the cricketing calendar, working to a tight budget."

"Evidently you are unhappy though, what is it. Wasn't it as easy as you thought it would be?"

"I didn't expect it to be easy, but I didn't expect to be sabotaged either."

"I think you had better explain!"

"Let's start with the emails, in my name, cancelling the photographer."

"Are we talking about that Leeds disaster again? India, you were so unprofessional that weekend I am surprised you are bringing it up again."

"Nick received an email cancelling him again for Scarborough. It was so late we would have been liable to pay him still and again it was at the shoot that the client was present for."

"You mean Nick wasn't there?"

"No Nick was there."

"No problem then."

"You emailed me to complain it was my fault when old photos turn up in the paper. Then someone else from this office had made sure he was in the papers even more."

"Well, the client was pleased with the results he saw in his sales."

"Is that why there were photos the next night? Is that why that photographer was waiting for him?" India watched Philip's reaction. She realised Philip already knew all about this.

"Yes, it is what the client wanted." India was floored by that sentence. She knew Tilly wouldn't agree to that, or would she? *Is that what she meant when she said it was her fault, that Charlie and I weren't speaking. Is that why she was so upset at how ill Charlie had been? She was the one that knew Charlie was in the hotel.* At her shocked silence, Philip continued.

"They are the client and the talent. They are not your friend. Time to grow up India."

313

India pulled herself upright in the chair. She was at a loss for what to say. Philip didn't have the same problem.

"If you check the accounts, you will see £1,000 for extra expenses. The client knew and paid for that service." A small tight smile escaped India, now she was certain that Philip was lying. She didn't speak. Philip had given her just what she needed. "India, you need to join the real world, and realise where your loyalties lie, or it is time to go home to mummy."

"Thank you." And she meant it. Now, in this moment, she had total clarity. The sleepless nights, the tears. In one sentence India realised that everyone had been right: it was time to grow up. It certainly wasn't 'time to go home to mummy'. She was going to leave this job she had fought so hard for, and she was going to do it now. This was so much easier than she thought. She sat at her desk, wrote her resignation, and signed it.

Jayne walked into the office and told India to pop out for milk and coffee. India sealed the envelope and addressed it to Philip as she stood up to put on her red jacket. Jayne decided to add biscuits to her list. India said nothing. She opened the top drawer of her desk and took out her fabled address book, a fountain pen, and her hand cream. She dropped them into her handbag and walked out the door.

Seeing her reflection in the windows of a shop as she walked towards the tube, she was glad she had dressed to impress today.

She texted Nick.

INDIA: You got a job?

NICK: Do you need one?

INDIA: I just left B&B

NICK: I'll put the kettle on – pick up some milk

NICK: And some biscuits

India laughed, but it made her realise she had no problem buying milk and biscuits, but there was something about Jayne's jobs.

Thirty minutes later, she walked into the studio. Nick was in the office, working on images of Charlie from Scarborough. They were images she hadn't seen as she was avoiding everyone that day. The one on the screen showed Charlie in his kilt, barefoot on the beach with his cricket bat. India couldn't drag her eyes away from it.

"Damn, have I left before all that was signed off?"

"No, this is extra work Joe commissioned that last day." Nick turned to study India.

"Well, you look much better than you did yesterday. How do you feel?"

"Brilliant!" Nick picked up a camera and started taking snaps of India. "I want you to remember how good today felt." A little unsure of herself now, India looked away."

"What next, Beautiful? Are you ready to give in to me or is Leeds calling?"

"Oh, it's calling alright, but I need to be sure. This morning in Philip's office it became so clear that it was time to walk away from there. No question. Now I can work on my next step. I have to tell my family and hope they understand."

"And if they don't?"

"Then I'll be sad, but I have to do this, I have to try." After drinking gallons of tea and brainstorming work options in Leeds, India headed back to her flat.

As she passed Stella's door, her grandma called out.

"We are in here. Come and tell us how it went." Filling her lungs with air that she let out slowly, India entered Stella's flat. Everyone was sitting around her table.

"Well, that is a much better face than last night. Do you feel better?"

"So much better."

"Did they listen?"

"No, but I left."

"Are you proud?"

"Yes, I am."

"Then we are proud of you too."

"I have something else to tell you and I hope you will still be proud."

"I'm sure we will."

Chapter 45

With a small backpack over her shoulder, India stood on the doorstep, clutching a peace offering of two bacon sandwiches from the shop around the corner. Shifting from leg to leg, her nerves were showing. As she pressed the doorbell, she immediately wanted to flee. There was a long wait and no sign of movement in the Victorian villa. Her heart sank. India didn't need to run away, so much for surprising him. It had taken so much for her to come north, to risk so much, but the last two weeks had taught her that not being with Charlie wasn't an option. She reached out to open the garden gate when she heard his voice growl out her name.

She spun round to find Charlie standing on his step in a pair of sweatpants and nothing else. She took all of him in. From his bare feet to his tousled blonde hair. This is why she had come. Charlie came down the steps towards her.

"Is it really you?" he croaked.

"It's me." India was recovering her breath.

"What? I…"

"You said I should knock on your door one day." Charlie stood stunned four feet away from her, running his hand through his bed hair. India's heart dropped some more. She had misread what he said.

"India, I meant, I mean, this is so soon."

"You didn't mean it?" her eyes downcast, not wanting to watch him reject her after everything she had given up to stand there.

"No… I mean…" he was fumbling. India decided enough was enough. She could just be his friend.

"Charlie, I bought you a bacon sandwich, not a set of handcuffs."

317

"I only got back home last night."

"I know. Do you want me to go? Let me just leave the sandwiches."

"Come in, I'll put the kettle on." India walked into the great room, put the sandwiches on the kitchen island, and took off her coat. Charlie was still looking shocked, shaking his head. *He was in bed! Fudge! What if he has a woman in his bed and I have come barging in with a bacon sandwich.* She had wanted to surprise him, and now she knew that was a massive mistake. They hadn't spoken since that last night. She had sent flowers for his mum, and she had talked to Robbie. Should she have done more?

Her heart sat inside her ribcage, like a metal bucket, heavy and empty. What did she do now? make an excuse and crawl back to her flat? Make polite conversation and ask his advice on where she could find an office? Numbly she followed him into the kitchen area to get plates, Charlie reached around her to pick up a teaspoon. As his arm touched hers, her skin warmed with his closeness, and her heart lifted. Turning towards him, her fingers reached to caress his bare chest and India knew she wasn't alone. Their eyes locked and Charlie slowly lowered his head, bringing his mouth millimetres from her lips. His hot breath blew across her cheek. He closed his eyes.

"India. I'm sorry..." India stepped away, but his hands shot to her waist and pulled her back to kiss her. It was a slow, gentle kiss, a kiss that explored. Their tongues slowly, carefully explored further. Charlie refreshed his grip around her, bringing her into his naked chest. Her fingers spread out exploring his smooth skin. Charlie lowered his mouth to her ear and whispered.

"I was going to get dressed but I get the idea you like me like this."

"It would be a shame to cover this," her hands dancing across the golden hair.

"You are a wicked woman. Why are you in my house tempting me like this?"

"I want us to have a proper chance. As soon as I arrived in London, I wanted to turn back, actually probably as soon as I stepped on the train."

"I have a match on Monday. How long do I have you for?"

"How long do you want?"

"India, don't mess with me!" It came out as a growl, telling India he did want her. It was time to stop playing with him, closing her eyes she took a steady breath in and out.

"I left Bentley & Bentley as soon as I got back. It had been a long time coming. That business with the vodka wielding woman was the final straw. When I saw what they did to you, I couldn't stay a second longer I walked out that day."

"So now what?"

"I have a few options, but I haven't had a break in a while, so first I'm taking some time out." Charlie kissed her again, this time his hands explored her curves. Did this mean he was happy she was there?

"Charlie…" His kiss strangled what she was trying to say.

"Uh-huh?"

"I don't have to stay here, I can…"

"I want you to stay." He tightened his hold on her as if she were walking away and he wanted to stop her.

"I…"

"India? are you hungry?"

"No"

"Good. I'll feed you after."

"After?"

"After this."

His hand under her bum, he lifted her off the ground, and her legs flew to his waist. Her arms tightened around his neck as he carried her towards the stairs.

"You may need to pinch me soon. I don't know how many times I've dreamed of taking you to my bed. I was in such a deep sleep when you rang that doorbell, I thought I was dreaming. I'm not convinced I'm not still asleep." The corners of India's mouth broke into a smile. She had been so worried she had made a mistake when he opened the door.

Charlie sat India on the bed and as she was taking in his room, he slipped down his sweatpants, leaving himself naked and proud in front of her. India blinked at the sight as he moved towards her and began unbuttoning her shirt.

"Beautiful," he whispered as he slid it off, revealing her black lacy bra. He fingered the straps that went over her shoulders.

"You are beautiful too, look at this." She spoke softly, as she reached out to touch his erection. Leaning forward, she touched her lips to the salty tip and looked up into his eyes.

"Now I know this is a dream, please don't let me wake up yet." Her lips opened and her tongue darted out to lick around the tip, her hands clutching the top of his huge thighs. India closed her eyes as her mouth slipped over the head of his shaft and she stopped with her lips gripping firmly just below that. One hand left his legs to hold the base still, allowing her to control the movement in and out as she flicked her tongue. All too quickly she was aware as the muscles in his leg tensed, and she knew she had seconds to enjoy this. She gently pulled her mouth away and held her hand around him to ease his release.

He laughed.

"You do love me! They treat you like dirt all that time, but when they start on me, you walk." His smile had spread across his face.

"Let's get you cleaned up," and he took her to his bathroom. In her daze, India didn't seem to notice he was undoing her jeans whilst she stood with two hands covered in his cum. As she stepped out of her jeans, she waved her palms in front of his eyes.

"It's only on my hands."

"I prefer to do a thorough job," he beamed as he turned on the shower.

"I like your thinking."

Under the rainfall shower head, Charlie took the time to wash her hair and all of her body, checking every inch carefully. His attention to her was intense as he caressed her skin. India was relaxed and happy, more than happy.

"Beautiful, maybe you better pinch me now." India pulled at his nipple, then stroked across his chest. The minty shower gel she picked up tingled her palms as she washed his trunk and down his arms. Slowly turning him around as she began to take care of him.

It was Charlie's turn again, and he lifted the hand-held spray to trace around her breasts, up and over her shoulders. Turning her away from him, he played the shower up and down her back, lingering more and more on her lower back. Finally moving the water lower and lower, the water trickling between her legs. India wanted to open her legs wider to give him better access and at the same time wanted to clench her thighs. A soft groan left her as Charlie pulled away, taking with him this piece of pleasure. She turned to face him, her face puzzled, and his lips found hers. This kiss was wet, inside, and out. Their shared passion was growing strong, and his erection was back.

As the shower head threw water down onto their faces, the kisses became heated. This new fervour had taken India by surprise. Touching Charlie before had been dreamlike. Slow and sensual. Now she had surrendered to this, the temperature had been turned up.

"Maybe it's the mint shower gel but my lips are on fire."

"That's not shower gel, that is all you and me, my angel. If you are moving in, I need to find a bigger shower. I want to pleasure you in here on a daily basis."

"That is such a corny line."

"It might be corny. but it's true. The idea of having you here every day is beyond anything I hoped for."

"You don't think you might tire of me if I'm here all the time." Shaking his head, he splashed water into her face, which he wiped away with his thumb.

"Not a chance."

He pulled her out of the shower, turned off the water and wrapped her in a large towel, and picked up a much smaller towel to dry himself. Charlie was in charge. India marvelled at the idea of living with someone who would look after her and what that could mean.

"Come here," he shouted as he bounced back on the bed.

"Hey, don't think you get to boss me around now." Still, she sauntered over to his outstretched body, trying to move slowly to tease him, she was torturing herself more than him. One knee at a time, she climbed up beside him.

"Is this close enough?" she teased him.

"I'm sure you could get closer," his voice vibrated through her.

Charlie jumped out of bed, leaving a puzzled India watching him dash to his closet. He pulled out a bag and began rummaging inside. With a look of triumph, he held up a condom. When he reached her carrying his prize, she took it from him. He offered no resistance as she pulled him down on the mattress beside her.

"Now where were we?"

"I wanted you to get closer."

Tearing the foil with her teeth, she lifted one leg over him until she sat astride him, resting gently on his thighs.

"Let me attend to this, and then we can see just how close we can get," she whispered, her voice husky with the promise of what was going to happen next. Charlie reached to move the wet hair from her face and then softly cupped her breast as India focused on applying the condom, stroking down his full length as she slid it on. Lifting herself up, she used one hand to place him at her entrance, then slowly lowered down until he filled her completely. The fit, the way they came together, was something she hadn't experienced before. She had boyfriends in university, and one or two since, but she had never lived with one and it never felt as right as being with Charlie.

As she sank down, she leaned forward to kiss him and his hips lifted in response, trying to get even further into her core. India eased her body haltingly up and down, teasing him. He held her hips, helping her to find a pace that worked for both of them. Their eyes were locked, the side of their lips lifted in the same smug smile. Their moods a mirror of each other. Eager to explore the possibilities now they had crossed that line.

In Scarborough, their lovemaking had been tentative, each equally scared of going too far, of letting go. This new beginning had a different energy. The increased intensity was reflected in the pace she set. No more languid strokes. It was a freer pace that was beyond what they had tried before, but this was the first time they were both certain. This was it. It was real and forever. No doubts, no testing the waters, this was them as one.

Since the moment she woke up at 5 am, India had been excited about this moment, so it -wasn't long before she found her joy. As the wave hit her, her back arched as she clenched tightly around him. His hands held her, keeping her moving through her climax as he searched for his. Charlie kissed her, his tongue wrestling with hers as his pace quickened and his hips lifted. The grinding found her sensitive spot, and a second wave washed over her, pulling another climax from her. As she clenched and tightened, he quickened and lengthened his thrusts as he too, found that second release. India collapsed forward onto his chest, fighting to find air for her lungs.

With a delicate peck to his lips, she rolled off him and laid by his side. As they stared up at the ceiling side by side, Charlie asked her the question that was bouncing around his head since he had seen her standing outside her house.

"Tell me again why you are here."

"I have left Bentley & Bentley and I'm taking some time out. I have rented a flat on Cardigan Road to see if Leeds will work for me. I don't want to push you into anything you don't want Charlie."

"India having you here, in my life, in my house, in my bed is what I have wanted for a long time."

"I don't understand, why did you push me away at the festival?"

"Because much as I want you here, leaving that job, your place in London, I wanted that to be something you decided without me. I really cursed myself for not saying out loud, come to Leeds, come live with me, just be with me. But I couldn't ask you to give up your life for me. How could I do that to you? I love you."

"Charlie, I was confused, then when you weren't there anymore, I realised being with you was the only thing that was important to me. It was all I needed. I love you too."

"Now might be a good time to pinch me again." India laughed and squeezed his nipple hard.

"Ouch." He stood up and went to deal with the condom. When he returned, he knelt beside her on the bed and started to tickle her, and she responded. A tangle of arms and legs. The laughter that spilt out of them made her sides ache. That laughter reflected the tension that had haunted their time together from the beginning. As the giggles subsided, they lay wrapped in each other. Both faces beaming. Finally, together, finally, all the barriers were gone.

Epilogue

India lifted two pizzas from the oven, taking them to the kitchen island for Zach to cut up.

"Do you think I should make any more, there is plenty of dough and marinara sauce. I guess we could have pizza tomorrow."

"Take a breath girl, let us see how these go and I can always jump on and put a few extra ones together if the guys are still hungry later. Didn't you say Tilly was bringing some cheesecakes?"

"Of course, when those turn up, people won't be looking at my food."

"These guys love your pizzas. It is all some of them were talking about in the showers. Now go get a drink."

Charlie was passing around drinks and trying to encourage some of the younger players to move outside. With India here, his house was now a home and his friends from the team were starting to consider it as a place to unwind, but today was special. April was turning into May and the British summer was on its way and with it came test cricket, the game they all loved.

Seeing India so at ease in the kitchen made his heart sing. It had taken him eight months, but in a few weeks, she would be giving up her flat and would be officially living here with him. To be honest, she had been living at his house since that day she knocked on his door. She had hung on to her place as some sort of safety blanket, and she used it as an office. Her father, the accountant, pointed out that paying residential prices when she could just rent an office, made no financial sense. Charlie took that to mean he approved of India living with him.

Their first few months together were rocky with her family, but something had made a shift and they seemed to realise they would lose her if they didn't change. India had never shown any doubt about her decision to move to Leeds to be with him. Today her brother and his wife would be coming to see them, too. Simple gestures like that meant a lot to her, so it was important to him.

Here she was, feeding his teammates and welcoming Zach to live with them. This time last year, things had all changed with one phone call. India told him that the bumps along the way, had simply helped her know that being with him was worth the changes she made.

The doorbell announced the arrival of Andrew and Autumn Barrington Jones. Daniel Woods with his long strides was first to the door. India froze as he opened the door and brought them into the main room. When Andrew saw her, his face broke into the broad smile she had grown up with, and that alone made India relax. She spread her arms and Andrew didn't hesitate to hug his sister as if they hadn't seen each other in a year. They had seen each other, but the silent barrier of disapproval prevented Andrew from touching or even smiling at India. Autumn was more reserved, but she had always been like that. She gave India a brief hug and a small kiss on the cheek. It was their first time to visit Ash Road, and she watched Autumn's critical eye sweep the room. India was relieved to see her nod and smile her approval. Much of her sister-in-law's reserve and judgemental attitude came from joining the Barrington Jones family. India felt if she could embrace a different approach to their expectations, then she too would be a happier person. Making a mental note to try to help Autumn relax into being herself, instead of what she thought she should be. She led them into the garden to introduce them to Ben Woods and his wife.

As India entered the kitchen again, the door opened and in breezed Tilly, carrying a plant and gift-wrapped box. She made a beeline for India in the kitchen. Hot on her heels was Joe with a stack of cheesecake boxes. Charlie collected a new bottle of prosecco and joined them all at the island.

Joe and Tilly emptied their hands, and everyone exchanged hugs and handshakes. India was hugged and kissed so hard she nearly keeled over. Charlie grabbed her elbow, then slipped his arm possessively around her waist, kissing her temple.

"Are you ready for a drink, my angel?"

"I am."

"And can I tempt you, now you are finally here?" He said to Joe and Tilly.

"Yes, please. Sorry, we got held up picking that box up from my father's." Tilly breathed out as she hugged Charlie's side. India's eyes lit up when she realised the gift was from Maxwell Sykes. Tilly pushed the box towards her.

"Well, open it will you." India picked up the box and gave it a shake. Something inside rattled.

"Just open it." Pulling at the ribbons, she did as she was told and found a bunch of keys and a sheet of paper. Max had generously offered to rent her an office on North Road, around the corner from Charlie's house. It was a great price and an easy out contract. It meant she could finally start to develop the business further. This was a huge step forward for her.

"Thank you, you don't know how much this means to me."

"Oh, I think we do. Anyway, when do you think you will have the office open?" asked Joe.

"A couple of weeks. Why?"

"We need to make an appointment to come and discuss a new project with you." Tilly gushed. India picked up on her excitement. "That is if you are both up for it." Her eyes bounced between India and Charlie.

"So now you have to tell me more. What is it?"

"We are taking Gym Away to shopping TV. We have a meeting at the studio in three weeks. So, are you in?"

Although they both answered at the same time, India said "YES" as Charlie gave an emphatic "NO."

Who will Tilly and India persuade to be the face of Gym Away on TV?

To find out what happens next, sign up for the newsletter and get a free bonus chapter all about the day India moves into her new office.

Email India for your copy india@booksbybelinda.com

Note from the author.

I have loved writing India and Charlie's story and I have many more such stories to tell you.

I promise you that my stories will be full of strong women who have their problems to solve and brave men that will join them on their journey. Most of all I promise you many, many happy ever afters.

As I send you this book, I must thank those who have helped me. The ones who have encouraged me, the ones who have written alongside me at silly times of the day and the ones who have helped me lick the story into shape. I have listed them here in alphabetical order. Ben, Christine, Di, Elaine, Emma, Helen, Katie, Joanne B, Joanne P, Linda, Mandi, Martin, Rachel, and Yvonne. Not to mention the lovely gentlemen who sat next to me at Headingley.

Come and find me on social media. Cheer me along as I write more. BEE

Find Belinda online at www.booksbybelinda.com

Facebook @BelindaEdwardsAuthor

Instagram @booksbybelinda

Twitter @BooksByBelinda